Living On A Rainbow – Calvin Wade

Foreword/Acknowledgements

'Living On A Rainbow' is my first fictional book release in almost two years and I am incredibly excited about having something new out for people to read. Harry 'H' McCoy and his friends and family have never been far from my thoughts in that two year period so I hope you enjoy bringing them into yours.

In all my fictional books, music plays a significant role in the writing process. To fully enjoy 'Living On A Rainbow', I would encourage you to listen to the many songs mentioned. They really help paint the picture of the moments described. I am particularly indebted to all involved with 'The Slow Show' who could not have been more supportive when I requested the use of the lyrics to their song, 'Ordinary Lives' in the final Chapter.

'Ordinary Lives' is written by The Slow Show. Lyrics by Robert Goodwin. Permission granted by J C Caddy Management & Rough Trade Publishing Ltd.

I would also like to say a huge thank you to Marley Junior Ellis-Brennan, a very talented young man whose piano playing introduced me to 'I Giorni' by Ludovico Einaudi. You have excellent taste, Marley!

Thanks also to Shaun McManus for introducing me to the music of 'The Slow Show', Stuart Napier for the introduction to Anna Nalick's Breathe (2am) and thanks to every other friend who has made a musical recommendation that has ended up in this book.

Once again, thanks to Antony at ebook-designs.co.uk for the cover art work.

A huge thank you also goes to Tracy Fenton for her guidance, error spotting and candid comments. Thanks also to Lisa Hall for taking the time and trouble to steer me on to a better path.

Finally, thank you to all my friends and family for your consistent and ongoing love and support. It is impossible to put down in words how much it means to me.

Calvin. 4th July 2017.

Chapter One

We are all fragile creatures. The loved ones that surround us now are temporary. Those that form the nucleus of our friendships and family bonds, at any given point in our lives, do not necessarily remain with us through time. There may be a variety of reasons for this. The relationships themselves may be fragile or their world may only ever have been intended to collide with ours for a short span of time. Ambition and love draw people in different directions, work lives can create nomadic pathways and loves journeys can take us on geographically diverse paths. Death may also arrive to cause its ultimate diversion or, as so often is the case these days, our mental health may become mental illness.

I never anticipated that I would become ill in the way that I did. At no stage should you ever think that I am an expert on mental illness just because I have experienced it. A woman who has given birth would not necessarily be expected to perform a complicated delivery of another woman's child. I do have my own theories but I expect anyone with any real knowledge on the matter would be quick to dismiss them. I believe, sincerely believe, that mental illness can act randomly or it can be caught. I don't exactly mean caught like chicken pox or influenza, but I mean it can slowly develop inside you like a bug when other people chip away at your soul. I believe that is what happened to me. In time, you will be able to judge for yourself. I will tell you my story and you can reach your own conclusions.

The part of the story about the incident on the Thelwall Viaduct is particularly perplexing as I have always had, for as long as I can remember, an aversion to heights. I think my type of vertigo is called 'suicidal vertigo'. Once I get to a certain height above ground, when I am exposed to a sheer drop, fear takes over. The fear is partially caused by an overwhelming desire to throw my body over the edge of the building, the hill or the bridge. Preservation then kicks in, preservation, agitation and panic. It's a horrible collection of sensations and I tend to avoid these scenarios at all costs. I avoid them when I'm well, anyway.

Bearing in mind I suffer from vertigo, standing on the edge of the Thelwall Viaduct, with my bare feet dangling over the side, would not have seemed like one of my brighter ideas, but rational thoughts had long since checked out of my brain like departing holidaymakers. They had just left their baggage behind.

I can't really recall much about the whole incident other than its finale. Andy tells me about it and when he does, I think I can remember other snippets, but perhaps all I am doing is painting a picture from the stories he tells. When you are at the bottom of the ocean, it is hard to see anything, even with your eyes open. Andy says the one thing that he remembers with the most clarity about that miserable day was the lack of compassion. There I was, a broken man, my brain cells raging an internal civil war to decide whether my future belonged in life or death and the average passing motorist was more concerned with the inconvenience I had caused them. Apparently the police had closed the southbound carriageway of the M6 down to one lane which was the major cause of frustration.

"If you want to do it, just do it, throw yourself off and do us all a favour, you fucking nutcase!"

This type of verdict on my predicament was allegedly common place. People have no sympathy for strangers unless they are terminally ill, young or very old. I was none of the three. I understand where they were coming from though. Five years ago, I would probably have felt exactly the same way. What sort of an idiot parks up on the hard shoulder of the Thelwall Viaduct, in the middle of a rainstorm then calmly clambers over all obstructions until he is standing on the edge of a motorway bridge looking a couple of hundred feet down to the Manchester Ship Canal and the uninviting, grey waters of the River Mersey? I'll tell you what sort of an idiot – an ill one, a mentally ill one.

When darkness overcomes the light, I guess all you can hope is that you have a friend who can turn up with a torch and thankfully for me, more often than not, Andy would turn up shining brighter than sunshine. Andy knows me better than anyone. I have known him longer than I have known my wife. To be honest, Andy has always seen the warts and all version of me, rather than just the presentable side. I've always felt comfortable enough in his presence to reveal my true self. For a long time I think I tried to keep the dark side from Cathie, but eventually it became impossible to hide. I certainly opened up to Andy about the fears and frustrations in my marriage a long time before I opened up to Cathie. With hindsight, that was one of the many things I managed to get wrong.

When Andy turned up on the bridge, the police allowed him through the cordon. I am not sure of the exact story, Andy makes subtle changes every single time he fascinates new people with it, but there is no doubting the police believed his tale that he would keep a safe distance away from me. I am aware this did not happen.

Andy said I greeted him on the bridge without drama, like he had just popped around to my house for a beer or a cup of tea. Knowing Andy like I do, I would actually have been more surprised if Andy ever did call around to my house for a beer or a tea, he is a red wine or champagne type of guy.

As Andy clambered over the framework to join me, probably being cursed at by a dozen watching police officers as he did so, he said I started talking to him about the weather and about my choice of shoes. I was frustrated that I had bought a new pair of black shoes that were too hard at the heel so I had swopped them for a battered old brown pair. I subsequently took them off and threw them into the water below. Andy took his own shoes and socks off too and dropped them down into the Mersey to empathise with my barefooted stance.

"You shouldn't have done that, Andy," I said, shaking my head, "you should have given them to me."

One of the many things we have in common is a shoe size. Andy can afford to lose a pair of shoes. He has more shoes than any man I know.

"What's all this about, H?" Andy eventually asked, once the formalities were out the way.

I wouldn't have been at a stage, at that point, that my speech would have been slow or calm, nor would I imagine, would it have been clear. I tend to either be silent or rambling when I sink very low. I apparently chose to answer Andy's question with a ramble that was very difficult to decipher. All Andy could make out was that something had gone.

"I'm not catching what you are saying, H. I don't understand what you are saying has gone. Tell me again. What's gone that has upset you so much, H?"

"Listen," I instructed, "a condom, a fucking condom. Not that I've done any fucking. The only thing I ejaculate these days is guilt."

I swear more when I'm badly depressed. The acceptability filter that gauges what I can allow myself to say and what is not permitted, seems to switch itself off when I am depressed. At that point, almost anything goes. I guess by then my brain has decided it has enough to worry about without trying to gauge whether a certain word is offensive or not. I'm told I never use the 'c' word though, which provides me with a little comfort.

"I still don't understand. Why does losing a condom make you stand on the edge of a bridge?"

Andy said I gave him a look which suggested I thought he was now the one who was not of sane mind.

Eventually I repeated myself clearly enough to be heard.

"I bought a box of twenty four condoms last Christmas. I was feeling optimistic. I've used two. There are twenty one left in the box."

I apparently shifted around as I was saying this so less of my feet remained on the edge of the wet road. I was standing on the drop side of a metal barrier with my arms pushed back through it to keep me from falling. If I had adjusted my shoulders and pushed my arms out, I would have dropped to my death. Andy said for those few split seconds he was concerned that was what I was about to do.

"Maybe you've miscounted, H."

I scoffed at this suggestion.

"Miscounted! Miscounted! I count them every day, over and over and over again. There were twenty two when I last counted, there are twenty one now. My marriage is finished, Andy. Cathie's with someone else now. I've driven her to it. Cathie and the kids were the last things I had worth keeping and soon they'll be gone too."

After that, I apparently stopped talking. I took my top off, stood up and just let it drop to the water below. Andy said I was really scaring him at this point. This wasn't a cry for help. It was irrational behaviour from a man with a confused mind.

When Andy tells this story, even now, I shake my head in disbelief. It is almost impossible to accept that the person sat with him on the bridge is me. For over thirty five years of my life I had been normal. Dare I say it, as I know it makes me sound like a bit of an arse, but for a long time I had seen myself as a cut above the rest. I was a little more intelligent than the norm, dressed a little better, had a better house, a better job, a better looking wife – I was going places that not everyone had the ability or the money to go to. I may have come across as a little arrogant to those that didn't truly know me, but in certain situations I felt I had good reason to be pumped full of self-belief. The person I am now hates a lot of the things about the person I was back then. I had a superiority complex. It gradually surfaced like a wart of the mind.

I had no idea back then that the good times would not always roll. I had never expected any drastic changes to my life but even if I had been forewarned, I would never have anticipated my inability to deal with it. I was like a carefully crafted piece of clay, I had always been lovingly handled and when life's pottery wheel started spinning too quickly, I was not expecting to be mangled up and tossed aside.

The bit about the whole incident I do remember and I can still visualise it clearly now was the rainbow. Around that time, after my darkest moments, there always seemed to be a rainbow. I think it was there retaliating against the demons in my head, aiming to allow the good to momentarily get the better of the bad. I have mentioned the Civil War that was going on in my brain and my mother and the rainbow were Oliver Cromwell and the Roundheads. It was a sustained fight and it wasn't an easy victory.

I can clearly remember seeing my mother looking down on that bridge. I could hear her calming voice. She always seemed to sense when I was most likely to do myself harm. On this occasion, I was giving her particularly strong clues. Slowly, in her beautiful, softly spoken London accent, I heard her say,

"This isn't how your story should end, my darling. We shouldn't seek out death. It will come to find all of us when it's ready but until that time, embrace life. Stop letting it get the better of you. You're ill, my love, you need to find a way to get better."

"I don't know whether I want to get better."

"Of course you do. This is why you're here, on this bridge. Don't you see? You're trying to be George Bailey from 'It's A Wonderful Life' and you want me or Andy or someone to be Clarence Odbody. You want someone to save you from yourself and pull you from the depths of despair. You want to be saved from jumping off this bridge. You want to be shown how the world is a better place with you in it, which it is, but this isn't Hollywood, you need to learn that for yourself".

"No, that's not it," I protested, "you don't understand."

"I understand better than you do, my darling. There is still so much for you to see and do. Think what you'd be sacrificing. Think for a moment about what you will lose when you leave, Harry. There will be no hugs from the children at bedtime. No sunny summer's evenings sipping wine in the garden as the sun goes down. No crackling of logs on the fire on a bitterly cold winter's evening. No Laurel and Hardy. No Cinema Paradiso. No music. I know how much your music means to you. Just imagine never being able to hear this again...."

Somehow, I don't know how, my mother worked her magic. Somehow she made me see my father, sat at a piano, playing Ludovico Einaudi's 'I Giorni', the most wonderful piece of music I have ever heard. I cried on that bridge when my father played, which is nothing unusual, I always cry when I hear that music. Somehow it encapsulates everything life is about. It is beautiful, emotional and at times, desperately sad. My tears were down to more than just the emotions of the music though. I cried because I was in such a lonely place. I cried because I felt such a fool. I cried for my mother and father. I gripped Andy's hand tightly, told him I was sorry and asked him to lead me to safety, which of course he did.

There have been many rainbows since that day, but they weren't the radiant ones that my mother lived on. After that day, her work was done.

Chapter Two

I am from Rochdale. If you are of a certain age you probably know it as the place that Lisa Stansfield comes from. I think she may actually come from Heywood which is a few miles up the road, but that's splitting hairs, she's definitely from the Rochdale area. If you are a little older, you might recall that it is the place Sir Cyril Smith MBE, the posthumously disgraced Liberal MP served for over twenty years (after his death I heard someone outside Peacocks in the town centre say that the MBE stood for 'Meddling Bastard Escaped' – from what I have subsequently read it appears he wasn't far wrong).

If you are of my father's generation, Rochdale is known for producing Gracie Fields, the star of cinema and music hall in the first half of the twentieth century, who was born above her grandmother's fish and chip shop in the town. When I was a child, my Dad says he took me to see Gracie come back to open the theatre that still bears her name. If you are too young even for Lisa Stansfield, you probably just know Rochdale as a rundown town to the North East of Manchester, Bury's dishevelled next door neighbour. Don't get me wrong though, I love the place. For those who do remember Lisa Stansfield, they'll remember her biggest hit was 'All Around The World'. If she did, in fact, go all around the world after quarrelling with her 'baby', I bet she never saw another place like Rochdale.

I suppose one of the things that sets Rochdale apart from elsewhere are the characters it possesses. Some of the loveliest people on earth come from Rochdale and admittedly some of the oddest. I'd like to think I fall into both categories. I'd say most people from Rochdale fall into at least one or the other, but the odd ones are not always 'good odd'. It is a place where most people do not have a lot, so they are prepared to fight for what they can get. I have never seen people fight for discounted produce like they do in Rochdale. I've seen grown men fist fighting over a 3p bag of sprouts in Tesco. It can be like pigeons fighting for breadcrumbs. Herbert Spencer probably came up with his 'survival of the fittest' comment, not only after reading Charles Darwin's 'On The Origin Of Species' as was reported, but probably after spending a few days in Rochdale too. Some people in Rochdale would give you their last penny and others would do whatever it takes to get yours. It's that sort of place.

Our family ended up in Rochdale by default. Not long before my mother discovered she was pregnant with me, my parents decided to get out of London, for reasons I will explain shortly, and move to Manchester. The only places they could afford to buy in Manchester were in areas they didn't want to live, so they ended up buying in Rochdale. My parents fell in love with the place as much as I did and remain there even in death, as Dad's ashes are next to Mum's coffin in Rochdale cemetery on Bury Road. They were known in their local pub as the 'Cockney Lancastrians', although technically Rochdale is no longer part of the Red Rose county.

My Dad wasn't a young man when he arrived in Rochdale as he was born way back in 1922. I didn't arrive on the scene until the back end of the blazing hot summer of 1976. Being relatively good at Maths from an early age, I wasn't far into my childhood when I calculated that my father was no spring chicken. He was fifty four when I was born and a pensioner by the time I started Secondary school, which always felt perfectly normal to me, but the older I was, the more aware I became of how weird it seemed to everyone else. The kids in our road used to call him 'Old Daddy Mack', whilst my mother had the much more pleasant nickname of 'Yummy Mummy Mack'.

What made outsiders look into our family with a particular sense of puzzlement and a dash of resentment was the peculiar bond between my mother and father. It was not just the fact that my Dad was old that appeared strange nor was it just this combined with the fact that my Mum was young. It was the fact that Dad was old and poor whilst Mum was young and glamorous. If you've ever seen the Bruce Springsteen video to 'Dancing In The Dark' when he beckons a young Courteney Cox on to the stage to dance with him, well that's what my Mum used to look like, like an English Courteney Cox. She had the black hair, flicked across to one side, blue eyes, dazzling smile and a bit of puppy fat in her cheeks which I think always helps you age better than if you have a thin face. All my friends used to fall in love with my mother, even Andy, on some level, was infatuated by her.

Normally, if a young, good looking lady marries an older man, it is presumed that the man must be wealthy, that he is going to lavish her with riches that she has never previously enjoyed. This was definitely not the case with my mother. My Dad has never been wealthy. My mother made herself considerably financially poorer by getting together with my Dad. Undoubtedly she made herself considerably richer in spirit though. If there was a better man on this earth that my Mum could have married, I can state, quite categorically, that I have never met him.

Admittedly, the age gap between my parents was a considerable one. My father was twenty nine years, three months and six days older than my Mum. As far as I am concerned, love is love and as long it works equally well for both parties and there is no mental manipulation of one person by another then it is wrong for anyone else to have a negative view. Whether love incorporates a bond between two men, two women, two people of different skin colours, two different religions or two vastly different ages is immaterial. People like to gossip though and, as a rule, gossip doesn't tend to seek out normality.

I was fourteen when my Mum first told me about her romantic history with my father. I would say both my parents were naturally quiet souls but each had their talkative moments and each would choose certain times to seek isolation. My mother was always a great fan of television, whilst my father tended to prefer an evening in the study listening to his beloved radio. Radio Four was his preferred option. As you will come to learn, I idolised my father and as a teenager wanted nothing more than to appreciate his programmes as much as he did, but they seemed alien to me, whilst Mum's TV shows like 'Birds of a Feather', 'Brush Strokes' and 'Bread' seemed funny and inviting. The only thing we watched on the television as a family was 'Only Fools & Horses' which my Dad loved as much as my Mum. It was the only show he would switch his radio off for other than old classics like 'Laurel & Hardy' and 'The Three Stooges'. It was always good to hear my father laugh as he was usually a serious man, certainly not stern, but definitely serious.

Anyway, one particular night, it must have been in 1990, Mum was in one of her chatty moods, which were very rare indeed. A lot of people are quiet with people they don't know but Mum was just quiet with everyone, with the possible exception of my father. She was nearly always quiet around me though. We could spend an evening together in front of the television without either of us saying a word to each other. On the rare occasions she did speak, she would never say a sentence if a couple of words would suffice.

On this evening in 1990 though, Mum was talkative. She initially just explained, during an episode of 'Bread' that her parents were still alive but once I queried why we never got to see them, she was more than happy to relate the whole story. Perhaps it was a way of getting out of watching the second half of 'Bread', which had peaked and was on the slide by then. If Mum ever uttered anything during 'Bread' it was to comment that it was no longer the same without the original Joey and Aveline.

It turned out that my Dad had been married before, which hadn't come as a total shock to me. I had always figured that this was a distinct possibility given his age, but had lacked the courage to ask my parents whether I had any half-brothers or half-sisters somewhere in London. I learnt that my Dad's first wife was called Irene and she had died of cervical cancer when she was 37 in 1960. My father and Irene had apparently always wanted children but Irene had never managed to conceive.

Mum said that my father thought that it was possible that Irene had miscarried early in pregnancy a couple of times as she had felt she was pregnant as her periods were late, but had bled heavily after around six weeks, before even making an appointment to see her Doctor. After Irene's death, my Mum said Dad had expected to live out the rest of his life as a widower and without children.

Irene and my father's closest friends were Joan and Kenny Craddock. Irene and Joan had grown up together in the same street in Finchley, apparently a stone's throw from North Middlesex Golf Club, which was where she met my father at a dinner dance. My father had apparently been an impressive dancer but more Fred Astaire than John Travolta, my Mum explained. Neither Irene nor my father had been a member of the club, but Kenny had been and my Dad had been invited to the function by his friend, who was apparently keen to act as a matchmaker for Dad and his wife's best friend. This was not long after the end of the Second World War and Dad and Irene were married after a twelve month courtship in 1947 at Saint John the Apostle Church in Whetstone.

Mum said Dad and Irene were happily married for thirteen years. Irene only became aware she was ill a few months before she died and once the cancer was diagnosed, it was too late to save her. When she passed away, Joan and Kenny were instrumental in ensuring my father coped with his tragic loss. Kenny would often call around at Dad's and encourage him to go to the pub with him and every Sunday Joan would invite Dad around for a roast dinner. It was always a busy affair around the dining room table as Joan and Kenny had five children, two sons and three daughters, who always called my father, Uncle George. The middle daughter, Catherine, was my mother.

No-one ever called my mother, Catherine, she was referred to as Kitty. The same happened to me. I was christened Harold, but throughout my life I have never heard anyone call me by that name, with the exception of the Registrar during my marriage vows. I am called Harry occasionally but never Harold. My Mum once said she didn't even like the name Harold but loves Harry and did not realise you could actually christen someone with the shortened version. To Mum's great frustration, over time my name was shortened even further to just plain 'H'. Dad liked me being called 'H' though, he always thought it was manly. To me, 'H' is who I am, not Harry and definitely not Harold.

So, my father was a regular visitor to my mother's house throughout her childhood, but she said there was no special bond between them and given Dad was forty when Mum was eleven, there was certainly nothing untoward. He was just a pleasant family friend to my mother's family. She said she did grow up feeling a little sorry for him as she knew he was a lonely widower, but did not give him a moment's thought when he wasn't around for dinner.

I have heard both my mother's and father's version of their coming together and both recount the tale in different ways, but both are agreed that it was my mother who was first to realise that there was potentially a romantic connection between them. My Mum was nineteen when this became apparent, which would have made Dad only a year or two short of fifty. Dad said that around that time, he began to appreciate how beautiful Mum was both in looks and spirit, but had he known of any romantic interest from my mother, he would, at that point, just have dismissed it as a brief crush. This was not the case. Although Mum has always been quiet she has also always been determined.

The event that apparently triggered a romantic feeling in my mother's brain and heart was a trip to the cinema. Mum was a keen reader, she must have read over a hundred books a year and when the Joseph Heller's novel, Catch-22 was made into a Hollywood film, starring Alan Arkin amongst others, my mother was desperate to see it, as it was showing at The Rex in East Finchley. Over dinner one Sunday, Mum was bemoaning the fact that her boyfriend had let her down as he had done once too often and on that basis she had no-one to accompany her to the cinema.

My father had just speared a sprout with his fork, but put down his cutlery and announced,

"Catch-22, you say, Kitty? I have heard that being discussed on the wireless. I haven't read the book myself, but the film sounds very interesting all the same. It's showing at the old Rex, is it? I'd happily come along with you to see that, providing you don't mind being spotted out in East Finchley with an old codger like your Uncle George."

My Dad was never a cunning or manipulative man so when he told me that he only offered as an innocent favour I have no reason to question his sincerity. Mum says she accepted the invitation innocently too, egged on, to an extent, by her parents. It was only through the course of the evening at the cinema that Mum became aware that the man she had called 'Uncle George' was a kinder, wiser, more gentlemanly man than she had ever spent an evening with before. By the time Mum arrived home that night, she had decided if there was only one man in the world for her, then that man was George McCoy. I don't know the full ins and outs of their courtship, but I know everything remained innocent at least until my mother reached the age of twenty one in 1972, long after Mum had revealed the intensity of her feelings. Apparently Dad dismissed Mum's feelings as 'ridiculous' initially, but when my mother continually repeated that he was the one for her and she was not going to change her mind, my father explained it would be entirely inappropriate to even contemplate 'courting', until Mum was twenty one. I think it may have even been 1973, after Mum's twenty second birthday that they eventually had a secretive first date.

The relationship didn't stay innocent forever. George McCoy and Catherine 'Kitty' Craddock were married on Wednesday 7th July 1976 at Rochdale Registry Office at Rochdale Town Hall. My Mum was eight months pregnant at the time. Despite never even glancing at another woman throughout their marriage, my Dad always retained an element of guilt about his relationship with Mum. To my mind, the guilt was ridiculous and once I was an adult, I often told him so. Dad made every second of his time with Mum a quest to ensure her happiness. He could not help feeling though that he had betrayed the goodwill of my Mum's parents. Joan and Kenny had welcomed him into their home after Irene's death and my Dad felt that when he had left London, he had taken one of their daughters away from them.

Kenny Craddock was a wealthy man. Along with his brother, Joey, he ran a successful scaffolding company called Craddock & Sons that had been started by Kenny's grandfather and father, operating in North London since before the Great War. There were stories that they had done extensive work on Buckingham Palace at one stage, but my mother was not sure if they were true. She said her father certainly didn't say anything to dispel them, rumours like that can only be good for business. Kenny and Joey ran a reputable firm but they had associations with all sorts of people. Some were the type who were prepared to carry out work of any description, including physical beatings and perhaps even murder, if they were paid enough money to do it.

According to my Mum, she only confessed to her parents that she was having a relationship with my Dad after their first sexual encounter, late in 1975, almost three years after their first date. My mother said it had been Dad's decision not to rush things.

My father had started working as a chef at The Royal Horseguards Hotel when it opened in 1971 and stayed for almost five years. He used to get the Northern Line tube every day from East Finchley to Embankment and on the days he worked breakfast and lunch, he would stop around four o'clock at The Old White Lion pub for a pint before walking home. Knowing this, on the day Kenny Craddock had heard his daughter's tearful confession of her relationship with my father, he headed down to The Old White Lion at half past three and waited for Dad to arrive. My parents said that Dad had a pint of Watney's Special Bitter waiting for him on the bar when he arrived. Kenny Craddock told him that it would be the last pint he would ever buy for his old friend. Dad was given an ultimatum, either leave town that night or sometime soon after he would be found face down in the Thames.

My Dad had known Kenny long enough to know that this was a very real threat. Dad went to the nearest red telephone box after leaving The Old White Lion and telephoned his boss at Royal Horseguards to tell him of his intention to quit without notice. Apparently his boss was far from impressed as Christmas was around the corner but Dad firmly stated he had no choice. He went home to pack his bags and unexpectedly, whilst packing, my mother arrived. He told her that he was leaving for Manchester without stating a reason. My mother adored my father as much as he adored her and despite protesting that he must leave alone, Mum would not listen. By seven o'clock, they were both on the Manchester Pullman from Euston to Manchester Piccadilly. It was the one and only time my parents travelled first class. It was fortunate for me that they did leave together. Just before Christmas 1975, within three weeks of arriving in Manchester, where they stayed in a bed & breakfast in Fallowfield, my mother discovered she was expecting me.

The following summer, on 18th August 1976, I arrived on the scene, weighing an unspectacular six pounds and two ounces. Joan and Kenny did not discover where my parents had moved to, or if they did, they made no attempt to contact them. A further thirty four years would pass before I finally got to meet them. They weren't bad people but if I could have one wish, it would be that I could turn back time and ensure that meeting would never take place. My life would have been so much easier without any contact with Joan and Kenny Craddock.

Chapter Three

Andy Corcoran and I were brought together by football. If either of us had actually been any good at that stupid game then a friendship between us would never have been formed. We went to the same junior school, Bamford Primary. Bamford was a reasonably large primary school with two classes to each school year. Andy and I were always in different classes, so didn't get to know each other in the classroom, we were introduced in the harsh world of the playground. During our infant years, I was unaware of his existence, it was only once we moved up to juniors that we became friends. Only juniors were allowed to play with footballs in the playground and it was only then that our misery began. It wasn't an immediate bond either, it was fostered through years of torment.

Every boy played football. Up until that point my closest male bond was with my father. Dad was a chef in Manchester, like he had previously been in London, but as a younger man he had been a lower League professional footballer with Brentford and Milwall. Although Dad was a North Londoner, football took him to West and South East London. He told me the coaching staff at Brentford saw him as being one of the greatest inside left's they had ever had at Griffin Park. He broke into the first team in 1938 and had made over twenty five appearances for the first team when Adolf Hitler decided to give him an altogether different career, a career in the army. In late 1939, Dad lied about his age to join up. Due to his footballing background, there were probably people in the Army who knew he was only seventeen, but I am sure they were prepared to turn a blind eye. Six years later, after two years fighting and four years in a prisoner of war camp, Dad returned to his footballing career, initially back with Brentford and then subsequently with Milwall. He had lost a yard of pace and a ton of spirit during the War years and said he was never the same player again. He retired from the game in 1950, aged just twenty eight. He blamed Hitler not football and was desperate for me to love the game as much as he did. The passion was never there.

My lack of passion for football was probably down to my lack of ability. Frustratingly, I wasn't good, I would even go as far as to say I wasn't bad either, I was absolutely hopeless. I believe the expression 'two left feet' signifies someone who kicks the ball with his stronger foot like most other people do with his weaker one. I was worse than that. I didn't even have the co-ordination to kick the moving object with either of my feet. I would swing one of my feet at it and, to much hilarity, the ball would creep under my foot or between my two legs.

The most humiliating moments in the playground at school involved two capable footballers being elected as 'captains' and then everyone else lined up on the school wall waiting to be selected for a team. In turn, the captains would choose one player each. People of all ages enjoy the feeling of being popular amongst their peer group and most, at the very least, are uncomfortable with the knowledge that they are unwanted. No matter who the two team captains were, Andy Corcoran and I were always the last two picked to join a side. This bothered me a great deal. It did not bother Andy a jot.

One day, Andy and I were, as usual, the last two sitting on the wall, as everyone else lined up in the two teams they had been picked to play in. Andy was doing something with his hands and legs which even as a ten year old struck me as very odd. He had his hands on the top of his knees and was moving his knees apart simultaneously to the left and right and then back together again. As his knees were about to touch, he would swop his left hand to his right knee and his right hand to his left knee and then as the knees were moving back apart, he would move his hands back again. Whilst he was carrying out this bizarre ritual, he was humming a song to himself. It wasn't a song I knew, I wasn't a great follower of popular music.

As Andy hummed and I looked on at him perplexed, the other boys were arranging where each of their team members were going to play in this important playground match. It had seemingly been forgotten that Andy and I had yet to be selected for either team. I suppose our impact on the game was going to be minimal anyway, so it mattered little whether we were picked or not. I used the moment as an opportunity to get to know Andy a little better.

"What are you doing?" I asked Andy. He later told me I asked in a manner that suggested I thought he was an idiot. He is probably right.

Andy Corcoran was an odd kid. I didn't really know him, but as far back as I could remember, I just thought of him as the odd kid in the other class. If my knowledge of the English Language had been a little more comprehensive at ten than it actually was, I would have described him as unconventional. As things were, I had to make do with 'odd'.

"I'm being Chevvy Chase," Andy replied, continuing his weird little sit down dance. The game of football had now started. I presumed we were destined not to participate.

"Who's Chuckie Chase?" I questioned. I would soon learn Andy knew a little about a lot of things that I didn't.

"Chevvy Chase, not Chuckie Chase, you dimwit. He's in the Paul Simon video for 'You Can Call Me Al'."

I was still none the wiser. I probably didn't even know he was talking about a music video. Paul Simon sounded like an actor's name to me and Chevy Chase like the name of a car.

"Oh, ok," I said.

I didn't like being picked last nor did I like being called a 'dimwit'. I was a sensitive soul and my feelings were hurt on both counts. I decided, at that particular moment in time, that I hated Andrew Corcoran.

"Hay-ch," one of the team captains shouted over at me as he ran past chasing the ball, "we need someone to go in goal."

Being picked second last is not quite as bad as being picked last, even if he did get my name wrong. Everyone called me 'Hay-ch', there is no such letter, it is 'Ay-ch'. Andrew Corcoran understood and to my surprise, decided to fight my corner. No-one had ever stuck up for me before.

"It's Ay-ch, Yozza, you numbskull!" Andy pointed out, "it's the letter after 'Gee' in the alphabet, Ay-ch."

"I'm not bothered. Just get in goal, will you?" 'Yozza' Hughes shouted over, looking a little taken aback.

This was the first of many times that Andy Corcoran would stick up for me. Immediately the hate I thought I had for him evaporated. I knew I was only picked ahead of him because my team needed a goalkeeper and Andy couldn't be relied upon to stand between the two coats that acted as goalposts. He had a tendency to wander off doing Michael Jackson dance moves when put in goal. I couldn't catch any better than I could kick, but at least I could be relied upon to stand between the coats.

That afternoon, as I was walking home after school, I heard a voice calling after me.

"Ay-ch! Ay-ch!" was the shout. The correct pronunciation was a big clue to who the caller was.

I turned around to seek confirmation and sure enough Andrew Corcoran was running towards me. He was tall for a ten year old and very skinny. I remember my mother subsequently used to refer to him as 'that gangly boy'. Most ten year olds had their shirts hanging outside their trousers by the end of the school day and their school tie lopsided or loosened, but Andy still looked like he did first thing in the morning. He ran slowly either because he wanted to maintain his immaculate appearance or possibly just because he was naturally slow. Andrew Corcoran was many things but an athlete was certainly not one of them.

"Hi Ay-ch. I was just wondering, are you going to play football again tomorrow?" Andy asked. He sounded breathless. He probably was just slow.

I thought about his question. Prior to being asked, I had never really considered that there may be an alternative. Like it or not, football at playtime was what the boys did.

"I don't know," I answered, "what could we do instead?"

"We could play chase."

"With just two? That'd be boring."

"We could get the girls to play."

I thought about it. I did not really know what to say to girls and I did not imagine for one moment that they would be easily persuaded by Andrew Corcoran. Even at ten years old I had some idea of what girls deemed attractive and appealing in boys and Andy did not seem to possess many of the necessary qualities.

"They wouldn't play with us, Andrew."

"Do you know how to knit?"

I thought this was a stupid question. My Mum didn't even know how to knit. I didn't have any relatives to speak of, other than Mum and Dad, but as far as I could make out from things on the television, knitting was a job for Nannas, bored Nannas.

"No!"

"I could teach you. I could bring my knitting needles in and some wool."

"No, thanks."

"Look Ay-ch, I'm trying to think of something good, but it doesn't even have to be good. I hate football. You hate football. It doesn't really matter what we do, as long as it isn't football."

Andy was right. I was a bit torn as to whether I liked this very unusual boy or whether I would enjoy the games he would want to play, but what did I have to lose? Football wasn't for me so I might as well try something different.

The next day I discovered my pre-conceived assumption that Andy would not be popular with the girls was completely wrong. The girls in his class absolutely adored him and once we stopped playing football, the girls made towards us like waves to the shore. My ability to interact with girls, up until then, was almost non-existent but Andy seemed to be on their foreign wavelength. We mainly played chase, tick, British Bulldogs or 'Blockie' which was a version of hide and seek but as the seeker, if you spotted someone you had to run back to the base point and shout 'Blockie 1-2-3' and if you were hiding, you had to get back to the base point before the seeker and again say 'Blockie 1-2-3'. If you were the first person to be spotted, next time around it was your turn to be the seeker.

I only remember deviating from these games when it was someone's birthday. If it was your birthday, you got to pick the game for the day but only after the 'Hen, Cock or Goose' ritual. This involved the birthday person being grabbed by the hair and having it pulled as many times as their age, so a ten year old would receive ten pulls. They would then be asked 'Hen, Cock or Goose?' If they answered 'Hen', the others would do it again, meaning another ten pulls of the birthday hair. 'Cock' would mean a knock on the head and if they selected 'Goose' the child would be let loose. I can't recall why, after the first time we did this, that everyone didn't just say 'goose', I can only imagine we mixed things up a bit. Playtime was transformed from a miserable time that I dreaded to my favourite time of the day.

Out of school, I started to spend a lot of time with Andy Corcoran too. We were still in third year juniors when Rebecca Fenton started calling Andrew, 'Andy' and pretty soon everyone else followed suit. The time I spent out of school with Andy was calmer and less excitable than our time at school, as it was mainly just the two of us rather than us being joined by a group of giggling girls. We would play computer games on the Commodore 64 or sometimes we would both read the same book at the same time and then we would discuss it chapter by chapter. Occasionally we would be brave enough to try something sporting but we were both so lacking in any co-ordination that we would spend more time picking up the ball than hitting, kicking or catching it. Within a few weeks we were good friends, within a few months we were inseparable.

The next twelve months seemed to pass in a heartbeat and all of a sudden preparations were being made for the 'Leavers Disco'. I was very excited about this event. It was 1987 and Andy had managed, over the previous year, to introduce music into my life. A chance to dance sounded fantastic and I couldn't wait to show the girls my moves. I wasn't confident about much but I had faith in my ability to impress the girls with my dancing. Andy had already told me I was 'gifted' when we had danced around his lounge to Wham, Michael Jackson and Duran Duran and I knew this was my opportunity to shine like I had never shined before. I began to imagine myself as England's answer to Michael Jackson and the 'Leavers Disco' was going to be my first step on the road to global fame. Those eleven year old girls would think back to the 'Leavers Disco' 1987 and remember what an impression I made on them and how it was no surprise to any of them that I went on to international fame. That was the plan anyway. From all accounts, that night at the 'Leavers Disco', I certainly made an impression.

Chapter Four

I was sitting on a chair in the corner of the school hall with my arms folded, my chin tucked into my chest and a scowl on my face. The 'Leavers Disco' had been a disaster. I was angry, upset and doing my level best not to humiliate myself even further by crying. I had sat there, on my own, for about fifteen minutes and the most upsetting thing was that no-one seemed to notice. Not one person, not even Andy. He was too busy strutting his stuff on the dance floor, surrounded by about six smiling girls in party dresses, shouting out the words to songs like Billy Idol's 'White Wedding' and Cyndi Lauper's 'Girls Just Wanna Have Fun'.

The whole build up to the night had been brilliant. The disco was on the first Friday night in July and the weekend before my Mum had taken me shopping into Rochdale town centre. For about two years, I had been asking if I could have a Sergio Tacchini tracksuit and the standard reply from my Mum was that they were far too expensive and it was ridiculous spending silly money on a brand name when Woolworths sold perfectly good tracksuits for a quarter of the price. I have no idea why but on the last Saturday in June, 1987, my mother had a change of heart and let me choose whichever tracksuit I wanted. It was always going to be a Tacchini.

That Tacchini tracksuit my Mum bought me that day was the best item of clothing I had ever owned. It looked amazing. I felt how Charlie must have felt when he found that 'Golden Ticket'. The top was largely light blue with a few navy blue features like the zip, collar, the famous Tacchini 'T' logo and two navy blue hoops on each upper arm. The bottoms were plain navy blue with a white logo.

"Thanks very much, Mum!" I said excitedly as she drove me home. I kept peeking into the plastic bag every thirty seconds to make sure it was still there and that I did really have my very own Tacchini tracksuit. We had an old silver Ford Cortina, that was probably about ten years old at that point, which Mum and Dad shared, but Mum mainly drove it. I always had to sit in the back, even if it was just the two of us, because Mum told me it was illegal for under thirteen's to sit in the front. To this day, I am unsure whether that was actually a real law or whether it was just one of those parental white lies you get told to protect you.

"You need to thank your father too," Mum replied, "we both got paid yesterday so your Dad gave me half the money towards it. Now don't talk to me anymore, Harry! I need to concentrate."

Before I realised my Mum was deemed attractive by my secondary school friends, I realised she was ranked in the world's worst drivers by my primary school friends. Andy and the girls would tease me about how terrible she was. If she ever picked me up from school, she would either park with a front and back tyre on the pavement or at a forty five degree angle to the kerb with a front tyre close to the kerb and the back end almost in the middle of the road. Our cars were always peppered with dents and scratches from various scrapes and bumps my Mum had managed to inflict upon it. My Dad was never angry with her, he just used to laugh.

"Goodness me, Kitty McCoy, what will we do with you?" he would say smiling.

When Mum and I arrived home that day from 'town', I ran straight up the stairs to my bedroom, changed into my tracksuit, then ran downstairs to show Mum.

"What do you think?" I asked, standing upright and proud in front of her.

"The top is lovely, Harry but the bottoms are too long. Do you want me to put a hem on them for you?"

"No thanks, Mum. They're fine. I'll grow into them."

I would rather my tracksuit bottoms were two inches too long than allow my Mum an attempt at altering them. Mum was no better at sewing than she was at driving and I could picture being handed back a pair of tracksuit bottoms that came down to my shins. There was no way I was going to let her anywhere near them. The greatest gift I had ever received required me to provide the greatest care I had ever given and that included keeping them away from Mum. A brief conversation ensued (most conversations with Mum were brief) where she pointed out that although the tracksuit was very smart, it was not the type of clothing I should be wearing for the 'Leavers Disco'. In my mind, it was exactly what I should be wearing for the 'Leavers Disco'. It was cool beyond belief and it was loose enough for me to properly dance in. Sometimes though, I relented just because I didn't like confrontation and I always felt subservient to my parents. In this case though, Mum was prepared to compromise and it was agreed that I could wear the tracksuit top with a pair of jeans. I would have liked a pair of new Levi 501s but the Tacchini tracksuit was £49.99 so I knew I would probably have to wait another two years before I could have them. Dad was a Chef at The Palace Hotel in Manchester and Mum was a school dinner lady (thankfully not at my school) so I understood when Mum told me 'they were not made of money'. I had two pairs of jeans to choose from, my pair of 'Wrangler' jeans which I had been given for Christmas and my 'Lee' jeans that I had been given for my tenth birthday that were now getting tight around the waist and only reached down to the top of my socks. I decided I would wear the 'Wrangler' ones.

Andy was just as excited as me about the disco but he didn't have to wait two years for anything. My parents, particularly my mother, described him as 'ruined', which I correctly took to mean 'spoilt'. His father was a dairy farmer on a farm near Ramsbottom and although they didn't live on the farm, as it was owned by Andy's grandfather, a lot of the money made seemed to filter through to Andy. My Commodore 64, for example, was bought second hand from someone advertising it in the Rochdale Observer, whilst Andy had a new ZX Spectrum Plus, a Commodore 64 and a BBC Micro computer. He had Nintendo and Sega stuff too, in fact not only did he have a bedroom, he had a games room upstairs for his computer stuff and a games room downstairs which had a table tennis table and a pool table in it. I hardly ever went in the downstairs games room though as we were both hopeless at table tennis and pool. Andy said that room was more his Dad's games room than his. He had a young Dad and Mr Corcoran would often have friends round for evenings to play pool and have a few beers. To me, that seemed like a very strange thing for a Dad to do. My Dad would never drink beer in the house and any friends he had were couples who were friends of both of my parents.

Perhaps one of the reasons that Andy and I related to each other, despite our very different upbringings was that we were 'only children'. We both felt we had found the brother we never had at home. Andy's parents didn't go with him to buy his clothes for the 'Leavers Disco', his Mum just gave him £100 about a month beforehand, to go into Rochdale and buy himself something. He asked me if I would go with him. He had a black leather wallet with five crisp twenty pound notes in and it felt like going into town with a football player or a rock star. I had never even seen a twenty pound note before and I was nervous when Andy let me inspect it. It had the Queen on one side and William Shakespeare on the other, with his fist tucked under his chin and his elbow leaning on some books.

"Are these real?" I asked.

"Of course they're real! I hope it's going to be enough to get what I want."

"You can probably buy everything in the shop for that, Andy!"

"I doubt that very much, I have expensive tastes."

It was an experience going shopping with Andy. My shopping experiences had tended to involve me going into one shop, buying the first thing that I liked and then going home. Andy was not like that. We must have trudged up and down the steep hill in Rochdale town centre about half a dozen times as Andy deliberated about what to buy. He tried dozens of things on, spent ages looking at himself in various shop mirrors and continually asked my opinion. It must have taken him four hours to choose but eventually he bought a pair of Levi 501s and a blue and white jacket which was a replica of the one Emilio Estevez wore in 'Breakfast Club', it even had the wrestling badge saying 'State Champion' on the arm. It cost something crazy like £70 but Andy wanted it so Andy got it. I'd like to say I wasn't jealous, but in truth, although I was extremely grateful for the parents I had, I wished they had the vast riches the Corcoran family seemingly had access to.

Once we had finished shopping that day, we returned to Andy's and he offered the two pound change to his Mum, who was having a glass of white wine and a cigarette in their huge kitchen. The ashtray on the kitchen table was full and the wine bottle was empty which indicated it wasn't the first glass or cigarette. She just shrugged and told him to keep it, so we disappeared to his room to listen to music on his compact disc player. Not surprisingly, Andy was the first person I knew who owned a CD player too.

From that day to the day of the 'Leavers Disco' it was countdown time. We built ourselves up to a frenzy of excitement and on the day itself, I dragged myself out of bed about six o'clock. It was like Christmas in the summer. I was the first kid to arrive at Bamford Primary that day and would have been there hours earlier if my Mum had agreed to walk me down. I was dressed and ready to go by lunchtime and every half hour in the afternoon I would ask if I could go yet.

At half past five, I finally got my way. My Mum had nipped down to the corner shop to buy a pint of milk, probably just to get away from my pestering, so I knocked on my parents' bedroom door, where my Dad was, to see if he would walk me down. Dad had a day off work and as I went in, he was sat upright on his side of my parents' bed, with his slippers on, listening to some classical music on his cassette player.

"What are you listening to?"

"It's 'Les Toreadors' from Bizet's Carmen. Do they not teach you anything at school these days?"

That's what he actually said, but all I heard was, 'It's blah, blah, blah. Do they not teach you anything at school these days?' I only figured out what Dad actually said when I started listening to classical music myself, many years later.

"Not stuff like this."

"Well, they should. What was it you wanted, H?"

"Can you walk me down to school now, Dad, please?"

My Dad was three months from retirement but he didn't look sixty five, he still had a head full of black hair which was just receding a little at the front and greying a little in the sideburns. His wrinkles were only noticeable when he smiled. He always dressed smartly too. He never wore jeans, trainers or t-shirts, it was always smart trousers, shoes and shirts with an added layer of a jumper in the winter. He always wore white vests beneath his shirt. As a child I was always told to wear a vest, as an adult, I don't think I have ever worn one.

"What time does it start?"

"Six."

"And what time do you make it now?"

If I could have made it, it would have been five minutes to six, but I told him the actual time not the time I had made.

"Half past five."

"We'll still be early if we go now, son. It's only five minutes' walk."

"Please, Dad. I want to be early," I begged.

My Dad took pity on me. He lifted himself up off the bed with a groan which I took not to be aimed at me, more at his aching body.

"OK then. I'll get myself ready. We can't leave until your Mum gets back from the corner shop though. I think she wants to take a few photos of you, before you go."

Within a couple of minutes Mum was back. There was a brief panic as the batteries were flat in the camera so the flash didn't work, but Dad suggested we go into the back garden to take the photos, as it was a fine, bright evening outside. We mixed up the combinations and took a few extra ones in case anyone blinked and then, eventually, Dad and I were each given a kiss on the cheek and were allowed to go.

Dad enjoyed walking. I think he was so fit for his age because of all the walking he did. He walked at least a couple of miles every day and more on his day off. I often used to go with him. My Mum didn't enjoy walking, especially on wet or windy days, as she was concerned that people would see her looking 'bedraggled', so it gave me a rare opportunity to spend time just with my Dad. I treasured every moment I spent with him, as he was such a wise, contented, peaceful soul.

I don't really remember too much about what we spoke about that evening, but I do remember walking along with me on the inside and Dad on the road side. Dad always walked closest to the road, whether he was with me or Mum. He told me it was gentlemanly to do this. I have always done the same with Cathie.

One thing I do recall my father saying was that he was relieved he wasn't my age now. He said he was glad he had been a teenager in an era of proper ballroom dancing and not disco music like nowadays. He said he had lived in the perfect generation for a man like him. My Dad always gave the impression that he had enjoyed his life. Even the four years in the Stalag prisoner of war camp were looked back upon with fondness. It had been an ordeal, Dad always said, but an ordeal endured with some of the finest men he could have possibly hoped to meet.

When I arrived at school, there was only one teacher, Miss Peterson and the caretaker, Mr Arthur, there. Mr Arthur was shining the floor in one of the classrooms with that special, circular, hairy, shiny, polishing machine only ever used by caretakers in schools.

"Goodness me, Harry, you're keen! Go and have a seat in the Hall until some of the others arrive. Do you want a drink of orange juice whilst you're waiting?"

Miss Peterson was one of my favourite teachers. She took me when I was in second year infants. She relied on hugs rather than shouts to get her message across. The children behaved because they loved her not because they were scared of her. Not all the teachers were the same.

"Yes, please."

Miss Peterson soon brought me a weak tasting cordial orange juice in a white plastic cup and I chewed around the rim as I waited for the others to arrive. Other children started drifting in about five minutes after me, looking very proud of themselves in their party clothes, but I had to wait twenty minutes before Andy arrived, looking like Emilio Estevez after he had been on one of those medieval torture racks. His 'Breakfast Club' jacket was, however, the coolest thing I had ever seen an eleven year old wear. I was relieved when I saw his tall head in the queue in the entrance hall. I chatted to lots of different people before Andy turned up, but I never felt quite as comfortable when he wasn't around. We were a team and everyone knew it, including me.

When Andy walked through into the Main Hall, a big smile broke out across my face and when Andy's eyes caught mine, he smiled back, heading straight across the centre of the hall to where I was sitting on the far side from the entrance. Andy stood out because of his height, his expensive clothing, but most of all he stood out because of his confidence in himself. As he walked over, he couldn't help but break out into a little Michael Jackson moonwalk. He did it well too, not quite Jackson standards but very impressively for an eleven year old. There was a certain Michael Jackson-ness about Andy back then. He walked as though his every step on the pavement lit the floor below him, like in the Billie Jean video.

"Hi 'H'. You're looking great. Love the Tacchini. Want a Juicy Fruit?"

"No, thanks."

I wasn't good with chewing gum, it made me anxious. As soon as I started chewing it, I started to worry about how I was going to dispose of it and how uncool I would look putting my fingers into my mouth to take it out. Wrapping up saliva clad gum into a little bit of silver foil wasn't the coolest either. Add to that the fear of choking and I quickly decided chewing gum wasn't for me.

As I was declining a strip of Juicy Fruit, the opening guitar of Prince's 'When Doves Cry' kicked in through the DJ's speakers. I remember the DJ was called DJ Ronnie and he had business cards above his speakers that said on them, 'Rochdale's Very Own Disc Jockey, Ronnie Roberts. Music For Every Occasion.' I know that as I collected a card as a souvenir from the evening, as he was setting up, and kept it in my bedroom drawer for years. Ronnie was about fifty with long straggly, silver hair and wore a tie-dyed t-shirt that was too small for a man with his belly and too colourful for a man of his age. On the whole, he had decent taste in music though and started with a medley of Prince's 'When Doves Cry', followed by Simple Minds 'Don't You (Forget About Me)' and then Bon Jovi's 'Livin' On A Prayer' at which point the music briefly stopped so Mrs Thornhedge, our headmistress, could thank us all for coming and tell us what wonderful children we had all been during our time at the school. She also mentioned where the fire exits were located.

Once 'When Doves Cry' started, Andy whooped with delight and shouted out,

"Come on 'H', let's dance!"

Andy strutted across to the middle of the dance floor, followed by me and shortly afterwards by about thirty girls. Every other lad just sat around the edge of the Hall chatting, laughing, staring at girls or playing a game of tick which involved them not getting up from their seats, just trying to angle their bodies away from the 'ticker'.

I loved both singing and dancing. I thought I knew all the words to most songs from the eighties but it turned out that I may have misheard a few. Gillian Sharp gave me a sharp prod in the ribs when 'Livin' On A Prayer' was playing because I sang,

"Gina wants to die in her old age," which apparently I'd got wrong. The music was too loud to hear what she thought the real words were, but I thought Gina wanting to die in her old age made sense. After all, at that age, I thought everyone wanted to die in their old age.

I don't remember every song that was played that night but remember for the first hour I danced enthusiastically to every one. I remember DJ Ronnie was taking requests so it was stuff like 'Take On Me' by A-Ha, 'Rio' by Duran Duran and 'Open Your Heart' by Madonna which I know was definitely played, as I remember Andy requesting it.

It wasn't until Kenny Loggins 'Danger Zone' came on, an hour into the party that things began taking a turn for the worse. In that first hour of dancing, I realised that I had feelings for Shilpa Gupta. Shilpa was in my class and I had always considered her to be sweet and happy, but at the 'Leavers Disco' she was wearing a very intricate, pink Saree and it took her levels of attractiveness to heights they had never previously scaled. She looked stunning. I kept trying to dance around her and as she became aware of this, she smiled shyly and giggled beautifully. For the first time in my life, I thought I knew what love felt like. It felt like a euphoric illness. I felt sick with delight.

Unfortunately, I was oblivious to the fact that cupid's arrow had been busy. I wasn't the only boy in school who had their passions stirred by Shilpa Gupta, it turned out there were several others. The keenest of the lot was Greg Stones, a confident boy from Andy's class who thought that the way to a woman's heart was to ridicule anyone who stood in his way.

Greg Stones did not know how to dance. I think he pretty much knew that himself, you could tell he looked uncomfortable. He was a stocky, dark haired boy with a heavy fringe. He came over to dance with Shilpa and me as we had given ourselves a little space from Andy and the twenty nine other girls he was dancing in the middle of. There was a sharp contrast between Andy's dancing which was flamboyant and extroverted with lots of thrusting arm movements and Greg's which solely involved him moving his feet from side to side. To try to distract Shilpa from his lack of grace on the dance floor, Greg tried to engage in a conversation with her. He did this by shouting very loudly. As I danced next to him, I was sure he was making me look good. There was absolutely no arm, shoulder, hip or neck movement to Greg's dancing, he just stepped like a novice skier going sideways up a hill.

Greg's language was more colourful than his dancing.

"Thought I'd come and teach the gay boys how to do it," Greg yelled across at Shilpa.

I smirked. I thought he had realised he was hopeless but I was mistaken, he actually thought he could dance. Shilpa didn't say a word. I presumed she was too classy to respond. To my mind, she was just giving him a token, uncomfortable, half-smile. Having failed with his first character assassination, a minute of stepping from side to side later, Greg launched a second attack.

"They'll probably be necking later," he yelled across to Shilpa, who looked puzzled and frowned at him.

"Who will?" she asked.

Greg Stones motioned his head towards me.

"Hay-ch and his bum chum. They'll be giving each other love bites and kissing each other's bottoms."

I don't think Greg was intending for me to hear him, as he was shouting into Shilpa's ear, but he was so loud I couldn't help but hear. I was slightly offended but it was easily brushed off, Greg was an idiot so his stupid comments were irrelevant. I had heard boys muttering about me before, ever since I had stopped playing football at break, but hadn't realised what was being said. I was anticipating an angry response from Shilpa. I couldn't imagine she would tolerate Greg speaking like that about me. She liked me, I know she did. Perhaps she might even have started to get the same feelings for me that I had for her, feelings of love. I waited but the angry response didn't come, in fact, quite the opposite, Shilpa just giggled and smiled, but this time not at me, at Greg Stones. I didn't know what to do. I stayed there a while, my heart felt wounded but I continued to dance in that awkward three some, watching Greg and Shilpa talking and laughing. They were both ignoring me now. I had become so insignificant I wasn't even worthy of insults. Reluctantly, I shuffled away from Shilpa and towards Andy's group.

Greg Stones awful, shuffling dance movements provided the catalyst for a lot of awkward, uncomfortable boys to lose their nervousness about dancing. They probably concluded, one by one, that it was impossible to move any worse than Greg, so over the next few songs, thirty or so boys emerged from the corners of the Hall on to the dance floor.

DJ Ronnie wanted to keep the dance floor full. He must have realised that if he kept on playing pop songs like Mel and Kim's 'Respectable', that the boys would soon return to the periphery. He had to dig deep into his music collection and bring out the songs in the box earmarked 'Any Old Fool Can Dance To This' or in our case, 'Any Young Fool Can Dance To This'. For a full half hour, he started playing songs that were perfect for eleven year old boys to jump around to. Old classics like 'Baggy Trousers' and 'One Step Beyond' by Madness, 'Should I Stay or Should I Go?' by The Clash, 'Come On Eileen' by Dexy's and Bad Manners 'Can Can' were all given an outing. Most of the boys loved it, grabbing hold of each other and hurling themselves around with wild abandon but this desperate tactic by DJ Ronnie backfired. It was the equivalent of 'Wet Wet Wet' taking up Heavy Metal or Johnny Mathis taking up rap. They might find a new audience but it would only be a matter of time before they lost their original following. After a few songs, most of the girls dejectedly stomped off, with the exception of Shilpa Gupta, who was bouncing around the dance floor with Greg Stones, who had been given an opportunity to move away from the side step and had moved on to jumping up and down. The boys who considered themselves 'proper' dancers, namely Andy and me, stomped off too.

"It's not fair," moaned Jenny Trescothick, sticking her bottom lip out as she did so, "just because boys don't know how to dance, they have to play songs like this."

"Some of us do know how to dance, Jenny," Andy protested.

"OK, you do," Jenny conceded, "but none of the others do."

"What about 'H'?"

Jenny Trescothick, chewing gum that she had probably been given by Andy, looked me up and down.

"No offence, H, but you've got less rhythm than anyone I've ever seen in my life. You dance like a kangaroo that is being electrocuted."

About a dozen girls simultaneously sniggered at Jenny's jibe. I had never seen a kangaroo being electrocuted but knew enough to realise that this was not a compliment. I could feel myself blushing. My face was the colour of humiliation. Girls who hadn't heard what Jenny had said were asking what everyone was laughing at, so there then followed a lot of whispering and then a lot of second hand sniggering. I felt embarrassed and I felt betrayed, not by Jenny, who was just stating her opinion, but by Andy, who had managed to convince me that the one thing in the world that I was actually good at, was dancing. He had lied to me. He had probably only pretended to think I was good, so I'd go and dance with him and make him look better. Andy had blown my ego up like a balloon and then let all the air out. I was deflated and flat. I wanted the ground to swallow me up.

Soon enough DJ Ronnie ran out of floor fillers for eleven year old boys, either that, or he was told by Mrs Thornhedge to calm things down a bit. 'Dancealong' eighties pop returned to the delight of the girls and the acceptance of the boys. Most of the lads didn't want to dance for the whole night, they just wanted to feel like they had made an effort and to a man, they had. All the girls dragged Andy back to the dance floor, he feigned reluctance for all of three seconds, but when they tried to drag me too, I fought against them and remained rooted in my seat. These girls were not my friends, they had all collectively been laughing and sniggering at me only a few minutes earlier.

Once the girls had gleefully danced away, it was the boys turn to have a go at me. On reflection, I guess I brought it on myself to an extent. Even though I was mad with Andy, I couldn't stop myself from sticking up for him. Greg Stones was more to blame than I was though. Buoyed by his success of sorts with Shilpa Gupta, he was sat in the middle of about five boys, looking red faced and sweaty. Michael Jackson's 'Thriller' was being played and Andy was in his element, acting out the moves from the 'Thriller' video that we had replayed a thousand times on the VCR in his bedroom. The girls around him loved his moves. The boys who looked on were jealous.

"I don't know who Andy Corcoran thinks he is," Greg commented bitterly, "look at him! I hate him. He think he's the 'King of Bamford', but all he is, is 'King Of The Puffs'!"

The four surrounding lads laughed and agreed. Once again, Greg wasn't speaking for my benefit, but his inability to adopt the right decibel level meant I heard every word from about six seats down along the row.

"You're just jealous because you dance like a space invader!" I shouted back across.

"What did you just say?" Greg asked, leaning forward and across at me, trying to intimidate me not to repeat it.

"You heard me. I said you dance like a space invader."

"Get lost Hay-ch! I knew you'd stick up for him because you're 'Prince of The Puffs'! Let's face it, you're in love with Andy Corcoran."

All the boys surrounding him, laughed, nodded in agreement and made affirmative comments. I was already emotionally vulnerable after the dancing insults, so this stung.

"He's just my friend," I protested, even though at that moment he didn't feel like much of a friend.

"Yeh, right. You want to have sex with him," Simon James added smugly.

I was shocked by Simon's input. He was a quiet, intelligent lad who had always been very pleasant towards me before, but I suppose he was anxious to fit into the gang so he was making sure he wasn't left out when it came to dishing out insults.

I have to confess I didn't really understand his insult. I was eleven. I was old enough to know what sex was. I couldn't really imagine my own Mum and Dad doing it, especially not my Dad, but I suspected they would have perhaps reluctantly agreed to do it just the once, in order to have me.

I could sort of picture my Dad saying,

"I am terribly sorry to have to ask this, Kitty, but we would both really like to have a baby. I know it's awful, but would you mind if we did that sex thing, just the once, in order for us to have a child?"

I had a basic sexual knowledge but presumed Simon James must not even have that if he thought two boys could do it. I thought I could put him straight.

"Don't be dense, Simon. How could I have sex with Andy? He's a boy."

"He could put his willy into your bottom. You'd like that, wouldn't you, Hay-ch? Andy's big fat willy up your bum. That would make all your dreams come true, wouldn't it?"

Those five boys laughed like they had never laughed before after Simon said that, side splitting, tear streaming, hysterical, laughter. They thought it was the funniest thing anyone had ever said in the whole history of the world. Cannon and Ball were nobodies compared to Simon James. He was the new 'King of Comedy' and I was the newly christened, 'Prince of the Puffs'.

I was smart enough to know I had lost this battle. It was five against one. If I had protested, it would have just made things worse. I just stood up, ignored any subsequent jibes, walked across the dance floor to the other side of the Hall, folded my arms and sulked. I remained in my own little world of indoor rain clouds for fifteen minutes until Andy came over to try to brighten my day. Andy would become an expert at managing my dark clouds and insecurities but at that stage he was a mere novice and despite the clouds producing rain so acidic Prince could have sang about them, he was there to pass me a brolly.

Chapter Five

It had taken Andy fifteen minutes to come over to the sulking spot, which, to my mind, was about thirteen minutes too long. By then he knew something was wrong, so crouched down in front of my seating position, putting his hands on each of my shoulders.

"What's the matter, 'H'?"

"Nothing."

I would never give a response like that these days. I would just come straight out with my issue. There would be no mind games. I find mind games annoying. Time and people have taught me that lesson but at eleven years old, I hadn't figured that out and was craving the attention I had been starved of. Saying 'nothing' was just a request for Andy to delve deeper. We both knew that.

"Of course there is! You've been sat there for ages with your angry face on. Who's upset you?"

"No-one."

Once again, just stupid mind games.

"Come on, H, you can tell me. We're like brothers. We share everything."

"You told me I could dance," I blurted out, "but everyone else thinks I'm rubbish."

Andy was old before his time. He had a very mature head on his shoulders for an eleven year old. He gave a measured response.

"Don't be so ridiculous, H. They're jealous, that's all. Everyone has their own style when it comes to dancing and yours is just too cool for them to understand."

I perked up a little.

"Really?"

"Yes, H, really. It's probably the type of dancing you'd see in Manchester or London or even New York and the rest of these kids are just very Rochdale."

I liked that. I could relate to Andy's point. Maybe I danced differently because my parents were from London. Maybe it was capital city dancing coming through in my blood. Perhaps it was just that the other kids didn't know talent if it slapped them in the face with a wet fish. If Michael Jackson himself had turned up at our school disco, with his sparkly jacket and white gloves and began 'Moonwalking', I could imagine the kids in our school would all look at each other and say,

"Who the bloody hell does he think he is? Swanning in here with his flashy clothes and his daft dancing, nobody dances like that in Rochdale. I can't be that mithered with all that fancy footwork either. He needs to calm himself down."

The truth was, I was no Michael Jackson. I was truly hopeless at dancing. I've not improved either. For a while, in my late teens, I convinced myself that I had, but I think in reality, I was about as good at dancing as I was at football. The point is though, if Andy turned on his charm, he could convince me I was brilliant at anything.

"So you think I'm good?"

"H, I think you're brilliant. The problem you've got around here is that you're a dancing shepherd, leading the way for others to follow and these numpties are all just sheep. Now are you going to put a smile back on that face of yours or what?"

I tried to smile but I wasn't ready. It turned out to be more of a grimace. I still had more that I needed to get off my chest.

"They said we love each other too."

"Who did? Anyway, who cares about that H? I do love you. You're my best friend."

"I don't mean like that, like bum chums, benders. They said I want you to put your willy up my bum."

"Who said that?"

"Loads of them."

"Like who?"

"Like Simon James and ...."

I should have said Greg Stones first, but I said Simon as he was in the forefront of my mind, as it had been his insults that had created the most hilarity and for me, the biggest humiliation. If I had known that Andy would set off seeking retribution, I would have stopped him. Simon was basically a good kid who was just trying to fit in and had said some thoughtless stuff in his attempts to do so. He wasn't the ringleader of hate. The ringleader of hate was Greg Stones. Andy should have set off in his direction.

Before I had even had chance to finish my sentence and explain the context of Simon's comments and that Greg had sparked the whole thing off, Andy had gone. He had spotted Simon James over in the far corner of the Hall, taking large handfuls of 'Monster Munch' and pouring himself a glass of cheap coke from a table that had been set up to provide children with refreshments. Andy began with a purposeful stride, but he gathered pace like a plane on a runway and by the time he was halfway across the Hall he was sprinting. I was fascinated. I had never seen Andy sprint before.

Andy's intention was to rugby tackle Simon to the ground and, as he put it the next day, 'duff him up', but he was momentarily forgetting how poor he was at sports and that he had never played rugby in his life. He had no idea how to tackle. Simon was oblivious to the imminent attack, as he had his back turned. A smattering of Monster Munch fragments were building up around his feet.

I would like to tell you that Andy rugby tackled Simon James so fiercely they fell on to the top of the refreshment table, spilt coke and watery orange juice, crushed all the crisps, rose like a victorious wrestler and sent a right hook in to the face of the already gobsmacked Greg Stones and justice was served. That is not what happened.

What really did happen was a pretty decent consolation prize. Running full speed in an ungainly fashion was something Andy had no experience of doing. He had always previously kept some speed in reserve to ensure he arrived everywhere in pristine condition, without a hair or an item of clothing out of place. Thus, as he ran ostrich-like, across the heavily polished floors, he slipped but could not help but continue running with his arms out in front of him for protection. He ended up pushing into the back of Jenny Trescothick, who had only stopped dancing momentarily to grab a drink of juice. Andy hit her with such force that she toppled head first on to the refreshment table, sliding across it, over the other end and hit the metallic school climbing frame that had been folded away behind it. Somehow she managed to get her left foot through a tight space between two metal bars and it jammed there, so she was left dangling with her feet in the air and her head about three inches off the ground. Her hair, hanging upside down, looked like a Ken Dodd tickling stick.

Thankfully, Jenny Trescothick eventually emerged from the incident relatively unscathed. She just had a slightly bruised ankle. The damage done was emotional rather than physical. In those brief moments that her world was literally turned upside down, the tartan skirt she was wearing was forced downwards and underneath were a pair of knickers that must have been passed down by an older sister. In bright white lettering on a black background it simply said 'Showaddywaddy'.

I had no idea what a 'Showaddywaddy' was nor was I exactly sure what the word said initially. Like half the people in the room, I turned my head upside down so I could read it. By this time, Jenny Trescothick had started to sob, probably through a combination of panic, pain and public humiliation. Miss Peterson and Mrs Thornhedge rushed to her aid and, whilst they did, Andy tried to dust himself off and blend unnoticed into the crowd of onlookers. Andy had never been and will never be someone who can blend into a crowd. Mrs Thornhedge had spotted him.

"Andrew Corcoran, don't you be trying to slope off anywhere. Once we get Jenny down from here, I shall be wanting a word with you, so you stay right where you are," she said this in a sinister tone that made anyone who liked Andy fear for his future.

Ten minutes later, the drama was over and all the girls were back dancing, including a puffy faced Jenny Trescothick, who had begun to put her ordeal behind her, with the only evidence being those puffy cheeks, a slight limp and the occasional sniff. She was not totally permitted to erase the incident from memory though. From that day forward, pretty much everyone who was in our school year at Bamford gradually forgot the name Jenny Trescothick, but they all remembered her nickname that was christened that night – 'Waddy'! At Secondary school, everyone called her 'Waddy'. At University, thanks to her having the misfortune of arriving at Warwick University and finding someone else from Rochdale in her Halls of Residence, she was called 'Waddy'. I have it on good authority that these days, even in the throes of passion, her husband calls her 'Waddy'. She hated it at first, but as she grew older she began to see the funny side.

As for Andy, he just claimed he was running for a drink and knocked into 'Waddy' completely by accident. It was a half-truth and Mrs Thornhedge had little choice but to take his word for it and he escaped with a warning to 'be more careful in future'. He certainly didn't heed that particular warning. He did make an effort to behave himself for the rest of the evening, but by the next day he was plotting to get revenge on Greg Stones for upsetting me (once I explained, Simon James had become less of a target).

The whole 'Waddy' incident helped me bounce back from my sulky mood and I was even persuaded by Andy to get up and dance again, but I moved without the same exuberance I'd had earlier in the night. I danced like I thought everyone was watching, but not in a good way. Andy too, danced like everyone was watching, but he adored the spotlight being on him. The sixty seconds after knocking 'Waddy' over were the only time I can ever recall when he didn't want the spotlight shining his way. My confidence, however, was dented after the 'Leavers Disco' and for a while, I attempted to move in the shadows. This proved an impossible task with Andy Corcoran as my best friend. I should have known that with Andy, drama is always around the next corner.

Chapter Six

There's something wonderful about trudging through muddy fields in Wellington boots, it gives you a certain feeling of invincibility. If you were wearing any old pair of shoes or trainers, you would be slipping and sliding in acres of mud, but in Wellington boots you can splash through them like a harvester through a field of corn.

Saddleworth Moor was muddy even in the summer. We had parked the car to the West of Dovestone reservoir and were heading North towards Greenfield reservoir. Often in the summer it was dry enough for shoes, but in 1987, even in July, it wasn't. It didn't matter though. It was a hike I could manage, come rain or shine, since I was eight or nine and one my Dad and I particularly enjoyed, so when he suggested I join him that Sunday, I was quick to agree. I hadn't realised it wasn't just companionship he wanted though. He wanted me there for a man to man talk. My father had decided it was time for our 'birds and the bees' moment.

I'm not sure if anyone does actually talk about 'birds' and 'bees' when they hand out sexual education talks to their offspring, but my father certainly didn't. We were heading down a clough by Greenfield reservoir, talking about football and about how Everton had won the League, which wasn't a particularly riveting conversation for me, but I had tried to keep at least a passing interest in football for my father's sake.

"So," he said after the footballing conversation had quickly dried up, "what exactly do you know about sex, H?"

To be asked this question by my Dad, the day after the 'Leavers Disco' seemed perfectly natural. I was about to move on from the cosseted, safe environment of Bamford Primary School and move into the big wide world and this was one step towards my father ensuring I was ready for it. It wasn't awkward or embarrassing having this sort of conversation with my father.

"Quite a bit," I suggested, "I know how a woman gets pregnant."

"How?" my father asked, as we walked along the wide, stony path by Greenfield brook.

"The man puts his erect thingmebob into the lady's parting and a liquid comes out with sperm in. When one sperm combines with an egg inside the lady's tummy, they combine to make a baby."

I had been taught all my sex education in the playground, beginning from around the age of eight. Some of the details had been a bit sketchy at first, but over three years, I had managed to separate the wild exaggerations and plain lies from the truthful aspects and had managed to develop a basic knowledge of sex.

"OK, so you understand the mechanics, but do you appreciate the context?" my Dad said. I had no idea what this meant.

"Pardon?"

"Do you know when people have sex?" my father said, this time choosing language that I would understand the meaning of.

"When they're married," I answered.

I could feel myself blushing after I said this as I knew it was the answer my father expected to hear from me rather than the right one. Scott Winter's sister was pregnant and she was only about sixteen. She certainly wasn't married. I thought the correct answer was that people had sex when they wanted to have a baby. It turns out that wasn't quite right either.

"Not necessarily, H. Most couples have sex a long time before they are married."

"Because they want to have a baby together?"

"Often that isn't the reason. Often a man and a woman just want to have sex as it is something that adults enjoy doing."

"Oh right."

I was genuinely shocked by this. I honestly thought most people had sex with a reluctant acceptance that it was something they had to endure to have a child.

"I think, as you get older though and you start having girlfriends, the important thing is to always remember the possible consequences of what you are doing. There are ways and means for couples to make sure they don't have a baby when they have sex, but they aren't always reliable and perhaps we should discuss them another time. The message I want to get across today, is that you should always think about the consequences. Sex is not just a physical act, there are feelings, emotions and dangers involved."

I picked up on the word 'dangers'.

"What sort of dangers?"

"What I mean is, if you are with a lady and she gets pregnant, then you both have a link for the rest of your lives. You will always be the parents of that child, whether you stay together or not. Always remember the possible consequences of what you are doing. If you don't love someone enough to want them to be the parent of your child, do not have sex with them. When you are old enough, you will need to make important decisions and the most important decisions of all are to do with sex. I am not sure if I am explaining myself very well here, H. Do you understand what I am trying to tell you?"

I thought I did.

"Only have sex if you really like someone," I suggested.

My Dad considered my answer for a few moments. I remember he was wearing a flat cap and his grey hairs shone out from underneath it. I thought he was the wisest man on the planet. I'll probably repeat myself regularly when talking about my father and using the word 'wise' but I don't seem to be able to think of one without thinking of the other. I didn't think of him as a genius, just worldly wise.

"Yes, to an extent that's right. Not just like them," Dad suggested, "you need to know them, trust them and adore them before you ever think about having sex with them."

"OK."

We walked along for a while without speaking whilst I took in this latest nugget of knowledge from my father. I then thought about something else I needed to ask him.

"Dad, can two men have sex? I don't mean with a lady. I mean with each other."

I'm not sure if my question concerned my father but if it did, he showed no outward sign of it bothering him.

"Why do you ask, H?"

I kicked a few stones along the pathway.

"Oh, it was just something some of the boys said at school. They said two men could have sex and I wasn't sure whether or not to believe them."

"Well...let me see how I can best answer that one...I suppose two men can have sex together...and for that matter, two ladies can have sex together...but of course it takes a man and a lady to create a baby."

"OK, thanks."

I let my father's answer sink in. I already knew two men would not be producing a child. I just wanted confirmation that two people of the same sex sometimes engaged in sex with one another and my father had just confirmed, in a round about way, that they did. Although I didn't find the conversation uncomfortable, there were certain questions I would have felt awkward asking my Dad, how two ladies had sex when they didn't have a penis between them was one such question. I presumed that they must just rub together and kiss. As for what men did, my father's affirmative answer was enough for me to conclude the boys at school were right.

"Do you prefer boys or girls?" my Dad asked matter of factly.

"I like both," I replied honestly.

"So you wouldn't mind kissing a boy or a girl?" my father asked, still not showing any outward signs of this being a problem.

The penny dropped. I hadn't realised he meant in a kissing type of way.

"Oh, to kiss? I wouldn't want to kiss a boy. I think I'd like to kiss a girl, but I've never actually kissed one."

I could feel myself blushing again after that confession. My Dad responded with some words of comfort.

"Things like that don't need to be rushed, H. You have your whole life ahead of you."

My Dad saying that sent a pang of sadness through my body. I did have my whole life ahead of me but he didn't. He was sixty five. In that moment, I truly began to appreciate how old my father was and I was suddenly gripped by the realisation that his role in my life could be a short one. This thought scared me. I needed him to be by my side throughout my life, teaching me right from wrong, passing his wisdom on to me, but I knew that unless he defied science, this was very unlikely to happen. I felt the need to hold him.

"Dad?"

"Yes, son."

"Can you give me a hug, please? I feel like I really need a hug."

My Dad smiled a warm smile.

"Of course I can."

We hugged and I held him tightly. I always felt he smelt of after shave, knowledge and experience. Dad and I hugged a lot. I'm not sure if that was unusual amongst his generation of men, I suspect it probably was, but then he was a very unusual man. He just seemed to me like a man who was dipped from head to toe in goodness every day of his life. I clung even tighter than usual to his re-assuring smell that day. I wanted to get older and have my life deliver the excitement that independence and experience bring, but not if it meant my father being taken from me. It seemed an unfair trade off. I would rather be perpetually stuck as an eleven year old than be in a world without my father in it. I was overcome with emotion and started to cry, which surprised my father.

"What on earth is the matter, H?"

"It's just...it's just...it's just that I don't want to get any older," I stammered through my tears.

My Dad must have assumed that this 'man to man' talk had scared me a little, but that wasn't the case at all. I had just seen the future and I didn't like it one bit. He attempted to re-assure me about something I did not need to be re-assured about, but at least it distracted me away from thinking about his mortality.

"I understand, H. Age brings with it responsibilities that you probably don't feel ready for right now, but we all adapt. When I was your age, I was a very shy boy. I hated the idea of going to Secondary Modern, which is what Secondary schools were called back then, unless of course you passed your eleven plus and went to a Grammar School, which I was never going to do," my Dad said, in a faraway ramble, like he had drifted off to a land of memories.

"Little did I know, at eleven," he continued, "that within six years I would be fighting in a World War. If I had have known, I certainly wouldn't have spent any time worrying about school. Much darker times lay ahead."

"Did you kill anyone in the War, Dad?"

Perhaps a lot of eleven year old boys would have romanticised a war killing and made it into something noble, but I didn't like to think of my honourable father as a killer, even in war.

"I really don't know, H."

"How come?"

"I fired artillery guns. We fired twenty five pounders back then. I was in a crew of seven. Thinking back, I'm pretty sure there will have been casualties but we didn't get to see close up the damage that we had done. It wasn't as if I had any choice in the matter, anyway, I just did what I was told to do, H. You didn't get people like me in senior positions in the British Army or even amongst the Yanks, for the matter. I wasn't leadership quality any way. I was just a young boy."

In my youthful naivety it felt better that the only killing my father might have done was at a distance, rather than in close combat. I didn't like the thought of him looking a man in the eye and then stabbing or shooting him, stripping him of his right to exist.

We talked a lot more about the War that day. My Dad fought in Palestine, in Africa and on Crete before he was captured in 1941 and spent the next four years in a prisoner of war camp south of Wolfsberg, Stalag XVIII A. We talked about the friendships he made and the friends he lost. My father was not just a wonderful man, but a wonderfully brave man too. I wanted nothing more than to be like him. It would have been impossible for any child to admire their father more than I admired mine. He was my idol and although my life changed and brought with it trials and tribulations I could never have expected, that one simple fact remained constant. I idolised my father and although he is no longer with us, I still do.

Chapter Seven

In Secondary school, the music tastes that Andy and I fostered at primary school changed. We didn't totally abandon our former loves, they just lived a more sheltered life. Artists like Madonna and Michael Jackson were still considered great but a whole new music scene was developing much closer to home and we wanted to be part of it. At thirteen and fourteen, we certainly weren't at the centre of all things 'Madchester', but we were happily on the fringes.

The biggest band that was emerging out of Manchester in the late 1980s had to be 'The Stone Roses'. Andy always claimed he 'wasn't fussed', but he was though, you could tell he loved them. Any time 'Fools Gold', 'I Wanna Be Adored' or 'She Bangs The Drums' came on the radio, he'd be singing along, knowing abstract lyrics you could only possibly know if you had listened to those records over and over again. Andy just thought liking 'The Stone Roses' was conforming. All the coolest kids at school loved 'The Roses' and Andy didn't want to share a common interest with them, he wanted to be alternative.

Andy's favourite band from Manchester were James. When we first started at Matthew Moss High School, in 1987, hardly anyone at school had heard of them and Andy loved that. They had been touted as the next big thing in Manchester and had released their first album 'Stutter' but word hadn't reached too many school kids in Rochdale at that point. By the time we left 'Matthew Moss High School', practically everyone had heard of them.

When we were in our third year at Secondary School, Andy had begun to go into Manchester, on a Saturday, once a month. He wanted to just go for a wander around, but he justified it to his Mum and Dad by saying there was a swanky hairdresser's, off Deansgate, where he needed to go to have his haircut. In reality, he would get the train to Manchester Victoria but walk through to some barbers near Oxford Road station. I went with him a couple of times. I didn't get my hair cut as my Mum insisted on cutting mine, to spare her the cost, but I sat there whilst 'Mad Harry' went to work on Andy's. He did an excellent job but it was a weird old room in a dilapidated building with ancient floorboards and more than likely ancient equipment. It was what I would imagine a barber's would have looked like in Victorian times. 'Mad Harry' was about eighty but seemed a pleasant, timid old soul. Andy would go home and tell his Dad that the cut cost him £8, but in fact he was only charged 80p a haircut, so he would pocket the other £7.20 that his Dad would give him. I told Andy I thought this was theft. He told me that he was merely being entrepreneurial. I would never have done such a thing to my parents but with an abundance of money comes a lack of appreciation.

Knowing he was always going to be £7.20 up from the 'Mad Harry scam', Andy would stay in and around Manchester shopping for music and clothes. In the city centre, Piccadilly Records was his favourite place for music and Afflecks Palace was his favourite spot for clothes. The latter was a trendy indoor market, popular amongst hip kids and students and in Andy's mind, if it wasn't bought at Afflecks Palace, it wasn't worth wearing. With the music, he was less exclusive but Piccadilly Records was Andy's favourite place for new compact discs and vinyl records, whether it was seven inch records, twelve inch records or LP's, which I learnt stood for 'long player'. For cheap second hand records Andy tended to go to Rochdale or a place called King Bee records in Chorlton-cum-Hardy.

Andy wanted to get hold of everything he could by James, whether it was singles, albums or limited edition four track recordings called EPs. James' lead singer was Tim Booth. He was arthouse cool like Lou Reed rather than rock star cool like Ian Brown from The Stone Roses. He spoke softly with a middle class lilt that suggested life had brought him to Manchester rather than having been raised there. He had masses of curly hair and danced, Andy pointed out, just like me, moving every muscle in his body to the music. Andy hadn't seen him performing live but they were often on late night music shows on Granada television or Channel 4 so he had all their performances on video.

We didn't have a video recorder at home, but Andy did give me a cassette version of 'Stutter' that he had recorded from his compact disc and on the other side of the cassette he put all the different James songs he had from his vinyl collection. I thought their music was a bit weird, it was very manic, but the more I listened to it, the more I learnt to love its obscurity. My very favourite track was called 'Johnny Yen', which seemed to be about a circus act setting himself on fire.

Andy would often record cassettes for me, not just of Madchester music but huge varieties of music going back to the forties and fifties. He would never record a new tape though until I could answer detailed questions about the one I had most recently been given, to prove to him that I had given it a proper listen. His music collection had grown to epic proportions by the time he was about thirteen. He probably had over a thousand CD's and even more vinyl records. It was lucky he had a huge bedroom as it wouldn't have all squeezed into mine.

If it wasn't for those cassettes though, a lot of songs and artists would never have entered into my consciousness. Brilliant mainstream songs like The Eagles 'Hotel California', Fleetwood Mac's 'The Chain' and The Beatles 'Eleanor Rigby' as well as slightly more obscure songs like Peter Gabriel's 'Games Without Frontiers', Velvet Underground's 'Venus In Furs' and my particular favourite, Leonard Cohen's 'Don't Go Home With Your Hard-On', were introduced to me and stayed with me forever. Andy loved the music emerging from Manchester, but his tastes were eclectic and he would buy magazines like Sounds, Record Mirror, NME, Melody Maker and Q to give him a detailed insight into bands and artists both modern and historical. He also listened to John Peel and Bob Harris on Radio One, all the time. He didn't like the more mainstream DJ's, but John and Bob were like Gods to him.

When we were in our first year at 'Matthew Moss,' Andy used to get a hard time from the older kids for being different. He was miles taller than everyone else, moved differently, acted differently, wore his uniform differently, everything about him seemed to shout out 'bully me' to the older kids but his reaction to bullying was different too. He was never intimidated, always unfazed. I remember once four lads in Fifth Form took an arm or a leg each and dropped him into a huge muddy puddle but he didn't cry or make a drama out of it. It was at the start of lunch break so he headed home, changed and was back for afternoon lessons. Despite being flamboyant, Andy knew when to take it down a notch or two.

By the time we reached the third year, the bullying had long since stopped and instead, Andy became a child the older boys wanted to talk to. Word had spread that he was into music in a big way and the fourth and fifth year lads would often seek him out to ask him questions about who were the rising stars and what music they should spend their money on. It was hanging around with the older kids at thirteen and fourteen years old that led Andy to start smoking.

Part of me was shocked when I discovered Andy was smoking. It seemed to be to be more of a 'sheep' thing than a 'shepherd' thing and it seemed out of character for Andy to take the lead from anyone else. At break and lunch time, when Andy used to go over and chat music with the older lads, I didn't tend to join them, for a number of reasons, including the fact that I felt out of my depth with a bunch of older boys and didn't like the idea of sneaking through a gap in the perimeter fence to 'enjoy' a sly cigarette.

One weekend, I decided to quiz Andy about why he would want to smoke. We were up in my bedroom, having a cup of tea. Andy was fussy when it came to tea, he would only ever drink Tetley tea and it had to be brewed in his own teapot, so if he came around to ours he would bring his teapot around with him, along with its purple knitted tea cosy that his Nan had apparently knitted for him as a Christmas present. He started to bring his own teabags too as my Mum usually bought cheap teabags, but once she found out he would only drink Tetley tea, she bought them and hid them from Dad and would only bring them out when Andy visited. We would bring the pot up to my room on a tray with a bowl of sugar and a selection of biscuits that Andy would bring with him. There were often macaroons, Wagon Wheels, Club Oranges, Club Fruits, Garibaldis and chocolate digestives amongst the vast selection. In our house, my Mum and Dad only ever bought plain digestives and fig rolls and as a treat, one big shop a month, my Mum would buy Kit Kats, which we had to ration. Mum was prepared to get the better teabags when Andy visited but not the better chocolate. Expensive chocolate was a step too far. We were offered a Kit Kit each if there were any left, but Andy would always politely decline.

"I don't understand why you've started smoking," I stated just as Andy was putting a third heaped spoonful of sugar into his second mug of tea. I didn't have sugar in my tea as all the sugar in the chocolate was enough to give me a sugar rush. It was probably the chocolate high that encouraged me to challenge Andy about his smoking.

"The inner me told me I was a smoker, H. Artistic people tend to smoke. History is littered full of entertainers that smoked. Humphrey Bogart, Nat King Cole, James Dean…"

"Those guys have something else in common," I pointed out.

"What?"

"They're all dead."

"James Dean died in a car crash."

"I know but lots of people who smoke die of cancer. Why do it to yourself?"

"It's not something I'll do forever. It's just something I feel like doing right now. Don't nag me about it."

I think I'd touched a nerve. I kept on pressing it.

"Michael Jackson doesn't smoke."

"Not that we know of. Michael Jackson might be cadging fags from Bubbles all the time in Neverland for all we know."

"Do you even like smoking?"

"I don't dislike it."

I took this to mean 'not really'. If he'd have enjoyed smoking, Andy would have said so.

"Do you not think about all the bad things it is doing to your body?"

"As a matter of fact, H, I do. One of which is stunting your growth. I am fourteen years old and six feet two. I need something to stunt my growth. I'm tall enough already, thank you very much!"

Andy was a September birthday so was fourteen soon after we started third year. I was an August birthday, so was one of the younger ones in our school year, eleven months younger than Andy. He was about a foot taller than me at the start of that school year. As time passed, I bridged the gap a little, perhaps to about seven or eight inches, but despite Andy's smoking he grew to be about 6 feet 5 inches tall. He still says if he hadn't started smoking he would have been over seven feet tall. He exaggerates. In many ways, Andy liked to stand out, but when it came to his height, he didn't enjoy towering over everyone. Although I thought at the time he was being tongue in cheek when he said he wanted his smoking to stunt his growth, I do think there was an element of truth in his comments. Perhaps it stunted the growth of his feet. They only grew to a size ten, the same as mine.

"Anyway," Andy continued as he peeled the silver wrapper back on a Club Fruit, "why do you always disappear when I hang around with the Fifth formers? You'd like them. They're more fun than most of the imbeciles in our year."

There were lots of little reasons and one major reason why I didn't want to join Andy with the Fifth Formers. I decided it was time to be honest, both to Andy and to myself.

"I don't like Lucas Glover."

"What's wrong with Lucas Glover? He's the funniest lad at our school. Tommy Cooper's coffin is shaking because he is worried that Lucas is his Second Coming"

Lucas Glover was no Tommy Cooper. What Lucas Glover actually was, was a hyperactive, loud mouthed idiot, who never shut up. He wasn't tall but his Dad owned a gym in Radcliffe, so he had spent twelve months pumping iron. He had a body like Sylvester Stallone in First Blood.

"He calls me Paki," and there it was, I'd said it, the truth was out.

Andy pulled a confused face like he had taken milk out the fridge and smelt the one that was a fortnight out of date.

"But you're not Pakistani."

"I told him that, so now when he doesn't call me 'Paki', he calls me 'coon' or 'golly'. He's told all the lads in their year that they should start calling me 'golly'. He's told them it's my new nickname."

"I don't get it. Why would he do that?"

"Maybe because I have brown skin?"

It was unusual for Andy to be slow on the up take. It turns out he was just confused as to why Lucas would single me out.

"So what? Half the kids at school have brown skin and you don't. Not really."

If you aren't from Rochdale, you may not be aware that Rochdale has a big Asian community, certainly even more so now than back in the late 1980s, but nevertheless, even then I'd say one in five kids at our school was Asian. It was the same at primary school, but prior to my teenage years, I had paid very little attention to the colour of anyone's skin, including my own. It was only a couple of years into secondary school that race began to get mentioned. All the kids in our school year just mixed in, regardless of colour, but for some reason the kids in the school year two years older tended to mix more with kids of the same racial background. The group of 'smokers' that Andy tended to hang around with were almost always just white kids. I had no interest in hanging around with a bunch of kids who smoked anyway, but the fact that Lucas Glover had been throwing insults my way, both at break times and on our walk home, cemented my determination to keep away.

My father is mixed race. By genetic association, I guess that makes me mixed race too. I haven't mentioned this earlier, because as I was growing up my father's age and wisdom were far more significant factors to me than the colour of his skin. My Dad's mother was a white, working class Londoner, his father was a black working class man from Trinidad & Tobago, who moved to London shortly after the First World War. They had three sons together. My Dad was the eldest and the only survivor. His youngest brother, Jimmy, was knocked down and killed by a delivery lorry when he was ten. His other brother, Desmond, joined the Army at eighteen in 1943 and twelve months later was killed during the Battle for Caen.

As for my grandparents, my grandfather died in the early 1960s, long before I was born, whilst my Grandma lived until I was four. I have one vague memory of her being at our house and watching a film on television with John Travolta in it. It caught my attention because he was living in a bubble. I remember Grandma laughing and crying her way through it. I remember her laugh too. It was a deep laugh with a smokers cackle. I remember the feeling of her laughing at me too, but not in a scornful way, more out of delight. My mother may not have kept in contact with her family once she moved to Rochdale but my Dad obviously kept in touch with his Mum.

Given 25% of my bloodline was Caribbean, I didn't look like the type of kid Adolf Hitler would want to invite around to duet on 'Tomorrow Belongs To Me'. I had brown eyes and dark curly hair, but not proper African-American hair with tight curls, it was just half way between wavy and curly. My skin was dark enough to confuse people about my heritage. I was often asked if I was Polish, Jewish, East European, Indian, Pakistani or black or amongst the less polite I was asked if I was a Paki, a Yid, a Jew-boy, a wog, a Camel jockey, a coon or 'touched by the tar brush'. It didn't even cross my mind to be offended until Lucas Glover spoke about my skin colour in such a manner that it finally dawned on me that comments about race could be hurtful. Prior to that, I had spent a miniscule amount of time thinking about how I looked. It was other people's fascination.

At this point in our conversation, there was a knock on the door. My mother entered. She was wearing cropped denim shorts that revealed most of her legs from the thighs down and a black T-shirt, with a silver pattern on the front, that looked a couple of sizes too small for her. I remember thinking that day that she looked like something out of an Aerosmith video (she had moved on from Bruce Springsteen). My Mum was skinny but she had a large chest and if you looked hard enough, you could see her nipples pushing against the T-shirt. I hadn't looked hard enough, other friends had pointed this out to each other when they had been around to mine and she had worn the same t-shirt. I guess she had the perfect figure for those teenage boys to lust after. She was black haired, blue eyed, busty, skinny, put a lot of make-up on and wore revealing clothes. Every teenage boy who came round had a tongue that dropped so far out his mouth when he saw my mother that it could have removed the fluff from his belly. Without telling them, I had banned them all. Andy was the exception. Andy didn't look at my mother lustfully. He looked at her like I looked at her, with a pleasant indifference.

"Do you want me to refill your teapot?" Mum asked. She didn't really know how to make idle chit chat with my friends but tried to be helpful.

"Yes please, Mrs McCoy, that would be lovely," Andy responded.

"OK, I'll bring it back up in a few minutes," Mum said as she grabbed the tray with the teapot on, "two teabags or three?"

"Three, please."

I watched Andy as he engaged in this brief conversation. His tongue wasn't out, he didn't stare at her breasts with a look that suggested he wanted to put his nose between them and then shake his head rapidly. He didn't watch her backside wiggle as she carried the tray out. Andy treated my Mum no differently to how he treated my Dad. He was just a polite visitor to our home.

"What do you think of my Mum?" I asked him after I heard her go downstairs and switch the kettle on.

"I find her interesting," he replied stoically.

Our other male friends, or rather my other friends as Andy and I didn't really have mutual friends that were male, would have gone with 'sexy', but I was intrigued to hear what Andy meant by 'interesting'.

"How is my Mum 'interesting'?"

"Well, she seems very shy and uncomfortable with attention but then wears clothes that attract attention. It's a strange paradox."

"Do you think she's sexy?"

Andy seemed appalled by the suggestion.

"H, she's your mother!"

"So? You can still find her attractive."

"Well, I don't, not in the slightest bit. You're not going to tell me you find my mother sexually attractive now, are you? That would just be hideous."

Andy pretended to throw up.

"No, course I'm not. I was just asking because a lot of kids do find my Mum attractive."

Andy regained his composure.

"I know. I've heard some of the reprobates in our year wittering on about it. I don't find her interesting in that way. I just enjoy trying to figure her out. I think she lacks confidence and maybe she wears the clothes she does to give herself a little boost. I'm not sure. I don't think she does it to attract other men as she seems to really love your Dad."

"She adores him."

"And so she should. Your Dad's the salt of the earth."

"I know."

We didn't dwell on this conversation. Andy soon moved our chat back to the Fifth form kids and the issue relating to Lucas Glover's comments. The whole episode seemed to have annoyed Andy even more than me. I could tell he was livid.

"Do you want me to have a word with him?" Andy offered.

"No, there's no need. I'm quite happy having nothing to do with him."

"I'll sort it out."

"Andy, I'm telling you, just drop it."

My Mum arrived back with the tea.

"Can one of you boys open the door for me please?" she instructed from outside the door.

As I went to the door, Andy repeated his intentions. He said it with a more menacing tone second time around.

"I'm telling you, I'll sort this out."

Chapter Eight

The first thing I knew about the fight was when I went past the Headmaster, Mr Redgrave's office. Lucas Glover and Andy were sitting outside, heads bowed. Andy had a tear in the left arm of his school blazer and both looked bloodied and bruised, surprisingly Lucas probably looked like he had come off worse. Just as I was about to go over to Andy to see what the hell had happened, the school secretary, Mrs Bousfield, came out the office and ushered both boys back through to see Mr Redgrave. Thankfully corporal punishment had been dispensed with by then. I remember Geoff Shatner telling me in first year that when his Dad was at the school, Mr Redgrave used to send fighting kids home looking like tigers after he'd delivered 'six of the best' with his trusty cane.

It was half way through school lunch time when I saw Andy outside Mr Redgrave's room. It was raining and our designated classroom during 'wet play', which even back then I thought sounded strangely sexual, had changed. I was wandering around aimlessly trying to remember where the new one was. Having failed to find any of my classmates, I decided to head to the school noticeboard. The noticeboard was on a narrow corridor outside the boys' gym changing rooms and right by the staff room, so there were plenty of wet kids in their white PE kits and teachers carrying briefcases busily moving in and out of the two entrances like wasps into and out of their nests. I tucked myself in close to the wall to avoid being struck by a stray bag.

I looked up to see which room 'Three Michigan' were in. There were eight classes in each school year and each class was allocated an American state beginning with 'M', so there was Maine, Maryland, Massachusetts, Michigan, Minnesota, Mississippi, Missouri and Montana. I was in Michigan. All the good looking girls were in Massachusetts. I was almost fourteen, my interest in girls on a romantic level, had really started to kick in.

When I say I was interested in girls, my interest was selective. Initially, there were three or four pretty girls in 'Three Massachusetts ', who I found attractive, but soon enough I found I was purely focused on one girl, Amy Garfunkel. My relationships with other girls remained on the platonic pathway that they had always been on. Amy was not initially aware of my interest, but I was very aware that there was a girl in 'One Maine' who was infatuated by me. Her name was Joanna Barry.

That day, as I stood looking up at the noticeboard, half concentrating on the task in hand and half thinking about what the hell Andy had gone and done now, I felt something on my hand. It felt like a cat was licking the palm. It was a dry tongued lick. Perplexed, I turned and looked down and sure enough, standing beside me was Joanna Barry. She was eleven, four feet six inches tall, had braces on her teeth and wore strange, light blue plastic framed glasses.

"Joanna, did you just lick the palm of my hand?"

"No," she said, without expression.

"You did, didn't you?"

Joanna didn't say a word, she just shrugged her shoulders. To me, this was tantamount to a confession.

"Bloody hell, Joanna! You're weird," I said laughing.

"So?" she paused before adding, "You're friend has been fighting."

Joanna had only started at school a couple of months before. She didn't seem to have any friends so within a couple of weeks of starting, she had taken to following me around. I hadn't done anything to encourage her, but once she started following me, I didn't do anything to discourage her either, it wasn't in my nature to be cruel to her. Most of the time, she just seemed to watch Andy and me from a respectful distance away. I would say the odd word to her, but most of the time I forgot she was there. Licking my hand was a new thing.

"Andy? Did you see him?"

"Yes, with Lucas Glover. They were fighting at the back of A6. There was a big crowd. He lost."

"I've just seen them outside Mr Redgrave's office. Lucas looked like he came off worse, if you ask me."

"He did in the end," Joanna explained, "but that was only because some Asian kid beat Lucas up when Andy was on the floor....I'm going for my dinner now, H. Do you want to come with me?"

"No, thanks, I've eaten."

"See you later then."

"Bye....and Joanna?"

"What?"

"Don't be licking anyone else's hand in there. They might send the white van for you."

"I won't. I only want to lick yours."

"Great!"

With that Joanna headed off. It was the longest conversation we had ever had, but I was glad of it, as she had shed some light on the fight. I didn't see Andy again that day until we were walking home. He was walking ahead of me, but was easy to spot because he was so tall. He seemed to be walking faster than he normally did. He was walking on the road to get past various groups of kids who were ambling home.

"Oi, Andy, hang on!"

Andy seemed to hear me, cranked his head to the side instinctively, half thought about stopping but then just kept going. I ran to catch him. Once I reached him, I realised why he was dashing to get home. He had the biggest black eye I had ever seen. His left eye was only slightly open, forced closed by a shiny, purple golf ball sized lump above his eye. I should have been sympathetic but my overriding emotion was annoyed.

"I told you not to try to sort my problems out."

"I didn't do this for you," Andy lied.

"Who did you do it for then?"

"For myself. When Noah was searching for a pair of idiots for his Ark, his problem was half solved when he came across Lucas Glover."

"So what exactly made you hit him?"

"I don't know. I think my right fist forgot that it belonged to me and thought it was attached to Muhammad Ali, so took on a life of its own and led me towards his face."

"I meant what caused the fight?"

"I told you, Lucas Glover was being an idiot."

"Joanna Barry told me you lost."

"Well, Joanna was obviously not aware of the rules. First one to fall on to the floor was the winner. Mr Redgrave gave me a winner's medal, that's why I was outside his office. There was a medal ceremony. They played the national anthem and everything. I'm surprised you didn't hear me singing. I was belting it out."

"You look like you got battered."

"Looks can be deceiving. Anyway, I wouldn't go as far as to say 'battered'. I would say, mildly injured from repeated blows."

"Stop trying to solve all the world's problems, Andy, you aren't superman."

"But I do look good in a cape."

"I'm being serious."

"I know you are but I'm not trying to solve the world's problems, just yours."

"I can look after myself."

"No, you can't. Look at you. The Munchkins were taller than you."

"Get lost, I'm average height, you're the one who is a freaky size like Herman Munster, not me. Anyway, this is what I look like when I fight my own corner," I said, pointing at my own, unblemished face," and that is what you end up looking like when you fight for me. Be my friend, make me smile, make me laugh, be there for me when I need you, but please don't fight my battles for me, Andy. You're a terrible fighter."

"I suppose you might have a point. I should have learnt my lesson after Greg Stones beat me up at Bamford."

I didn't know anything about that.

"When was that?"

"A few days after the Leavers Disco, remember when I was off school for a few days because I had a rash on my penis?"

"Yes."

"Well I didn't have a rash on my penis. I had a badly bruised face but I figured if I said I had a rash on my penis, it would be embarrassing enough for people to not think I was lying. Being beaten up by Greg Stones is more embarrassing than having a poorly knob."

"Did your Mum and Dad not go into school?"

"No, my Mum nearly did which was a bit of a shock as she normally just ignores me or gives me a few quid to go away. I had to beg her not to go in. I might not get away with begging this time though."

I was surprised Greg Stones hadn't been bragging about his victory at school, although beating Andy Corcoran in a fight wasn't really something to brag about. It would be comparable to beating Stan Laurel or even Duncan Norvelle.

"Look, it's not that I don't appreciate what you've done for me. I do. I really do, but I just don't think, even though you're massive, that you are any better at fighting than me. If we need to get back at people, we need to find a smarter way of doing it. Otherwise we will end up getting a lot more bruises and black eyes."

"I suppose you're right," Andy reflected, "it's just in my mind I'm a great fighter, but in reality I'm not. Did you hear Mo Iqbal battered Lucas?"

Mo Iqbal was a Fifth former. He was 'the cock of the year', which also meant he was 'the cock of the school'. This meant he was the toughest lad not the biggest dick, often the two were not mutually exclusive, but to me, Mo Iqbal always seemed to be alright. He tended to hang around with the other Asian kids, but a couple of times I'd been in the same detention classes as him and he came across as a decent lad. No interest in school whatsoever, but a decent lad all the same. He wasn't the brightest kid at school, but then I was no Albert Einstein myself. It appeared to me that Mo Iqbal would be fine with you as long as you didn't cross him. Lucas had obviously done something to piss him off.

"I'd heard it was an Asian kid, I didn't know who though. Why did Mo Iqbal get involved?"

"No idea. I'm glad he did though. Lucas had landed the punch that did this to my eye and my world was moving around like I was a giant spinning top, so I had fallen to the floor to try to stop it. If Mo hadn't intervened, I reckon Lucas would have picked me up and pressed down repeatedly on the top of my head to get me spinning even faster."

"Why didn't Mo have to go to see Redgrave too?" I asked, puzzled, as it was only Andy and Lucas that I had seen outside the Headmaster's office.

"He did. He went in first. Have you not heard?"

"Heard what?"

"He's been expelled."

Chapter Nine

I have previously mentioned that all my friends were in love with my mother with the exception of Andy. When we were in the Fifth Form, the very same thing could be said about Amy Garfunkel, all the boys loved her except Andy. He said he could never be interested in a girl who I liked, but there was more to it than that. Whereas I had started to become a bit obsessive about girls by the time I was fifteen, Andy never mentioned them, certainly not in a romantic sense anyway. I began thinking that there may well be a possibility that he was more attracted to boys than girls, but thought if he was he would tell me when he was ready to. My infatuation with Amy Garfunkel interested him though and he encouraged me to feel positive about my chances.

"You should just ask her out," Andy declared one Saturday afternoon as we came out of the newsagents on Bury Road in Bamford, each carrying a can and a bag of penny sweets. Andy's can was a Barr Cream Soda and I had a Shandy Bass. As Andy pulled off the ring pull to his can, half the drink exploded out of it and he stretched his arm out in front of him as the liquid fizzed out and on to the floor like a sugary waterfall.

"If this goes on my Calvin Klein jeans, I'll go loopy. I paid seventy quid for these! I knew that'd happen when I dropped it," he moaned.

I wasn't interested in Andy's can or his new jeans.

"Do you think so?"

"Of course, it always happens. I should have got another one when I dropped it off the shelf."

"No, I meant do you think I should ask Amy Garfunkel out?"

"I wouldn't hesitate for a second. Procrastination will get you nowhere. I don't think she is going to be the type of girl who will be staying in on a Friday night practising the cello, if you don't move quickly someone else will. Anyway, you'll be fine, she likes you, I can tell."

As soon as Andy stopped speaking he took the brave option of putting his mouth over the top of the can to stop any more of its sugary contents going to waste.

"You can tell. How?"

My heart was pounding, but Andy had a mouth full of cream soda so he made hand signals to me that he was trying to swallow the liquid frothing around in his mouth and throat before he could reply. I was desperate to hear proof that my love might be reciprocated, but I was sceptical about whether Andy would provide it. He was my biggest fan. He would pretty much see the positives in everything that involved me. Finally, Andy managed to swallow his drink, other than a few stray drops that escaped down the side of his chin. He took a white handkerchief out his jeans pocket and wiped his chin before speaking.

"It's blatantly obvious, H."

"In what way?"

"In lots of ways. She smiles when you speak. She holds her glance when she looks at you, longer than when she looks at anyone else. She goes into the girls toilets to check her appearance in the mirror just before she has a lesson with you."

My heart felt like it was flipping around like a pancake but I was doubtful Andy's last point could be accurate.

"Come off it, how would you know that?"

"I've obviously known you've liked her for a long time so I've been watching her, really just to ascertain, for my own peace of mind, that she's good enough for you. In my humble opinion, she isn't, but that's by the by, the point is, I've noticed she goes into the girls toilets before every class you're in with her."

"OK, stalker, two questions."

"Fire away."

"Firstly, how do you know that she isn't just going for a wee?"

"She isn't in there long enough for a wee. They don't just pull a zip down and pull it out like us, there is a whole complex procedure of pulling everything below the waist down. She isn't in there long enough for all that. She just wants to take a moment to re-assure herself that she looks fabulous and then out she comes."

"Could be for someone else's benefit?"

"I doubt it. Have you not noticed who you do Biology with?"

I thought about it. They weren't the most handsome or charismatic of people.

"OK, point taken. Possibly just for her own benefit then?"

"Possibly, I've no doubt she loves the mirror as much as the mirror loves her, but take it from me, there's a pattern to what she's doing and in the centre of that pattern is you."

"I'm not sure."

"Look H, if you want to ignore what I'm telling you, feel free to, I won't be offended but I'm telling you, she likes you."

I could feel myself getting goosepimples, but I still had my second question to ask.

"So come on then, tell me why you think she isn't good enough for me."

Without hesitation, Andy replied,

"She's pretty loud. She's crass. She's bubbling with confidence and self-assurance but in an arrogant rather than self-confident way. Amy Garfunkel knows she's pretty. I think she likes you better than anybody else, but she likes male company and flirts a lot. I'm not sure, with your sensitive nature that you will cope very well with the interest she generates from other boys. You're too good a person for her, but she's a stronger character with a more steely disposition than you. I'm worried she might hurt you."

"The last bit sounds very gay."

I didn't like to hear Andy's list of negatives about Amy and I just sort of blurted out my reaction. Given I still hadn't worked out what Andy's sexual tendencies actually were and given it didn't matter to me anyway, I immediately felt it was the wrong thing to have said. If I had been aware of the word 'homophobic' when I was fifteen, I would have been concerned that was how I was appearing. Andy showed no signs of reacting negatively though.

"I don't care if it does. What sort of friend would I be if I thought something but didn't say it and then saw you get hurt?"

I think, once Andy said this, that I immediately decided that I would stop even trying to fathom out whether or not Andy was gay. All I did know for certain was that Andy wanted nothing more than to be a good friend to me. I was proud to have him around.

We walked back up to Andy's house, chatting, joking and laughing. Once we were there, we headed up to Andy's room. Back in the early 1990's, we weren't reliant on the internet, social media or mobile phones to keep in touch with our friends. We just knocked around at each other's houses or quickly phoned each other to arrange a meeting place. Once we were together, we weren't distracted by interacting with others via WiFi, we just listened to music and talked to each other. By Fifth form, James had released two more studio albums, 'Stripmine' and 'Gold Mother', which had a more commercial feel to them than 'Stutter'. I preferred 'Stripmine', but although Andy really liked it, he thought it wasn't in the same league as 'Stutter' or 'Gold Mother'. As I was a guest at his home, he agreed to put Stripmine on first on his record player. After he'd played my favourite track, 'Are You Ready', I asked him to pick the needle up and take it back to the start of the track. I think I made him play that track half a dozen times as I thought James were passing subliminal messages to me about how I should handle Amy Garfunkel. After the sixth play Andy carefully put the record back in its sleeve, holding it around the edges to avoid finger marks. The conversation that I had deliberately put on pause, resumed.

"Did you hear John Dunphy is having a party tonight?" I asked Andy.

"No, you're forgetting you're the only male friend I have left. If it was a girl's party, I'd have known about it, but a lad's, not a chance."

I was sort of expecting that answer. I knew that Andy had long since fallen out with most of the lads from our school year. He hadn't gone to any great lengths to fit in from the start and having spent the third and fourth year hanging around with either me or the older lads, those potential bridges of reconciliation had long since become driftwood.

"Do you fancy coming?" I asked out of politeness. I fully anticipated the response I received, perhaps worded a little differently.

"I would rather lick my grandmother's incontinence pads than go there," Andy said with a dramatic flick of his hand, "but don't let me stop you going. I expect you are going to tell me that Amy Garfunkel also has an invite to this soiree."

Andy knew me too well.

"I expect so," I answered a little sheepishly, "she likes John Dunphy a lot more than you do."

"Yes, I have heard they are very close," Andy said stressing the last two words. There was a touch of Julian Clary about the way he delivered his lines, poised, not overly expressive, but with a dramatic effect. It was a dig at me. Andy was put out that I was intending on going to a party without him, but everyone has to have a certain level of independence and I was concerned that perhaps Andy and I were too interdependent. I think Andy had always also enjoyed the fact that he provided the strength in our friendship too, in that he was the outgoing, strong minded, flamboyant one whilst I was the reserved, fairly shy and sensitive one. I wasn't meek though. I also had a little bit of steely resolve in my DNA. I wanted to go to this party and I knew I would be going whether Andy went or not. Andy had always done his own thing when he wanted to, including hanging around with the older kids, so I did not feel duty bound to reject the invitation.

"They are close but just as friends," I clarified.

"Of course, I wasn't suggesting anything else," Andy replied in a caustic manner, "I very much doubt anything salacious was going on between them, I was merely commenting that they are very close. I am pleased you are going to the party. I hope it is a wonderful night. Just keep your wits about you and be sure not to drink too much."

"You sound like my mother!"

"Oh, I'm not saying it for the good of your health. I'm saying it for the good of your memory. I know if you end up getting inebriated you won't remember a thing and I want to hear everything, every single juicy detail, especially the bit that involves you finally getting it together with Amy Garfunkel. No tongues though, 'H', a first kiss should be just a little moist and gentle. It should definitely not include the use of that fleshy, muscular organ. Keep it in your mouth and keep your other fleshy, muscular organ inside your underpants too. Irrespective of whether or not Amy Garfunkel is a lady, you need to make sure you always act like a gentleman."

They were wise words. I wish I'd have listened. I don't think there's ever been a time I have acted less like a gentleman than at John Dunphy's party.

Chapter Ten

John Dunphy lived on a farm near Rawtenstall. How much farmland there was and what animals they kept remains a mystery to me, as it was dark when I arrived and I didn't really think to ask. All I do know was that the house his family lived in wasn't overly large. His Mum and Dad had gone away overnight to visit friends up in Newton Aycliffe, wherever that was and they had foolishly agreed to allow John to have a small gathering. They were far enough out into the sticks that they thought it unlikely that a hundred uninvited guests would attempt to gatecrash. It was sound reasoning, but it turned out to be wrong.

The concession granted to John, by his parents, to have a party came with certain stipulations. Firstly, no-one was allowed upstairs. Mr & Mrs Dunphy mustn't have trusted John's friends to abide by this ruling as they had borrowed stair gates from friends with younger children and put one at the foot of the stairs and one at the top. The one at the top had a bicycle padlock wrapped tightly around it, which circled the stairgate and the bannister, to ensure it remained tightly shut. The only possible way to open it would have been to enter the padlock number and John explained he faced execution if the top secret number was revealed.

The second stipulation Mr & Mrs Dunphy made was that their eldest son, Patrick, should remain at home to ensure things did not get out of hand. Patrick, at nineteen, was three years older than John, but as we found out later in the evening, age does not necessarily bring maturity along with it.

I had been told at school the day before that the party would be starting at eight o'clock, so I asked my Dad if he would drop me off. He was the slowest driver on earth, but I didn't mind, it was an opportunity to spend some quality time with him.

"What time will you want picking up?" Dad asked as he drove painstakingly slowly out of Bamford and towards Rawtenstall.

"About half eleven, if that's OK, although if you carry on driving at this pace, Dad, we'll be lucky to arrive before midnight!"

"Cheeky bugger!" Dad replied with a smile.

I had never heard my Dad 'properly' swear but as I got older, he would utter the odd mild curse in front of me. Words like 'bugger', 'crap' and 'piss' were now deemed acceptable. My Mum said she had never heard him say any of the 'full fat' swear words either. Sometimes, if they were to have a rare argument, she claimed she would throw them into her phraseology just for shock value. I had never witnessed any of these arguments my Mum said they occasionally had and wondered if my Mum had just made them up so their relationship didn't appear too saccharine sweet.

I enjoyed teasing my Dad about his driving. I teased him a lot about his age too and he would just chuckle. I knew not to cross the unspoken line, so never made jokes about skin colour, the armed forces or Mum, as he was particularly proud of all three. When I say he was proud of his skin colour that isn't entirely correct. He was proud of his family tree. He was just sensitive to criticisms that anybody made based on skin colour. My Dad rightly pointed out that brains are all the same colour. He was a firm believer in equality and could never understand why anybody made judgements based on race, religion, sexual preference or gender.

"The best candidate for a job is the one best suited to the role purely based on factors like intelligence, aptitude and experience. How light or dark your skin is and what you do with whatever you've got between your legs when the lights go out, should have no bearing at all," was how my Dad used to sum things up.

To my father, a mixed race man who served in the army, sacrificed a lot for his country and subsequently for love, there were just certain things you didn't joke about.

"Anyway," my Dad pointed out as we continued our journey at 'Popemobile' pace, "better to arrive safely than not at all."

"True, I don't mind really. I was only joking."

"Is Andy not going to this party? I could have given him a lift."

"No, he's not going. He's not really friendly with John Dunphy."

"Any fit girls going?"

This question sounded so wrong coming from my father. He was too old to be asking questions like that.

"Don't call them 'fit girls', Dad."

"Why not? I thought that's how young people referred to good looking young ladies these days."

"We do, but it sounds wrong when you say it. It makes you sound like a pervert."

"Charming! OK, I shall re-phrase it for you, 'H'. Are there any good looking girls going to this party then?"

"I imagine there'll be a few."

"Just remember to be confident but to treat them with dignity."

Dad was beginning to sound like Andy.

"OK, Dad. I shall open doors for them and put my coat over any puddles."

"I'm not suggesting you do that. All I'm saying is treat them with dignity. Girls like to be treated with a bit of dignity."

Plenty of the girls that I knew who were going to this party did not want to be treated with any dignity at all. I discovered when I was in my thirties that most women over thirty want to be treated with dignity, whilst I discovered in my teenage years that most teenage girls were far more interested in the bad guys than the good ones. There seemed to be an almost universal misconception that the bad guys were more fun. After fifteen years with a collection of idiots, the women who had chased the 'bad guys' began to change their minds about the sort of man they wanted. Back then though, I was considered a 'good guy' and most girls just wanted to be friends with me rather than flirt with me. I was just hoping Andy was right and Amy Garfunkel was the exception to the rule. That night, I knew I was likely to find out one way or the other.

Eventually, having spent half an hour feeling like we were being over taken by milk floats and old ladies with those little tartan shopping bags on wheels, we arrived at John's house. As my Dad pulled the handbrake on the car, I came out with a suggestion.

"Maybe it's time you bought another car, Pops."

I have no idea why I suggested that. My Dad could have borrowed Ayrton Senna's Formula One car and he wouldn't have driven any faster.

"I'm holding out for a year or two," my Dad replied.

"Why?"

"Well, it'll probably be my last car so I want to keep putting a bit of my pension away each month, so I can get a decent one."

My heart sank when my father said that. His last car. I knew what he meant, but I still asked him to explain himself.

"Why will it be your last car?"

"Well, I'm seventy now. If I buy a new car at seventy two, I should make it last a good eight to ten years because your Mum and I don't do a lot of driving. So, even if I'm lucky enough to last longer than the car does, I can't see me driving past eighty. I'll hand over the keys to your mother and she can drive your old Dad around after that."

I looked at his face. He seemed to have aged a lot in the five years I'd been at Secondary school. His hair had thinned and the wrinkles that used to only gather below his eyes had now spread across his face making it look like a brain with features. I immediately felt anxious about going to the party for no other reason than because I felt I was neglecting my father. I hadn't spent as much time with him in Fourth and Fifth form as I had when I was younger. I had even allowed my appearances on his walks to tail off. I felt consumed with guilt. He was living out the last few years of his life and I had been neglecting him. I should have been more aware of how little time he had left. I couldn't bring myself to get out of his car. My Dad spotted my deliberation.

"I'm confused, 'H'. You've just spent the whole of our journey moaning about the time it's taking and now we're here, you're not getting out. What's going on?"

"I'm not sure I want to go any more."

"Do you know what? Your mother said earlier that you might say this."

I was now puzzled too.

"She did?"

"Yes, she had an inkling Andy wouldn't be coming to this party and she thought you may be nervous going without him. Just go in and enjoy it, son. Savour every moment. You're only young once."

"That's not the reason, Dad."

"What is it then?"

I realised I was being ridiculous. I couldn't spend every moment of my life with my seventy year old father just in case he didn't live to see tomorrow. For all I knew, he could live until he was a hundred. Dad wouldn't have wanted me to sacrifice my early years to try to savour his later years.

"Oh, it doesn't matter."

"Good. I'm telling you, go in there and have a brilliant night, that's an order! I'll be back to pick you up at half past eleven."

"Thanks Dad. I will. Are you not going to tell me not to drink?"

"I trust you to make the right decisions yourself, 'H', without me nagging you."

"Dad…"

"Yes?"

"I love you very much."

I used to hug my father a lot, but along with the walks, the hugs had also dwindled. As for saying, 'I love you', I couldn't even remember the last time I'd told him. It must have been at least five years before, probably more. It felt uncomfortable to say and that pained me.

My father smiled.

"I know you do, 'H'. I love you very much too. Now go on, get yourself in there before we both start crying like a pair of babies. Have a wonderful time!"

"I will. I love you, Dad," I repeated as I got out, closed the car door behind me and walked confidently towards John Dunphy's house. It felt far easier to say second time around, as if a barrier had been lifted. Abandoning masculine traditions, from then on I would carry on telling my father I loved him for the rest of his life. I realised that day that it's impossible for a father to hear those words too often from his son.

Chapter Eleven

A few minutes later, five years on from the 'Leavers Disco', I was once again sat in a corner at a party feeling uncomfortable about Andy Corcoran not being there and wishing he would arrive. The difference this time was that I knew he would not be swanning in, in dramatic fashion. I would be sailing this ship alone. Whether there would be stormy waters or calm seas remained to be seen.

There were around a dozen people there when I arrived. A group of about eight boys were in the kitchen, sat around a huge wooden table, making a start on a vast array of beer cans lined up on one half of the table. It was a long, rectangular table with twelve chairs around it and the cans of beer had been artfully arranged so they spelt out, 'Let's Get Pissed'. When I went to grab a beer, about three of the lads yelled in unison to get one from the spare pile on the work top rather than ruin their masterpiece.

At that stage of my life, I wasn't really a drinker. I had had the occasional shandy with my Dad, but had never had a proper drunken experience and was keen to avoid starting at John's party. I had decided in advance that I would have a couple of beers and then call it quits. I took a can of Carling Black Label and watched silently as the other lads played a drinking game with a pack of playing cards, on the half of the table that wasn't covered with cans.

"Take a seat, 'H', we'll deal you in," John Dunphy suggested in friendly tones as he slurped the froth off the top of the beer can he had just opened.

I was never very good at cards and was keen to avoid joining in. I made up a quick excuse.

"No, I'm fine thanks, I was going to go through and say hello to the girls," I replied.

I could hear familiar girls' voices from one of the other rooms and was keen to discover if Amy Garfunkel was amongst them.

"OK, bud. Keep away from Lottie Gilchrist though. She's spoken for."

"Yeah, I know!"

Lottie and John had been together about six months by then. There were rumours around school that they were having sex but I didn't tend to get involved in rumours. I didn't know whether it was true or not, so it wasn't worth repeating. I wasn't sure whether the universal opinion was that it was a good thing or a bad thing. Personally, I thought it was both a risky and daring thing to do. I hadn't even had a girlfriend by then and any proper kisses I'd managed had only come about through a third party spinning a bottle or holding mistletoe above me and the girl at Christmas.

Other than the kitchen, there were two other rooms downstairs. The biggest room was a large square lounge with plenty of family photographs of John and his brother, in various stages of childhood, adorning the walls and mantelpiece. At this stage, that room was empty, but the female voices I had heard earlier were coming from a front room, off the lounge. I headed towards their jovial sounds.

The door was shut so I knocked, out of unnecessary politeness and entered. I was a little disappointed to discover that there were only three girls in there, sat on one of the two settees talking away excitedly. They were Lottie Gilchrist, Mussarat Miandad and Cathie Squires. They must have been talking about something that they did not want me to hear, as their conversation petered out on my arrival and they looked at each other awkwardly, barely disguising nervous smirks. All three were in our school year at 'Matthew Moss' and were in a group of about a dozen girls who were classed as 'pretty but swotty' by the majority of the lads. They weren't the 'cool kids' like the group Amy Garfunkel was in, but they were warm hearted and friendly and everyone seemed to like them, with the exception of Amy's gang who were oblivious to their existence. If I was making a Grease analogy, they would have been the 'Sandra Dee's'.

"Hi! Sorry am I interrupting?" I asked, knowing I obviously was.

"Of course not," Cathie said patting the settee, "come and sit down."

Cathie Squires was a motherly type. By this I don't mean a quiet, unassuming motherly type, like my own Mum. I just mean a ringleader and caring type, sometimes prone to being obstinate. Like me, she had elderly parents, but in her case both were advanced in years rather than just one. I think her mother was forty five when she gave birth to Cathie and her Dad was a few years older again. Cathie was the youngest of five girls, her eldest sister had already had a son before Cathie was born, so she was an Auntie the day she arrived in the world to a nephew who was three years her elder. I didn't find Cathie overly pretty, she was slightly overweight and it seemed to me that someone had pushed her in at the front until it came out the back, as she had no boobs and a sizeable bum. Her features were pleasant though, she had very deep blue eyes and curly blonde hair which didn't seem to have been organised into a style. It was just left to run wild like Japanese knotweed. Out of ten in looks, she was about a six, some of the other lads may have argued a seven, but they weren't as fussy as me. She wasn't in Amy Garfunkel's league. Amy was the fittest sixteen year old in Rochdale.

"Can I ask you something, H?" Cathie said, "Something I've been dying to ask you for ages but Andy's always with you, so it's been impossible to ask."

I knew what she was going to ask, so gave her an honest answer before the question was even out of her mouth.

"You can ask me, Cathie, but honestly, I've got no idea."

Cathie gave me a look like Arnold out of Different Strokes would have given Willis.

"I haven't even asked the question yet!"

"You were going to ask me whether Andy is gay."

I said it seriously but all three girls started laughing.

"How did you know?"

"Because I get asked it all the time!"

"Because everyone thinks he must be," Cathie explained, as though it needed an explanation.

"He's very effeminate," Mussarat chipped in, "not that I'm saying that's a bad thing, he just is."

"He's DEFINITELY gay," Lottie added with so much authority you would have thought that she had already witnessed him in the midst of a sexual act.

"Look, all I know is that Andy's a one-off. He's loyal, he's funny and he's intelligent."

The girls looked at each other with those smirks back on their faces.

"What?" I queried.

"It sounds like you fancy him," Cathie explained.

Perhaps that's what people thought. In fact, I suspect that was exactly what they thought. That Andy and I were gay lovers. People like to tittle tattle and perhaps we had somehow given them something to gossip about. I wasn't in the least bit concerned.

"Think what you like, I don't mind, I honestly don't, but the truth is, if you'd have let me finish without exchanging glances, I'd have said that Andy is a good friend and regardless of whether he is attracted to boys, girls or both, it's not going to make me like him any more or any less."

As I finished saying this, I realised how like my Dad I was sounding. I saw this as a good thing. I wanted nothing more than to be like my Dad.

"One day the truth will come out," Lottie suggested.

I don't know whether she was suggesting the truth would come out about Andy and me as a couple or whether she meant Andy's sexuality would not be a secret as he got older. I plummeted for the latter.

"I don't think Andy's hiding the truth. I just don't think he's interested in anyone at the moment."

"That's impossible," Cathie said shaking her head, as if I'd stated the world was flat, "we all have feelings and desires. It's part of who we are."

Mussarat agreed with Cathie, but pointed out why Andy may be concealing his feelings or at least why she would conceal hers in a similar position.

"I like men, but if I liked women, which I stress I really don't, but if I did, I wouldn't let anyone know."

"Why not?" Lottie asked.

"Well, apart from the obvious cultural reasons, I'd think I was a bit weird. I mean, it's not natural, is it? We're designed to be attracted to people of the opposite sex."

"Are we?" I questioned.

"Of course we are, 'H', don't be dumb. If we were all gay, there would be no future generations."

I didn't like the fact that I was being called 'dumb'. I wasn't the cleverest kid at school, not by a long stretch, but in this matter, I definitely wasn't being dumb.

"I know that Mussarat, but is every single one of us here to re-create? Could it not be possible that say 90% of us are designed to be attracted to people of the opposite sex and 10% of us are designed to be attracted to people of the same sex? If Andy is gay, and hand on heart I don't know if he is or if he isn't, but if he is, he hasn't chosen to be gay just to be different. It's just how he's designed."

"OK, calm down, we were only asking a question, 'H'," Lottie said in conciliatory tones. She could obviously see I was getting riled.

There was an awkward silence for about thirty seconds after this as no-one, including me, knew what to say next. It was down to Mussarat to put this particular conversation to bed. She took my two hands in hers and simply said,

"I hope Andy appreciates what a good friend he has in you, 'H'. Not everyone would stick up for a friend like you just did. You're completely right. His sexuality shouldn't matter, it's what sort of person he is on the inside that counts and you see him as a very good one."

Prior to that evening, I had never made any effort to speak to Mussarat. The only thing we had in common was that people pronounced our names wrong. I was 'Hay-ch' instead of 'Ay-ch' and Mussarat was pronounced with a silent 't' at the end so was 'M-Sara' but anyone who hadn't been made aware of this, like a new teacher at school, would always go for 'Muss-a-rat', which would cause guffaws amongst classmates.

I now decided I liked her, liked her in a platonic sense. I wasn't used to being praised by anyone other than my parents and Andy, so I was flattered to have been praised from a new source. I was transformed from feeling defensive to being buoyed with confidence. It's amazing what good a bit of flattery can do, especially to someone with a fragile ego like mine. I now felt more than worthy of Amy Garfunkel's affection and tonight was the night I was going to prove it.

Over the next twenty minutes, the party got into full swing. When John's parents had made the assumption that very few people would turn up to a party out in the sticks, they did so without appreciating how rare opportunities were for parties amongst fifteen and sixteen year old kids from Rochdale. At best, I knew of three or four in the previous twelve months, so most people (with Andy being one exception) wanted to make the most of it. In total, I would say over a hundred of us turned up, of which about twenty had been officially invited. They ate, drank and destroyed everything in their path like a swarm of locusts in a field of barley.

When you are fifteen or sixteen year's old, any periods of supreme confidence tend to be fleeting. This time mine only lasted until quarter past nine, the time that Amy Garfunkel arrived. These days if you saw a photograph of Amy Garfunkel on Facebook or Instagram, you would wonder what all the fuss was about, but back then she had all the finest physical features of Erika Eleniak, Maryam D'Abo and Catherine Oxenberg. She was a fair haired stunner. When she walked into that front room, bristling with confidence, my own positivity crumbled quicker than a Cadbury's Flake in a cheese grater. Karen Carpenter may have sung about being on top of the world in the 1970's, but when it came to beauty in the 1990's Amy Garfunkel occupied that prime location at beauty's highest peak. My millions of tiny offspring were desperate to abandon my body the moment I glanced at her.

Amy Garfunkel was no shrinking violet. She exuded confidence. I don't think I had even heard the word narcissism at fifteen, but I was aware she was probably more than a little selfish and self-obsessed but I couldn't help myself adoring her. She walked like a ballerina, so the heels of her feet never touched the ground, which gave me the impression that she floated around the room. She seemed central to every conversation and her punchlines seemed to trigger every bout of hilarity. Girls felt it would boost their status to be seen with her and the boys didn't exactly crash our ships on to the rocks as we gazed at her beauty but as a collective bunch of horny young men, beer was spilt, ash was dropped and hearts were broken.

When I made comparisons to beautiful women of the era, you may have noticed that I chose ladies of Nordic-like charms. Amy was a blond haired, blue eyed goddess. It would have been more appropriate if Amy had possessed a seductive voice like that of Marilyn Monroe, but in reality she had a reasonably harsh voice like that of a teacher in a class of unruly children. We were prepared to forgive this slight diversion from perfection. I imagined myself being Rex Harrison and Amy being Audrey Hepburn in Rochdale's Pygmalion. Like Eliza Doolittle, the voice could be changed but the beauty was here to stay, at least for several more years.

Once my confidence evaporated previously unnoticed obstacles seemed to appear in front of me. Without Andy there, it seemed like I was peripheral to every group and every conversation I joined in. I tried to be a social butterfly but as I moved from one small group to another, I couldn't help feeling my departure wasn't mourned by those I left behind or my arrival welcomed by the new group. My social inadequacies did nothing to stimulate my romantic bravery from within me and as I watched Amy Garfunkel grab centre stage in every group she was in, I started to doubt whether we were suited. To try to escape from my sense of awkwardness and low self-esteem, I quickly drank a second can of lager, swiftly followed by a third and then a fourth. By the time I had had my sixth can, I was back in the game or at least I was drunk enough to regain the belief that I was.

I remember sitting on a settee on my own, cracking open a seventh can and watching two separate sets of events unfold before me. First of all, I was watching how Cathie Squires was being charmed by Keith Corden on the other settee. Keith had begun by walking over confidently, made a comment that I couldn't hear but it was obviously witty as it had made Cathie laugh, then he perched himself down on the settee next to her so the back of his bottom was only just on the seat and then, as the conversation progressed with a continued positive response from Cathie including increased eye contact, Keith moved further back into the settee, edging Cathie into the corner, so her right side was pressed against the settee's arm. In frame by frame movements, Keith's right arm crept around Cathie's shoulders so eventually it was fully around her back with his hand touching her right shoulder. Once Keith had succeeded in this movement without any signs of negativity from Cathie, Keith's momentum quickened. Their eyes were now constantly fixed on each other's and after a genius move where Keith closed in, pretending to remove a fictional object off Cathie's cheek, their heads seemed to simultaneously tilt to a 45 degree angle and a kiss began. I felt like standing up and applauding Keith's mastery of the art of seduction. There was a tinge of jealousy too, despite already having only scored her six out of ten for physical beauty, Cathie was one of the better looking girls at the party and she was no longer an option. I quickly brushed that feeling off and turned my attention to my primary target, Amy Garfunkel.

Amy was standing in a group of three girls and three boys. They had initially been talking, laughing and joking but had now moved on to solely singing songs. The music that had been playing in the kitchen was only blasting out on a cheap portable CD player, so the noise wasn't carrying to the other rooms. In my inebriated state, it amused me that none of the songs they were trying to sing ever reached a conclusion. Someone would begin a popular song, others would join in, everyone would know the chorus and then it would be left to one or two to maintain the momentum, but normally they would get lost in the lyrics somewhere in the second or third verse. There was a mix of old and new songs. 'American Pie' was one, 'Daydream Believer' was another, 'Sit Down' by James was belted out, during which they amused themselves by sitting down and that was followed by a few Stone Roses and Happy Mondays songs. They particularly struggled with the Stone Roses songs probably because a lot of Ian Brown's lyrics are almost undecipherable. There was no Google to fall back on in those days. I remember thinking that if Andy had been there, he would have steered them in the right lyrical direction.

I was just an interested observer in their singing until one particular song brought me to my feet and gave me the impetus and confidence to join in. I'm not sure who it was, but one of the girls randomly started singing Michael Jackson's 'The Way You Make Me Feel'. In a long list of Michael Jackson epics, 'The Way You Make Me Feel' is somewhere in the middle. It's not exactly a hidden gem, after all it's on the 'BAD' album, which sold tens of millions, but if you stopped a hundred people on the street and asked them to tell you their favourite Michael Jackson song, undoubtedly they'd say songs like 'Billie Jean', 'Thriller', 'Smooth Criminal' and even 'Don't Stop 'Til You Get Enough' long before they'd mention 'The Way You Make Me Feel'. It doesn't stop it being a brilliant song, but it did stop those half dozen people in the 'Singalong Gang' in John's front room getting past the first couple of lines. That's where I came in.

In a strange way, I felt I owed it to Andy to get up and sing. Several years previously, we had sung it around his house and on our walk home from primary school often enough. We'd watched the video of it thousands of times too. Michael's dancing in that video was beyond sublime and his love interest in it had the sexiest figure I had ever clapped my eyes on. I often had an uncomfortable bulge watching her strut away from Michael's advances.

I also saw that song as a sign. I could relate to the lyrics and thought they were prompting me to show a level of bravery and persistence that Michael showed in that video. Someone, I think it may well have been Amy, as she had led the singing in most of the songs, began to falter after the first few lines and rather than let them move on to another song, I took my cue, got to my feet, joined the group and took over.

I don't have the greatest voice in the world, Andy's for example, is far better than mine, but I can hold a note. I guess the alcohol was largely responsible for my lack of trepidation, but I just went into a little 'H' zone, not really caring what was going on around me, but I was aware there was a stunned silence. I wasn't someone that these kids had ever seen hog the limelight before. I was enjoying myself though and as my confidence grew, I began throwing in a few of Michael's moves, as when we were younger, Andy had taught me them and I'd almost mastered the moonwalk. When I reached the chorus, each line needs repeating so I used my clenched fist as a pretend microphone and prompted a couple of the girls to repeat the lines. When the song finished, I'd like to say everyone in the room got to their feet and roared their approval, but in reality, there was no more than a ripple of applause from a few supportive females. Cathie Squires had even stopped kissing Keith Corden to watch.

"Wow, H!" Cathie said encouragingly, "That was fantastic! Who taught you to dance and sing like that?"

"I don't know," I shrugged, "I just can."

I felt a bit guilty for not passing the plaudits to Andy. It was, after all, him who had taught me or at least encouraged me. The last time I could remember dancing in front of an audience of sorts was at the 'Leavers Disco' at primary school and I had been universally ridiculed after that. I began to think maybe Andy had been right back then after all, perhaps I really was ahead of my time. It turned out to be a false dawn. I've never been complimented about my dancing ever again. I peaked at fifteen.

Disappointingly though, Amy Garfunkel didn't seem to have been impressed. She hadn't been one of the girls who had clapped, hadn't joined in with the chorus and she had swiftly moved on to her next song, 'Too Many Walls' by Cathy Dennis which once again was soon aborted as it was yet another song with a bunch of tricky lyrics. As you may have realised by now, I was always picking up on the words in songs, thinking they were meant just for me, so as I listened to Amy singing the first few lines, I decided not to go chasing after her. Maybe it was because I felt there were too many obstacles in my way or maybe it was because she didn't sing it in the soft, tender way that Cathy Dennis did.

I may not be entirely sure what my reasoning was to abort my mission to capture Amy Garfunkel's heart, alcohol tends to make my recollections a little blurred, but whatever it was, I recall it was after that 'Too Many Walls' song. Despite Andy not being there, I was starting to enjoy myself and probably just didn't want to spoil my good mood by getting knocked back. John Dunphy came in at that point with a four pack of beer and offered me one. I pulled it off the plastic holder, opened it, clinked it with John's to say 'Cheers' and then took a huge gulp. It was icy cold and tasted great. I decided I loved beer and it loved me. It had magical qualities. It even made me dance well. If I wasn't going to get lucky, one thing was for certain, I was going to get drunk.

Chapter Twelve

The songfest was brought to a halt when some lad who I had never seen before, until he took my spot on the settee, leant forward and began vomiting all over John's carpet. He seemed too zoned out to realise what he was doing as after thirty seconds of resurrecting the contents of his evening meal, he tucked himself into a ball on the settee and went back to sleep. I had expected the rancid smell would have led everyone to flee to the other rooms, but they all just seemed to edge over to the other side of the room. The only two people it seemed to have a real impact on were John Dunphy and me. I was concerned because the stench was making me gag and John was concerned because he knew it fell upon him to clean it all up.

"Oh my God! Who is that?" John asked, whilst staring at the culprit, who was now sleepily rubbing the trail end of his vomit off his mouth and on to the settee.

"Don't know, but he was in the kitchen before with your brother," someone explained.

"Fuckin' typical! Well my bloody brother can clear it up then. Where the hell is he? This night is turning in to a fucking disaster."

John Dunphy stormed out the room in search of his brother. Teenage parties were always a disaster for the host. I didn't understand why anyone was stupid enough to think it was a good idea to have one at their own home. You gather together a group of people who are at an age when their selfishness peaks, their tolerance of alcohol is at its lowest level and are then somehow surprised when everything goes wrong.

The smell in the front room became too much for me so I wandered out in to the lounge. There must have been about seventy people in there, including about twenty lads who were jumping around drunkenly to 'Smells Like Teen Spirit' as someone had brought the portable CD player through. They were bashing into irate bystanders and tensions were mounting as some boyfriends were going in to overprotective mode. Rather than finding myself in the middle of a fist fight, I decided to seek liquid sanctuary in the kitchen.

The kitchen, which had earlier been a hive of activity, was now empty but bore witness to its previous role as the epicentre of drunken activity. Beer cans and food were strewn across the floor along with some discarded broken glass. The impressive dining table had playing cards spread across it, like an army in disarray, many soaked in spilt lager. Some wag had drunkenly arranged the non-crushed empty cans to spell out, 'JOHN IS A TIT', another example, like everything else in the room, of how little respect was shown to the host and his home.

I felt bad for John. I was drunk but not heartless. I'd overheard someone saying that John's brother had invited a few mates around and they were getting stoned upstairs, so his parents naïve view that he could be relied upon to ensure things wouldn't get out of hand had proved to be wrong. As I was surveying the damage, John briefly rushed in, collected various cleaning products from the cupboard under the sink, muttered something about his brother being the biggest arsehole on the planet and then rushed back out, broken glass crunching under his feet as he did so.

After John left the room, I went to the cupboard under the sink myself, grabbed a couple of black bin bags and started to tidy the place up. It didn't take me long as it was only a case of binning the cans and bits of food, as well as sweeping the glass up and washing down the work surfaces. Within ten minutes, the kitchen was spotless. Just as I finished, the kitchen door opened and Amy Garfunkel slid in. She stood with her bottom tight against the door which I took as a sign that she wanted no-one else to intrude. If backsides can be compared to wines, this was no Liebfraumilch, it was more a Chevalier Montrachet Grand Cru.

"Haych, I wondered where you'd got to. Bloody hell! Have you cleared this all up?"

I nodded. I forgave her mispronunciation of my name immediately. I looked her up and down. She was petite with a big personality and an immaculate dress sense. For her slender frame she had an ample bosom which was always a bonus in the mind of a teenage boy and meant she went in and out in all the right places, both at the front and at the back. She wore a light blue dress with a floral pattern that was well above the knee but she wore black tights underneath. They had a ladder in them, on the left leg that stretched down from her thigh. I also noticed Amy was wearing more make-up than I had ever seen her wear before, but the light blue eye shadow only served to accentuate her beauty. I was mesmerised but was desperate to do everything I could not to show it.

"Arrhh! Aren't you sweet?" Amy continued.

Coming from anyone else, I may have considered this condescending, but uttered from the lips of Amy Garfunkel, it had its own unique charm.

"Thanks. Everyone seems to be trashing the place which seemed dead tight to me, so I thought I'd clear up."

"That's lovely, Haych."

In time, I would tell Amy how annoying it was to be called 'Haych', but not then, not that night.

"Thanks! Most decent people would do the same."

"I'm not so sure they would."

Without asking, flinching or appearing uncomfortable, Amy just walked straight up to me and began to hug me. As I've mentioned before, I'm not the tallest person in the world, I had sprung up to be average, but I felt tall with Amy's diminutive figure cuddling in to me, as she couldn't have been much taller than five feet.

As I wrapped my arms around Amy, I began to ponder what this hug actually meant. Was it a 'thank you for being a good friend to John' hug or a 'this is my excuse to cuddle up to you because I fancy you' hug. Left to my own devices I probably never would have worked that one out, but barely had my brain registered the question when Amy looked up at me with her big doe-eyes, puckered up and moved in for a kiss. I'm glad I didn't have time to think as that meant I didn't have time to ruin everything, I just instinctively kissed back. It felt wonderful, there were no tongues, it wasn't too sloppy, but there was a certain smell, an alluring, pleasant smell that I hadn't come across before. I could taste it too. I told myself it was the smell of desire mixed with the taste of electricity. In reality, it was probably vodka on Amy's breath. She had quite a thin upper lip but a really thick lower lip which I felt added to her sensuality.

"That was good," Amy said as we pulled out of the kiss, before taking hold of my left hand and adding, "Let's go into the back garden. There's a bench at the bottom of the garden, I noticed it earlier before it went dark. We'll have more privacy there."

Before I knew it, I was being led outside. I couldn't believe my luck. Why the hell was this happening? I wasn't overly tall or good looking and had barely spoken to Amy that night or previously, but here I was being dragged to a bench for passion by the fittest girl in Rochdale. I half thought it was some sort of honey trap and once I arrived at the bench, half a dozen Sixth Formers, mates of John's brother maybe, would pounce on me and beat the crap out of me, but my nervousness was misplaced. Without even the briefest of small talk, we arrived at the bench and our kissing continued. After a couple of minutes of snogging, I concluded that I must have somehow ended up in a Meat Loaf song and was probably hallucinating in a ditch.

As it transpired, I was thinking of the wrong Meat Loaf song but it was Amy not me that was rushing through the bases. My fingers had been more than happy trying to tune Amy's left nipple in to BBC Radio One, but as we kissed, Amy grabbed my other hand and placed it firmly underneath her dress which led me to discover they weren't tights but suspenders. When I subsequently clumsily failed to find the two erogenous zones hiding below, I was given a guided tour.

Amongst all this excitement I didn't want to pull out of our lingering kiss as I feared if I did, I would feel too awkward to allow my fingers to remain in exploration mode. I was both fascinated and aroused by this new sensation but didn't really know what I was expected to do. I figured that perhaps the deeper my fingers went inside Amy, the more benefit she would reap. It soon became apparent that I had drawn the wrong conclusions. As I delved deeper, Amy initially began kissing with less passion and subsequently removed herself from our clinch altogether.

"You're hurting me," Amy whispered softly, but it still made me feel like an incompetent fool. No matter how tenderly she said it, it was still a complaint.

"Sorry," I replied guiltily. I hated myself for being so inept.

I was about to confess that this was all new to me and I didn't have the foggiest idea what I was supposed to be doing, when Amy spoke again, just in time to spare my blushes.

"Just be gentle. Use the tips of your fingers and just slowly move them inside and out and then back in again. Part them and bring them together. When I'm ready for you to do something different, I'll let you know. I'm not going to be shy about guiding you, Haych, I know what my body wants."

Receiving a sexual talking to from Amy Garfunkel should have been a whole lot better than having a sexual conversation with my father, but bizarrely this talk felt several degrees more cringeworthy. Perhaps it was because I was meant to be clueless when my father discussed things with me, whilst now, I was meant to know what I was supposed to be doing. It had now been firmly established that Amy knew what she was doing and I did not. I was glad we could barely see each other in the darkness as I could feel my face flush with humiliation. I put my fingers back to work hoping they would not be abject failures second time around. I was now at a point that I had stopped enjoying the experience, I just felt pressured to get things right. I was concerned that if I failed again, Amy Garfunkel would head straight back to the party and tell a captivated audience how I had bruised her fandango.

Thankfully my mind was soon put at ease. We had started kissing again, but it began as uncomfortable, passionless kissing, as if both of our minds were elsewhere. My fingers were following instructions and after a couple of minutes, Amy briefly stopped kissing to utter encouragement.

"That's better, Haych. That feels nice. Keep doing that."

Amy hadn't exactly turned into Meg Ryan but at least I felt a little less of a fool. I still wasn't comfortable or relaxed about the whole thing though. I was being taught a lesson in love but the natural beauty of the moment seemed to have been stripped away. I persevered, kept kissing, kept feeling my way around Amy's body, but not instinctively, just doing what I was told. If there had been such a book as 'An Idiot's Guide To A Woman's Vagina', I was being read the first few pages. I moved faster and slower as I was told and when I made a false move, Amy took my hand and led it to where it should be. I was getting to play with the private parts of the most beautiful girl in Rochdale, but given the choice I would have rather have been playing Super Mario. I was good at that. With this, my mind kept telling me I was a sexual dunce.

Despite my brain not enjoying this new sexual experience, my body was giving outward signs to the contrary. As Amy began to take pleasure (or perhaps fake pleasure) in my improved movements, she moved one of her hands across the top of my jeans and couldn't help but notice my heightened sense of arousal.

"Oh wow, Haych, that's a monster," Amy almost squealed. Everything she did seemed to contrast with my coyness.

My emotions were all over the place now. Amy's compliment about my manhood made me feel proud, uncomfortable, ridiculous, a little embarrassed and invigorated with a new sense of desire.

"I need to see this fella in the flesh," Amy was saying as she began to undo the buttons on my jeans.

I could feel my heart pounding in my chest. I took Amy's statements and actions as indicators that I could stop trying forlornly to find her mysterious 'G' spot, as it was her turn to do things to me. I took my fingers out from inside Amy's body and along with my other hand, let it fall to my side, as my body slumped a little on the bench. Before I relaxed too much, I looked anxiously back towards John's house. The light from the kitchen was barely allowing us to see each other, but more of a concern to me was that someone else may come out into the back garden and spot us. The coast was clear for now.

Amy stood up off the bench, turned to face towards me and then went down on her knees in front of me. There were white pebbles all around the bench and they made a crunching sound as she kneeled into them.

"Spread your knees apart, Hay-ch," Amy commanded.

I did so. I knew what was about to happen and my mind was now in overdrive. I tried to take my thoughts back to Andy's Paul Simon and Chevvy Chase 'You Can Call Me Al' knee dance but stopped myself from crossing my hands over the top of Amy's head. She shuffled into the gap between my opened legs and went back to work on the top of my jeans, undoing the rest of the buttons and then pulling at the waistline.

"Sit up a little so I can get them off," Amy instructed.

I hesitated.

"Someone might come out and see us," I said nervously.

"We would hear them before they could see us," Amy explained reassuringly.

"OK."

I did what I was told. I was dizzy with both fear and excitement. Was this really happening to me when fifteen minutes before I had been washing the dishes? I lifted my bottom off the seat and did not sit back down until I could feel my belt below my knees. I can't remember what boxer shorts I was wearing but given they would undoubtedly have been purchased by my mother, they would have been an unspectacular supermarket 'own brand' pair. It didn't matter. Amy wasn't concerned about the wrapping she just wanted to get to the present. I lifted up temporarily once more. My boxer shorts were around my shins soon after my jeans. Amy took a moment to inspect what was on offer, running a thumb and finger up the shaft of my penis. I don't think it had ever stood prouder.

"That's a fine specimen you have there, Haych."

I could make out Amy's smiling teeth through the darkness. The muscles in my face were frozen with fear so I couldn't smile back. I just remember her blonde hair moving downwards like a sinking duster. This was it! This was the moment. The moment I had been dreaming of since I had set eyes on the magnificent, pocket sized features of Amy Garfunkel. From the top of my head to the tips of my toes, I began to gently shake. I felt like I had been plugged in and was now being sexually electrocuted. I knew exactly what was about to happen. Amy was going to kiss a place that had never been kissed before.

That was the last thought I had before it all went wrong. It was all too much for my dirty mind and innocent body to cope with. In uncomfortable second by second spasms, my body prematurely let go. As I twitched, my brain bungee jumped off the bridge of sexual desire into the valley of emptiness. Before I had even begun the race, I had been disqualified for a false start. There was collateral damage too. Amy was too close to the epicentre of the explosion. Her painful reflection would stay with us both forever.

"Ow...ow...I can't see! It stings, it really, really stings!"

"What's the matter?"

"What do you think's the matter, you idiot? I've got jizz in my eye."

Chapter Thirteen

"So you've never heard it called 'jizz' before?" Andy asked.

"No, but I knew exactly what she meant. It was pretty obvious."

"Yeh, there were a million little clues written all over her face," Andy said drily.

Neither of us laughed but I could tell Andy was stifling a grin. It was the morning after the night before and I was around at the Corcoran's house, relating to Andy in minute detail how the evening had gone and how it had literally reached an unfortunate climax. Andy was aware of how uncomfortably embarrassed I had been and was sensitive enough not to mock my humiliation too much. Humour was barely acceptable, laughter would have been inappropriate.

"So what happened next?" Andy asked.

"Amy just got up and ran into the house with her right eye still closed."

"Was she OK?"

"I've no idea. There was no way I was going back into the party in case she'd told everyone what had just happened. I just went around the side of the house, opened the side gate and started walking home."

"Walking home? To Bamford? From Rawtenstall?"

"Well, I knew I wasn't going to make it all the way home. I just needed to get as far away from there as I could," I explained.

"So how did you eventually get home?" Andy asked.

"I'll tell you in a minute, something else happened before I made it home."

"What?" Andy replied, with intrigue in his voice. He loved a drama and the previous evening had been nothing if not dramatic.

"Well two things actually. After Amy had stomped off back into the house like an angry pirate, I headed around the house, like I said and I was only a hundred yards up the road when I heard the sound of a woman's shoes behind me. Girl's shoes actually. Guess who it was?"

"Not Amy?"

"Nope, she would still have been bathing her eye in the sink at that point. Guess again.

"I've no idea.

"Guess."

"Dannii Minogue."

"Don't be stupid!"

"I told you I had no idea. Just tell me."

"Joanna Barry," it seemed like an anti-climax after Andy had guessed Dannii Minogue.

"Really? Our little stalker! What was she doing at John's party?"

"Stalking me, probably. She said she had gone there with a few friends from her school year but it freaked me out that she had spotted me leaving. I mean, if she saw me going, she might have known why I was leaving."

"You mean if she saw you going, she might have seen you coming."

"Thanks! Seriously though, you know what Joanna's like, I just wouldn't put it past her to have watched my every move from the shadows. I didn't even realise, at any point in the evening that she was even at the party."

Joanna's relentless pursuit of Andy and me had eased over the previous twelve months as she had found a few other misfits from her year to hang around with. She'd still appear unannounced from time to time – standing behind us in the school canteen or following us around the school playground but once either of us spotted her, we would always engage her in a brief conversation, after which she would happily go on her way. There was nothing unpleasant about Joanna, she had a good heart and a dry sense of humour like Andy and would often make us laugh. She was just a bit odd. As Andy would often say, who were we to condemn the girl for being odd, when I was a bit odd and he was outrageously odd? He had a point.

"What did Joanna have to say then?"

" She trundled up to me on heels too high for her and just said, 'Shit party,' then asked if I was OK and when it became apparent that I wasn't, she refused to go back to John's and said she was going to walk back to Rochdale with me, to check I was alright. We walked about half a mile, hardly speaking, until we got to a telephone box. I then rang my Dad to see if he'd come and pick us up."

"And did he?"

"No, my Mum answered. My Dad had fallen asleep and she didn't want to wake him, so she came to get us. Typically, I started puking up about a minute before she turned up, so she arrived with me on my knees, retching into a gutter, trying to get the last few carrots out, with Joanna stroking my hair as I did so."

"Bless her."

"Who? Joanna or my Mum?"

"Well," Andy explained, "I meant Joanna but bless your Mum too, for letting your Dad sleep and for coming to get you."

"So that's you updated with my two things. Joanna turning up and me throwing up. The weird thing was, Mum gave Joanna a lift back to Rochdale and I've never heard her say so much in my entire life. She chats a bit to my Dad but not like this. I sat in the back so I could lie down and Joanna went in the front. Her and my Mum were jabbering like two old friends."

"What about?"

"I don't know, I was pissed. Girly crap. Relentless girly crap, all the way home. When my Mum came down to breakfast this morning, she said, 'I like your little girlfriend. She's lovely!' I had to point out that Joanna Barry is not my girlfriend."

Andy took a cigarette out of a packet of Benson & Hedges and lit up. He had gone past the stage, by now, where he tried to hide his smoking from his parents. Their concession was that the only place in the house that he was allowed to smoke was in his bedroom and only if his window was open. It seemed to me to be a bit of an odd arrangement as both his parents smoked, but perhaps they felt that, at sixteen, Andy was too young to be joining them.

"Perhaps," Andy said, after blowing out a couple of rings of smoke, "your Mum was an ugly duckling too, before developing into a beautiful swan. Maybe she can identify with Joanna."

"Maybe. I'm not bothered what the reason was. It was just nice to hear her chatting and laughing. I never know what to say to her. My Dad's my best friend, my Mum's just my Mum."

"So what about Amy then? Do you think there's any chance you'll see her again?"

"See her, like in a date sort of way? No chance!"

"How come?"

"Well, given how we left it, I really can't see that happening. It's more likely that Michael Jackson will beat Mike Tyson in a boxing match than it is that Amy Garfunkel will ever go out with me."

"It could happen," Andy said, trying to sound optimistic, "Michael Jackson wouldn't let Tyson get anywhere near him. Even Stan Laurel won a boxing fight once."

"Only because the other boxer knocked himself out with a horseshoe!"

We both loved Laurel & Hardy but I was drifting away from the point.

"Just be positive," Andy said. He had the utmost faith in me, no matter what the circumstances. I just didn't have faith in myself.

"No, Andy, I've blown it."

Andy smiled.

"Perhaps not the wisest turn of phrase that. You never know though, she might just surprise you. For all you know, she might even be the type of girl who likes that sort of thing."

I thought Andy had properly gone crazy.

"Like it? Given the way she was screaming in pain, I somehow got the impression she wasn't exactly enjoying herself! Anyway, surely no girl in the world likes a boy splurting out their sexual juices on their face."

"You'd be surprised," Andy said knowingly. Andy was far cleverer than I was and when he knew something that I didn't know, he had a certain expression on his face. A knowing expression. There didn't seem to be any reason why he would know. It was at this very point that I became convinced that he must be crazy. Crazy or delusional. He was better at chatting to girls than any other boy in our school year but for him to even suggest he had ever had any sexual contact with a girl was frankly ridiculous.

"How exactly do you know this?"

"Porn."

"Porn?"

At just short of sixteen I had never seen anything pornographic, not a magazine, not a video, not a thing. For Andy to suggest that he had, seemed to me like the weirdest thing that he had ever said. He had previously never given me any inclination that anything sexual was of interest to him. Yet here he was suggesting he was familiar with pornographic content.

"Yes. Don't look so shocked."

"When have you ever seen porn?"

Andy stubbed his cigarette out in his ashtray, got up off the chair he'd been sitting in and went over to the door. He opened it, checked no-one was within earshot and then shut it again.

"Well, because my Dad has loads of the stuff," Andy said quietly.

This wasn't a brag. It was said with sadness in his voice, like Andy was ashamed of his father. I certainly would have been ashamed of my father if I'd ever discovered he owned a stash of pornography. Andy's Dad wasn't much more than half my Dad's age, but it was still creepy.

"Magazines or films?" I asked pretending to have some sort of knowledge of the porn industry. The fact that I knew there were porn magazines and porn films was as far as my knowledge stretched.

"Both. There's a ledge at the top of the cupboard in Dad's bedroom and he keeps everything up there. I don't know whether my Mum knows about it, I presume she must do. I discovered it when I was about eleven, when I was looking for Christmas presents."

"How did that make you feel as an eleven year old finding out your Dad had a load of pornos?"

"Disgusted."

"And now?"

"Still pretty much the same. It's all very sordid. You like to think of your father as someone who is almost permanently celibate, having only ever got his codger out for reproduction purposes."

That was still how I saw my father at fifteen. He was tactile with my Mum but I liked to imagine the activity never strayed beyond a hug and a kiss.

"How come you watched it?" I asked. I would have expected Andy to be repulsed by sex rather than intrigued.

"I didn't watch it when I was eleven. I went back up there recently when I knew my Mum and Dad were out. I only did it because I was curious. I'm an only child, I knew nothing about what girls look like down there and I knew nothing about sex either. I think I know too much now. It was all very unpleasant. I can't ever imagine me getting pleasure from doing those things."

I didn't know what to say to Andy so I chose to say nothing. His problems seemed worse than mine. My short-term future seemed to involve me avoiding Amy Garfunkel whilst Andy's long-term future seemed to involve him avoiding sex altogether. I had a father who I admired more than any other man on earth whilst Andy just had a dirty pervert for a Dad. Creepy Mr Corcoran (as I christened him that day and always referred to him that way in my head subsequently) had left Andy sexually scarred whilst Amy Garfunkel had only left me with a bruise that would heal. Perhaps it was just convenient for Andy to use his father as a scapegoat for his sexual inhibitions. Perhaps there had never even been any porn. I certainly wasn't going to ask for any evidence.

The following Monday we were back at school. My plans to spend the rest of Fifth form avoiding Amy Garfunkel were immediately ruined at first break when she marched over to me by the

Tuck Shop (thankfully without the black eye patch I had envisaged her wearing) and politely asked if she could have a word in private. She still called me 'Haych' but frankly, at that moment, that was the least of my worries.

Chapter Fourteen

Even though I knew I was in for a tongue lashing off Amy Garfunkel, the first thing I did after we sat down in an empty cloakroom in 'D' block was admire her beauty. She wore her long blonde hair in a ponytail for school and she pulled off the sexy school uniform look to perfection – skirt a couple of inches higher than it should be, black stockings (those less intimate with Amy may have thought they were tights), a thin tie (with the thick end tucked under her blouse) and a couple of buttons undone at the top. Even the way she sat, upright with her arms crossed and her chest out was giving me the horns. I was canny enough to know that outwardly I should be displaying an impression of regret and remorse not one of lust. I was remorseful too. Friday night should not have concluded the way it had.

"So come on then, Haych, who've you been blabbing to about Friday night?"

This opening statement caught me off guard. I had been anticipating a telling off about leaving the party or the angry pirate debacle, I hadn't anticipated this. I immediately felt like throttling Andy. The whole unsavoury incident was probably all around the school now thanks to his big gob. It didn't sound like Amy was totally sure I was the source of any revelations, so whilst there was some uncertainty I had no intention of confessing.

"No-one."

Amy gave me a hard stare but the coats probably saved me from a punch to a delicate area as the cloakroom was poorly lit and they darkened the surroundings further. If it had been lighter, my blushing face would have been a dead give away.

"Honestly?"

"I swear I've not told a soul. What makes you think I have?"

"I don't know. Maybe my mind is playing tricks but I've felt like everyone around me has been discreetly pointing and sniggering. Are you absolutely certain?"

"Of course I am. What would I have to gain by talking about it? I'm the one who comes across as the biggest idiot in all this. It's not exactly something for me to brag about."

"Thanks," Amy said, but not in a tone of gratitude, more one of sarcasm, as if I was suggesting that getting together with her wasn't something to show off about, which it most certainly was, if I hadn't sexually overheated.

My eyelashes on my left eye twitched violently, an annoying bodily by product of feeling nervous and uncomfortable.

"I don't mean getting off with you isn't something to brag about, it is, it most certainly is. I just mean, you know, getting the stuff in your eye and then running off. They weren't exactly my finest moments."

Amy seemed to accept this.

"Oh right. And you swear you haven't told anyone?"

My eyelashes twitched again, even more crazily this time. I prayed Amy hadn't noticed as she may have felt I was mocking her injury.

"I swear," I lied, "I swear on my life."

"On your mother's life?"

Amy obviously regarded my mother to be more important to the human race than I was.

"I swear on my mother's life," I said without hesitation, but immediately felt guilty that I had betrayed my Mum so readily. It was all mumbo-jumbo anyway but if Amy had asked me to swear on my Dad's life I don't think I would have been able to. In my mind, my Dad was only ever clinging on to life by his fingertips and I didn't want to be held responsible for treading on them.

"OK, I believe you," Amy said, "perhaps it was someone who saw me run into the bathroom who has started spreading rumours."

"Or maybe you're just being paranoid," I added.

I felt bad. Not only had I ejaculated into this poor girl's eye, ran off and then blatantly lied about not telling anyone, I was now trying to suggest she was half crazy.

"Possibly," Amy agreed.

"Is your eye OK now?"

"It's fine. I'm sorry I called you an idiot when it happened. It was just that it really hurt."

"Don't worry. I am an idiot," I said sheepishly. For more reasons than I cared to explain.

"Don't be silly, it's not as though you did it on purpose. It wasn't very gentlemanly of you to run off though. You should at least have waited to check I was alright."

"Sorry. I was drunk."

Not the best excuse in the world, but the only one I felt able to utilise.

"There was a rumour going around that you'd got off with Joanna Barry."

Brilliant. Just brilliant.

"Joanna likes me, but I don't like her, not in the same way anyway. I do look out for her though. When she started at 'Matthew Moss' she had no friends. It must be hard that, being surrounded by hundreds and hundreds of other kids every day, but not feeling that any of them are your friends. Andy and I took her under our wings a little. Anyway, you must have known that wasn't true."

I meant because my orgasm would have taken any sexual interest away, but Amy took it to mean that after being with someone as fine as her, I wouldn't possibly have stooped so low as to go with someone as mediocre as Joanna, which I guess in our harsh teenage world had some truth too.

"Yes," Amy responded, "I don't mean to brag but she's not in my league, is she?"

I didn't bother to explain.

"So what happens to us now?" Amy asked after an uncomfortable period of time had elapsed in silence.

"How do you mean?"

"Are we going to go out?"

"On a date?" I asked, expressing genuine shock.

"Yes. Why not?" Amy said forcing out a smile. She looked uncomfortable but I didn't understand why. I only realised years later that acting in an extroverted manner is sometimes a way of masking your insecurities.

I felt like saying, 'because my sperm used your eyeball as a goldfish bowl', but I just answered tactfully but honestly.

"Because I thought I had ruined everything on Friday."

This time it was Amy's turn to make light of what had happened.

"No, it's fine. I'll get a pair of those protective glasses from the Chemistry lab for our next date."

"Very funny!"

Amy seemed to take a little delight from her own joke. She laughed a lot louder than me and took a few seconds to contain her subsequent giggles.

"I thought it was....where are you going to take me on this date then?"

I thought about it briefly.

"Do you fancy getting the bus into Bury on Friday night?"

"Yes, that'd be nice. I'll write my phone number down. Ring me."

Amy took a pen out of her school bag and wrote her number down on a scrap piece of paper and passed it to me.

"Thanks."

I could feel myself growing in confidence. My eyelashes had even calmed themselves down so I decided there were a few things I needed to clear up. Amy stood up ready to go.

"Amy," I said, "before you go can I ask you a couple of things?"

"Will it take long? My drama lesson starts in like two minutes."

"No, I'll be as quick as I can. Firstly, why me?"

Amy looked puzzled.

"What do you mean?"

"You're gorgeous, you know you are, you could have had your pick of any lad you wanted, so how come you are interested in me?"

"You're a nice person, Haych. I've been out with a couple of lads recently who haven't been so nice. I needed a change. The bad boy thing hasn't worked out well for me."

"OK."

I wasn't the only 'nice' lad out there but if that was the reason, I was fine with it.

"Anything else, Hay-ch? I really need to go to drama now. I'll get bollocked if I'm late."

I never understood why the girls used words like 'bollocked' or 'I saw her bollocko', it made no sense and irritated me. I had something else that irritated me to get off my chest.

"It's Ay-ch not Hay-ch. Call me Ay-ch."

"That's what I always say! Anyway, I've really got to run, Mrs Murphy already hates me. She says I don't listen. Ring me. Don't forget."

Amy Garfunkel was the fittest girl in Rochdale. I was never going to forget.

Chapter Fifteen

Our date didn't start well. In fact, the day hadn't started well. I had woken up that Friday morning to discover a massive spot had invaded my face overnight, protruding outwards from the middle of my chin. As it grew larger and larger throughout the day it felt like some living creature was going to burst out of it like something out of an Alien film. By the time I was home from school it had peaked and it had a big yellow head on it that was begging to be squeezed out. I asked Mum whether it was massive and she said you could only see it if you stared at it which no-one was going to do. I knew this was a strategic lie to lessen my anxiety, but it wasn't appreciated so I went to the bathroom, pushed hard around my facial intruder with two fingers and in no time the yellow and red spray fizzed out all over the mirror.

The issue I had subsequently was that the wound refused to stop bleeding. After mountains of invisible anxiety oozed from my body, along with the several pints of blood that drained from my face, the spot consented to run dry. I scoffed at whichever idiot had decided that schooldays were the happiest days of your life.

Within minutes of my cavernous wound healing, the doorbell rang and I ran down the stairs to ensure Amy was not confronted by my inquisitive parents. As it turned out, I was the one who was met by an inquisitive parent-in-law at the door.

"Good evening," said a tall, overweight man with a salt and pepper beard and a beer belly large enough to open its own brewery.

I looked at him bemused and then spotted the radiant good looks of Amy next to him, looking like she had just walked off a Scandinavian art house film set with her blonde hair flowing down to below her waist and wearing a heavily embroidered white lace dress that I was immediately doing my best to see through.

"Are you not going to ask us in?" Amy asked smiling. Her teeth weren't as tiny as the rest of her. Amy always seemed to be smiling around me whilst I always seemed to looking back with a frown. I told myself that I needed to relax a little. With her father standing before me, however, this seemed like a difficult time to start.

I wasn't sure what I was expected to do. It was a first date. Did first dates normally involve the girl's father meeting your parents? I suspected not. When Amy had said on the phone that her Dad would drop her off, I was anticipating him doing just that. I decided I had best not get on the wrong side of him from the outset.

"Oh sorry, of course, come in."

What followed was an embarrassing five minutes of stilted conversation. My Dad had done something to his hip in the week, bending down to pick his slippers up, so was looking even more geriatric than usual, whilst my Mum, despite just wearing casual, around the house, clothing, almost matched Amy for beauty but had none of her social skills . Amy had obviously inherited her chatty, outgoing nature from her father, whilst my quiet, unassuming parents, who had not been expecting visitors, seemed constantly uncomfortable.

"I didn't want to appear rude by dropping Amy off at your door and then abandoning her, so I thought I would pop my head in and say hello. I'm Geoff," Amy's Dad said extending his arm and shaking my Dad's and then my Mum's hand.

"Hello Geoff, I'm George and this is Kitty. Can we get you a hot drink? A tea or coffee?"

"No, no, I'm not stopping. I'll leave these two lovebirds to get on with their night out."

I thought that meant Geoff was signalling his imminent departure but unfortunately not. What followed was a further five minutes that seemed to last forever. Geoff talked a lot, mainly about himself, about his job running a solicitor's practice and skiing holidays in Zermatt and Moritz. He had such a bulky frame that I couldn't imagine him skiing. If that belly hit a snowy hillside, I am sure they would have had to signal the avalanche warnings very promptly. I figured that Amy would look good in salopettes though. I had already long since concluded that Amy would have looked good in anything and even better in nothing.

Mum and Dad didn't really talk back to Geoff. They just forced out friendly smiles and nods. Eventually, after telling Amy to behave herself, which I think was more of a veiled warning to me, Geoff left. I didn't know where to take Amy after that, I wasn't comfortable taking her up to my room and I didn't want to sit in the lounge, making further small talk with my Mum and Dad, with them having to ask daft questions to keep the conversation alive like whether she liked school and what her future plans were. So, I made what I thought was a sensible decision to head straight out to the bus stop.

"I can give you a lift to Bury if you want, H?" Mum offered.

"No, honestly, we're fine Mum, we'd rather get the bus."

As we reached the bus stop, having walked there without touching, but me walking closest to the road like Dad always did with Mum, Amy made the stereotypical error.

"I didn't know your Grandad lived with you," Amy commented.

I obviously knew exactly what she meant and I guess I could have politely explained, but tactless remarks like that had always managed to get my back up a little, so I played along.

"He doesn't."

"Oh right, was he just visiting your Mum? Your Mum is gorgeous, by the way. She doesn't look old enough to have a kid our age."

"Sorry, are you saying the man you just met at our house is my Grandad?"

"Yes. Is he not your Grandad?"

"He's my Dad."

Amy may have been a great looking girl, but what she gained in looks, she lost in diplomacy.

"Get lost! Don't take the mickey out of me, Haych!"

She'd already forgotten it was Ay-ch too.

"I'm not, I'm being completely serious. George is my Dad, Kitty is my Mum. They are a couple, a very happily married couple despite the age gap."

"Honestly? You're not winding me up?"

"I wouldn't do that," I said, sounding serious, which I was. What sort of sick pervert would suggest their mother and grandfather were married? I'm guessing no-one.

"Shit! I've put my foot in it there, big style, haven't I?" Amy said, putting her hand over her face. I don't think she was actually as embarrassed as she was trying to pretend to be.

"Don't worry. People do it all the time. They don't look like a good match but surprisingly they are."

This statement was true. People mistook them for father and daughter all the time. I suppose it was a natural assumption for people to make, despite the fact that Dad was mixed race and Mum wasn't, she was dark haired and was certainly young enough to be his child. It didn't normally bother me, but it did that night when Amy did it. It was our first proper date and I wanted things to go well.

After that, things thankfully improved. I liked Amy a lot, but on reflection, in those fledgling stages of our relationship, my infatuation was largely based on looks. We didn't have a lot in common. Like her father, Amy talked a lot, but like her father, a lot of what came out of her mouth was garbage - egotistical, rich kid, garbage. I just accepted it at the time as a sort of endearing quirkiness. It was only when I reflected on it later in life that I remembered it less fondly.

We went to see Basic Instinct at the Warner Bros cinema in Pilsworth. It was quite a sexy film, probably not the ideal choice given our previous encounter and to be honest, I didn't know what was going on half the time. Amy seemed to enjoy it though.

"Did you see her Tinker Bell when she was getting interviewed?" Amy asked.

"Her Tinker Bell?"

"Yes, it was in all the papers that you could see her Tinker Bell when she had that white top on and was crossing her legs? Have you not read about it?"

"No and even I had, I wouldn't have been looking," I said, trying to sound chivalrous, hoping it wasn't too obvious that the second part of my answer was a lie. I was gutted I hadn't heard about it. Sharon Stone's character, Catherine, was a complete loon ball but Sharon Stone was sexiness personified and I would have liked to see what I could see. Without the prior knowledge to look intently, I hadn't seen a thing. I'm sure that Catherine's bits would have been too womanly to be called a 'tinker bell'.

"I couldn't see much either. It was a big fuss about nothing. It wasn't like there was this big hairy vulva smacking the audience in the face."

I hadn't heard the word 'vulva' before to describe female parts, but it was obvious that was what Amy was referring to. I wasn't sure if it was a pretend word like 'Tinker Bell' or a proper biological word. I looked it up in my 'Collins Mini Dictionary' when I was back in my bedroom and it transpired it was a proper word. I felt informed.

Unlike the characters in 'Basic Instinct', Amy and I behaved like a proper lady and gentleman that evening. We did nothing more than hold hands other than a quick snog outside her front door. After everything going off too quickly, in every sense, at John's party, I felt it necessary to slow things down and this time around, Amy unsurprisingly seemed happy for me to keep my trousers on.

Amy lived in Shawclough, which is a couple of miles from Bamford, so I had to walk back from hers, as I didn't have enough money left after the cinema and bus journey to get a taxi and I wasn't phoning my parents again after the previous weekend's dramas. I had plenty of time for contemplation on that long walk home and felt the evening had been a success and there was no reason to doubt that we would be seeing each other again.

As it turned out, we stayed together for another eighteen months. We developed a solid friendship and I would say, after about four or five months, we fell head over heels in love. It didn't last though, things untangled and, like so many teenage relationships, it had a messy end. I think ours was significantly messier than the norm.

Before all that though, in fact even before we had a second date, there was a far more dramatic event. A horrible, life changing event, that took my life in a completely new direction. A direction I did not want to go in. I still have nightmares about it to this day. I still question why I didn't do something, anything, differently. It happened two days after my date with Amy. What I thought would be a normal, lazy Sunday turned out to be anything but. It was, still is and will always be, the worst day of my life.

Chapter Sixteen

Breakfast that Sunday was not really different to any other Sunday. It was early April and it was going around in my head that maybe it was about time that I started revising for my GCSEs. It was a few more weeks before the idea became a reality, although I'm sure everyone would have been very sympathetic if I had announced I wasn't going to do any revision at all.

My Dad and I were up by half past seven that morning and, as usual, Mum didn't rise until about nine. Mum needed much more sleep than we did. I hadn't seen much of Dad the day before as I'd had an unusual lie in after my date with Amy and Dad had been out walking early. By the time he returned home, I had gone around to Andy's, as Dad was out for hours. He shouldn't really have been out at all with a bad hip but rather than give in to the problems it was causing him, he was battling against it. He had tried, unsuccessfully, to walk as far as he normally did. As a result of his stubborn refusal to give in to signs of old age Dad was looking particularly uncomfortable that Sunday morning. Wincing at times with pain, he asked me to get the breakfast plates and cereal bowls out as he couldn't bend down to get them out the low cupboard where we kept them.

"Are you coming with me on my walk today?" Dad asked as I started to lay the table.

"For goodness sake, Dad, can you not rest up for a day? It's obvious you're struggling."

"I'm fine," he stated firmly, although he very obviously wasn't.

"I'll tell you what," I said as I poured my cereal into my bowl, "I'll come with you, but only if we go for a short walk around Rochdale rather than going for miles around Saddleworth.

"OK son, you have a deal," my Dad said without even giving it a second of contemplation. He was obviously pleased with this compromise. He had the look of a relieved man.

"So," he said, "your young lady friend seemed very nice, easy on the eye too. Funnily enough, I said to your mother after you went out, that she was the type of girl that would have caught my eye at your age. Is her mind as pretty as her face?"

"Yes, it is."

It actually wasn't but I didn't know that back then.

"Good. That's nice to hear. Is she the girl that Mum gave a lift home to after the party last week?"

"No, that was Joanna Barry."

"Two girls in a week," Dad said, chuckling to himself a little.

"No, Dad, I didn't get off with Joanna. She's just a friend."

My Dad ignored this fact.

"'H', you're young, you're single and you're free to do what you want. You don't have to justify yourself to me."

"I'm not. I'm just telling you the truth. Joanna is just a friend."

"Whilst Amy is your girlfriend?"

I wasn't quite sure if Amy quite classed as my girlfriend yet. We had 'got off' with each other at the party and had only had one date since, but it felt like she was becoming my girlfriend. As well as the date, I had spoken to her on the phone for an hour on Thursday and for half an hour on Saturday evening, once I'd returned home from Andy's. In my whole life I had never spoken to anyone on the phone for longer than five minutes before that.

"She's not my girlfriend yet, but she will be," I concluded.

"Do you love her?"

I looked up from my cereal bowl towards my Dad. It wasn't a serious question, he was grinning from ear to ear. He was just winding me up a little.

"Stop taking the mickey out of me! You're just jealous."

"I'm not jealous at all, 'H'. I love your mother."

After breakfast, I went back up to my bedroom for a while. Andy had become a voracious reader and often passed books on to me, telling me that I must read them as they would change my life. I would regularly start to read them, pack them in after an hour or two and realise the only change was that I had wasted a couple of hours when I could have been doing something else.

'The Engineer of Human Souls' by Josef Skvorecky was different. I loved it from the moment I read the first page and felt I could identify with Danny Smiricky, the teenage hero. He may have grown up in Communist ruled Czechoslovakia rather than Rochdale, but his primary focus was on meeting girls and falling in love, just like most teenage boys. I was reading 'The Engineer of Human Souls' that morning and although I loved it, I found myself falling asleep on my bed after an hour of reading.

I mustn't have slept for more than ten or fifteen minutes, but I could feel that I was dribbling out the corner of my mouth, which woke me back up. I was also conscious of the fact that my hair was sticking up. My Mum had said the previous day that she would cut it after my Sunday evening bath. I had wet it already that morning to stick it down at the sides, but had fallen back to sleep with it still damp and I could feel that one side was sticking back up. I walked drowsily through to the bathroom to re-apply some water feeling the world was against me. When I was on the landing, I could tell the kitchen door was open, as the voices of my parents drifted up the stairs like smoke.

"What a gorgeous morning," I heard my mother saying cheerily.

"It is indeed. 'H' and I are going on a walk soon. Care to join us?"

I pulled a face when I heard Dad's offer. I didn't want Mum to come, she would spoil it. I knew it wouldn't be father and son conversations if Mum came with us, it would be husband and wife conversations with me walking a yard ahead or behind, just occasionally being brought into the conversation out of sympathy.

"Are you in any fit state to be going walking with that hip?" Mum asked, concerned.

"You sound just like your son!" Dad laughed, "I'm fine. We aren't going far, just local. Come with us."

"Don't," I thought.

"I might just do that, just to keep an eye on you."

"Damn," was my next thought, as I cursed my bad luck even more and headed through to the bathroom to sort my mad hair out.

A couple of hours later, as predicted, I found myself walking slowly along Bury Road in Bamford, whilst Mum and Dad held hands and chatted lovingly. I was having my own little conversations in my head, asking myself why I had even bothered coming out, I should have just left them to it. We reached the crossroads where we could have just kept going straight along Bury Road, left would take us uphill towards Rochdale's football ground, Spotland, on Sandy Lane and right would take us down along Roch Valley Way.

"Which way, Kitty?" Dad asked.

"You choose, honey. Only you know how much pain you're in and how far you can manage."

Dad was obviously struggling more than he was letting on.

"We'll just go up to Spotland then and then turn around and come back. Perhaps if I don't ache too much, I'll come back out later."

If it had been just Dad and me, he would have given me the choice and I'd have walked down Roch Valley Way. It irked me that once Mum decided not to make the choice, Dad didn't then ask me. It was because he didn't even know I was there, I concluded. Despite his age, Dad was still like a silly little lovestruck schoolboy around Mum. I suppose that's what happens when you marry someone young enough to be your daughter and pretty enough to be a film star, I told myself.

"Perhaps we could nip in to the Cemetery for a swift half when we get back here. Give you chance to rest up," Mum suggested.

"I like how your mind works, Kitty McCoy!" Dad enthusiastically responded.

Once again, to my annoyance, I was not consulted. Mum and Dad weren't agreeing on having a glass of beer in Rochdale cemetery, which was on our left as we began walking up and down the undulations of Sandy Lane. They were referring to the aptly named 'Cemetery Hotel', which my Dad liked because of the good quality beer in there. He was always saying one of the benefits of moving North was that the quality and range of beer in the pubs was far better. I would rather have headed straight home and I decided on the spot that I would decline any invites to join my parents in the pub and would walk home alone, whilst they stopped to enjoy their liquid refreshment. I would rather carry on reading my book than watch them whisper sweet nothings to each other in full view of the locals.

Back then, as now, Rochdale had a reputation as a rundown town, with its multi storey blocks of flats that cast their shadow over the town centre like concrete dinosaurs and its multitude of terraced homes that were created to house the workers from a booming industrial revolution. It wasn't all grey and miserable though. There were many leafy, rural areas and Sandy Lane, Rochdale may not have been Barbados, but as we walked up the slow incline, a mass of old trees on both sides of the road bowed to greet us like a collection of charming pensioners.

To enhance the picturesque scene, after we passed the cemetery, two horses each pulling a cart, could be seen emerging through the sunshine, coming towards us down the hill. As they grew nearer, we saw that a man sat alone on the first cart, whilst on the second there was a boy in his early teens alongside a girl who must have been no more than ten.

"What a beautiful day!" my Dad reflected contentedly.

I am not a believer in higher powers and an all powerful, perfect deity. There are too many stillbirths, cancers and tumours in the young for me to worship a flawless creator. Up until the early twentieth century apparently around one in thirty women died in childbirth, no amount of praying or selfless devotion could prevent it. What sort of loving God would have allowed millions of years of female genocide purely based on his own creative flaws? Perhaps it would be easier to believe in a creator who toyed with his human creations purely to satisfy a wicked sense of humour. That would at least go some way to explaining what happened next.

The air of calmness was invaded by a loud bang. It may have been the sound of a gunshot, a car backfiring or something exploding on a garden fire, but whatever it was, it scared the living daylights out of the second horse. It was making a distressed sound, the likes of which I'd never heard a horse make before, halfway between a neigh and a human scream. The teenage boy was doing his utmost to placate it, but the horse was repeatedly trying to defy gravity by balancing purely on its hind legs and each time gravity took control, it sought to defy it again.

Despite the boys urgings the horse was not calming down. It continued in its frenzied reaction until it managed to topple the cart behind it on to its side, tipping the young man and the girl we assumed to be his sister out on to the road. Once this had been achieved the horse galloped away frantically, dragging the toppled empty carriage along with it. There was only one direction it could possibly run and that was downhill. It jinked to its right to avoid the carriage in front and then gathered momentum as it sped down the hill towards us. The man in the front carriage tried to grab the reins as the horse passed him, but having failed to get a grip he jumped off and began a vain pursuit.

We were less than one hundred metres away from the initial incident, so it must have only taken ten or fifteen seconds for the horse to reach us, but each of those moments seemed to play out in slow motion. My parents were in front of me, so were nearer to the horse than I was. My father, as was customary, was nearest the roadside. I don't know whether he just froze on the spot or whether he decided our best chance was to stay still, but he remained rooted to the spot.

Aware my father could not move quickly because of his age and particularly his problematic hip, I shouted to my mother,

"Open the gate, Mum!"

The noise of the horse's hooves and the carriage rattling on the road was growing increasingly loud. It felt like our only option was to go into the front garden of the house we were standing beside, but as Mum tried to push and pull the gate nothing was happening. Hoping it was just jammed rather than locked from the inside, I went to help her. Frantically, I pushed and pulled too, as Mum stood to the side. Still nothing happened. There was barely any time left, as I looked over my shoulder I could see the horse was now less than twenty metres away. I contemplated picking my Dad up and throwing him over the hedge into the garden but that would have taken too long. I just stepped forwards in front of him, spread my arms and legs wide, stared into the flaring nostrils of the distressed horse and waited for the inevitable impact.

The impact I then felt was not that of a seventy stone horse hitting me at full pelt nor was it the impact of a wooden carriage. It was a push, a human push, pushing me into the hedge I had been stood beside. Moments later, whilst adjusting to the sensation of a thousand tiny thorns scratching at my body, I heard a sound which had vague similarities to a sound I had heard before. The sound lodged in my memory banks was the sound of a coconut being smashed against tarmac after I had won it at the school fair. This time however, as I stepped out from the hedge, I was soon to discover it had not been a mere coconut cracking on the tarmac. This time, it was the back of my mother's skull.

I didn't see my mother dragging my father in to the hedge to save him. I wasn't even aware that shortly afterwards she would save me too. All I felt was her hands on my shoulder. I would never be blessed by the touch of my mother again. The police tried to comfort us by telling us that it would have been instant, that my mother would not have felt any pain, but it was no comfort. No comfort at all. At forty one years old, my mother was dead. No matter how many times I told myself she was dead, it just didn't seem real. An ambulance took me and my father to hospital to treat us for shock and I just kept expecting my Mum to turn up in the car, kiss us both on the forehead and then drive us home. I had never even heard of the five stages of grief or Elisabeth Kubler-Ross before that day but soon I would feel that despite never having met us, that she knew me and my father better than we knew ourselves.

Chapter Seventeen

Thirty seven people attended my mother's funeral, exactly thirty seven. I knew that because as I stood at the pulpit, ready to deliver my mother's eulogy, I felt like I was about to cry. Her dead body was there, in a shiny, solid redwood coffin in front of me and I could feel the emotions building up inside. I had cried plenty of tears since Mum had died, but this was not the time to add to the collection. To distract my brain from passing on the 'go' signal to my tear ducts, I quickly counted the number of heads looking up at me. There were twenty five plus two rows of five people in the choir, the Vicar and me. Thirty seven, not including Mum. All of us would play her role sometime in the next hundred years it was just a question of when. It was a sombre thought but around that time sombre thoughts were commonplace.

I took out my pieces of paper from the inside pocket of the unwanted new suit that my father had bought me especially for the occasion. After a head count, sombre thoughts and a few gulps of air, I began to speak. For the next few minutes, for the most part, my grief was postponed. I don't know how and from where I summoned the strength of character to get through it, but I did. My father told me that evening, before we retired to bed, that I had started that speech as a child and finished it as a man. Perhaps it was a cliché, but I felt there was an element of truth in what he said.

I don't recall exactly what I said in that speech. For the most part, those few weeks after Mum's death were lost in a dark cloud of grief, but I did manage to hold on to a few memories from that time, especially from the day of the funeral itself. I remember starting in a faltering, nervy voice but after a couple of paragraphs of reading from my sheets of paper without even glancing up, my nerves and emotions settled and I was able to meet the eyes of my audience.

My Dad, as could only have been expected, took Mum's death very badly. Cancer had robbed him of his first wife and now a tragic accident had taken Mum. There were a lot of 'what ifs'. Dad blamed himself for choosing to head up Sandy Lane when we could just as easily have headed straight along Bury Road or taken a right at the crossroads down Roch Valley Way. He also blamed himself for being a 'stubborn old fool' and not resting his troublesome hip that fateful morning. I tried to deflect blame by pointing out that it had been me that suggested having a walk locally rather than heading up to Saddleworth as he often did, but Dad just dismissed my words as 'nonsense'.

The owner of the horse, the man on the first cart, was arrested at the scene but he was never subsequently charged. I don't really remember why that was. Perhaps it was because Dad didn't want him to face charges. I do recall him saying to a police officer that Mum was not the type of lady who would have sought vengeance for an accident. He said he was sure the poor man would have felt bad enough already.

Dad did have these moments of incredible mental strength after Mum's death but they were fleeting. I remember during one of his other strong moments he had told the undertakers and the Vicar that he was intending to say a few words at the funeral, but the day before the service my protective instincts took over and I suggested that I take that burden away from him. He protested initially but I was insistent and said I would make sure I made a speech that would have made Mum proud.

I spent the afternoon before the funeral around at Andy's. His Mum and Dad rarely engaged in conversations with me when I was around there, but that day they both made sure they came into Andy's room to say that they were very sorry to hear about my Mum and if there was anything they could do for me, I only had to ask. As I considered his Mum to be a bit of an alcoholic and his Dad to be a smutty, sexual pervert, I didn't intend to be asking them any time soon but thanked them anyway.

Andy had more idea what to write in a funeral speech than I did. I don't think it was down to any sort of experience in the matter, he was just using that worldly wise gift he had. He suggested that all I needed to get across was what a lovely person Mum had been and how much she loved my Dad and me. I clearly remember him saying that it was going to be a gloomy enough day anyway, so I should try and put in a few more light hearted sections. There was a paragraph that Andy wrote about Mum's London accent and how she said 'GR-ARSE' instead of 'gr-ass' and 'PAR-TH' instead of 'p-a-th' which made a few of the largely Northern members of the congregation smile the following day. To put it in context, I was saying how she loved the people of Rochdale and they loved her. I mentioned that she was a quiet soul, not one for throwing parties or standing out in a crowd but everyone she met here seemed mesmerised by her. I said I didn't know if it was her kindness, her beauty or the way she spoke and then I mentioned how she pronounced things.

Overall, I think I stumbled my way through the whole speech rather than delivering it with any degree of eloquence but everyone there, especially and most importantly Dad, seemed proud of me for giving it a go. When I went back to my seat after finishing, my Dad his put his arm around me, whispered in my ear that my Mum would have been so proud and then we just sobbed. For a long time, we both just sobbed.

Outside the church, a few of the ladies hugged me and several of the men shook my hand, including Joe the landlord at 'The Cemetery' who squeezed my hand tightly before saying,

"You're a braver man than me, Harry. I could never have got up and spoke like you did at my mother's funeral. If you're ever looking for work, give me a shout, I'm always looking for strong characters to work at my place."

These gestures did temporarily make me feel a little better. Life does have a way of putting a plaster over emotional cuts and despite the service being as distressing as I had envisaged it would be, the funeral reception, held at the inappropriately named 'Waggon and Horses', at the bottom of Roch Valley Way, was a further comfort. Old friends and a few of Dad's family were there to boost our flagging spirits.

Andy was my only friend that attended the funeral and the reception. I thought for a while about asking Joanna Barry too, as she had chatted with my Mum after John Dunphy's party, but then realised it was probably inappropriate. I even thought I saw her in there when I scanned the congregation but my mind was probably just playing tricks.

At the reception, Andy managed to sum the whole experience up in his own, unconventional style. Everyone was sitting around tables, drinking beer and reminiscing, when Andy, out of nowhere, began to sing. He sang the Crowded House song, 'Four Seasons In One Day'. For the first few lines, the general chatter only lowered slightly, but after a while there was a general hush as everyone listened. Andy had leant me 'Woodface', the album the song was on and although I quite liked it, I hadn't bathed myself in the lyrics or seen it as anything more significant than a pleasant pop song. Andy changed my perspective on that song. 'Four Seasons In One Day' is not just a melancholy song about the changes in the weather, it is a genius of a song about the fragility of life. I didn't know that. I would never have known that without a best friend called Andy. He sang it wonderfully, with a smooth, easy tone, very much like Neil Finn (the singer in Crowded House), but when he finished no-one clapped. Some people probably just saw it as an unwelcome distraction, but not me. For me, in less than three minutes Andy had summed everything up. Things can change in an instant in life, so treasure the moments you are basking in its sunshine.

In the days after the funeral, I remember feeling a mixture of emotions but the predominant one was guilt. I felt guilty for having spoken at the funeral. She was my mother, should I not have been as distraught as my Dad? I felt guilty for taking Mum for granted. She was twenty nine years younger than my Dad and I had stupidly assumed I would have nearly a whole lifetime with her, but nowhere near as long with Dad. I felt guilty for resenting her relationship with my father.

I also felt ashamed. I was ashamed that I allowed myself to be jealous of her. I was ashamed that I took her love for granted. I just hoped that she realised that I was just being a stupid kid and deep down I loved her just as much as my Dad did.

A further emotion that was prevalent around this time was worry. I worried about how my father would cope with such a tragic blow. I was deeply troubled by Mum's death but I was young and knew I could ride this storm. Along with Andy, Dad was my best friend and my hero, but he was old and frail. He had bounced back before, but he was a much younger man back then and I was worried he may not have the strength of spirit to bounce back this time.

Finally, and perhaps most concerning, I had a lot of anger. I was angry with Mum for saving me instead of saving herself. I was angry with the man who owned the horse for putting his two children in charge of a horse and cart. I was angry with life. I was angry with death. The bulk of my anger, however, was directed towards Mum's family. No-one from Mum's family had been at her funeral. I was angry that they had all let her down. Her father should never have asked her to make a choice between them and my Dad. They should never have forced my Mum and Dad to move away. Mum's family had sacrificed the love of the kindest, prettiest, most unselfish woman on the planet just because she had been brave enough to fall in love with the most humble and most wonderful man. I took a long, long time to forgive them.

Chapter Eighteen – Twelve Months Later

"Where do you fancy going tomorrow night?" Andy asked as we left Hopwood Hall College that Thursday afternoon and headed towards the bus shelter.

Andy had stopped growing by then. He was six feet five inches tall, but still hadn't filled out so looked even taller. I was still growing, I was about five feet nine at that point, so always had to crank my neck upwards when we talked. He was growing a moustache but it was a feeble attempt at carrying it off. My Dad had noticed it and commented that he hoped Andy didn't suffer from hayfever as one sneeze was likely to blow it right off. I could have grown a pretty substantial moustache by then but Amy had persuaded me not to, saying it would tickle when we kissed. I had begun regularly shaving too, once a day and certainly felt more of a man than a boy. The feeling of being a man now was partly due to my physical appearance but also due to the adversity that I had faced which I suppose would naturally accelerate maturity.

"I'm not bothered where we go. You choose," I responded.

"Bury then, we'll go to Bury. It's more upmarket than Rochdale. We could go to The Roxy."

Personally, I preferred going out in Rochdale. We used to run into people we knew in Rochdale, more people from Sixth Form, but Andy thought the pubs and bars were classier in Bury which I suppose they were. They were more likely to ask me for ID in Bury too, so I would have to borrow a driver's licence from someone in Upper Sixth. Given his height, bouncers never asked Andy for ID. Andy suggesting 'The Roxy' was meant to be a sweetener for me as he knew I liked it in there. It was a massive nightclub which could fit over a thousand people in and always had a good vibe. One of its many claims to fame was that 'Hitman And Her' was often broadcast from there.

Andy was keen to keep me occupied and upbeat as he knew the coming weekend would be the first Anniversary of my Mum's death. It had been a year of ups and downs. Initially, after Mum died, I had two weeks off school. I couldn't face going in for that fortnight and neither my Dad nor the school tried to force me in before I was ready. When I eventually returned though, I found it was a welcome distraction. Everyone knew what had happened, of course they did, but after telling me how sorry they were, they soon moved on to discussing music and girls. Within a couple of months it was GCSE time and I probably studied harder than I would have done if life had remained uncomplicated, as revision was a further distraction from a house without Mum. I ended up surprising myself and passing six GCSEs. They were all Grade C passes but as far as I was concerned a pass was a pass. Following on from the GCSEs, I stayed in further education moving to Hopwood Hall to do 'A' Levels in History, Economics and English. Andy passed all nine of his GCSEs with A's and B's so headed to Hopwood too.

At home, my Dad tried his best to give me the impression he was managing without Mum. He didn't lose his sunny disposition and learnt to do things around the house that he had always previously left to Mum, like using the washing machine and ironing the clothes. I learnt too as I didn't want a man of Dad's age having to do it all. Between us, we turned a few white t-shirts pink and burnt a few holes into favourite shirts and trousers, but overall, I like to think we coped admirably.

It was only when Dad was in bed that he let his guard down. I was often woken up in the early hours of the morning by his uncontrollable sobs of despair. At first, I went to his room to try to comfort him, but as time passed, I realised he didn't want me to share these desperate moments with him, so gradually I left him to manage his low moments alone.

Amy Garfunkel, for all her imperfections, some of which I was yet to be made aware of, was a huge help in the twelve months after we lost Mum. Andy used to call around to our house much more frequently than he had whilst Mum was alive too. This was not because he didn't love my Mum, just because he understood the importance of not frequently leaving Dad all alone. It was Amy's presence though that used to give Dad the biggest boost.

Dad had always loved female company and Amy made a real fuss of him when she came to our house. As I say, Amy had her faults, but a lack of compassion for my father certainly wasn't one of them. She would always ask how he was feeling, would be quick to give out sympathetic hugs and would always invite him to join us if we were heading out anywhere.

"She's an absolute treasure, that girl," Dad would often say to me after Amy had been around.

I adored Amy too. She was the first girl I had ever dated, first girl I had properly fallen in love with and I had developed such an infatuation that I would gladly have spent twenty four hours a day, seven days a week with her but Amy sensibly always pointed out that we needed to make time for our friends too, so I would see her in the evenings on Tuesdays and Thursdays during the week and on Saturday afternoon and evening at the weekend.

"So, are you seeing Amy on Saturday night?" Andy asked as we stood at the bus stop outside Hopwood Hall. Amy hadn't stayed on at Sixth Form, she was doing 'Youth Training' at the local job centre.

"I am. Same as every other Saturday, I'll be seeing Amy."

Andy didn't say anything, he didn't need to, for twelve months he had made his views on Amy perfectly clear and his face sneered every time her name was mentioned.

"I know you don't like her, Andy," I added, "but I love her and my Dad loves her too, which is important."

"How is your Dad?" Andy asked, happy to move the conversation away from Amy.

"You only saw him on Monday!"

"I know. I mean with it being the Anniversary of your Mum's death this weekend. Have you seen any noticeable signs of a mental deterioration? I was intending on staying in on Saturday night, but I could call around with a take away pizza and sit with him and watch Noel's House Party."

"Can you really see my Dad watching Noel's House Party?"

"Well, I'll listen to Radio 4 with him then and discuss whether Jiang Zemin will prove to be a sound choice of President for the People's Republic of China and the implications for Hong Kong."

"Even my Dad might not know what you're on about there."

"Don't doubt him. Your father is a wise old soul."

"I know he is. Anyway, it's fine, Amy and I were intending on just staying in with Dad."

"What about tomorrow?" Andy asked.

"What about tomorrow?" I queried.

"Well, should we be going out leaving your Dad on his own?"

"He's used to it."

"But this weekend?"

"He'll be fine, Andy. I didn't want to leave him on his own for both nights, but one will be fine."

"Are you sure?"

"Positive."

"Why doesn't Amy see you both nights at the weekend?"

The only time Andy liked talking about Amy was when he was wanting to point out all her faults to me. I imagined that that was what he was about to do. I wouldn't say he hated her but he definitely disliked her with a passion.

"You know this. We do our own thing one night at the weekend and see each other on the other. Normally we spend Saturday afternoon and evening together."

Andy started walking around the bus shelter as if he was a barrister about to deliver a speech to a jury.

"It's a little bit weird though, don't you think? I mean the likes of Cathie Squires and Keith Corden are with each other all week at College and they still want to see each other every moment they can at the weekend. They're infatuated with each other. You and Amy obviously aren't."

I knew what he meant. He meant Amy wasn't infatuated with me. He knew full well that I was infatuated with her.

"You always say Cathie and Keith make you want to spew."

"They do. I would rather put cocktail sticks up my urethral orifice than watch the pair of them bursting each other's spots and licking each other's faces in the Common Room, but from their perspective, they are mad about each other and don't care if everyone knows it."

"I love Amy. I told you that a minute ago."

"I'm not saying you don't love her."

"So you're saying she doesn't love me?"

Andy pondered my question. I could tell he was scratching around the corners of his brain looking for an eloquent response.

"Perhaps not as much as Cathie loves Keith. I think she needs his love like a car needs petrol. She can't function without it. Perhaps it's not even his love that fuels her perhaps it's the various liquids his body produces. There is a strong possibility that Cathie Squires is an alien from out of space and the only way she can survive on earth is by regularly refuelling on Keith Corden's saliva and other assorted juices!"

"Has anyone ever told you you're a lunatic?"

"I'm a lunatic? I'm not the one going out with Amy Garfunkel."

"She can't win with you. If I saw her all the time, you'd be calling her a bunny boiler and saying she'd ruined our friendship. You'd hate anyone I went out with."

"Don't flatter yourself. I'm sure I'll love your next girlfriend."

"There may never be another girlfriend."

"You're not going to tell me you're a jobby jabber, are you?"

"A 'jobby jabber'?"

"A homosexual. I think it's Scottish. The Scots call a poo 'a jobby'."

I gave out a brief laugh. It was a funny term that I hadn't heard before. It was a laugh tinged with an awkward feeling of embarrassment though as it seemed odd that Andy would be using slang words for homosexuality when everyone I knew presumed he was gay.

"I meant I may never have another girlfriend as I could be with Amy for the rest of my life," I explained. Andy wasn't fond of my explanation. He winced like he had begun that exercise with the cocktail sticks and the urethral orifice.

"Stop right there. I'm prepared to accept this little dalliance with Art's daughter but I promise you if you ever married that crazy, narcissistic bitch, I swear I would never speak to you until the day you come to your senses and applied for a divorce."

I was shocked by Andy's vitriol. I was acutely aware that he didn't like her but I wasn't aware that his feelings ran so deep. I was both hurt and annoyed by what he had said but did my best not to show it.

"That's a bit harsh, Andy, even for you."

"I'm just being honest with you. If you ever married her, our friendship would be dead."

"Let's hope I never do then."

Andy could change his mannerisms and tone of voice in the blink of an eye. This was one of those moments. He swiftly went from being really animated and passionate to calm and collected.

"I don't even know why I'm getting so het up. Let's face it, H, you're more likely to walk on the moon in flip flops than marry Amy Garfunkel. For starters, she doesn't love you enough. For main course, your Dad isn't rich enough and for pudding, you're not daft enough. It may take a while for this fog of romance to clear, but once it does you'll come to your senses."

I didn't like it when Andy was all knowing and superior. I thought he had it all wrong. For a number of reasons, I hoped it was Andy that was mistaken and that one day he would realise Amy was a wonderful person and the best thing that had ever happened to me. I hoped he would apologise for making such a poor judgement and speaking so wrongly about her. That's what I hoped. In reality, there weren't many reasons for optimism. Andy had always been trying to split us up, even at the very start. He confessed that he had 'accidentally' told a few girls about the 'angry pirate' incident after John Dunphy's party. I was convinced that he spread those rumours to ensure we didn't get together.

My memories of that Friday evening in Bury are fairly vague. I do recall that we never made it to 'The Roxy' and that there was an incident at a bar when some bloke in his twenties called Andy a 'gay boy' and Andy, in his own inimitable way, responded by saying that was an assumption rather than a statement of fact whilst if he were to call this man 'a wanker' this would be a statement of fact. The bloke was with his girlfriend or wife and didn't take kindly to being ridiculed in front of her, so tried to grab Andy by his Paul Smith white floral shirt. Andy evaded his grasp and, despite being six feet five, somehow managed to blend into the crowd and sharply head towards the exit. We laughed about it once we were in the safety of another pub, but I can remember spending the rest of the evening anxiously looking around in case the bloke re-appeared, even though it would have been two against one, I wouldn't have fancied our chances.

A further thing I remember about that evening was walking into our kitchen, armed with a half eaten doner kebab with chilli sauce. It was about one in the morning. At the table, with an empty glass and a more than half empty bottle of Glenfiddich, was my father.

"Hi Dad," I said as I went to the sink to pour myself a sobering glass of water, "You haven't drunk all that tonight, have you?"

My Dad picked up the whiskey bottle and smiled a little.

"No, don't worry. I couldn't sleep so I just came down to have a quick tot. Did you have a good night?"
"Yeh, it was good. How come you couldn't sleep? Is it because it's a year on Tuesday since Mum died?"

"Mainly, but also, probably because of what happened to Mum, I settle better when I know you are home safely."

This made me feel guilty that I was so late home.

"Sorry Dad. I'd have come home sooner if I'd have known you were worrying."

"No, no, don't be silly, H. You need to live your life. I want you to be happy."

Overall, despite losing Mum so tragically, I was happy. I had a good looking girlfriend who I loved, a best friend who never failed to make time spent with him feel like a fun adventure and Sixth Form life at Hopwood Hall was enjoyable too. I rarely thought about Mum other than when I was at home. At home, it was impossible not to think about her. Dad still went for his long walks, his dodgy hip flared up from time to time but thankfully it didn't appear to be deteriorating but there was a natural and fully understandable air of sadness about him. A few kind hearted people popped their heads in to say hello from time to time, but these visits became less frequent as time passed.

"I am happy, most of the time. I want you to be happy too, Dad. I don't expect you to be laughing and joking every second of every day, but as much as I would love her to, Mum isn't coming back and you need to find a way of distracting yourself from your grief."

"You kebab smells awful, H. I have no idea how you eat those things. So, what are you trying to suggest, H? That I accept Mum is dead and go out and find myself a new woman."

"I'm nearly finished," I said, pointing at the wrapping of my kebab, as I took a large mouthful.

"Put the wrapper in the outside bin when you're done then, otherwise the kitchen will stink to high heaven in the morning."

"OK. I'm not suggesting that you get a new girlfriend, Dad, just that you find a new hobby."

"Walking is my hobby."

"A less solitary hobby, Dad. If it has to involve walking, join a rambling society. If not, go and watch Rochdale football team every week or go down to the pub. Just do something that will help you stop thinking about Mum."

My Dad poured himself another whiskey. It was a long measure. I began to suspect that he had lied to me and perhaps the Glenfiddich had been freshly opened that evening.

"I think that's the point though, H. I don't want to stop thinking about her. I was blessed to have Kitty in my life and the memories of all the times we spent together are what get me through the day."

"You can't just live in the past though, Dad."

"Why not? I'm 71 years old, believe me my past is a lot more exciting than my future."

I was stuck what to say at first. Part of me wanted to agree with him.

"Because Mum wouldn't have wanted you to."

I'm not sure whether it was down to the whiskey or down to it being the anniversary of Mum's death or a combination of the two but for the first time since Mum died, Dad started crying in front of me. It caught me off guard.

"It should have been me, H," he said through his tears, "I still don't understand why it wasn't me. I'm still annoyed with your mother for sacrificing her life to save mine. I'm old, I've had a full life. Your mother's life was only just beginning. Every moment we were together I felt like I was living on a rainbow, but everything has been stolen from me. Now, I feel more like I'm stuck in a tornado. A tornado that continually spins me around and will never let me go until the day I die. I don't think I want to be here anymore, H. I'm so lonely. My life is empty without her."

I put my doner kebab down and went over to give him a hug. Still being just shy of seventeen, my ability to empathise was tempered by an element of selfishness. There was a feeling of frustration that despite all my efforts for the past year, Dad was still declaring his life empty. Dad seemed to read my mind.

"Don't think I don't appreciate what you have done for me over the last year though, H. At times you've had to lift me up and carry me through it. Your speech at Mum's funeral was both the saddest and happiest moment of my life. It was agony letting Mum go, but I couldn't have been any prouder of you."

This wasn't the first time Dad had said he was proud of me over the last twelve months, far from it, he was always telling me, but he didn't normally specify any of the reasons why.

"Dad, I need you to hang on in there. Try to keep your spirits up. I know it's harder for you than it is for me, but we need to keep pulling each other through this."

"I'm not saying it is harder for me, H. You and your Mum were my world, but she wasn't blood to me like she is to you. It's just that I find the fact that she has gone so hard to take in. It wasn't as though she had been ill. It doesn't make sense that she was killed by a horse and carriage. This is bloody Rochdale, for Heaven's sake, not some Quaker backwater in America. I don't think I've seen a horse and carriage before or since in Rochdale. It was as if it was sent by the devil."

It struck me as a strange thing for my Dad to say. He had a quiet Christian faith as a younger man, which he hadn't managed to pass down to me, but he seemed to have lost all faith since Mum's death. Suggesting Mum's death was the work of the devil though seemed illogical at best. We were just in the wrong place at the wrong time. It was logical to blame ourselves or each other or even the man on the other horse or the horse itself but not the devil. I reckoned he'd definitely had that half bottle of whiskey to even suggest it out loud.

"We've been over this. It was just bad luck, Dad. If your hip hadn't been bad we'd have been at Saddleworth and Mum probably wouldn't even have been with us. If we'd have kept on Bury Road or gone down Roch Valley Way, we'd have been fine too. Same as if we'd gone out five minutes earlier or later or the bloke on the horse had. It's all ifs and buts and maybes but it's happened Dad and we can't change any of it now."

Dad looked at me with the small pools of tears still in his eyes.

"But I wish we could."

"So do I, Dad, so do I."

"Right, I'm going to bed. I promise you tomorrow will be a better day, son. If I die in my sleep, never forget how much your mother and I loved you."

"I won't Dad. Goodnight."

Every time he headed to bed after Mum died he had said that same thing. 'Never forget how much your mother and I loved you'. He said it any time I went out anywhere too. At first, I thought it was because he was going to overdose on some pills or find some other way to knock himself off, but eventually I realised it was nothing of the sort. It was just because Mum had never had the opportunity to say her goodbyes and no matter when Dad's final curtain call came, he wanted to make sure he had said his.

Chapter Nineteen

It was a Saturday afternoon in August. Amy's Dad had been to Rochdale's first home game of the season, so Amy had jumped in the car with him, rather than getting the bus to ours. She had phoned me as she was leaving and I'd arranged to meet her outside the Cemetery Hotel. Although I always insisted Mum's death was just bad luck, something within me, whether it was superstition or emotion I'm not sure, but something kept me from ever walking along Sandy Lane again. Logistics meant that I had to go past the spot where Mum died from time to time in Dad's car, but I tended to look straight ahead at the road or to the other side rather than stare directly at the hedge.

I could tell Amy was in a bad mood as soon as she arrived outside 'The Cemetery'. Her mouth seemed to be drooping at both sides and she was uncharacteristically quiet.

"What's the matter?" I asked in a tone of concern.

"Nothing," Amy answered in a tone that indicated that there obviously was and I would have to continue to act out the annoying charade a little longer before she would tell me.

"Do you fancy having a drink in here?"

Amy shrugged, "Not bothered if we do or we don't."

"Come on," I said trying to inject a bit of enthusiasm into my voice in an attempt to lift the mood, "let's go in and I'll buy you a drink. Looks like you could do with cheering up."

We went in and I ordered a Mann's brown bitter, which is a bottle of Mann's brown ale and half a bitter. It was a drink I only drank until I was eighteen to try to look older than I actually was - an attempt to age myself by ordering an old man's drink. I suspect everyone in 'The Cemetery' probably knew I wasn't eighteen but also probably knew that I was George McCoy's lad and given I had lost my Mum, they were prepared to turn a blind eye to my underage drinking.

"So come on, tell me, what's up?" I asked again once we sat down on stools at a little mahogany table that had Whitbread coasters to preserve it.

"Nothing, I'm fine," Amy once again insisted unconvincingly.

"Well you're obviously not."

"Andy," Amy said and in one word the charade was over.

"What about Andy?"

"He hates me."

"He doesn't," I protested, but this time it was my turn to be unconvincing as I was aware that Amy was pretty much on the button, "what makes you say that?"

"I went to Boots last night after work and he had a right go at me outside afterwards."

"Andy did? Why?"

"How am I supposed to know? I've no idea. Called me every name under the sun and said I wasn't fit to be with someone like you. Do you think he might fancy you, H? It felt territorial, like a warning to keep away from his man."

"No, don't be ridiculous. We're just mates. That's what mates do, look after each other."

"Having a go at someone's girlfriend isn't looking after, H, it's bullying."

Amy seemed to brighten up once she had released all her pent up frustrations about Andy. I was confused though. Although I knew Andy had never liked Amy, it seemed totally out of character for him to launch an unprovoked attack. A provoked attack would have been very much in character though and without wanting to trigger another bad mood in Amy, I kept bringing the conversation back to what may have caused Andy to have an outburst.

"H, honestly, I didn't say anything or do anything. I'm not sure why you don't appreciate this, but I am the victim here. Stop looking for reasons to justify what Andy did. There is no justification. I just walked out of Boots and he was there outside, waiting for me, snarling like a rabid dog. I do have a bone to pick with you about that, as a matter of fact."

I have always been a bit paranoid so immediately started inventing potential issues in my head and immediately thought how I would respond to them. The real reason was out in the open soon enough.

"Why what have I done?" I asked, not innocently though, just inquisitively.

"Andy said during his crazy rant that he wished I'd never forgiven you for what happened at John Dunphy's party. You promised me you didn't tell anyone, H. Swore on people's lives."

I felt sick. I would have loved to have been able to look her straight in the eyes and tell her I didn't have a clue what she was talking about but I was a nervous liar. I suspected my eyelashes would twitch or my whole face would if I tried to lie my way out of this. Lying was what had delivered me to this awkward moment in the first place. I paused for thought.

Amy looked like a princess with her long blonde hair, smooth complexion and beautiful blue eyes. Not only all that, she had the body of a gymnast but with the bonus of a chest that could have belonged to a topless model. She had brains too. She was a dynamic package. A dynamic package with a sting like a scorpion when she needed to use it. Amy was using it now. I was being punished for my indiscretion. The cat was out the bag and it was scratching my face.

Amy was clever enough not to say it outright but we both knew what she was implying. I had sworn on my mother's life that I had not revealed details of our private encounter to a living soul. It was a lie and my mother was now dead. The two may not have been mutually exclusive. Amy was blowing up the balloon of guilt in my brain. She was cleverly suggesting that there may have been a reason why my Mum had died. My big mouth may have murdered my mother.

Chapter Twenty

I called around to Andy's the morning after Amy's outburst. On arrival, he told me Sunday was a day for crumpets with honey on, so he made about six and smothered them in honey so it rolled down the side like the oil in the Castrol GTX ad. We took them up to his room with his ubiquitous teapot and after honey stuck to my unshaven face like cotton wool to a fresh cut I tactfully made him aware of Amy's accusations.

"That just goes to show what a bitch she is. Get off your throne Alexis Carrington Colby, a new Queen is in town," Andy said, with more than a hint of panache. I wasn't sure whether Joan Collins had ever visited Rochdale, but I understood the point he was trying to make.

Amy's insistence that Andy hated her was showing no signs of being false. I hadn't been telling him about her hatred though just that she had implied that my loose lips had caused my Mum's death. At some stage, with some cunning detective work that I hoped would be dynamic enough to impress Inspector Morse I was going to discover why he had made his true feelings known to Amy outside Boots on a Friday evening.

"I mean," Andy continued, becoming increasingly demonstrative, "for that cow to even strategically suggest you may have killed your mother is just plain disgusting. How dare she accuse you of that?"

"I didn't say she directly accused me, Andy. I just said that she reminded me of the promise I'd made to her about keeping the eye accident to myself. It was me who concluded that my big mouth may have been responsible for Mum dying."

I was defending Amy but I had come to the same conclusion as Andy. Amy mentioned my promise to make me feel guilty about Mum's death and question my role in it.

"You don't seriously believe that though, do you?" Andy asked as he put his honey sodden plate down and reached for a cigarette, "That telling a white lie to Amy may have led to your Mum being killed?"

"I don't know. Have you heard of the butterfly effect, whereby each little thing we do contributes to everything else that happens subsequently?"

"Of course I have, it's in chaos theory. Edward Lorenz coined the phrase."

I'd never heard of Edward Lorenz or chaos theory but I wasn't surprised that Andy knew all about it. There was very little I knew that he didn't.

"Well, maybe if I hadn't lied, Mum would still be alive."

"Possibly, but that could apply to absolutely anything."

"What do you mean?"

"Well, I could say if my Mum and Dad had decided to have a bit of rumpy pumpy five minutes earlier or five minutes later then I might never have won the race to the golden egg and we wouldn't be sitting here now. This is just the path we are on and we'll never know how much influence we have on changing events. It's probably easier to accept that when it comes to birth and death everyone has their time to arrive and their time to go. This was just your Mum's time to go."

Andy's logic comforted me a little.

"So you reckon my Mum was destined to die when she did?"

"I don't know, H, I'm just saying it's probably the best way to look at it. At least looking at it that way stops you torturing yourself over what might have been."

"True. What made you mention the eye accident to Amy anyway?"

Perhaps blurting out the question wouldn't have impressed Inspector Morse all that much but it seemed an appropriate time to ask. Andy briefly looked at me then glanced away. It was unusual to see him look uncomfortable.

"I'd rather not say."

"Why not?"

He stubbed his cigarette out, as if he was trying to find something other than this conversation to occupy his mind.

"I just wouldn't."

"Am I going to have to prise it out of you?" I asked jovially, trying to lighten the mood as it had very rapidly darkened.

"H, this is not a game. I'm not telling you. Get Amy to tell you."

"I would but she says you just had a right go at her and she has no idea why."

"That'd be right," Andy scoffed, "poor old innocent Amy."

"Come on, Andy, we're mates, just tell me. I'm not taking sides, I wouldn't do that. I just don't understand what's going on."

"It's because we're mates that I'm not telling you. I'll just say this, my instincts about Amy Garfunkel proved to be right. Tread very carefully."

"I think I know what I've got myself into."

"H, I really don't think you do. I can tell you until I'm blue in the face that she's a scheming bitch but you'll never believe me. As much as I hate having to do this I am just going to have to sit back and watch you find out for yourself."

Chapter Twenty One

The mutual hatred between Amy and Andy seemed to gather pace after that confrontation in town. Every Friday when I saw Andy I couldn't mention Amy without a sigh or a scowl and each Saturday when I saw Amy, she would find any opportunity she could to make disparaging comments about Andy. It was clear Amy wanted me to end my friendship with Andy and equally clear Andy would be far happier if I finished with Amy.

Several months passed when I continued my weekend routine of seeing Andy on a Friday evening and Amy on a Saturday. Then one Thursday, as we were heading home from Hopwood Hall, after a day at college, Andy asked if we could swop.

"It's just one weekend, H! Surely she won't mind just for this weekend," Andy said as we took our usual seats at the front, on the upper deck of the double decker.

"It's not that simple," I replied, probably giving away the fact that this request had made me feel agitated, "it's Thursday already. It's a bit late to spring this on her now."

"Why? What does she do on a Friday?"

"Nothing. She just stays in."

"So why can't she just swop? She could stop in on a Saturday night instead."

"Because it's not what we do. We do our own thing Friday and see each other Saturday. We've always done things that way."

"I can't make Friday this weekend though. It's my Dad's Auntie's 80th over in Halifax and we're stopping over at her house. We won't be back until mid-afternoon on Saturday. For God's sake, H, I don't see what the problem is. Stop being such a pushover and just tell her you're seeing her on Friday this weekend."

I instinctively ducked as some overhanging branches from some large, roadside trees hit the front of the bus. I was probably just as annoyed with Andy as he was with me. It was Thursday afternoon surely his Auntie's 80th hadn't just been arranged at the last minute. Why did he have to spring this on me now?

To a large extent though, I was annoyed with myself because I knew Andy was right. I didn't like the idea of suggesting to Amy that we swop nights. Amy was temperamental and small issues could trigger big problems. Suggesting to her that we swop weekend nights seemed like the sort of thing that could trigger a drama, especially if it came to light that the reason that I wanted to change was to fit in with Andy's plans. I decided I'd rather take the safe option.

"Look mate, I'm sorry but I'm not swapping. We'll just have to leave Friday this week. I'll call around to yours on Sunday instead or come to mine if you like."

"You're a mug, H. She's a manipulative cow and she's got you wrapped around her little finger."

"No she hasn't," I protested despite knowing Andy was right.

"Just suggest it and see what she says!"

"No!"

I felt bad about letting Andy down but it made me think more about the arrangements I had with Amy. Why did we only ever see each on Saturdays? If all she ever did was stop in on a Friday, why did she not occasionally suggest we meet up? She knew I saw Andy every Friday and by suggesting I saw her rather than him, it could potentially drive a wedge between Andy and me, something Amy would be more than happy to do. So why hadn't she suggested it? Not even once.

The following day, when I arrived home from College, I decided I was going to surprise Amy by calling around. I had nothing else planned, with Andy being away, so tried to tell myself it was a romantic gesture but it wasn't. I was checking up on her. I also felt I was testing our relationship. If I turned up unannounced and Amy was pleased to see me that was a good sign, if I turned up and she was angry or annoyed with me then that was bad. I was starting to take some of the things Andy said about Amy to heart and I didn't like the thought of Amy thinking I was a pushover. I knew I needed to be stronger but not in an overly macho, domineering way. I just wanted to regain parity in our relationship which I knew I'd lost. As things stood, Amy called the shots. I loved her and didn't want to lose her nor did I want my Dad to lose her as she was fantastic with him, but I had nagging doubts about the direction our relationship was going. I feared I was being a love-struck fool. I wasn't exactly sure how turning up on a Friday evening was going to resolve that but it was something I felt, for a variety of reasons that I should do.

Chapter Twenty Two

"So explain to me again why I'm taking you to Amy's on a Friday? I thought you two only ever saw each other on a Saturday," Dad said as he drove along, at his normal pedestrian pace, towards Amy's.

"Andy's gone out to his Auntie's or Great Auntie's 80th, so I thought I'd surprise her."

"Does she like surprises?"

"I guess I'm going to find out soon enough."

"Well, let's hope she does......H, have you noticed a change in me recently?"

"What sort of change?" I asked which sort of made it obvious the answer was 'No'. It wasn't as though I had been particularly looking for signs of a change.

"Do you not feel I've been a bit jollier?"

I thought about it. It hadn't crossed my mind but now he'd come to mention it, it was a long time since I'd heard him crying or since he'd said life was no longer worth living. I immediately feared he was going to announce that somehow he had met a new lady friend. I shouldn't have begrudged him that anyway, but the thought terrified me.

"I haven't really thought about it, Dad, but yes, I suppose you have."

"Good. I think so too."

"Is there any reason why?" I asked, fearful of the answer I may get.

"Nothing specifically," Dad said, "I've just been trying harder. It was very hard coming to terms with your mother's death. When I was young, I always thought life was like a book and you'd go through all these Chapters before reaching the end, but life doesn't appear to work like that. Life can end in the first Chapter or halfway through a sentence in the middle or, if we are extremely lucky, it can reach the natural ending we all hope we get to have. I've realised now that I'm never going to come to terms with losing your Mum, but at the same time, moping around all day every day doesn't achieve anything either. I'm not sure when the story of my life will end, but whilst it is still being written, I want it to be cheerful."

I got the general point of what Dad was trying to say and it pleased me that he was trying to adopt a brighter approach. I felt sorry for him that he didn't have Mum anymore and it made me feel a sudden enhanced appreciation of what I had with Amy. As we were talking we drove past a florist's. A lady was collecting in some of the flowers that she had on display outside the shop front.

"Dad, can you just pull over for a few minutes?"

"Why, is everything OK?"

"It's fine. I just want to get Amy some flowers."

Dad slowed down, if that was possible and put his indicator on, before pulling over to the side.

"You'll have to be quick it looks like they are shutting."

"I know. I said as I got out the car and ran back towards the florist's, feeling for my wallet in my pocket as I ran.

It was probably only fifty metres up a slight slope back to the shop but I was panting as I arrived. The florist, who looked in her fifties, was smartly dressed and heavily made up. She was carrying a black plastic bucket full of flowers back inside.

"Excuse me," I said, "would it be possible for me to buy some flowers?"

"Now?" she asked.

"Yes."

"I'm shutting, love. I could take an order from you and you could pick them up in the morning."

"Oh," I said and in those two letters I managed to convey my feelings of disappointment.

"Did you want them for tonight?" the lady asked sympathetically.

"Yes, I was hoping to take them around to my girlfriend's now. My Dad is parked up down the road. He's giving me a lift."

"Go on then!"

"Thanks very much!"

"Well, you need to come in and let me know what you want and then you need to go and tell your Dad he's got a ten minute wait. My husband will be wondering where the hell I am. I've not stopped today. I don't know what's come over the men around here, suddenly gone all romantic."

Fifteen minutes later, I was back in the car proudly clutching a bouquet, which was made up largely of pink and white flowers. I couldn't tell you the names of those flowers but they had a pink bow at the bottom and were in a see through wrapping at the front, with a white papery type backing. To me, they looked expensive and cost me ten pounds. The lady told me they should actually have been £18, but given young, romantic men were the long term future of her business, she was happy to make a concession.

Soon after, my Dad dropped me off in Shawclough, at the top of Amy's road. Amy lived in a cul-de-sac and there were often cars parked at the bottom of the road which made it difficult to turn around. Given Dad's age and cautious approach to driving, a three point turn in such circumstances often became an eleven point turn and I had watched anxiously before as the manoeuvre had taken him up to five minutes. Wisely, he now suggested he dropped me off at the entrance to the road.

"What time shall I pick you up?" Dad asked as I carefully stepped out the car with the bouquet.

"If I don't phone you, could you come back about half past ten, please?"

"That's fine. Do you want me to park up whilst you make sure she's in?"

"No, no, she'll be in. She says she's always in on a Friday. If not, a couple of lads from Shawclough go to Hopwood so I can always call around at theirs."

This was only partially true. A couple of lads I knew from Hopwood did live in Shawclough, but I had no idea where so I couldn't possibly call around to their houses. I just didn't want Dad hanging around. If Amy was out, I'd feel guilty about asking him to drive me over, so decided I would rather walk the couple of miles home rather than feel like I had made Dad drive me over unnecessarily.

"As long as you're sure. Hope she likes the flowers, son."

"Thanks Dad! Cheers for the lift. See you later!"

I closed the passenger door behind me and started walking towards Amy's house which was in the bottom right corner of the road. As I recall it, Dad then sped off towards home, burning rubber as he went, but your mind plays tricks on you over time and realistically I know that he would have trundled off home.

I was about halfway down the road when the fuzzy glow I had been feeling from buying the flowers started to evaporate quicker than a pond in the Sahara. I was sure I spotted a group of about four lads, of similar age to me, walking down Amy's drive, to the side of her house. She lived in a large bungalow which had a pathway running down the right side of the house. Her Dad always wanted visitors to enter through the back door, into their utility room, as the hallway was carpeted and his obsessive cleanliness meant he fretted about people getting mud on his expensive carpets if they came into the house from the front.

Puzzled, I started walking a little faster and as I got closer to Amy's house, I noticed it wasn't just four lads. There were lots of small groups of people, dozens in total, all congregating on Amy's path. My first thought was that she must have arranged a party. Her parents' cars were noticeably absent and there was no way her Dad could possibly have been at home if this 'riff raff' were getting together on his driveway. This was by no means a pleasant conclusion to draw, as it was a party to which I had not been invited but as I took a proper look around the groups, it became evident that something more sinister than a party was taking place. Every single person gathered on the Garfunkel's driveway was a teenage boy.

I stood at the very front edge of the driveway, still holding my flowers tightly and surveyed the scene. To the left, queuing in single file against the side of the house, were at least twenty lads and then a further twenty were in small groups, standing to the right, next to the garden fence, chatting over cigarettes and a few cans of beer that were being passed around. As there were no familiar faces, I decided to join the back of the queue on the left. The lad in front of me, a tall, dark haired, square faced guy with unfortunate levels of acne and unattractive, patchy facial hair, turned around after he spotted my flowers out the corner of his eye.

"Waste of time bringing flowers, mate," he chided, "people have tried that before. Only ever works if you're good looking and no offence, pal, but there's better looking lads than you here."

"Only works for what?" I asked, already feeling confused and offended by the opening sentences of this ugly young man whose intelligence and beauty appeared roughly on par.

"Yeh right, as if you don't know turning up in your smart shirt with a bunch of flowers."

"Just pretend I don't know then."

"Stop trying to be clever, pal. There're people in this queue who like nothing more than kicking the shit out of a smart arse. You know why you're here and you know I know why you're here. You're here for 'The Friday Night Romp'."

"The Friday Night Romp?" I repeated. My emotions were everywhere. This lad was irritating me but more importantly my worst fears were being realised. I could feel myself getting upset. I was naïve but not naïve enough to fail to realise something sordid was taking place. Something sordid that could only involve Amy. Amy or her mother and if I was taking bets I would have given you a million to one on her mother. Geoff wasn't the easiest guy in the world to love but I couldn't imagine Mrs Garfunkel would ever resort to this.

We started shuffling forward a few feet, which temporarily distracted 'Spade Face', but once the forward momentum stopped he was happy to turn around again and resume the conversation.

"So, tell me the truth now, did you really know why you were here?"

"I honestly didn't."

"Get lost! Swear on your mother's life."

"I swear on my mother's life," I said, figuring I couldn't kill her twice.

"So do you still not know what's going on here?"

"Not the foggiest idea."

"Are you taking the piss out of me?" 'Spade Face' queried.

"No, straight up, I have no idea what is going on."

"No way! Why the flowers then?"

"I'm just delivering them."

"Seriously?"

'Spade Face' pulled an even stranger than usual face. He was more confused than me now.

"Absolutely."

"No way!"

This whole little game of me insisting I hadn't a clue what was happening and 'Spade Face' insisting I did know was growing tiresome.

"I tell you what, you just tell me what is going on because at the end of the day, does it really matter if I know or not?"

"Fair enough. Doesn't mean I believe you though."

"Just tell me!"

"OK. On Friday nights there's a bit of a ritual around here. The fittest girl in the village, Amy her name is, invites lads into her house, one by one, takes a photo of them on her Polaroid camera, then once everyone has had their turn, she picks one."

"Picks one?"

"Yeh," 'Spade Face' said getting annoyed with me for being slow on the uptake, "for a romp. She comes outside and tells us who's won, he goes inside and everyone else goes home."

I felt sick to the pit of my stomach. We started moving forward again so we reached the back corner of the house. I looked behind me and about half a dozen more lads had joined the queue.

"How long has this been going on?" I asked, once we had stopped moving forwards. I was trying to keep my composure as best I could as I felt I would be more likely to hear the truth from 'Spade Face' than I would from Amy.

"I don't know. I've been here three weeks now. Not been picked yet, but this Amy girl puts either a tick, a question mark or a cross on every photo. If there's a cross, you don't bother coming back. I've had a question mark the last two weeks. Kinky bitch too, apparently, uses baby oil. God, I'd love it if she picked me tonight."

It was all too much. I saw red. I took no notice of this ridiculous queue of disgusting, perverted young men and started heading towards the back door.

"Oi! What do you think you're playing at? There's a queue here," 'Spade Face' shouted out.

The shouts of injustice alerted those in front of him. I had moved in to the garage, three feet from the back door, when two lads who were about Andy's height, seemingly with a propensity to devour spinach, blocked my path.

"Don't even think about barging in front of us, pal. We've been here half an hour."

"I need to see Amy," I said, choking back tears.

"We all need to see Amy, mate, but you have to wait your turn like everyone else. So go on, be a good lad and get to the back of the queue before one of us decides to knock you out."

I was angry and upset but I still wasn't stupid. If I'd have tried pushing past Rambo and Robocop I'd have got my face kicked in. I considered just edging into the queue behind them, but the glares they were giving me meant that wasn't an option, so I trudged back disconsolately. As I did so, I decided upon Plan B. I kept walking, not to the back of the queue, but to the front of the house. If the door was open, I decided I was just going to walk right in and if it was locked, I was just going to bang on it like Benjamin Braddock in The Graduate until Amy turned up. Thankfully, for all concerned, it was open.

As I pressed the handle down on the door and pushed it open, I started to question why I was even bothering going inside. 'Spade Face' had told me all I needed to know. Was I just torturing myself by seeking some sort of confrontation? My relationship with Amy was over. She had made a complete fool of me. If I had mentioned to the waiting mob of sexually charged perverts that I was Amy's boyfriend they would collectively have laughed in my face. I should have listened to Andy's warnings. He had always been smarter than me. I had been a mug, a complete mug.

After a brief moment of reflection, I decided the reason I wanted to do this was because I wanted Amy to know that I was aware of her deceit. I went through into the hallway. There were two corridors leading off to the left and right. The left one led towards the kitchen, dining room and lounge. The one that led right went towards the bedrooms. Straight in front of me was the utility room and the back door, which was accessed from the outside via the integral garage. I was expecting a trail of teenage boys, like worker ants, leading the way to Amy's bedroom, but everything was eerily quiet, which I soon concluded was because Amy must have made everyone wait outside before taking them inside one by one. I stopped in my tracks and listened for sounds. I could hear Amy's voice but it wasn't coming from her bedroom as I had anticipated, it was coming from the lounge. There was a male voice too. The tones were friendly, even jovial. Their laughter felt like it was personal, as though they could sense my sadness and it amused them. I headed left along the corridor and paused outside a half open lounge door whilst I tried to summon some courage.

"So tell me why you think it should be you tonight?" I heard Amy asking.

"Well, I've been coming here every Friday for the last six weeks and each time I speak to you I feel we have a connection, yet, as you know, I've never been picked. The thing is though, you keep going through this same procedure every week and I reckon that's because you're still searching for Mr Right. Stop searching Amy. Pick me and put an end to all this."

That was my cue. My cue to storm in on Amy Garfunkel and angrily tell her that she'd already found her Mr Right but now she'd blown it. That it was all over and she was dumped. I hesitated once more though. I wanted to feel angry but the only feelings I could muster were those of humiliation, fear and sadness. Everything was over with Amy but I couldn't understand why. Other than that first night at the party, I had only ever acted like a gentleman towards her so why had she gone and done this?

"Right, smile for the camera," I heard Amy saying whilst I still procrastinated outside the door.

"You know what I look like already, Amy," the male voice protested, "do you have to take another photo?"

"Yes, I do," Amy said with insistence, "it's part of the process."

Once that photo was taken, that bloke, whoever he was, was going to walk out the door and stand face to face with me. I didn't want that. I wanted to confront Amy. I needed to go in. I strode into the lounge just as Amy clicked the button on the camera. The door was right behind where a good looking young man with a mass of fair, curly hair was sat. The Polaroid spat out its square photo, probably of the back of the bloke's head, as he turned as I entered and stared at me, perplexed, as I stood there silently clasping my bunch of flowers.

I wanted to say something authoritative like 'What the hell is going on here?' or 'The game's up, Amy' or something else that would exit the lips of a scorned lover on an American soap opera, but I didn't say or do anything. I just stood there looking pathetic, like one of those characters in Awakenings, frozen in time. A tear rolled down my cheek.

"H, oh my god, H!" was all Amy needed to say. I dropped the flowers and fled. I ran out the lounge, through the hallway and out the front door. I kept running up the cul-de-sac, past a few stragglers who were late joining the queue. Once I reached the top of the road, my run became a walk, but I didn't walk in a calm, day to day manner, it was more a tearful, sobbing, out of breath walk. I probably only managed a hundred metres at most before I sat on the kerb with my feet on top of a gutter, put my two hands on top of my head, my lower arms from wrist to elbow covering my face and I bawled in a self-pitying, teenage way. Life just seemed very, very unfair.

Chapter Twenty Three

After a couple of minutes of sobbing, I felt a gentle hand on my shoulder.

"H, look I'm so sorry. This wasn't the way I wanted you to find out," Amy spoke in calm, comforting tones that seemed somewhat inappropriate given the circumstances.

"I've just witnessed fifty lads queuing up outside your house, hoping to be the one you pick to shag you. How exactly did you want me to find out about that?"

"You don't understand, H. It's..."

"Too right I don't understand. It's cheap and dirty and sordid and it's not you, Amy. All of this isn't you."

I stood up. For the first time ever in our relationship I felt I had Amy on the defensive and it didn't feel right that she should be allowed to look down on me. Not that there was a relationship any more. As I looked at her, the fact that we were finished still upset me. Why did she have to be so beautiful and so uncaring?

"It's complicated, H. Come back to the house and I'll try to explain over a cup of tea."

Amy tried to hold my hand. I shook it off. There was no way I was going to be holding her hand. If I hadn't arrived unannounced she'd have probably been sharing her vagina with the winner of the pervert competition within half an hour.

"With fifty lads watching on? No, thanks!"

"There's no-one at ours any more, H. I've sent them home."

This made sense. Through my tears I had heard a lot of footsteps and voices.

"I don't even want to try to make any sense of this, Amy. It would be impossible. We're finished. There's no way back from here. How could there possibly be?"

The last sentence was for my own benefit. I wanted there to be a way. I wanted this to be a huge misunderstanding and it all to turn out to be an innocent game of scrabble played between Amy and half the male population of Shawclough, but the likes of Andy already thought I was a fool for dating her. How would he feel if he knew I was sharing her with fifty others?

"I know that, lovely. I'm not trying to save our relationship. I know I've ruined everything and I'm truly sorry I've hurt you. I just want you to understand why I did it. Come back to mine. Please?"

A warped part of my brain was still telling me to go back. It was still trying to convince me that something could be salvaged from the wreckage of this bomb that had just landed into the middle of our relationship. Maybe we could stay friends. Thankfully, my brain and my heart were then flooded with bitterness.

"Stop insulting my intelligence. I'm not coming back to yours. In the next sixty seconds, I am going to dry my tears and head off home. If we never see each other again that will suit me just fine. Where the hell are the rest of your family anyway?"

"They've gone up to our caravan site in Brompton on Swale. They go every Friday after work and come back on Saturday afternoon. I've told you that, you just don't listen."

Amy had never told me that. If she had told me, I would have been uncomfortable about her being on her own every Friday. Being totally honest, if I'd have known she was on her own, I would have tried to get around there to sleep over whenever I could. Amy didn't tell me because she didn't want me there.

"How come none of your neighbours bother to tell your Mum and Dad that you're running a brothel in their absence?"

"It's not a brothel. It's a selection process and anyway, all the neighbours hate my Dad so it probably amuses them to think his daughter is betraying him whilst he's away."

"Betraying me too," I added.

"I know, honey, I know. I'm sorry for that, I really am. I love you, H and I love your lovely Dad too."

"Then why do this to us?"

"I'm seventeen years old. I'm a beautiful creature with wings that need to fly. I know I won't always be this beautiful, this attractive to so many people. I love the calmness and sensitivity you bring to my life, but I also like the sense of adventure of my Friday nights. I love having all these young men desperate to be with me, desperate to be chosen. You don't know what it feels like to have forty or fifty sexual beings all overcome with their desire for you, sometimes even fighting over you. Watching two people fight to be with you is such a wonderful feeling. It makes me feel so wanted, so attractive, so alive."

I wiped my face. This girl wasn't deserving of my tears.

"Amy, that's all just arty bullshit you make up in your head to find some justification for being a slag."

Amy had the audacity to be offended.

"Don't you dare call me a slag, H."

"Then don't act like one."

I would see Amy again, in pubs and bars in Rochdale and occasionally in Bury or Manchester, but we never spoke to each other again, certainly not in full sentences anyway. I would find it within myself, despite how much she hurt me, to nod and say 'Hello'. Many years later, I even found it within myself to accept her Facebook 'friend' request, but that was just inquisitiveness temporarily prevailing over common sense and after a few weeks of having a social network friendship, in which time I had ample opportunity to check out how time had changed her, whether she married well and what her children looked like, I unfriended her. I took great satisfaction in the fact that the sands of time had not been kind.

That Friday night though, our relationship ended with a slap across my face. 'Slag' is such an awful word to describe anyone, so I suppose, in a way, I had it coming. I understand some people live their lives, and particularly their sex lives, in complicated ways. Those people, I guess, must feel the positives outweigh the negatives when it comes to polygamy or they wouldn't embroil themselves in such crazy games, but I didn't want any of that. I just wanted a monogamous relationship with someone I loved. I am too emotional and too insecure to cope with anything more. Thus, the experience with Amy set me back. It took quite a while for the wounds to heal and the scabs on my emotions to fall off.

Chapter Twenty Four

The death of my relationship with Amy Garfunkel triggered off the birth of my rebellious years. I didn't rebel against my father. It was more a case of rebelling against my sensible side. I had tried to be a good, honest, sensitive soul and all that seemed to bring with it was misfortune and manipulation so I tried to toughen up. I made a decent job of it too, for a while, but unfortunately the pendulum eventually swung too far and rather than being hurt by others, I became the one who was inflicting the damage. At first it was physical damage as I started to get myself into a few drunken scrapes but that was followed by emotional damage, which I knew from experience lasted longer than a fat lip or a black eye.

It was easy to get into fights when your best mate was Andy Corcoran. All I needed to do was keep my eyes and ears open. People would call him all sorts of names due to his tone of voice, dress sense or affectations. Whilst Andy would get into a war of words, I would want my fists to do the talking, the problem being that they often spoke in little more than a whisper. As Andy became accustomed to dragging me away from a potential flare up or watched on helplessly as I attempted to trade blows with a host of local idiots, he became more and more exasperated with my pathetic attempts to be aggressive. He pointed out that when we were at primary school it used to be him that did the fighting not me. He said he'd progressed and I'd regressed. It didn't stop him from coming out with me every Friday night but his condemnation of my actions meant that I grew to avoid trouble when he was around. To compensate, I started to go out on my own on Saturday nights and would select places that I thought would be hotbeds of violence. Most weekends there was very little trouble in the pubs, but there were often flare ups after kicking out time, normally between two lads fighting over a girl and then groups of friends would join in. It was just a case of picking a side and wading into the melee. I lost far more fights than I won as I didn't choose my battles with the intention of winning. I just wanted to take part.

Within a few months, I realised I wasn't achieving anything for my own mental wellbeing but my regular physical damage was causing my father far more upset than he deserved. Like Andy, my Dad was dismayed by how I was reacting to Amy's infidelities. He grew to understand that any trouble I became involved in tended to be on a Saturday night, so one Friday when I arrived in from a night out with Andy, Dad must have decided it was an opportune time to have a word.

I wasn't late arriving home that Friday. It was probably as early as eleven o'clock. Our 'A' level exams were nearing and although I was just about doing enough work to get by, Andy was throwing himself into his studying with the same passion and exuberance he threw into life. He wanted to get up early the following morning to do some revision so had wanted an early night. We had been out in Ramsbottom and as I was enjoying the 'bonhomie' in the various pubs we frequented I was tempted to carry on drinking without him when Andy suggested heading for the last bus home, but knew that would mean paying for a taxi and I wanted to save some money so I could venture out once more the following night. Reluctantly, I jumped on the bus.

Dad was still listening to the radio in the kitchen when I arrived home. He had dispensed with the reliance on alcohol by this point, so I think he would have been drinking coffee or possibly Ovaltine as he enjoyed that before going to bed.

"Good night?" he asked as I did my usual post-boozing trick of wandering through and making myself a glass of water from the kitchen tap, only the pretentious and the rich drank bottled water back then.

"Yeh, it was good thanks, Dad. You can't help but feel entertained when you go out with Andy. He's been telling me about some big fall out he had at College today with a girl called Waddy."

"Waddy?"

"That's her nickname anyway, her real name is Jenny Trescothick."

"Over what?"

"I can't remember. Something political I think. They're both doing Politics 'A' level. From what I can make out, her views are very left wing and his are fairly right, so they are bound to clash but importantly I think she is the only girl in College who is more intelligent than him and he doesn't like it."

"I can imagine. Isn't she the girl he knocked over at the party at primary school? The Showaddywaddy knickers girl?"

"That's right, that's her! I'd forgotten about that. I suppose she has good reason to hate him."

Dad saw this as an opportunity to move the conversation on.

"You shouldn't hate Amy though, son. You know that, don't you?"

"Dad, do we need to talk about this now? It's three months since we split up. I'm trying to move on."

Dad felt his face with the fingers and thumb of his right hand.

"You're not making much of a success of that though, are you?"

"What do you mean?"

"I mean the Saturday night fighting. The Sunday morning cuts and sores. It doesn't strike me that you're turning into Sugar Ray Leonard. I know Amy has hurt you but it's an emotional hurt, being physically hurt won't resolve it."

My Dad had pretty much hit the nail on the head. Mum's death and Amy's betrayal had left me with emotional injuries, internal emotional injuries. There was nothing to show how much I was hurting. It wasn't logical, but for some reason I wanted to feel some physical pain and I wanted my outer self to display that hurt. It was self-harming without taking a razor to my own skin.

"I know," I agreed with Dad, "for a while I just thought it might."

"So you've finished with all of that now?"

"I think so."

"Good. Amy wasn't a bad person, H. She just craves attention."

"She's a slag."

It was rare for my Dad to give me a look of contempt but very briefly that was what I saw. His facial expression indicated that he believed I had made a comment that was beneath me. His spoken words backed that up.

"No, no, she's not. Don't call her that. She has a good heart and she helped me a lot after your Mum died. She's just a kid trying to find herself in a mixed up way. You weren't married to her, H. She didn't sign any exclusivity contracts with you. Technically she's done nothing wrong."

"I was her boyfriend, Dad. Don't defend her. She made me into a laughing stock."

"Has anyone laughed at you about it?"

"No, but that's not the point."

The only person I'd told about the whole incident was Andy. He hadn't laughed. To my annoyance, he had actually confessed to seeing it coming, obviously not on such a grand scale, but it transpired that his whole argument outside Boots had stemmed from him catching her buying condoms. I had questioned why he hadn't thought they were for my use and Andy replied that they were flavoured condoms and he knew me well enough to know that I would never have worn a flavoured condom. I didn't tell him but this wasn't true. I wouldn't have chosen to wear one but if Amy had asked me to, I would have done. I would have done anything for Amy. I loved her.

"Son," my Dad continued, "I'm not defending her. She treated you badly and that wasn't right but get it into perspective. You weren't married to her. There's no messy divorce. You are seventeen years old, for goodness sake, dust yourself off and move on. There are plenty more fish in the sea."

"Yeah, but it puts you off going deep sea diving when you've just had your heart ripped out by a great white shark."

"Be more careful next time then. It's like that tale of the scorpion and the frog. You've heard that one, haven't you?"

I shook my head. Up until then I hadn't heard it, but I've heard it many times since. Told it myself many times since.

"No."

"I can't remember exactly how it goes but a frog is on a river bank and a scorpion comes along and asks the frog if he'll carry him over to the other side of the river. The frog refuses and when the scorpion asks why, the frog says because the scorpion will sting him. The scorpion promises he won't because if he does, the frog will stop swimming and they will both drown, so it serves no purpose. Thus, the frog allows the scorpion on to his back. Half way across, the frog feels a sharp sting and just before he dies, he says, 'why did you do that? We'll both die now' and the scorpion replies, 'I can't help it, I'm a scorpion, that's what I do'.

If you don't want to get hurt, H, think more carefully about the type of girl you are going swimming with. Next time don't pick a shark or a scorpion, pick a dolphin!"

Dad smiled as he said this. I think he liked his own analogy.

"Good night, Dad!"

"Good night son. If I die in my sleep, never forget how much me and your mother loved you."

Chapter Twenty Five

"A large Doner kebab, please, with lettuce, tomato and onion, please, but no sauce."

It was midnight on Saturday night and I had just ordered a friend to accompany me home, Mr D Kebab. I'd had a really good time, had managed to bump into several groups of lads and girls from Hopwood Hall in town and, as was common at the time, had drunk much more than I had intended to. The kebab was a belated attempt to sober myself up. As I was hazily watching the man behind the counter strimming the edges off the elephant foot into my pita bread, I heard a familiar voice.

"Oi, McCoy!"

I turned towards the entrance and standing there was the bulky figure of Mo Iqbal, former 'cock of the school', subsequently expelled for beating up Lucas Glover. Behind him stood seven or eight others, presumably his friends, of both sexes. Mo looked much older than I remembered him. He had a moustache now, but not a typical teenage moustache, a proper man's moustache like Daley Thompson's or Tom Selleck's. My immediate thought was that he may link me to his expulsion from Matthew Moss and seek retribution. I was particularly concerned as I felt as though I had recently announced my retirement from acting as a human punchbag. My fears were unfounded.

"How's it going, Mo?" I responded nervously.

"Fuckin' marvellous, my friend. Great to see you man!" Mo said, slapping me on the shoulder, which stung more than I let on.

"Is your mate not with you? Bloody hell, I can't even remember his name now. You know who I mean. The strange one. Acts a bit gay."

I knew exactly who he was referring to.

"I'm not sure who you mean," I replied innocently.

"Yes, you do! You know. Stop winding me up, man. The big tall guy. He was into The Smiths and The Roses and stuff like that. Crap fighter."

"Oh, Andy Corcoran."

Mo clicked his fingers.

"That's the fella, Andy Corcoran. Big long string of piss. Are you still mates with him?"

"Yes, I was out with him last night."

"Good for you, man, good for you. Is he not out tonight?"

"No, he's studying."

"He's a swot, is he?"

"A bit."

Mo laughed loudly at this.

"Funny how I got expelled for helping a swot! Bit ironic when I'm not the brightest myself. Well, not at school stuff anyway. I'm street smart and I've got business sense and I reckon that's more important.

I never really liked that Andy kid, bit too weird for me. It's good your still mates with him though. Loyalty in life is important. He was loyal to you and you're loyal to him, I like that. "

Mo was confusing me a bit. I had always assumed he must have liked Andy because he saved him from a beating. Perhaps he had just felt sorry for him.

"Why did you help him, Mo? If you didn't like him much, why help him?"

By this time, I had paid for my kebab and been handed it. I picked a bit of the kebab meat off the top whilst I listened to his answer.

"I just think it's important to stick up for the minorities. We need each other's help."

I was shocked. In fact, shocked is playing it down. I was flabbergasted.

"So you helped Andy because you think he is gay?"

Mo Iqbal looked at me with a mixture of humour and confusion. He started laughing again.

"No, man, I wasn't helping him. I was helping him help you. I heard your mate Andy say that Lucas Glover had called you a 'Paki'."

"You know I'm not Asian, don't you?"

"Of course I do, man, but you're not 100% Anglo Saxon either, are you? If Lucas Glover wanted to go all Ku Klux Klan, then he deserved a good hiding."

I wasn't overly comfortable with his reasons, I'd rather he helped Andy because he understood Andy was a good guy, helping a friend out and maybe that was part of the reason, but I suppose if you have an image as a hard man to protect, you don't confess that.

"Well, whatever the reasons were. Thank you!"

"No problem."

"How come you got expelled? Did you not tell the teachers what had happened?"

"They wouldn't have listened to me. I'd only been back a couple of days after a two week suspension for bringing an eighth of weed into school. I told them it was medicinal for my glaucoma but they didn't believe me. The teachers hated me at that school. I was happy to leave. Beating up Lucas Glover was the final straw for all concerned.....can I just have a portion of chips, please?"

Whilst Mo was paying for his chips, I paid more attention to the people he was with. There were actually only five others with him, three other Asian guys who I vaguely recognised from when they went to our school and two girls. One of the girls was Asian, the other was white, they too were familiar but I wasn't sure where from.

"Recognise any of these guys?" Mo asked, joining me slightly away from the queue.

"I recognise them all, Mo, but I'm pretty pissed mate so don't be expecting me to remember any of their names."

"I'll introduce you..."

"He doesn't need introducing to me. I used to adore Harry McCoy," said one of the girls stepping forwards from out of the queue.

I looked at her intently as she smiled back at me. It was the white girl and she was wearing a cropped pair of faded blue jeans, with a collection of rips in and a white t-shirt that only came down to just above a bare, flat stomach. There was a picture of Mickey Mouse on the t-shirt which struck me as the type of thing a seven year old would wear, but somehow it seemed to work. She had perfect teeth, something that I would not normally notice. She was undoubtedly pretty but her looks were tempered slightly by the significant amount of make-up she wore, especially around the eyes. She had brown hair in a bit of a non-descript style, the best way I can manage to describe it, is like that of a monk but without the bald spot. There was a confidence and zaniness about her. She was very tall, but overly slim.

"This is embarrassing," I said apologetically, "I know I should be able to place you but I can't. I mean it's not like there've been many girls who've adored me. At school there was only ever Joanna Barry and you're not Joanna Barry."

The girl started laughing. It was a quirky laugh. It brought back memories.

"Bloody hell! You are Joanna Barry!"

I instinctively gave her a quick hug but then backed off a little timidly once my brain kicked in.

"Hello, H."

I looked her up and down. She was fit, perhaps not quite in Amy's league, but not far off.

"What's happened to you in the last couple of years? The last time I saw you must have been at John Dunphy's party and you were like this big."

I indicated about five feet nothing. She was now about five feet eight.

"I was a late developer."

"You're telling me! Those braces didn't half do your teeth good too. Look at them!"

Joanna good humouredly opened her mouth and clenched her teeth together to show me them all.

"A fine set of gnashers! And what's happened to the glasses?"

"Contacts," Joanna said, pointing to her eyes.

Mo briefly interrupted.

"H, once these lot have got their food, we're off to a party in Milnrow. Fancy coming?"

"Yeh, that'd be great. How are you getting there?"

"We were going to get a couple of taxis. We can take another with us, no problem."

"Brilliant. Count me in. I just need to go and do something first. I'll meet you back here in five minutes."

There was no way I was going to turn down that invitation. As I ran over to a BT phone box, I reflected on the fact that I was now physically attracted to that little nutcase, Joanna Barry. I'd have never thought that was possible. Before I went to Milnrow though, I needed to phone my Dad. It wouldn't have been fair on him if I'd stopped out until the early hours without warning as I knew he wouldn't have slept. He was fine about it and said he'd leave a front door key under a plant pot around the side of the house.

I remember when we arrived at the house, the door opened and a massive cloud of smoke drifted out into the night sky with its distinctive smell of cannabis like freshly laid wood mulch. As we entered the hallway and went down the stairs to the kitchen, my eyes scanned around for familiar faces but I didn't spot any. Most of the people there seemed older than me. I'd guess most were in their early twenties. There seemed like a pleasant vibe though, it wasn't like a teenage party where everyone just wanted to get completely pissed and trash the place. This was cooler, friendlier and more hip.

The house was an old semi-detached property with four floors. Most people congregated in the basement as the kitchen was down there along with the beer and the stereo system. On every level though, there were plenty of people milling around. Joanna and I ended up sitting on the landing on the first floor with a can of Carling Black Label each and a spliff that one of Mo's friends had given us. Joanna looked like she had smoked one before so I was trying to give off the impression that I had too. We kept taking drags on it and passing it to and fro. I was already drunk but smoking pot made me feel even more lightheaded. It also gave me a feeling of euphoria like meeting up with Joanna again was the best thing that had happened to me in my whole life.

"This is good shit!" I said, as I passed the spliff to Joanna. I didn't really know whether it was or it wasn't but that's what people seemed to say in films.

"It really is," Joanna replied, breathing in deeply then blowing out.

"It is SO great to see you, Joanna. You're like a swan. A fucking beautiful swan!"

Joanna laughed, a little forcibly I would say, but I still found it endearing.

"Are you saying I used to be an ugly duckling?"

Our legs were touching and we were talking with our faces barely divided. Joanna would touch my hand with hers when she spoke. Neither of us was playing hard to get.

"Maybe a swan is a bad example. You're like a lily then."

"A lily?"

The laugh re-appeared. I laughed too.

"Well, you know, when lilies are growing they look like they're going to be pretty but only when they open up do you see exactly how beautiful they are."

"You're so sweet, H McCoy!"

Joanna put her arm around my waist. Talking random bollocks, I was soon to discover, is compulsory when stoned, but there is always time for sombre reflection. I thought Joanna was making a move towards a kiss but I read the signals wrong, temporarily anyway.

"And how are you?" she asked, moving her hand from my waist and cupping one of my hands in between both of hers.

"Other than a little spaced out, I am fantastic."

"No, I mean since your Mum died. That was such an awful thing to happen."

"Just bad luck," I said, shrugging my shoulders stupidly, like my mother's death was a minor event rather than a devastating, life changing disaster.

"I thought she was lovely when I met her."

"She was lovely. I just feel bad that I didn't appreciate her as much as I should have done. I obviously didn't realise I was going to blink one day and she'd be gone."

"I heard your speech. I thought it was amazing."

I had been avoiding eye contact whilst we had been having this particular conversation but once she said this, I turned and faced her. Our eyes almost collided.

"You were at Mum's funeral?"

"Yes, I was devastated for you. I felt an urge to go."

There had only been thirty seven people at Mum's funeral. I vaguely remembered thinking at the time that one was Joanna. I felt it was a very kind thing for her to have done. It made me feel very emotional.

"Thank you. Did you go to the Waggon & Horses after"

"No, I went home afterwards. I smoked a spliff, listened to some sombre music and reflected on what a shitty God we must have if he thought it was right to take your Mum away."

"Andy sang 'Four Seasons In One Day' in the pub. You'd have enjoyed that. It was strange and melancholy too."

"How is Andy? I miss him."

"Andy's great. He's not changed. I can't see him ever changing."

"Why should he? The best thing about Andy is that he doesn't compromise himself for the satisfaction of the masses."

As soon as she said that I kissed her. It wasn't a slow motion, tilt of the head, look into each other's eyes type of kiss. It was a zoom in before either of us has a second to think about it type kiss. A frantic kiss. Joanna didn't object. She kissed back with the same force and passion. I'd never kissed a smoker before and for a few seconds it felt like kissing a discarded firework, but our mouths seemed to produce enough saliva to flush it out. As I was kissing, tenderly nibbling her bottom lip with my eyes closed, my mind kept warning me that I was kissing Joanna Barry. She may not have been a scorpion or a shark, but she wasn't a dolphin either. I started thinking of the type of sea creature Joanna Barry could actually compare to and I came up with a clown frogfish, a sea cucumber and a dumbo octopus - something weird. When I sobered up was this still going to seem like a good idea?

When we pulled out of that kiss, I really didn't know what to say. I remember there was a small awkward pause, which I accept is common place after several minutes of spontaneous kissing. To break the silence, Joanna came out with the first of what became known between us as 'Barryisms', random words that made no sense to me until they were subsequently explained. Like Andy, Joanna Barry was on a completely different intellectual plain to me.

"Are you more of a Dali or a Picasso?"

With my cheeks and chin feeling wet with Joanna's misplaced saliva, I didn't really feel like a painting of any description. I then questioned myself whether Dali and Picasso were actually painters. I was about 80% sure that they were. The part of my brain that was particularly stupid was telling me that they were composers. Whatever they were, it was a strange icebreaker after five minutes of what was formerly known as 'necking'.

"Are you asking me if I'm a painting?"

"Of course I'm not, H! I'm asking you how you treat ladies."

"I still don't understand," I confessed.

Joanna didn't want me to understand. I'm pretty certain she knew full well that the chances of me adequately responding to her question were miniscule. It was a thinly veiled boast. Not that I minded, I was happy to be educated and I would have only broken the silence by asking something mundane like whether she was fifteen or sixteen now.

"Pablo Picasso treated women like pawns in his game," Joanna explained, "he treated most of them badly and rarely only ever had one on the go. His most famous partner was the photographer Dora Maar, but even when he was with her, he had several other women on the go too.

Salvador Dali, on the other hand, fell in love with his wife Gala, the first time he saw her and spent most of his life in love with her. I guess what I'm asking you, H, is whether you are a romantic or a seed spreader?"

I reflected on my relationship with Amy.

"I'm definitely not a seed spreader. I've had one girlfriend and she left me for half of Shawclough.

"She did what?" Joanna asked, sounding genuinely shocked.

I didn't want to start telling her all about it. I was too drunk and stoned to tell the story with any sense of perspective and would have probably started feeling sorry for myself.

"Oh, I'll tell you about it some other time," I answered.

Was this me paving the way to future dates? I wasn't sure. I surprised myself when I said it.

"Could you be a Salvador Dali?"

I thought this Picasso or Dali thing was all a bit pretentious. It had interested me fleetingly but I didn't want to dwell on the subject.

"I've no idea, Joanna. I suppose I'm a romantic, more than most lads anyway, but I'm not saying just because we've snogged once we are going to stay together for the rest of our lives."

"I'm not saying that either. I always thought you were more of a Dali anyway. That's why I turned Mo down, I saw him as more of a Picasso. I'm not interested in Picasso's...."

"Whoa! Whoa! Whoa! Rewind a minute, Joanna. Did you just say you turned Mo down?"

I was sobering up all of a sudden.

"Yes."

"When?"

"All the time."

"When was the last time you turned him down?"

"Last night."

"Shit, Joanna!"

"What?"

"Where is he now?" I said, springing to my feet.

"I have no idea, in the basement, probably."

"Why didn't you tell me all this before you kissed me?"

"I didn't think you'd want to know he was in the basement."

"Very funny. Why didn't you tell me that Mo fancies you?"

"Because you wouldn't have kissed me. I've wanted to kiss you for years, H. It was me that spotted you in the take away. That was why we all went in, because I wanted you to come to the party."

"Joanna, Mo is going to kick my head in when he finds out about this."

"He already knows," she said matter-of-factly whilst also getting to her feet.

I was really panicking now. Sweat was gathering on my forehead like a coward's tears.

"What do you mean 'he already knows'?"

"I keep my eyes open when I kiss. Mo came past us about ninety seconds into it, then he stormed off."

"Fucking hell! Why didn't you tell me?"

"You looked like you were enjoying yourself!"

"That was before I knew Mo Iqbal fancied you. Have you seen the size of him? He eats bricks for breakfast. How did he look when he saw us? Mad? Crazy?"

"Crestfallen. Crestfallen and betrayed."

"Bloody marvellous! He's going to kill me. He's probably gone to get a baseball bat or a knuckle duster or something. I need to get out of here quick."

"No you don't. Stick around. Fight for my honour. Show some balls."

I looked at her like she was the most stupid woman that had ever lived.

"Who the hell do you think I am, Joanna? I'm not friggin' Peter Cetera! Show some balls? I won't even have any balls once Mo gets hold of me."

I noticed Joanna was almost laughing.

"You're enjoying this aren't you?" I asked.

"Very much so. I'm excited. I've never had two men fight over me before. I hope you win. I like you more than Mo."

"Joanna, there's no chance I'm going to bloody win! He's fucking huge!"

"He's only the same height as you."

"But three times as wide. He'll kill me!"

"Fight for me, H. Be my matador against the raging bull."

"Not a chance!"

I gave Joanna a quick peck on the cheek and then I was off. I ran down the stairs in that house like it was the 'Towering Inferno'. There were two ways of getting out. There was a door on the ground floor and one in the basement. I had no idea where Mo was, but as soon as I reached the ground floor, I was out of there. Just as I slammed the door behind me, I heard the intimidating sound of Mo Iqbal's voice.

"HARRY!"

"Shit!"

The house where the party was, was in the middle of a long row of Victorian houses. Back in the nineteenth century they may well have been huge detached homes for the upper classes but now they were mainly semi-detached with all the gardens divided by well established and well maintained hedges, all about four feet high. Being drunk, stoned and scared, I decided I didn't have time to run to the top of the path and instead became some sort of weird mix of Red Rum, Ed Moses and Forrest Gump. I ran at the first hedge, hurdled over it or at least hurdled through the top and just kept going.

"H, wait you dickhead!" was the cry from behind which just prompted me to run faster.

This was realistically never going to work as I was no sportsman. I had hurdled, leapfrogged or clambered over six or seven hedges and naively my confidence was growing. As I went full pelt at the eighth, in almost total darkness, I hit something on the landing side. It felt like a brick wall and I initially thought I must have jumped into the side of someone's garage. A moment later, I realised it wasn't a garage at all. It was Mo Iqbal's chest. I slithered down it and on to the muddy grass below.

"What are you playing at, H?"

"I'm sorry. I am truly, really, really sorry," I begged.

"Why did you just jump those four hedges, man and then turn around and come back? You're a fucked up kid."

I was so pissed, stoned and scared that I must have become disorientated. After jumping the fourth hedge, I must have somehow lost my bearings and done a semi-circle before jumping the same four hedges again. Straight back to where I had started and smash bang wallop into Mo Iqbal.

Begging seemed like my only option now.

"I'm so, so sorry. I swear I didn't know."

"Know what? What are you on about, man?"

"That you fancied Joanna."

"Which Joanna?"

"Joanna Barry," I clarified.

"You think I fancy Joanna Barry?"

"Yes, I didn't know. Honestly, I didn't. I would have kept well away. Not that much happened. I barely touched her. I swear."

With one hand, Mo lifted me to my feet. I was all set for the knockout blow. Dad was going to go mad.

"I appreciate your sense of decency, H, but I don't fancy, Joanna Barry!"

"You don't?" I queried, suddenly feeling like I had been given a reprieve from the hangman's noose.

"Of course not, she's just my crazy little mate."

"She told me that you fancied her."

"She's winding you up, H. She's got a wicked sense of humour."

"Wicked as in funny or wicked as in cruel?"

"Funny. Cruel. I don't know, both I guess."

Mo started laughing.

"Stop laughing Mo or I'll have to sort you out!"

He knew I was joking. I had hit him at full pelt and had just bounced right off.

"Ok, I best stop then. Wouldn't want a night in Casualty."

"That's right. You know when you've met your match. Why were you chasing after me then if you weren't going to kick my head in?"

"I wasn't chasing you. I just saw you leaving so came over to say 'Bye' and then watched from the top of the path as you turned the place into fucking Aintree. You're a bloody lunatic, mate!"

"Well, I'm glad someone found it funny. You don't understand how unfit I am. I'm bloody knackered."

"So you fancy my mate Joanna then, do you? I saw you getting close on the landing."

"I'm not sure how I feel about her at this very moment."

"Well once you come to your senses, if you do decide that you fancy her, make sure you treat her well. She has a heart of gold that girl. She's a nutcase, there's no doubt about that, but I'm telling you man, she has a heart of gold."

Chapter Twenty Six – Six Months Later

"Joanna, this is my Dad, Dad this is Joanna. Be very careful around her, she's a bit of a lunatic."

"Thanks for the warning, H, but I'm sure I'll be fine. Very pleased to meet you, Joanna."

After the party in Milnrow, I didn't rush in to a relationship with Joanna. We both decided to take things slowly. A couple of weeks passed before we went on a date and I then arranged to meet up with her in town, once or twice, as she was working in a card shop over the summer, before starting at Sixth Form College. I'd say it took us about three months to actually be 'going out' and even then I wasn't sure how much I wanted another relationship, so we tended to meet on neutral ground most of the time. About five months after the party, I met her Mum and it eventually became time to introduce her to Dad.

"Pleased to meet you too, Mr McCoy," Joanna replied in an almost angelic tone that I had never heard before, "I met your wife. She was lovely."

"She certainly was. Please don't call me Mr McCoy though, Joanna. George is just fine."

"OK."

"And this must be Cilla. Isn't she beautiful?"

This introductory scene did not take place in our house, but in a very windy setting out on Saddleworth Moor. Joanna's Mum and Dad had a Doberman Pinscher called 'Cilla' and I suggested we bring her out for a run on the Moor. We arrived separately to my Dad, as I was now the proud owner of 'wheels'. Over the summer, I had managed to pass my driving test first time after only half a dozen 'proper' lessons and about eight weeks of ten or twelve hours tuition from my Dad. My father was a very calm instructor. He would pass on little tips, like if you are parking in a space with cars on either side, he would tell me to concentrate on keeping as close as I could to the vehicle on the driver's side, which would mean I was a safe distance away from the car on the passenger side. Once I passed, Dad lent me £1,000 so I could buy an 'E' reg Toyota Carina from an old guy in Norden. He had had it since new, but he'd just used it as a little run around, so it had only done 16,000 miles so the fact he was only charging £995 meant it was a bargain. The poor old bloke was 83 and couldn't afford the insurance anymore. His two sons were apparently keen for him to stop driving too. When I went to pick it up, they were both there and they looked relieved whilst Bernie looked emotional. Having your independence stripped from you must be one of the worst parts of growing old.

Once I had wheels, I started looking for work. For Dad's sake, I had taken my 'A' levels, but I knew I wasn't going to be going to University. I wasn't clever enough nor focused enough and anyway, I would never have felt right leaving my Dad on his own or putting him through the expense. I failed Economics and passed History and English with a 'D' and an 'E' which I'm sure wouldn't have got me in to Oxford or Cambridge. Andy put his genius to good use and ended up with three 'A's and a 'B'. His extra 'A' was in General Studies which I received a 'U' in which apparently stood for 'Unclassified' which I think is the educational equivalent of missing the board in darts. Andy probably could have gone to one of those fancy Universities, but settled on going to the University of Hull to study Law. I was pleased for him but it scared me a little that he wasn't always going to be nearby.

My first job was delivering pizzas for a take away called 'A Little Pizza Heaven' in Bamford. I worked from Thursday to Sunday, 6pm to 1am and was paid the princely sum of £25 a night plus tips. Tony, the owner, would also give me a tenner a week for petrol which didn't cover the cost, but I was a bit intimidated by his fiery Latin temperament so I always just took it without objection. I gave Dad £100 a month for my keep and a further £100 as a payback on my loan. I then had £200 in my pocket, less the small petrol loss, which seemed like a small fortune.

"So when was it you met Kitty?" Dad asked Joanna as we walked along.

"I'd been up to a party in Rawtenstall. H was there. He was the reason I went, if I'm honest. I've always had a thing for 'H'. When most kids were giving me a hard time at school when I was eleven, H and Andy were my knights in shining armour and I've never been able to shake off that soft spot since. Anyway, at that party, H was very drunk. He'd had some sort of row with a girl and was storming off so I followed him just to make sure he was alright. Mrs McCoy came to pick him up and she gave me a lift home too. I'm not just saying this because she was your wife or anything, but she was the most beautiful woman I have ever seen. I had thoughts about your wife that I never thought I would ever have about a woman."

I was sorely tempted to cut in at this point to tell Joanna to shut up. My girlfriend seemingly telling my father that she had lesbian fantasies about my dead mother appeared to be jumping with two feet outside of the circle of decency, but I waited for Dad's response. He just smiled.

"I remember that night!" Dad said, "Kitty was very taken with you too, Joanna. She thought you were lovely."

"Thank you, Mr McCoy, I'm really pleased to hear that. I can see why she went for you. You're a real old fashioned gentleman. I'm sure she always felt safe around you."

I was walking behind Joanna and Dad at this point, trying to keep an eye on Cilla who was excitedly scampering around, with her nose to the floor, sniffing every blade of grass like it smelt of after shave. I grimaced as Joanna made this point. Ultimately Dad hadn't kept Mum safe. He didn't seem to make the link though or if he did, he chose to ignore it.

"I hope she did. I hope H makes you feel that way too."

"He does, very much so. He tries to keep me on the straight and narrow and I try to lead him astray. Not too far astray, Mr McCoy, but we're only young once and I think a sense of adventure is a good thing."

"So do I. Now remember what I said, it's George not Mr McCoy . I don't like Mr McCoy, it reminds me too much of how old I am."

I was beginning to realise Dad had a soft spot for the girls I introduced to him. I don't mean that he acted in any way inappropriately, but the young man in him returned when he was around young women. His disposition was much sunnier and he was always charming.

After the walk, Joanna dropped Cilla back at her home, I waited in the car as her Dad was home and she said he was in a foul mood. We then went back to mine. We went up to my bedroom and I put on Miles Davis' 'Kind of Blue'. We just kissed, hugged and chatted like any teenage couple. I thought Amy was tactile but Joanna took it to another level. I suppose when you are in your late teens, you have reached a stage where you have supressed physical intimacy for a few years because you go through that early teenage stage of being embarrassed by family hugs, so once you get a boyfriend or girlfriend, you want to re-introduce intimacy to your life, but on a whole new level. After one mammoth kissing session, Joanna pulled away from our kiss and immediately stated,

"I bet you're Mum and Dad were hot in bed!"

I couldn't help but laugh.

"Thanks for that, Joanna! That isn't a thought I particularly want to be conjuring up."

"Why not? It's perfectly natural. You wouldn't be here without them."

"Do you like the mental image of your parents having sex?"

"It doesn't bother me. My Dad is only ever nice to my Mum when he's after sex. You can tell when he's had his way because he's back to being a grumpy sod afterwards. My parents aren't like yours. Mum's OK, but Dad's not a nice man."

"In what way?"

"He just isn't. "

Everything suddenly seemed awkward and uncomfortable. I decided not to press her for an explanation. Talking about my Mum and Dad having sex had become a welcome distraction.

"Anyway, I'm obviously not as open minded as you. My Dad's pretty old and my Mum's dead, so perhaps that has something to do with me finding it weird to imagine them getting jiggy in their birthday suits."

"I think," Joanna said running her hand through her hair in a manner that I found self-confident and sexy, "they would have had a special chemistry. I bet your Dad was very tender but when your Mum wanted it hard, I bet he gave it her hard!"

Enough was enough.

"Right," I said grabbing Joanna playfully, "stop it now! I really don't want to be having this conversation. Can we talk about something else, please?"

"We can talk about 'shagging' if you like?" Joanna suggested, sucking the little finger of her right hand like it was the crumbliest, flakiest chocolate in the world.

"We can if you like, but can we not refer to it as 'shagging'?"

"Why not?"

"It's coarse."

Joanna reached up and kissed me tenderly on the lips.

"Harry McCoy, you are such an old woman! How do you want to refer to it then? 'Making lurrvve'?" Joanna said mockingly, having said 'making love' in her best Barry White voice. I didn't think it was very lady like but I failed to stifle a reflex giggle.

"Sex is just fine."

"OK," Joanna said, interlocking fingers with me on both of our hands and then, in a very female way, she started trying to exert force, as if we were playing 'Mercy'-the game kids played at school when you bent each other's fingers back until someone begged for 'Mercy', "why have you and I not got around to having sex yet? It's certainly not down to me. You've been holding back. I think it's about time the groin ferret got a taste of the honey pot."

I really don't know if the sex talk was meant to turn me on or whether it was just Joanna's candid style, but I can't say I liked it. To me, and maybe it is just me, a girl lying on a bed in sexy underwear, is more attractive than a girl lying there naked with everything on show. There needs to be a bit of mystery in sex, but Joanna was squeezing everything out. I decided to implement a delaying tactic and I had a convenient one to hand.

"I'm not sure why I've not been ready. Perhaps the whole Amy thing has dented my confidence a little."

"Were you not sexually compatible?"

I didn't think it needed spelling out. I had previously mentioned it, after all, but I was wrong.

"Well, I thought we were but maybe if Amy felt like she needed to screw the whole neighbourhood then perhaps I wasn't quite as good as I thought."

Joanna brought her face very close to mine, left it there for a few seconds so we could feel each other's breath between nose and chin, then leaned forward and kissed me once more, this time on the cheek.

"I would never cheat on you. You know that, don't you? I adore you too much to ever even think for one moment about hurting you. If I hurt you, I think it would break my heart before it broke yours."

Joanna said this in an unusually serious tone. I believed every word.

"I know."

Joanna was pretty but not as pretty as I had originally thought when I stumbled into her in the take away. Alcohol carries beauty up a few rungs of the ladder. Perhaps I am doing her a disservice when I say this, because she had a very quirky attractiveness, but I couldn't imagine half a village queuing up outside her door. Individuality and loyalty, at that time, however, were huge turn ons. I trusted Joanna. I just didn't trust myself to provide the sexual performance that would have satisfied her physically and me mentally. Joanna sensed this.

"I'm not expecting perfection first time you know. We can grow into this together. Practice makes perfect."

At the time, I assumed by 'first time' that Joanna meant our first time together, but perhaps, looking back on it, maybe it was her first ever time. She was only sixteen. A late flowering sixteen too. I guess I will never know. She was certainly more confident than me. I had slept with Amy a few times but they were rushed and forgettable. I wanted it to mean more this time around.

Once Joanna had comforted me though, I felt ready. I was an eighteen year old boy and blood was surging to all the right places. If I had been sure that my Dad wasn't going to walk in with a tray of tea and biscuits, I would have been happy doing it right there and then, but that uncertainty was convincing me that I had to wait. I really wanted Joanna to know how much desire I had for her though, so started to kiss her hungrily on the mouth at first then on her neck. My hands began wandering around her body. Joanna gave me nothing but encouragement with gentle moans and reciprocal hand movements. After a few minutes of breathless cavorting, Joanna thrust her tongue into my ear as though it contained the remnants of a cake mix, before whispering into the wetness,

"If you want to undress me, I'm all yours, H. Don't worry, I'm on the pill. It will all be OK."

My lust was painful by this stage. It battled with my sense of morality. Morality can never defeat lust in a young man though. Until a man gets to his mid-twenties lust holds all the aces. After that things gradually calm down. My morality did put up a valiant fight though.

"My Dad's in, Joanna. He could walk in here at any moment."

Joanna dismissed my objection.

"I'm telling you now your Dad is coming nowhere near this bedroom. We've been in here two hours and haven't heard a peep out of him. He's been eighteen, H. He knows he could face an embarrassing moment if he walked in unannounced. It would be more embarrassing for him than it would for us. I'm sixteen, you're eighteen. We aren't breaking any laws."

"He trusts us."

"Trusts us to do what?"

"Behave."

"I don't think so. I think he trusts us to be careful, H. If we were at mine, that'd be different. My Dad might come in to protect his daughter's virtue, but this is different."

I gave it a brief thought. It didn't really know whether Joanna was right or not, but I wanted her to be right and that was all that mattered. I convinced myself that my Dad wouldn't be trying to catch us out. Thinking back to when I was dating Amy, Dad would only ever come in to my room with prior warning. He'd always shout up and ask if we wanted a drink. At this very moment, we had not long had one.

I clapped my hands together. I am not entirely sure why when we were trying to be discreet.

"OK, let's do this."

Joanna seemed surprised by my sudden change of heart.

"Really? Are you sure?"

"Absolutely."

"Great! Right, I'll undo my bra whilst you do my knickers. I'll need the support act to test the sound system out before the star of the show arrives, if you know what I mean."

I wasn't always the quickest on the up take when people were talking in code, but this time I understood.

"OK," I said, anticipation making my voice falter a little.

"I'll give you the nod when I'm ready for the big entrance."

Two minutes later, the show was on the road.

The main act didn't perform for long but he did manage an encore. It was the start of a live concert tour that was on the road for a couple of years. He played regularly but almost exclusively in the Rochdale area, with the odd summer performance in Blackpool, Llandudno and the Lakes. Everything went well at first. Performances improved and sometimes he even got a standing ovation. Fame is fleeting though. Two years later, things began to change. Daily performances became weekly ones. Performances that used to seem thrilling were now taken for granted. The performer, although he had enjoyed every moment, grew restless. He started to cast his eye around for new venues. He would always look back fondly on playing in 'The Cavern' but other theatres beckoned and he understood that those artists who only ever played one tune in one venue would sometimes look back with regret and wished they had toured the world.

Chapter Twenty Seven – Two Years Later

The sound of my own cough woke me up. My whole head seemed to shudder inside as I did so. It wasn't so much a banging headache as a brain quake. It hurt so much that my brain only permitted one eye to open to check light was allowed to enter. Before I even knew where I was, I knew I had a hangover of epic proportions.

I was in unfamiliar surroundings and was desperate to know my location. I scanned the room for evidence. I was in a double bed, on my own, in a room so small that it felt the walls were about to high five each other. There were posters on the walls with dried up bits of old blue tack surrounding them. I recognised a few of the iconic movie scenes that they depicted. There was one from 'My Own Private Idaho' with River Phoenix looking moody on the back of Keanu Reeves motorbike. Then there was John Travolta and Samuel L Jackson's characters pointing their guns in 'Pulp Fiction' and Harry Dean Stanton's walking along a railway track, looking like a tramp in 'Paris, Texas'. I thought how easily I would go crazy if a woman as beautiful as Nastassja Kinski ever left me and our son. My favourite one though was the one of Jean-Hugues Anglade looking cool as fuck in 'Betty Blue'. I imagined you had to be a cool fucker like Zorg to be able to make love to a woman like Betty. My mind praised me for having become enough of a movie buff over the last twelve months to have recognised most of the scenes. Andy would have been proud.

It was only when I wiggled my toes to ease the pins and needles that I spotted it. The physical specimen that was about to be awarded iconic status in the sexual department of my brain. It was a bottom. Not just any old backside though, it was the finest naked backside that I had ever seen. I didn't know it then, but its number one position was never subsequently rivalled. It would go down in the memory banks as the most wonderful bottom in the history of me.

I had never been a connoisseur of fine bottoms. In male adolescent chatter about 'tits or arse', I had always confessed to being a 'tits' man. There had always seemed something asexual about saying you liked bums more than boobs. Boobs were unique to the female form and there was a hint of mystery to them. Their naked appearance could be very different to their appearance supported by tight clothing and a good bra. You could be fooled into positivity like falling in love with someone you had only ever seen in designer sunglasses. They were like the final chapter of a physical story. Things could go horribly wrong but if they were right they were unforgettable. As you may well have guessed, as a young man I was infatuated by breasts. If eyes were the window to your soul, breasts were the cushions of the female heart. A backside was nothing in comparison. They were just there to aid the process of sitting and shitting.

That particular backside was different though. It was a sporty, well crafted bottom that sat below a thin waist, slender hips and was the pinnacle of a pair of long, shapely legs. The girl who owned this mesmerising bum had her back to me, brushing her long, straight black hair that flowed down her back like a silky waterfall. Her naked back was a perfect tone of light brown, as was that never to be forgotten posterior. My stirring and coughing alerted her.

"Good morning, sleepy head!"

There was, of course, a tone of familiarity to that friendly greeting. Young women don't tend to brush their hair in the nude in front of complete strangers. The accent was a Yorkshire one but when she looked over her shoulder at me with a wide smile, I could see she had a slightly lighter colouring than me, but seemed to be of Asian rather than Afro-Caribbean descent.

To be candid, and it still embarrasses me to confess this to you many years later, I had no recollection of who she was. I also have no idea how I could have been so drunk to forget the latter half of the evening but still mentally astute enough, in those forgotten hours, to attract someone that beautiful in to bed with me. Life would have been easier if my overriding emotion that Sunday morning had been pride, but it wasn't. I was, instead, overcome with guilt. I still had a girlfriend back home in Rochdale who loved me unconditionally and trusted me implicitly and I was manipulative enough to spend the night with someone else. A beautiful stranger whose name I couldn't even remember.

It transpired her name was Prisha. She was from a place in Leeds called Alwoodley, where her mother had also been born and raised. Her father was originally from Calcutta but had been a Doctor in Bradford Royal Infirmary for over twenty years. Perhaps the fact that Prisha was mixed race had been a factor in attracting the drunken me. She was studying Law herself at Hull University but was a first year, not a second year like Andy. We had met in the Student Union, on the dance floor. I had apparently made a grab for her when the DJ played 'Back For Good' to round the night off. I wasn't aware of any of this whilst I was in Prisha's bedroom though. Andy filled me in later over coffee.

Prisha was astute enough to know that I look perplexed by my surroundings. Without even a shred of awkwardness, her naked figure turned to face me.

"You look confused, H."

It was like waking up inside someone else's head. I could offer no explanation as to how this person I didn't know was familiar with who I was. Well, no explanation other than drink.

"What exactly happened last night?"

I don't know if I was asking a question that related to sex or just a general question. Either way Prisha looked unimpressed.

"How drunk were you?"

"Extremely."

"Oh my God, H! Can you even remember my name?"

Given Prisha was before me in all her naked splendour it seemed churlish to confess that I didn't remember her at all. Initially, I only told her as much of the truth as she needed to know.

"No, I'm really sorry, I don't. What is your name?"

"Oh my God, H!" Prisha repeated, but this time she looked more upset than jokey, "I thought last night was a special night. We talked, we kissed, we slept naked side by side and now you don't even remember my name! I naively thought we might be friends for life after last night and now you don't even remember my name. Oh my God!"

She seemed to like saying 'Oh my God!' and once I had done my name revelation, Prisha immediately looked ashamed to be naked before me. I was feeling pretty ashamed too. She started putting on some clothes. I waited until she was dressed before I made my full confession.

"Look, I can't tell you how sorry I am but I don't remember anything. I truly wish I did."

"What can you remember about last night? The whole evening can't just be one big blank."

"Well, I remember getting to the Student Union. I was with my mate, Andy and half a dozen of his Uni friends. We'd drunk a lot before we came out and smoked some weed too. I remember going to the bar when we arrived. I remember dancing to 'Sunday Bloody Sunday'...."

I paused trying to remember what happened next. No further memory of the evening was forthcoming.

"And that's it?"

"I think so. I vaguely remember 'Whole Of The Moon' getting played. I think I fell over on the dance floor during that and Andy had to pick me up."

"So you don't even remember meeting me at all?"

I thought that we had already established that.

"I wish I did but I don't. Please tell me your name. I'd like to try and repair some of the damage before I go."

"I don't want to tell you now. You should know."

"I haven't done this deliberately! I just can't remember. I'd love to be able to remember. I'm from Rochdale and girls that look like you aren't ten a penny in Rochdale. They probably aren't ten a penny anywhere. I'd love to have been able to wake up this morning and been cool with you, but I'm just being honest, I can't remember anything."

"Is Joanna as pretty as me?"

Shit! I'd told her about Joanna.

"Joanna's a beautiful person."

Joanna wasn't as pretty as Prisha but through the course of this conversation we seemed to have fallen out, so I wasn't going to give her the satisfaction of telling her.

"Then why are you here?"

"I wish I knew."

"Do you want me to tell you what you said last night?"

"You can if you want," I answered matter of factly. I was very interested in what I had said but didn't want to appear desperate to hear.

"You said you don't love her romantically anymore."

This came as a shock to me, even in drink it didn't seem like something I would say. I didn't know whether or not to believe her. Joanna and I had been together two years. I did love her. Along with Andy she was my best friend.

"You said you loved her like a best friend but couldn't see her being the woman you would spend the rest of your life with," Prisha continued.

Oh. My guilt was escalating.

"Did I sleep with you?"

"Not in a sexual way, no."

Good. I felt bad enough about all this already. Having sex and forgetting it would erase all the pleasure but still bring all the guilt. At least there was a minor positive to be taken from all this. I had been faithful. Sort of faithful. I presumed kissing someone and sleeping next to them naked wasn't going to win me any 'Boyfriend of The Year' awards.

"Is that a good thing or a bad thing?" I asked. I didn't want to look too pleased about it, in case I was supposed to look sad.

"Neither, H. It's a statement of fact."

She must have been a lot warmer towards me the night before for me to end up back here. I suspected I had been a fair bit more charming too. Charm and hangovers go together like gravy and Angel Delight.

"Did you not want to or was I incapable?"

Prisha started tidying around as she answered. It was probably a hint that I had outstayed my welcome. I wasn't ready to leave yet though. There were questions in my head that I wanted answers to.

"Probably both of those things came into it, H. I've had a happy but a relatively strict upbringing. A one night stand would not be something my parents would ever condone. Perhaps for that very reason I was interested in doing it. A chance to rebel. A bit like having a tattoo but without the permanency that entails. I didn't have the courage to see the adventure through though. Neither did you."

"What reason did I give?"

"You said it was down to respect. You had been hurt by another girl, Amy, doing the dirty on you and you said you didn't want to end up like her, being selfish, only ever thinking about what's good for you and not how it impacts on everyone else. You came across as a lovely guy, H, but if I'm being honest, it's really bugging me that you can't remember. I bared my soul to you too, H."

"You can tell me again now if you like."

It was a half hearted offer. I'm not good with hangovers. Alcohol can take me to a very high place, but it tends to drop me on the floor in a heap the day after.

"No, I think you should go. You should have just pretended you remembered, H. I wouldn't have felt so stupid then."

"You shouldn't feel stupid. I'm the idiot here, not you. Please don't feel bad."

"Just forget it. We needed each other last night. We don't need each other today. My head's banging. I'm going to get back in to bed and go to sleep. I can't face the day yet. Do you mind getting up, getting dressed and getting going? I don't want you to still be here when my housemates wake up."

I got out of there as quickly as I could. One of Prisha's housemates was in the lounge as I walked through, eating a bowl of cereal in her pyjamas.

"Good Morning!" she said with a mouthful of Corn Flakes as I walked by.

"Morning!" I replied. At that stage, there felt nothing good about it.

As I stood at the bus stop waiting for a bus which I hoped would take me back towards Andy's, I pictured myself being outside Amy Garfunkel's after I caught her cheating and the words I said back then came back to me.

"..I don't understand. It's cheap and dirty and sordid and it's not you....all of this isn't you."

Chapter Twenty Eight

Andy was having a cup of tea and a cigarette when I walked into his student house. I had surprised myself by even remembering where it was, but the fact it was just off a main road behind a Threshers off licence was what had triggered my memory. One of the lads in the house, 'Swarbs', had let me in and told me Andy was in the kitchen. My head hurt but I still smiled when I saw Andy's familiar teapot and tea cosy.

"The wanderer returns," he said as I walked through the kitchen door, "do you want me to pour you a cup of tea? It should still be warm enough to drink."

"Have you put sugar in the pot?"

Andy had developed a habit of putting about ten spoonfuls of sugar into the bottom of the teapot with three teabags. He liked his tea 'strong and sweet' but it was too sweet for me.

"No, I've stopped doing that."

"Good, I'll have one then, thanks."

"I take it you have a bad head, you dirty stop out."

"Yes, it's banging."

"Well don't be expecting any sympathy from me or be expecting me to condone your behaviour. I love Joanna. Fucking her about is unacceptable."

"I didn't fuck her about!" I tried to protest, as Andy poured my tea into a large mug that, for some reason, had 'Campbell's Chicken Noodle Soup' written on the outside.

"Don't give me that! I was there, remember? I saw you gyrating your hips next to Prisha and then I saw you go in for the kill when the 'slowies' came on."

At least I now knew her name. I didn't confess to not knowing.

"I'm glad one of us remembers that. So you know Prisha then?"

"Know her? Everyone knows Prisha. Half the lads on my course have slept with her. She has a penchant for rugby players too. Apparently once she's had the scrum half she's completed the 1st fifteen."

Any blood left in my pale face soon drained out on the news that Prisha hadn't succumbed to my charms but was in fact succumbing to everyone's.

"Honestly?" I asked anxiously.

"No, I made that up. She's on my course. Well, a year below me. Lovely girl, beautiful looking but that's not the point. The point is that you're with Joanna, the perfect person for you. What even possessed you to cheat on her? I'm devastated."

Andy had always been a drama queen. How exactly this had become about him and his feelings I'm not entirely sure, but he was acting like I'd cheated on him rather than Joanna.

"I didn't sleep with Prisha, by the way. I'd like to say the whole night is a blur, but it's not even a blur, it's a blank. What was that shit we were smoking?"

"I don't know. Shaggy got it from his regular dealer. It was strong but good quality gear. Don't be trying to blame your actions on Shaggy's gear. I suppose I'm partially to blame, I should have done more to stop you."

Andy had always done what he could to look after me but there were certain times he had to let go of the reins.

"Andy, we're twenty years old. I can make my own decisions."

"You can, but if I can see that they're bad ones, I'm still going to feel the need to put you back on course. So what next?"

"What do you mean?"

"I mean do you just get the bus home to Rochdale later and pretend none of this happened or is this thing with Prisha a game changer for you?"

"I don't know."

It had taken less than a minute for Andy to decide I was going in the wrong direction and that he needed to steer me back on course.

"Bloody hell, H! You should know. Last night all you did was make an error of judgement when you were stoned. You put a stop to it before it became too severe. Don't wreck everything you have with Joanna just because you've been a drunken fool."

"So you're suggesting I pretend this never happened?"

"Too right I am. Joanna's lovely. She's besotted with you, if you tell her, it'll destroy her."

"I'm not sure, Andy. Is being honest not a better way to go?"

"Not unless you want to be force fed your own boiled penis. Joanna's wonderful but part of what makes her so wonderful is that she is a few sandwiches short of a picnic. You've no idea how she would react to news like this."

"Not well."

"Not well at all," Andy stressed.

"What an absolute moron I am," I said with despair.

"Couldn't agree more."

"Why do you think I did it, Andy?"

"Half a bottle of vodka, eight pints of snake bite and black and a nice chunky spliff may all have played their part."

"That's no excuse though."

"I'm not excusing you! I'm just saying they may have played their part."

"Prisha says I told her that I don't love Joanna any more."

"Well of course you'd say that to Prisha! You were trying to get into her knickers. "

"Maybe. Maybe there's more to it though. Maybe that's how I really feel."

"Is it how you really feel?"

I thought about it.

"I don't think so."

"Then shut up then! H, promise me when you get home you aren't going to start acting all morose and awkward in front of Joanna, because I'm telling you now, if you do, you'll ruin everything. Despite being a Grade One idiot at times, you are still the nicest bloke I know and Joanna is the nicest girl. You belong together. Don't blow this."

"I'll try not to."

"Don't just try. Make sure you don't."

"OK. OK. I get the message. What about you, Andy?"

"What about me?"

"Have you not met anyone since you've been here?"

"I've met plenty of people. You were out with about a dozen of them last night."

"You know what I meant, romantically."

"No, have I heck. I don't need that sort of drama in my life, H. I'm studying hard. I want to finish here with the highest grades on my course. I don't need distractions. Anyway, I get enough drama every time you come over to last me a lifetime."

"No women caught your eye?"

"I've just told you! NO!"

"What about men?"

"What about men?"

"Any romantic interest in a man?"

"Here we go! This old chestnut."

"It's alright to be gay these days you know. Most people are very liberal. From an outsider's perspective, there's a lot to be said about being gay. I imagine there'd be lots of sex. Then there's hormonal stability. No fear of pregnancy when you're dating someone you don't want to marry."

"H, shut up, will you! I've told you, I'm fine on my own. I don't want to be with anyone else right now. When I'm ready, if I need you to play cupid, I'll let you know. For now though, I just want to work hard in the week and have a few beers and a laugh at the weekend. Is that OK with you?"

"Of course it is. If you're happy, I'm happy."

"Good. Now let's talk about something else."

Chapter Twenty Nine

Joanna was waiting for me as my National Express coach pulled in at Rochdale bus station, adjacent to the monstrosity of a council office building known as 'Black Box'. The bus from Hull had been less than half full so I had managed to grab a window seat without having the inconvenience of having to make occasional polite chit chat with the person in the aisle seat. The seat next to me remained empty throughout the journey so I tried to ease my headache by grabbing short doses of sleep but couldn't really settle as I was conscious I might sleep all the way through to Liverpool.

As our bus pulled in to the bus station I could see Joanna scanning the coach, looking for my familiar face and then her mouth breaking out into a broad smile once she spotted me. She waved excitedly. I smiled and waved back with far less vigour. I'd like to say I felt guilty or awful but the only accurate way to describe it is to say that I felt like a complete twat. Joanna had been a wonderful girlfriend and had done nothing to deserve this act of betrayal. I felt I had two options, tearfully confess or act like nothing had ever happened, learn from this gigantic mistake and treat her as she deserved to be treated from now on. Whether it was purely down to cowardice, I'm not sure, but I quickly decided to go with the latter option.

When I stepped down off the coach, Joanna came over and hugged me tightly, kissing me on the cheek before kissing my mouth several times. She would have been up for a full-on snog but she knew I didn't want to be one of those couples that have huge public displays of affection. Holding hands in public or a kiss on the lips was about as far as I was ever prepared to take it.

"It's so good to have you home. I know it's only been a couple of days, but the days don't half drag when you're away. Maybe I'll have to come with you next time."

I wished Joanna had come with me this time. Any drunken passion would then not have come with a whole load of guilt.

"Yeh, we'll have to go over together next time. Good idea."

This was a lie, it was a terrible idea. I never wanted Joanna to come to Hull with me. I could already imagine some ugly confrontation between Joanna and Prisha.

"Did you enjoy yourself?"

"It was good but I've got a stinking hangover now though."

"Oh my poor baby! Is Andy a bad influence on you?"

"Yes, it's all his fault!"

I laughed a little as I said this. My head still hurt when I laughed.

"Is he OK?"

"He's really good. Working hard as you'd expect."

"Not got himself a boyfriend yet?"

"No!"

Like many other people Joanna was convinced Andy was gay. She was strong minded and in her head it wasn't even up for debate. I had no firm opinion on Andy's sexuality but would sometimes tease Joanna by insisting I knew he was straight. I claimed to have seen him 'get off' with loads of girls. Joanna would scoff at this suggestion.

"Andy is no more straight than the Eiffel Tower is English. In fact, he's about as straight as the Leaning Tower of Pisa."

"You don't know that Joanna."

"I do know it. My heart and my mind both tell me he's gay. I don't even know why he doesn't come out. Either he's ashamed which he shouldn't be or he's in denial and soon enough he'll be true to himself."

We walked from the bus station to Joanna's car. She had passed her test about seven months after her seventeenth birthday. She drove a lot faster than me and a lot closer to the car in front. When she first passed, I would tell her to slow down and stop driving so close but Joanna would just argue with me, subsequently driving faster and closer, so I learnt to keep my mouth shut. She had a red Ford Fiesta that was always knee deep in rubbish.

"Is your Dad home?" Joanna asked as we got into her car.

"No, I rang him as I was leaving Hull and he's out tonight. He's gone to the cinema with a couple of friends from the 'Rambling Society'. They've gone to see 'Braveheart'."

"That's nice he's making new friends. Good for us too. Do you fancy going back to yours for some naked catch up?"

Despite having a hangover, a headache, pangs of guilt and feelings of physical and mental tiredness that made me ache from head to toe, I was twenty years old and had a complete inability to deny myself a sexual opportunity two nights on the trot. You wouldn't put a white rabbit in a cage with a python and just expect the snake to stroke it.

"Do I even need to answer that?"

"I'll take that as a 'Yes'."

As soon as we were through the door of my house, we pounced on each other. Joanna liked a little bit of rough play, so I pushed her down on the stairs and climbed on top of her. As we kissed, I put both arms under the back of her top, feeling the top of her smooth shoulders and then moving down with the intention of unclasping her bra. There was no bra.

"No bra, hey?" I reflected.

"I came dressed for action," Joanna giggled, "you may well discover that a little lower down there are no knickers either!"

I didn't want to wait to find out. We pulled at each other's clothes. I lifted Joanna's top over her head and she unbuttoned mine then undid the top couple of buttons on my jeans which allowed her the flexibility to move her hands inside and grip the cheeks of my backside. At that stage of my life, despite my lack of exercise, I had firm buttocks, a flat stomach and, if caught in the right light, traces of a six pack. Joanna nibbled on my ear lobe and then whispered,

"Let's just do it right here, H. I need to feel you inside me. I've been building up to this moment all weekend. God, I love you so much, Harry McCoy."

I was never the most spontaneous of people. The thought of having sex on the stairs brought with it a whole host of negative thoughts, as well as the obvious more positive ones. What if my Dad returned home unexpectedly and saw my bum going like the clappers on his staircase? What if a neighbour came to the door and did likewise? You could see through the glass in our front door and although one of our neighbours had never called around on a Sunday evening, what if tonight was the first time? It didn't need to be a neighbour, it could be anyone. Someone from Dad's 'Rambling Society' might want to drop a map in. There was too much risk involved. There was absolutely no way I was going to have sex on the stairs.

"I love you too, Joanna, so much, but it doesn't feel right doing it here. Can we not go up to my bedroom?"

"Really? Why?" Joanna asked with more than a hint of disappointment.

"It'll be more comfortable."

"I'm comfortable here."

"Well, I'm not."

"Why?"

"I just think Dad might come back."

"He won't leave 'Braveheart' halfway through to come home to check up on his twenty year old son! Don't be so ridiculous."

"I'd just be more comfortable in the bedroom."

"Come on then."

Joanna led me by the hand up the stairs and through to my bedroom.

"We're leaving the light on though, H," she warned me, "we always have to do it in the dark when your Dad's around. I want to see what we're doing this time."

"That's fine with me."

It was Joanna now who was taking the dominant role. She pushed me down on to the bed, so I was looking up at her eagerly, admiring her naked breasts. She kneeled on the bed next to me and then leant forward and started kissing my neck. I made a moaning noise because it tickled and I moved my head instinctively in circles, hearing the sound of tiny bones clicking as I did so.

Joanna unbuttoned the remaining buttons on my jeans and with gentle kisses started making her way down from my neck towards my waist. I was growing increasingly excited as she gently moved down my naked upper torso. Part of me wanted her to arrive at the destination point, whilst part of me enjoyed the anticipation. She put her tongue in my belly button, briefly circling before continuing downwards along the line of hair that bridged the gap between the crater left by my umbilical cord and my sexual organs.

Joanna slowly pulled my boxer shorts down. I was more than ready for action. I ran my hand through her hair lovingly. I was ready to think determined thoughts to prolong the pleasure when, without explanation, Joanna just stopped. She shook her body like a wet animal and sat bolt upright. She pulled my boxer shorts that were almost down to my knees back to their starting point.

"I HATE YOU, HARRY MCCOY!" she yelled out so loudly that my ears rang out in protest.

"What?" I asked, trying to grab her but Joanna had wriggled away from me, before standing up. I stood up too.

"What's the matter? What have I done?"

Joanna slapped me across the face. Hard.

"What the hell was that for?"

"You know exactly what it was for. You're a complete bastard, that's what it's for. For being a complete bastard."

Joanna was crying now. I didn't really understand why, but fear was making my voice falter too.

"Joanna, please tell me what's going on. What is it? What have I done?"

Joanna was trying to continue her journey away from me. She marched out the room and then picked her top up off the staircase and threw mine at me. She couldn't get out of there quick enough.

"We're finished, H. I loved you so much but I don't any more. I hate you now. I really hate you."

After saying this Joanna screamed. It was a scream full of pain and anguish like that of a mother in childbirth. After she had finished screaming, she turned back towards me and slapped me again.

"Stop hitting me!"

"You deserve it."

"Why? What the hell is it you think I've done?"

"I know exactly what you've done!"

"I haven't done anything!"

"LIAR!"

"Joanna."

"Look!"

Joanna pulled my boxer shorts back down and then with a finger on her right hand she prodded my left groin.

"That!" she said, "That's lipstick, H and it's not my colour!"

Chapter Thirty

In her heart of hearts, I knew Joanna didn't want to break up with me. She felt it was morally the right thing to do, but she was trying her damnedest to find justification to keep our relationship going.

"Does it have anything to do with your Mum dying?"

"Does what have anything to do with my Mum dying?"

"You cheating on me. Your Dad told me that before we got together, you went through a spell of being a loose cannon and kept trying to get yourself into fights. He thought you wanted to hurt yourself in some way. I just wondered whether this is the next phase in your grieving process? Trying to sabotage our relationship to make that pain emotional rather than physical."

I took a salt and vinegar crisp out the packet and sucked the salt and vinegar off it whilst I pondered the question. We were in a pub. I'm not exactly sure where that pub was, but it was next to a canal on our way from Rochdale to Formby. I remember the pub was called 'The Saracens Head'. I recall wondering what a 'Saracen' was and why anyone would name a pub after his head.

For a few days after the lipstick incident, Joanna wouldn't answer my calls. Her home phone would go to answer machine and I would then leave pleading messages for her to call me back. Her parents must have thought I was a nutcase. I was tempted to call around, but Joanna's father was an intimidating bloke with a host of tattoos and a drinking problem so I made my advances from arms length.

It took until Thursday to get a response. I had stopped ringing for 24 hours so I may have caught her off guard when she finally answered. After several periods of uncomfortable silence and a few sighs, Joanna agreed to meet up with me. She suggested I drive her over to Formby beach but we never quite got that far. We stopped for lunch at 'The Saracens Head' and afterwards decided to head home. It was our conversations about my infidelity that led us both to conclude that a long walk on the beach was not going to lead us to putting all the fragments of our relationship back together. Given the circumstances, a romantic stroll had probably always been too optimistic.

"Joanna, you can try to get into my head and work this all out or I could just tell you what you want to hear, that my Mum's death led me to do this one-off crazy thing, but the truth is, I have no idea why I did what I did. I'd like to blame it on some deep rooted psychological problems, but I don't think it would be fair on you or my Mum if I did that. I know this is going to sound like bullshit but I can't remember anything at all about 'getting off' with that girl. Honestly, the first time I knew of her existence was when I woke up in her bedroom the next morning. The only reason I think I did it was because I was stupidly drunk and all logic had gone out the window."

"That's not a good enough reason, H."

"I know."

We sat in silence for a minute after that. Joanna pushed a few pieces of scampi around her plate. I had eaten my mixed grill and was still hungry so had returned to the packet of crisps I had half eaten when our food had arrived unexpectedly quickly. I was tempted to ask Joanna if I could have her scampi if she wasn't going to eat it, but concluded that would be a bit tactless.

"Do you think I should stay with you, H?" she eventually asked.

"Yes, I do."

"Why?"

"Because we love each other."

It was a stupid reason. I should have said something bolder like 'I had made a terrible mistake but it had made me realise how much I had to lose and knew now I would never do anything that stupid again'. That probably wouldn't have worked either but I was setting myself up saying what I did. It drew the expected response.

"We loved each other on Saturday but that didn't stop you going to bed with someone else."

"You're making it sound like I slept with Prisha, which I didn't."

I shouldn't have used her name. That wound Joanna up more.

"Prisha? Was that her name was it? Pretty name. A pretty name for a girl who likes to suck someone else's boyfriend's cock."

Joanna said that loud enough for me to worry whether anyone else had overheard.

"That didn't happen," I said quietly.

"How do you know?"

I wanted to say I would have remembered that, but it didn't feel a safe thing to say, so I just said, "I just know."

"She left a lipstick mark on your groin, H!"

"That doesn't mean anything sexual happened."

"Really? Anyway, she might as well have done."

"You can't say that. Surely things would be a lot worse if something sexual had happened."

Joanna gave me a look which said she strongly disagreed. A look that threatened my face with that plate of scampi.

"I'm not sure it could be any worse. What happened was a betrayal of trust. That's why I feel so hurt and angry, H, because you betrayed my trust. To me, it's pretty immaterial whether that betrayal involved you activating your knob. You danced with her, kissed her, hugged her, went back to her house with her, stripped naked with her and then stayed the night with her."

"None of which I remember."

"So?"

"So it wasn't as though I was sober enough to think straight."

"I don't care, H! How would you feel if it was the other way around? What if I went out one night, got smashed and then ended up in bed with some lad I'd never met before? Would you be alright with that as long as I was too smashed to remember?"

"No."

"No, of course you wouldn't. Do you think you would ever forgive me?"

I thought about it. I answered honestly, but once I gave my answer I knew we were never going to move on from this.

"I'd try to, but deep down, I don't think I ever would."

PART TWO – Adulthood - MESSING UP

Chapter Thirty One – August 2007

Andy was still smoking. The teenage habit that he insisted wouldn't last into his twenties, had now stretched into his thirties. He had even stopped saying he was going to pack in now. Surprisingly, I had pretty much stopped nagging him about it too. He was working as a barrister, which must have been stressful and living on his own in a luxury flat in Manchester, which must have been lonely, so if his nicotine habit was providing him with some comfort then what business of mine was it if it was slowly killing him?

We were sat on a bench attached to a wooden table outside The Bamford Arms. A smoking ban in bars and restaurants had come into force the month before so we had to come outside to allow Andy to smoke. He'd bought a bottle of champagne, as he typically did, so we were catching up with each other's lives, whilst quaffing champagne. Andy will have been quaffing his anyway, I would have been swigging mine. It was a warm summer's evening. Andy was back visiting his Mum, who had been living on her own for five years, ever since his smutty father had done a runner with one of the younger neighbours, back in 2002. I was still living with my Dad.

"Did you just feel a spot of rain?" I asked, holding the palm of my hand out in an attempt to seek further clarification.

"No," Andy replied, "I'm not going back inside until I've finished this fag. Not unless it belts down. They're shrewd the government though, aren't they? Introduce a smoking ban in the summer whilst it isn't too bad to have to traipse outside. Imagine what it's going to be like come January when it's lashing down and blowing a gale. It's going to be a nightmare."

"They're trying to make it anti-social," I explained, "Have you ever read that Garrison Keillor short story about the last of the smokers?"

"No, can't say I have," Andy replied.

I wasn't too sure if I would get to the end of this brief tale before Andy's attention would stray. He was a much better talker than he was a listener and if he wasn't enquiring about something that interested him, you could often tell by the look on his face that his mind was wandering. I decided to tell a shortened version. I had already given myself a warm buzz by discovering a book I had read that Andy hadn't.

"It imagines a world in the near future where there are only a few smokers left. They are hidden in a cave, dragging desperately on their last cigarettes whilst police helicopters are circling above them, trying to drive them out."

"Quite prophetic," Andy said, savouring his own cigarette as if was his last, "it's heading that way here now."

He stubbed his cigarette out and re-filled both our champagne glasses.

"How's your Dad doing?" Andy asked once our glasses were full.

My Dad had had a hip replacement at the start of July. He'd been putting it off for years but he finally gave in to the pain when his mobility was so impaired that he could not even manage a walk to the local shops.

"He's doing really well. He's off the crutches now, he just uses a stick."

"A pogo stick?" Andy asked jokingly and for a split second I think we both pictured my old Dad on a pogo stick, pogoing around Rochdale.

"A walking stick, as well you know."

"Well, that's good. It's a big operation for George to go through at his grand old age. How old is he now? 82? 83?"

"Eighty five."

"Wow! Don't think I'll ever get to eighty five. I'll have succumbed to lung cancer or boredom long before then."

"There're things you can do to avoid both," I stated, immediately realising I sounded a little patronising.

"Oh shut up goody two shoes and drink your champagne."

I did as I was instructed. I hadn't been out for a drink since before Dad's operation so was enjoying the luxury.

"How's work?" I asked as I took another swig of my champagne. This was our second bottle, both bought by Andy. I could tell drunkenness was beginning to kick in. I'd already asked how his Mum was doing so work was the natural next subject. We didn't have the convenience of talking football.

"Work is work," Andy answered dismissively, "if my philandering father happened to die tomorrow and left me with his millions, I don't think I'd bother with work. I just do it to fund my champagne lifestyle and allow myself the luxury of snorting a few lines of coke off the backsides of rent boys, as and when the need takes me."

A few heads on surrounding tables turned themselves towards us to see who had come out with such an outrageous comment. I presumed Andy had just said it for effect. The volume of the statement was louder than anything else he had said all evening. As far as I was aware he was still living the same celibate life, at thirty one, that he had always lived.

"Good for you," I said in response. I saw a woman on one of the other tables shake her head.

"Thank you. I feel it is my civic duty to get involved with some of the kids from the magistrates court."

Andy was aware that he had managed to rile the poor woman and would have kept pushing the point until the woman felt compelled to comment. It seemed cruel to me so I looked to move the conversation on.

"Shall we talk about something else?"

"If you insist," Andy said, pulling a frustrated face, "how is your work and, more importantly, how is the lovely Sandy?"

"Work is still work for me too and thankfully, Sandy is still lovely."

"Can I hear the distant sound of wedding bells?"

"She's not that lovely!"

"Spoilsport. You are aware that you are in your thirties, I take it? Time is passing us by. I'm sure I could whip up the most hilarious Best Man's speech ever, at very short notice, if needs be."

"I've no doubt you could, Andy, but you're going to have to hold fire on that one for now."

"Hmmmmm," Andy said in a slow and very deliberate way, rubbing his chin. I knew him well enough to understand he was prompting me to delve further, which I then did.

"What?"

"Is your reluctance to commit anything to do with this Facebook thing?"

"What do you mean?" I queried innocently despite having more than an inkling of what Andy was about to suggest.

"Well, after you text me about signing up to this Facebook malarkey, I did as requested but then had a nosey through your other friends. Lo and behold, amongst your thirty seven friends there just happened to be a certain Cathie Squires."

"So what?" I replied defensively, "Cathie's married, has a little boy and lives in Australia."

"According to Facebook she's still Cathie Squires," Andy pointed out.

"OK, she's as good as married, has a little boy and lives in Australia."

"Is she still with Keith Corden?"

"As far as I know," I said, not wanting to reveal that I knew full well that she was.

"If they've been together since College and they've had a child together, it seems strange that they've never married. Why do you reckon that is?"

"No idea. It seems strange to me too."

That was the truth. I had wanted to Facebook message Cathie with that very question but given our history I knew it would have been inappropriate.

"Did you add her as a friend or did she add you?" Andy wanted to know.

"I added her."

"Thought as much," Andy said in an annoyingly knowing tone.

"She lives 10,000 miles away, has a little boy and lives with someone," I stressed.

"Doesn't stop you having feelings for her!"

"Stop winding me up, I don't have feelings for her. Well, just friendly feelings."

"You used to have feelings for her."

"Ages ago, mate. Ages."

"So if you don't have feelings for her, why keep in touch with her if she lives 10,000 miles away, has a little boy and lives with Keith Corden?"

"Same reason I keep in touch with the other thirty six people, because she's a friend and I like to see what she's up to."

"Just in case she splits from Keith?"

"No, because we went to school together, there's nothing more to it than that."

"Oh, ok."

"Is that all you are going to say, 'oh ok'?"

"Yes."

"Good."

"I believe you."

"Good."

I knew Andy didn't believe me. I wasn't sure I had convinced myself either.

"So if Cathie Squires isn't the reason, what is the reason you don't want to marry Sandy then?"

"I didn't say that I didn't want to marry Sandy. I just said not yet."

By the time we had finished our third bottle of champagne, which I had offered to buy but Andy was having none of it, the truth was out. I wasn't sure whether I ever wanted to marry Sandy Josephs. She was a very pleasant, attractive lady but there was no spark between us. She never did anything that surprised me, never made me laugh, we never argued, our very irregular sex was routine and the very thought of spending the rest of my life with her filled me with dread. I drunkenly explained that I had a sweet tooth and being told I was going to stay with Sandy forever was like being told I could only ever eat Digestives for the rest of my life. Plain digestives too, not the ones with chocolate on one side.

After that third bottle, Andy walked back with me to our house. He wanted to see if my Dad was still awake so he could say a quick hello but unfortunately Dad had already gone to bed. He had taken to going up to bed about nine o'clock and then having a read in bed. He was always awake in the morning before me though. I had bought us the 'Sky' satellite package the previous Christmas so most mornings when I woke up, he was sat in the lounge having a coffee and watching Sky Sports. Since his operation, because he wasn't able to get up the stairs, he had been sleeping on a bed in the lounge. When Andy came back to ours, we saw the lounge light was off, so headed into the kitchen.

Before he walked back to his Mum's, I offered Andy a cup of tea. I don't even know why I bothered. He was always going to turn it down. The loyalty to his own teapot remained strong. I then offered him a glass of water which he accepted.

For the next fifteen minutes, whilst we tried to dilute three bottles of champagne with two glasses of water, I rambled on about my love life. As far as I recall, I spoke very little about Sandy though. My focus was on 'the one that got away' – Cathie Squires. Andy had heard it all before several times but was prepared to sit there and listen once more. For a couple of months before she emigrated to Australia I had slowly become convinced Cathie was 'the one', very little had happened to me since to make me question my judgement. I had missed my chance and back in 2007, I thought I was going to regret it for the rest of my life.

Chapter Thirty Two

My first job, as a 'Pizza Delivery Boy', stretched out long enough so by the time I left it I was a 'Pizza Delivery Man'. It lasted three years from aged eighteen to twenty one and I would probably be still working at 'A Little Pizza Heaven' now if my Dad hadn't found me something new. It was easy money. The only thing that was remotely awkward was Tony, the owner and his fiery temper but whilst I found it intimidating at eighteen, by twenty one his temper just amused me. It made the shift more fun if Tony was kicking off and if an evening passed without a Tony meltdown, it was a little disappointing.

Driving back and forth, to and from 'A Little Pizza Heaven', four evenings a week, Thursday to Sunday, listening to music in my car that I'd recorded on to cassette tapes from mine or Andy's CDs, was an enjoyable way to earn some money and the time always passed quickly. On some nights, especially at weekends, I could be given more than £10 in tips. I was always in with a better chance of getting a tip if the cost of the delivery was £9 something or £19 something as people would often say, 'keep the change, son' when they handed over their ten pound or twenty pound note. The drunks at the weekend could be my best or worst customers, sometimes they would tip me a fiver but sometimes they didn't have any cash at all. Tony would let the regulars pay next time if they couldn't stump up the cash but if it was a new customer he would get me to pick him up and take him back round there and would pester the life out of them (and their neighbours) until they somehow found the means to pay.

I had a separate jar in my bedroom for 'tips' money and would try to save it for special occasions. It was primarily meant to be for birthday and Christmas presents, but as I didn't have many people to buy for, there was always more than enough so I started using it for trips away. Whilst I was still with Joanna it funded several overnight stops to Llandudno and Ambleside. After we split up, it was used for the occasional date, but for a spell I didn't get close enough to anyone to justify a trip away.

Once I reached the age of twenty one my Dad probably felt it was time I got off my backside and started working a bit harder. Although it was never discussed, I suspect I needed to provide more money to the household finances too, as, by 1997, Dad had retired. He phased himself out of work by working part-time for eighteen months, just going in Friday to Sunday, but after the busy Christmas period of 1996, he finished altogether. On the first Thursday of every month though, he would get the train into Manchester and meet up with some of his old work colleagues for lunch. One Friday morning, at breakfast, he passed a note across to me with a name and number on.

"What's that?" I asked once I had swallowed my mouthful of Rice Krispies and milk.

"It's someone I want you to ring," Dad explained.

"What for?"

"The night manager at our Hotel, Ben, has bought himself a bar in town and he's looking for staff. I suggested to him that you'd be ideal."

I looked again at the name and number. Dad referred to Manchester as 'town', whilst for me Rochdale was 'town'. I sought clarification.

"Manchester?"

"Yes."

"And what would I be ideal for?"

"Working behind the bar."

"Dad, I don't know anything about bar work."

"Yes you do. You like a drink so you know what all the different drinks are and you've done a job that requires you to handle money and be polite to customers. I think you'd be good behind a bar and more importantly, when I told Ben about you, he thought you'd be good too. He's refurbishing the place, turning it into an Eighties bar, so it won't be opening for another three months apparently but he wants you to ring him today. He wants to meet up with you. Says if you seem like a decent lad he'll give you a role as a Bar Manager and you can start working there before they open, helping him get set up, recruiting staff and getting a bit of insight into how the business works."

It was all starting to sound a bit more interesting but doubts still kept popping up in my head.

"How would I get into Manchester every day?"

"Same way I do. Jump on the train."

Dad was now at the stage where he would only drive to local places he knew well.

"I couldn't. If I was there until after midnight there'd be no trains."

"Well you'll have to drive then."

"It's a nightmare getting into Manchester in the car. I like it where I am."

Dad could have let out a deep sigh or shouted at me for being an imbecile. He could have pointed out that I had a lousy job with no future but he was too diplomatic for any theatrics.

"Just speak to him, H and then see what you think. If you don't fancy it after you've spoken to him then just keep doing what you're doing but just have the courtesy to speak to him."

"OK. What's the bar going to be called?"

"Halcyon."

"Halcyon? What does that mean?"

"I think it pretty much means 'the good old days' but I'd check it in the dictionary just in case I've got that wrong."

After a bit of deliberation, I spoke to Ben early in the afternoon and within a couple of minutes I knew I wanted to work for him. He was a Southern guy, from Petersfield in Hampshire. He caught me off guard initially by asking me about football. He asked me which football team I supported and when I said I wasn't really interested in football, he said if I was going to work for him and didn't have my own team, then it was compulsory I supported 'Pompey'. I had no idea who 'Pompey' were. I found his vibrancy and enthusiasm compelling and thought it would be good fun working for him. I agreed to meet up with him in Manchester the following week, we hit it off straight away and that evening I handed my notice in to Tony at 'A Little Pizza Heaven' who took the news with a surprising calmness, shook my hand, wished me well and then asked if I could work another week or two whilst he found another driver.

I ended up working for Tony for another six weeks but I am delighted I did as on the fourth week I would make a delivery that would change my life. It was a Saturday night and I had to deliver two twelve inch pizzas (a Margerhita and a Pepperoni) and a nine inch garlic bread to an address in Norden. I rang the bell and went through a pretty standard routine of hearing a little dog yapping and then someone shouting through frosted glass that they were just going to put the dog away. Eventually, the door opened.

I didn't recognise the young woman who opened the door immediately but I was instantly overwhelmed by her beauty. She had a mass of long, blond curly hair, dark blue eyes, smooth skin on a perfectly made up face and a bright, white smile.

"H Mc Coy!" she cried out in delight.

I had three boxes of pizzas in my hands but instinctively took a step back and squinted my eyes to take a better look at her. It felt a little like the time I saw Joanna Barry in the chip shop. Girls obviously change more significantly than boys. It took a couple of seconds for me to make the correct association. It was Cathie Squires. She was a million miles better looking than she had been at school. At school, she was just pleasantly attractive, now she was stunning. I thought Joanna had been transformed, but Cathie had blossomed into a Goddess. I had often seen girls I went to school with out and about in Rochdale and I noticed the looks of some of the prettier ones were already on the wane, but Cathie was completely the opposite. I was shallow enough at twenty one to fall in love with her on that doorstep based on looks alone. Thankfully, she had a personality to match.

"Cathie Squires! I'm so sorry, I didn't recognise you for a minute. You look fantastic!"

"Fantastic? Get away with you. In these shabby clothes?"

Cathie was wearing a pair of grey tracksuit bottoms and a pink t-shirt. The clothes weren't anything special but if she could look that good whilst slobbing around the house, I shuddered to think what she could look like when she was all dressed up. It felt like meeting a film star. I was in awe. I knew I wanted to be with her for the rest of my life. It turned out the feeling wasn't mutual. Cathie was really pleased to see an old friend but her feelings ran no deeper than that.

"How come you're stopping in on a Saturday night?" I asked, genuinely puzzled. This felt like a Cinderella moment. I was already hoping I was going to be her Prince.

"I have to," Cathie replied, pulling a bit of a 'poor me' face, "I'm saving up. Mum and Dad are buying the pizzas."

"Right. What are you saving for?"

"I'm emigrating."

"Wow! Really?" I said, trying to sound enthusiastic although I was secretly gutted. I had just found the girl I wanted to marry on the spot and despite my brain passing on the messages of unconditional love to my heart, I was now being told there was no reason for hope.

"Yes, to Australia. Keith moved out there six weeks ago. He's got a job as an architect. I'm just going through the process of applying for a visa and then I'll be joining him."

Keith? Who was he again? Then I remembered, Keith Corden, 'Slobber chops'. His manoeuvre on the settee at John Dunphy's party sprang to mind. I remembered admiring his ability to wriggle his way into Cathie's tonsils. The admiration turned to bitterness. She was far too good for him. What was she doing moving half way around the world to live with that cocksure numpty?

"So you're still with Keith?" I don't think I masked my disappointment too well when I asked that question.

"Don't sound so surprised! We've been together more than four years now. Here, let me take those pizzas off you. How much do we owe you?"

"£16.50," I said as I passed across the boxes.

Cathie put her hand into the back pocket of her tracksuit bottoms and passed me a twenty pound note. I immediately wished that it was my hand feeling the curves of that beautiful, pert bottom. I knew someone or something had flicked a switch in my brain and sent me into 'lecherous' mode, but I couldn't help myself having these thoughts. Whilst trying to tell my brain and body to calm down, I fished around in my little bag looking for £3.50 in change. There was no offer of a tip but I presumed, because it was Cathie's parents who were paying, that she wasn't in a position to offer one.

"There you are," I said as I passed back her change, "so when are you off to Australia then?"

"It took Keith about six months to get everything sorted visa and job wise, so hopefully I'll be all sorted in three or four months too. What about you, 'H', are you still 'going out' with that girl from our school?"

I presumed Cathie meant Joanna. She would have known who Amy was, so wouldn't have referred to her as 'that girl'. I could have spun a tale to avoid discrediting myself but decided candour was the way forward.

"No, she finished with me. Quite a while back now. Not really been seeing anyone since then."

"How come?" Cathie asked, looking genuinely interested.

"How come she finished with me or how come I haven't been seeing anyone?" I asked for clarification.

"I meant 'how come she finished with you'?"

"I got very drunk and did something I regretted," I confessed sheepishly.

"Harry McCoy! You naughty boy!" Cathie admonished me but in a tone I hoped was not really serious.

"I know, I was an idiot but I've learnt my lesson now."

I was keen to stress it was a one-off, despite Cathie's plans to emigrate to Australia I still wanted her to think of me as a nice guy rather than a typical lad.

"Well, she couldn't have been 'The One' if you were willing to cheat on her. I'm presuming that's what you did."

I nodded guiltily.

"As I've said, I was very drunk. There was no sex involved."

"You don't have to explain yourself to me, H. Tell yourself fate intervened because she wasn't 'The One' and don't beat yourself up about it."

"OK," I replied smiling a little. I felt Cathie had a point. I liked Joanna a lot but there was more than one reason that we split.

My thoughts moved on to Cathie's pizzas and the fact that they would be starting to go cold.

"I best leave you to have your tea," I added.

"You and I should go out," Cathie said enthusiastically which for a very short while made me think all my Christmases had come at once. She clarified her situation soon enough though.

"Go out?" I said, playing it as cool as I possibly could when inside I felt like leaping into the sky and punching the air like an exuberant footballer.

"When I say 'go out' obviously I don't mean in a romantic sense."

"Obviously," I repeated, as if that had been obvious to me from the outset, as it should have been given Cathie had already told me she was emigrating to Australia to be with Keith. I just fooled myself momentarily into believing she was after a bit of fun before she left.

"I just mean to keep each other company over the next few months. We could go and watch the odd film together or go for a drink or something to eat occasionally. I used to spend all my time with Keith so I've been at a bit of a loose end since he went to Perth. If it seems weird going for nights out with a girl just on a platonic basis, then just say 'No', but if you want a friend to do things with before you find 'The One' then give me your phone number and I'll give you a ring."

The things I was imaging doing with Cathie were undoubtedly very different to the things she was imagining doing with me. I gave her my number without a second's hesitation and watched lustfully as her backside wiggled back into the house in search of a pen, before her smiling face re-emerged, tearing a piece of cardboard off the pizza box to jot it down. Not for one second did I want that relationship to be platonic. I was on a mission. A mission to convince Cathie that moving to Australia was a terrible idea and staying here with me was the answer to both of our prayers.

Chapter Thirty Three – Three Months Later

"I can honestly say I've never fancied Australia myself," Dad was telling Cathie, one Saturday evening, "it'd be too hot for me. I've never been a fan of the heat. I'd rather live in Iceland than Australia. Cold I can handle, heat not so much."

Cathie was around at our house, as she had often been in the months that had passed since we met back up on her parents' doorstep. I loved bringing her to ours. Every girl I ever brought to the house always managed to find their way into my Dad's heart, but Cathie was different to the rest. He was beyond enthusiastic when Cathie was around. He was like a young child with a toy. He didn't want to share her with anyone, including me. Cathie pandered to him in a loveable way. She was aware of my Mum's tragic death but once she discovered that Dad had lost his first wife tragically too, she looked upon him as the most adorable man that had ever lived. Their relationship was never inappropriate, but there was a strange sort of flirtatiousness from both parties that made me a little jealous.

"The sunshine is what I'm looking forward to most, George," Cathie said in response, "it's so dismal here. We have long dreary winters and get excited if we have a couple of back to back sunny days in August. I can't wait to get home after a day in work, put my 'cozzie' on and go for a swim."

I mentally pictured Cathie in a bikini. The one I imagined her wearing was light blue with little white and red flowers on it. I could picture her coming out of the sea, like Ursula Andress in Dr No, running her hand seductively through her tight blonde curls whilst singing and then picking conch shells from the sand. My imagination went to town and I imagined myself running towards her. I had bulked up a fair bit and my newly found muscles helped me when I lifted Cathie up like a ballerina and span her around as we gazed adoringly at each other in our skimpy gear.

"H, H," Cathie was moaning sexily as we kissed and I sucked on her bottom lip then much louder and more angrily she shouted, "HARRY!"

It was the shout that brought me back to reality. It had been a real shout.

"What?" I asked, realising Cathie had probably been trying to get my attention for a while.

"You were in your own little world then! I was just asking whether you'd ever fancied Australia?"

"I'd like to go for a holiday, but I wouldn't want to live there."

"How come?"

"I'm scared of spiders."

Cathie nudged me playfully, "You big girls blouse!"

"And I couldn't leave my Dad here."

"Your Dad would come to Perth if you and I both lived there, wouldn't you, George?"

"Of course I would. I'd have no choice if my two favourite people were over there."

The last three months had flown by. With Andy at University, it had been great to have some regular company with someone else my own age. I had begun working at Halcyon five days a week, preparing for its grand opening, but initial optimistic forecasts of an opening date had been put back. We had, however, reached a stage where the staff had been selected, the bulk of the refurbishment had been completed and we just had to complete some of the finer details before we were good to go. It was due to open the following Friday, which was why I had suggested to Cathie that her, my Dad and I should go out for a meal on my final work free Saturday night. Cathie was more than happy for me to involve my Dad. She was always referring to him as a 'proper, old fashioned gentleman.'

At no stage during the previous three months did Cathie ever give me a sign that our relationship was developing into anything other than a platonic friendship but I still clung to the hope that at some stage it might. She talked about Keith a lot, wrote letters to him constantly and spoke to him on the phone two or three times a week, but from what I knew of him, I still didn't think he was deserving of her and I lived in hope that one day she would come to realise this. These hopes were soon to be severely dented.

As the night was meant to be celebrating my new job, Cathie and Dad let me choose the restaurant. I chose Pizzeria Bella Italia in Bury, mainly because when I asked Cathie, she said she'd never been there and I didn't want to take her somewhere that would have reminded her of Keith. It's top quality too. A proper family run restaurant that is still open to this day.

Cathie had arrived at our house looking better than I think I had ever seen her before. She was wearing a figure hugging, high neck navy blue lace dress with high heeled silver shoes and a sparkly silver handbag. My Dad at the end of the evening, after Cathie had left us, described the dress as being the length of a 1960s mini skirt but for me it was just pleasingly short. Dad drove, slowly as ever and I did the chivalrous thing and sat in the back with Cathie.

Absolutely everything about the evening was going perfectly. When Cathie was chatting in the car on the way, she kept touching my hand or leg with hers when she made a point which made me feel, just in the moment, that we were a couple. The food was great, I had Tagliatelle, Cathie had lasagne, I have no recollection of what Dad had but remember him ordering a bottle of Sauvignon which only Cathie and I drank as Dad was driving. It was only over coffee that things took a turn for the worse. It wasn't that there was a big row or Dad didn't have the money to pay the bill or anything like that, it was just life started to get back in the way.

"So," Dad asked Cathie, "how long is it now before you go to Australia?"

It wasn't Dad's fault. It was a just a friendly question but the answer made my heart sink.

"If my visa comes through, which I'm hoping should be any day now, I'm going to book the first flight I can."

"How wonderful!" Dad enthused.

By this stage I had stopped even pretending to be pleased or excited about Cathie's departure. I didn't say anything, I was taken aback she could be leaving soon though. I let Dad and Cathie chat away about Australia whilst I tuned out and drank my coffee sullenly. For the first time in three months, Cathie's departure seemed imminent. I had to do something.

"Hang on," I said, after their conversation had run its course, "are you saying if you're visa comes through on Monday, you could be leaving within a couple of days?"

Cathie laughed.

"No, not quite that fast. I'd need to get myself organised but I'd certainly be leaving within two or three weeks. Keith's been out there for nearly five months now, I really miss him. The sooner I can begin my life with him over there the better."

Desperate times called for desperate measures. I decided I needed to make Cathie feel guilty about going.

"What about your Mum and Dad?" I asked.

"What about them?" Cathie replied, drinking from her coffee as she did so.

"Well, aren't they a similar age to Dad?"

Dad was seventy five at this stage, I knew they weren't as old as him, but I was trying to put them in the same age bracket.

"Mum's sixty six, Dad's sixty nine. Are you saying I'm a bad daughter for leaving them?"

"I'm just asking how you feel about leaving them?"

"Well, I know when it comes to it, I'm going to feel terrible but I think I'm going to spend the rest of my life with Keith and he's moved there, so I need to support him."

"So you reckon Keith's 'The One'?" I asked. It seemed a logical question given Cathie was always saying how Joanna wasn't 'The One' as far as I was concerned.

"I'm sure of it."

I shouldn't have said what I said next. It was a dead giveaway. I had played the platonic friend role to perfection for three months but at that moment, fuelled by a lot of Sauvignon Blanc, I let my guard down.

"Well, I hope for your sake he is," I said spitefully.

My feelings were out. Cathie didn't say anything but I knew it wasn't a nice thing for me to have said and she will have questioned why I said it. Thankfully, she had drunk as much wine as me, if not more and I don't think the reasons behind the comment properly registered. Dad, on the other hand, was stone cold sober and he knew exactly what I was doing. I was in love and I was clinging to the hope that I could do something that would make Cathie stay.

I don't think I sulked through the rest of the evening but it was hard to put a brave face on it. With Andy in Hull, Cathie was the only proper friend in Rochdale I had and I couldn't help but see the situation purely from my own perspective. Once Cathie left, there would be a huge hole in my life. I decided whilst on the car journey back to Rochdale that I couldn't just sit by and let this happen. I had to say something. Before she left, I owed it to myself to tell Cathie I was in love with her. I thought there was virtually no chance of my feelings being reciprocated but then, out of nowhere, something totally unexpected happened and all of a sudden I was in with a chance.

Chapter Thirty Four

News of the game changer arrived on the Tuesday evening following our night out at Pizzeria Bella Italia. It must have been well after nine when the doorbell rang, as Dad had already gone to bed with his normal farewell ('Good night son. Never forget how much you were loved by your mother and me') and I remember I was sat on my bed reading Graham Swift's 'Last Orders'.

There is always a momentary sense of panic when the phone or doorbell rings unexpectedly at an unusual hour of the day, but with Dad safely tucked up in bed I knew it couldn't be anyone bringing bad news to our door. As I lifted myself off the bed and headed to the hallway, I had narrowed the 'unexpected caller' suspects down to Andy (who could have been surprising me with a rare visit back from Hull), Cathie (to excitedly announce her visa had arrived and that she would soon be jetting off into the sunset to fall into the arms of her lover, Keith) or it could be a neighbour who needed help pushing a car or some similar minor catastrophe.

When I pulled the door open and saw Cathie standing there in a high waisted pair of ripped denim jeans and an oversized, unbuttoned plaid shirt over a navy blue t-shirt with the Reebok logo on the front, I forced out a lips together, mouth closed smile. Internally, however, I felt only sadness, as I sensed an air of bad news. I was losing her.

"I'm so sorry," was all Cathie said initially and, without speaking, I motioned like a traffic policeman for her to come in.

Once Cathie was inside, before either of us had a chance to say anything further, she hugged me. Hugs weren't uncommon in our friendship. We would hug and then kiss each other's cheeks after a day or evening spent together, but this was a far more desperate hug than those that had come before it. Cathie held me more tightly and for much longer than she had ever done before.

"Are you OK?" I asked but no reply was forthcoming. Cathie just continued to hold me tightly and then she sniffed a couple of times which made me think she'd been crying. I was worried for her and almost as worried for myself.

"What is it? What's the matter?"

"Keith..." she said but her voice was cracking as she said his name so she didn't attempt to say anything further. Still holding me, Cathie buried her head under my neck so I could only see the top of her head. She's only three or four inches smaller than me, we're both pretty average height for our sex, but her shoulders were rounded and her head was bowed.

"Take a few breaths then calmly, when you're ready, tell me what's happened to Keith."

I didn't really have any fond memories of Keith Corden. At school, he was extroverted, over confident and a bit of a bully with the weak kids but I still didn't want to hear any news of him coming to harm. An arrangement whereby he stayed safe and well in Perth for the rest of his life and Cathie stayed safe and well in Rochdale with me, would have suited me fine. The waters of my life do not tend to run that smoothly though. When Cathie said nothing further for the next couple of minutes, impatience got the better of me and I decided I needed to push the conversation along.

"Is he OK?"

"He's fine," Cathie answered. I was taken aback that she had answered so promptly.

"Then why have you been crying?"

"Who said I've been crying?"

"The snot on that shirt was a giveaway."

I could feel Cathie's head tilt as she inspected her shirt.

"I'm joking, Cathie! It was obvious. Has Keith upset you?"

Cathie didn't directly answer my question but slowly began to explain.

"He phoned me half an hour ago. It's early morning in Perth...tomorrow morning, not this morning...but he couldn't sleep. He was out last night, I mean tonight, last night for him...anyway, he was out with friends in Perth....can we sit down?"

"Of course we can," I said very calmly although I hoped Cathie didn't continue to tell this story whilst repeatedly trying to decipher the time difference as frankly it was immaterial.

We went through to the lounge and sat beside each other on the settee. By this point, I had realised there was a distinct possibility that whatever was upsetting Cathie may not be all bad news for me. As soon as we were sat down, she blurted it straight out.

"He's slept with someone else."

My desire to do cartwheels around the lounge was tempered by the fact that my lack of sporting grace would have made them very unimpressive.

"Another woman?"

Cathie gave out a quick teary laugh.

"Well, it wouldn't be a man!"

Pity, there'd be no going back from that one.

"Sorry, it came out wrong. I meant has he fallen in love with another woman?"

My mind was all over the place and as well as the naturally jubilant feeling for myself, I also felt very sorry for Cathie. I wanted to be a supportive friend but the mix of jubilation and empathy just made me come across as bumbling and awkward. Girls in films seem to like that Hugh Grant style but Cathie seemed to be finding it annoying rather than endearing. She scrunched up her face .

"I said he'd slept with someone not that he'd fallen in love with someone else, H. You did it to Joanna. I thought you, of all people, might know the difference," Cathie said curtly.

I have always been a sensitive soul and given my feelings for Cathie, it felt like a low blow. I really liked Joanna but we'd never made plans to move halfway around the world together. I hadn't ever felt she was 'The One'. Keith was the bad guy here not me. I could have told her from the start that he was a player. As I was self-sympathising, I remembered how much it hurt when Amy had done the dirty on me and realised I probably lashed out irrationally too. I needed to pussy foot around Cathie, just whilst she calmed down.

"Look," I said choosing my words carefully, "I'm obviously saying all the wrong things here. I'll just keep my big mouth shut and you tell me exactly what's happened and how you feel about it."

So she did.

Up until that point in my life I considered myself to be a good listener, but as Cathie told Keith's story, in the most intricate of detail, I just wanted her to cut to the chase. A story that could have been told in two minutes took over twenty minutes to tell. Details I never wanted to know about Keith Corden were revealed; where he was born (East Anglia, his Dad was stationed at an RAF base at the time), his parents names (Joyce & Bernie), where he lived in Western Australia (Kwinana, halfway between Perth and Mandurah), the fact he was circumcised (as a baby) and the fact that sex never lasted longer than two minutes with him unless he was drunk (six pints and he would go on forever, eight pints or more and he couldn't raise his game). The latter details were probably revealed because I opened up a half bottle of vodka and some coke two minutes into the tale and by the end of it, it was gone. To be fair, I drank as much as Cathie, as it stopped me pulling my hair out whilst I was waiting for her to get to the part about Keith's infidelity.

Eventually, the only part of the story I actually wanted to hear was reached. Keith had been out with three male work colleagues (an Icelandic guy, another English guy and a lad from Perth, if that matters) after work. They all ended up very drunk (based on previous information, I'm guessing Keith had about seven pints or whatever the schooner equivalent of that may be) and ended up in a nightclub. He hit it off with a girl from Queensland who was studying at Edith Cowan University. Her name, which apparently Keith was reluctant to confess to Cathie as it didn't matter, was Belinda. She was equally drunk as she had been out with a group of University friends since lunch time. Keith went back to Belinda's student accommodation in Mount Lawley, did the deed and then guiltily rang Cathie a few hours later after he had woken up and started to head home. I didn't ask, but I presumed he must have had the Wednesday off.

"So how do you feel about it?" I asked, once the tale was over, before biting into my left cheek, as soon as the words came out, as this could have been deemed another stupid question.

"Upset, obviously."

"Yes obviously but I mean is it an angry upset or a relieved upset?"

The scrunched up face was back. I was still a long way from perfecting the 'shoulder to cry on' lark. Michael Parkinson's job as a chat show host was definitely not under threat from me.

"Why would I be relieved to discover that my boyfriend had just slept with someone else?"

"I don't know, maybe just because it's happened now," I began to explain awkwardly, "better to find out he's a cheat before you fly halfway around the world to be with him."

"Oh, I'll still be doing that," Cathie stated with, what seemed to me, an illogical degree of certainty.

"You will?"

Then, as now, I found a woman's mind unfathomable.

"Of course."

"Why?"

"He confessed. Keith could have lied or he could have just kept quiet about it, but he didn't, he confessed. We've been away from each other for five months, H. Either of us could have been up to all sorts and the other one would never have known. The fact that he feels so bad that he has to unburden his guilt to me, tells me has never cheated on me before and will never cheat on me again."

"Seriously, that's what you think?"

I totally disagreed. I was quite happy to try my best to be a shoulder to cry on, but I wasn't prepared to sit back and let Cathie do something stupid without, at the very least, being the Devil's advocate.

"Yes, don't you?"

"I don't know. You said before that after eight pints or more Keith was incapable of doing anything, so he couldn't have been all that drunk. Why didn't he become overridden with guilt when they started kissing or when she was taking her bra and knickers off or when he was putting his..."

Cathie stopped me there.

"Alright! Alright! I get your point. My point though isn't that he was doing it because he was drunk. My point is that he was doing it because he was lonely."

I sighed. It was a proper deep, exaggerated sigh.

"I'm sure he is lonely, Cathie, but if you go over there, are you going to have to be with him every second of every day to make sure he doesn't get lonely again? What if he works away over night? Will that make him lonely?"

"We've been apart five months, H. You just don't understand."

"You're right. I don't."

"He's 'The One' for me. You've yet to meet the person who is 'The One' for you, so I can't tell you how he makes me feel. When it happens to you, you'll know. We need to be together. Once we are together, everything will be different, things will be fine."

"OK."

I could not say any more at that point than 'OK'. I was shell shocked. I thought Cathie was a strong, independent character and hadn't expected that she would allow Keith to walk all over her emotions like this. If she forgave him once, would he not just keep repeating the same crime? I thought Keith's cheating would have been the death knell of his relationship with Cathie, instead, it seemed to have made her keener than ever to get over to Perth to be with him. I didn't understand, I didn't want to understand. In my mind, Cathie was being an idiot. I felt that if I had ever been given a chance with her I would have loved her too much to cheat on her, whether we were apart for five months or five years. Cathie wasn't Joanna. Would confessing how I felt about her make any difference?

We stayed up in the lounge for another couple of hours just talking. I opened a bottle of my Dad's Muscadet and told Cathie, who was feeling guilty about us taking it, that I would buy him a new one in the morning. He preferred red wine anyway so he wasn't going to be too bothered. White wine was for guests, I explained and Cathie was a guest. By midnight, we were both very drunk and weary. It had been an emotional evening.

"Shit!" Cathie exclaimed out of nowhere.

"What?"

"How am I going to get home now? I can't drive. I've drunk way too much."

"Stop here," I suggested without masking my drunken excitement about the prospect.

"No, no, I'll get a taxi."

"Don't be daft, you've told me before that the motion makes you want to throw up once you've had too much to drink. Stay here, you can have my bed."

"How very chivalrous of you, Mr McCoy, but where will you sleep?"

"I'll sleep here," I said pointing to the settee we were sitting on.

"I don't want you giving your bed up for me, H. We could both sleep in your bed. We could top and tail."

Cathie had no idea how hard it was for me to decline that offer.

"No, it's fine. It's too small. It's only a single. I'll sleep in here. You've had a bad day. You'll need your sleep."

I learnt something that night. If you chase rainbows you will never catch them, but if you act like gold doesn't interest you, someone will bring a big pot of it to your door.

Cathie took hold of one of my hands and stared right at me with her drunken, tired, beautiful deep blue eyes.

"I don't want to be on my own tonight though, H. I'm upset. My head's all over the place. Can you please just sleep in there with me? It'd be nice to have someone to cuddle."

"I'm not sure it would be a good idea."

"Please."

Chapter Thirty Five

You might possibly have thought that sharing a single bed with Cathie, at that stage in my life, would have been a dream scenario but it turned out to be a bit of a nightmare. I was as hopeless at understanding the subtleties of women as I was at playing football, so had no idea whether Cathie's suggestion that we share a bed and cuddle was simply a request to do just that or whether this was an invitation for things to go a whole lot further.

I had no experience of having to interpret female signals. When I had first got together with Amy, she had cordoned off the area so I knew I couldn't fail whilst with Joanna, I was aware of her historical infatuation so once again knew my chances were high. This was a whole new ball game but yet again a ball game I wasn't very good at. Things were complicated. There were several things I needed to take into consideration.

Firstly, there was the 'boyfriend in situ' conundrum. Despite Cathie's insistence that she felt Keith was 'The One', his actions seemed to suggest otherwise. Cheating partners was something I did actually have a little bit of experience in. To my mind, Amy had cheated on me because I wasn't 'The One' and then I had cheated on Joanna because she wasn't 'The One' either. It seemed to me people tended to cheat because they felt, perhaps subconsciously, that there must be someone out there better matched to them than the person they were already with. Cathie may have felt that Keith was 'The One', but somewhere in his mind Keith was still searching. Wedding vows contained the line 'forsaking all others' for a reason and if he wasn't prepared to do that now, their future wasn't rosy. This seemed obvious to me but Cathie seemed to be steadfastly refusing to accept it. I did recall however, how Andy had to let me discover Amy's foibles for myself and perhaps I was going to have to let Cathie do likewise, even if it meant waving her off to Australia. With regards to the night ahead, however, I felt if Cathie wanted to exact some revenge on Keith by sleeping with me then Keith had brought his bad luck upon himself.

The second thing my mind was focusing on was how things would look in the morning. Emotions had been running high. Cathie had been upset and we'd both been drinking. If we ended up sleeping together, how would we be with each other in the morning? Could we act like it never happened? Probably not. Would I want us to act like it never happened? Definitely not. Would we remain friends? It would certainly be difficult. Would Cathie immediately dump Keith and insert me as his immediate replacement? It was unlikely.

These questions going around in my head linked into another issue for me. The issue of trust. Even if everything worked out perfectly, Cathie dumped Keith and ran straight into my open arms, would I subsequently be able to trust her? Perhaps this might seem like a stupid question but I was still more than a little jaded from the Amy incident on that fateful Friday night. If Cathie was prepared to cheat on Keith, who she had consistently stated her 'undying love' for, could she not subsequently do the same to me?

Finally, all these scenarios that were spinning around in my drunken head were based on the premise that Cathie actually wanted something to happen between us. What if she didn't? What if I made a move to kiss her only to discover all that she wanted was a consoling friend?

It was about one o'clock in the morning when we eventually headed through from the lounge into my bedroom. I was half expecting Cathie to go to the bathroom to change and then appear wearing a thick woolly jumper that stretched down to below her knees. There was no such disappearing act and no woolly jumpers were magically created by the laws of Sod. We just took our positions either side of my bed and whilst I nervously undressed down to my boxer shorts, Cathie stripped down to her underwear as if I wasn't there.

I was pretending to be purely focused on my own routine of undressing but once I caught a glimpse of Cathie in her underwear, my attempts to keep a lid on my sexual desires were made a million times harder. Those pieces of underwear had incredible charms. They weren't just your bog standard black, white or miss matched pair. They were quality undergarments. A navy blue embroidered lace pair with heavily detailed white lacy bits at the top and bottom of the bra and at the top of knickers. A gentleman would perhaps have looked away but I was a young, inebriated, lustful man and I stared like I was a contestant on 'Screen Test' who had to remember every image that played out before my eyes.

It was no surprise to discover Cathie had a washboard stomach but was taken aback that whilst admiring it I noticed she also had a pierced naval. At school, Cathie had always been a bit of a 'Goody Two Shoes' so this act of rebellion seemed out of character. I loved it though. I had never been much of a saint myself nor had I ever felt a suppressed sense of lust as I did right then. As the next few minutes passed, however, Cathie still managed to turn the temperature up further in the furnace of my loins.

I clambered into bed, ignoring any need for chivalry as there was a greater need to avoid detection of the inevitable consequences that were taking place inside my shorts. I mirrored the reaction down below by sitting bolt upright as Cathie was standing beside the bed, circling her neck to alleviate a very different type of stiffness.

"I didn't know you had your stomach pierced," I said casually. My thoughts at that stage were anything but casual.

"Yeh, I had a wild summer last year. I've always been 'Little Miss Prim & Proper' but at some point last year I decided I was sick and tired of pretending to be someone I wasn't and it was time to let the naughty side out."

Wow! Just 'Wow!' I absolutely love the way beautiful women have the power to render any man speechless and Cathie was feeding me little fragments of her new identity piece by piece. I was mesmerised by her mannerisms and enthralled by her new naughtiness. There was even more to come.

"Do you like it?" Cathie asked, but she must have known the answer as I was probably salivating more than one of Pavlov's dogs on a trip to the butchers.

"I love it. You have to be fit for a stomach piercing and you are....physically fit I mean."

That was not what I meant but whilst I hadn't managed to ascertain what was really happening, I still needed to keep up the pretence.

"Thanks 'H'. It gave me a buzz having it done. I'd never really rebelled against my parents before. Not that they know! My Dad would be mortified if he knew but because I felt so pleased with myself for doing it, two weeks later I took things a whole lot further.

Don't ask me why, probably because of all the testosterone I was overdosing on at that point, I had an image in my head of what Cathie was about to reveal next. I should have just kept this image to myself but the vodka and excitement made me blurt it out.

"Don't tell me you've had the lips between your hips pierced!"

Cathie looked at me aghast.

"What? 'The lips between my hips'? NO!'

She then giggled. An incredibly sexy, infectious giggle which made me laugh too.

"What on earth made you think that?" Cathie asked once her giggles were stifled.

"I don't know," I said feeling my face blush, "I was shocked by your belly button piercing and from what you were saying I was just expecting you to reveal something else even wilder. That was all I could think of."

"I did do something wilder."

"What?"

"I had a tattoo done."

Tattoo? Cathie was in her bra and knickers. There was no sign of a tattoo. My guess seemed to make more sense than a tattoo.

"No, you didn't!"

Cathie turned the top of the world's most sublime knickers over slightly. On the left side, at a midpoint in the triangle between hip, groin and vulva, there was a discreet tattoo in small lettering and decorative handwriting. I leaned closer to see what it said, which was simply, 'La joie de vivre' in black ink.

"La joie de vivre," I said in a clumsy attempt to say these French words, "the joy of...."

I hesitated. I had never done French at school.

"Life, living. The joy of living," Cathie said, finishing my sentence off.

"That's what I thought," I quickly stated, not wanting Cathie to think I was stupid.

"Well?" Cathie said as she climbed into bed next to me.

"Well what?"

"What do you think?"

"Of the tattoo? I think I've discovered a side of you that I never knew existed, Cathie Squires!"

"I'll take that as a compliment. Keith hates it though."

"How come?"

"He says when I'm getting bed bathed at ninety when I'm doubly incontinent the carers are going to laugh at the irony. Keith doesn't agree with tattoos on women. He says they look cheap and it means I am making a pact with life never to change because if my tastes change I'm lumbered with it."

"What a miserable bastard!"

It was a statement that wasn't meant to be funny. If anything, I was being truthful but it set Cathie off laughing again and I found myself joining in. Once our drunken giggles subsided, I switched the light off. My bedroom was never the darkest, there was a street light just outside my window and the curtains were pale blue. I liked it that way when I was younger as I wasn't keen on the dark and since Mum died we'd never replaced them. I could still clearly make out Cathie's silhouette. We chatted for a few more minutes but we were both growing weary.

"I'm going to have to go to sleep now," Cathie announced, "I can hardly keep my eyes open. Give me a cuddle before I do."

Facing each other we wrapped our arms around each other's backs. Cathie kissed my cheek and I kissed the hair on the side of her head. I meant to kiss her cheek but it wasn't quite light enough to see where everything was so I somehow managed to miss. I cursed inwardly at my inability to get anything right. I loved the feel of Cathie's smooth, naked flesh pressed against me though. I loved the smell of her breath. I loved the enticing small of her perfume. I just loved her.

"Good night, beautiful man," Cathie said kissing my cheek once more.

This was my last chance. My mind was screaming 'Kiss Her, Kiss Her, KISS HER!'

I held back. I was too scared of failure.

"Good night, gorgeous," I said in response but all the other things I intended to do or say remained in my head.

Instead of opening up the window of opportunity, I had put a mortice lock on it and then thrown away the key. I turned to face away. By fearing failure, I had managed to walk, head first, right into it.

Chapter Thirty Six

I don't have the strongest of bladders so I would have been stunned if I'd made it through the whole night without stumbling across the landing to the bathroom at some point. A quarter of a bottle of vodka and half a bottle of Muscadet had sealed my fate. It was however, Cathie's wanderings at an ungodly hour that had woken me up initially. At first, she had attempted to find the doorway in the semi-darkness but after feeling several sections of the wall with both hands and inadvertently almost walking into a fitted wardrobe, she switched the light on.

"Sorry! Sorry!" Cathie apologised as the bright light lit the room and prodded my eyes like a pair of fingers.

I watched her backside disappear and after a flush of the loo, I watched the front side of her beautiful body with its radiant face reappear. Cathie switched the light back off and clambered into bed. At that point, I should have hauled myself out of bed too but I was warm and cosy. I didn't feel as though my bladder was giving out any distress signals so decided it could wait.

I felt like I had only dropped back off to sleep for a few minutes when I was disturbed once more. I opened my right eye first and then the left. The curtains were open which seemed odd and bright lights were streaming through the window. I was wondering whether I had somehow managed to sleep through until the morning but the clock on my sideboard was showing half past three and Cathie was still asleep. I decided I would pull the curtains closed once more so whatever the brightness was wouldn't disturb Cathie and I could get back to sleep.

The closer I moved towards the curtains, the sharper the brightness was. I squinted and ducked my head slightly to protect my eyes. Sometimes police helicopters would fly overhead, chasing joyriders, with a powerful searchlight and until I looked out the window, I suspected that's what the light may have been.

I could have just pulled the curtains together but my natural inquisitive nature was always going to force me to look out. When I did look, despite it being the middle of the night, I witnessed the largest, clearest rainbow I had ever seen. I remember being taught at school about rainbows and recalled they had something to do with refraction and reflection. A rainbow certainly shouldn't be appearing in the middle of the night. The colours seemed right though, 'Richard of York Gave Battle In Vain', Red, Orange, Yellow, Green, Blue, Indigo and Violet. The sky wasn't blue or grey though, it was black. The sun wasn't out, it was a clear night sky filled with a crescent moon and stars but the rainbow was there illuminating everything. It made no sense, but when I saw a smiling, familiar face perched on the top of the arc and heard the comforting softly spoken Southern tones, I knew what was happening. This was not the real world. My mother was appearing to me in a dream.

"Hello, Harry, my darling."

I looked up at her. The rainbow was very close by, just beyond the houses across the road, so I could make out my mother's features really clearly. She was back to her pre-accident best. I shouldn't have been able to hear her from where she was, through a closed window, but then my Mum shouldn't have been able to sit at the top of an arc in a rainbow at night time. Rainbows don't appear at night and my mother just happened to be dead.

"Hi Mum. This is weird. Is it a dream?"

"This is whatever you want it to be my beautiful boy."

"Well in that case, I need it to be a dream. Your resurrection on a rainbow would be a bit too much for me to cope with in real life."

My Mum's smiled broadened.

"That's fine, Harry, if you need it to be a dream, we'll call it a dream."

"That's good. Are you OK? Dad and I miss you terribly. I feel guilty too."

"Don't feel guilty, Harry. There's no reason for guilt."

"Yes there is. I should have stopped that horse hitting you. That's not all. I should have been a better son too. I was always good with Dad but I didn't try hard enough with you. "

"You were young. I understood."

"Are you OK though?" I asked again.

I understood this was a dream but I wanted to be re-assured Mum was happy.

"I'm very well. I miss the closeness I had with you and your father. I can see you though. I watch you both all the time."

I was a young man who did things young men do. I didn't like the idea of being constantly watched by my mother.

"All the time?"

Mum laughed. It was so weird hearing my Mum laugh again after all this time. It was definitely her laugh.

"Don't panic! There are certain things that we aren't permitted to watch."

"Like what?"

"Sex, masturbation, toilet trips, showers, baths – things like that are not acceptable to watch. Respectability rules on the rainbow."

"Good! There are certain things I wouldn't want you to see."

"I'm aware of that. I've always respected your privacy, Harry."

"I know. What's with the rainbow, Mum? I don't understand."

"I don't really understand myself, love. As far as I can work out from my interaction with other departed souls, the rainbow acts as an interim dimension before we properly pass on. We are only permitted to interact with the living at times when their minds aren't switched on. Like now when you're asleep. Even then, there has to be a good reason for us to appear."

"You've been there a long time."

"In the whole swing of things, love, I've been here for no time at all."

I thought about that. If time is no longer finite then my Mum was right, a few years are nothing.

"OK I get that," I said but there were other things that were still confusing me, "so if you need a good reason to appear to me, what's specifically made you appear now?"

"I felt you needed some guidance from me."

"Do I?"

Thinking back, my Mum provided guidance subtly and without me really being conscious of it. If I was ever to seek out advice, I would always have gone to Andy or my father. I didn't feel there was anything I especially needed her help with at that particular moment but I was soon proved wrong.

"You do. You need someone to tell you to back away from Cathie. You mean well but you're suffocating her. You're also acting in a conniving manner too which is making me feel uncomfortable. It's not becoming of you, Harry. I would have left it to your father to tell you this but he's even lonelier than you are and he's comforted by Cathie's presence. He doesn't want Cathie to go to Australia any more than you do. In the morning, your father will tell you to open up to her, tell her how you really feel but you need to ignore that advice. You can't mess with Cathie's emotions like that. The timing is all wrong. If she is 'The One' like you think she is, her life's journey will lead her to your door but if she isn't you will have the satisfaction of knowing you did the right thing. It is wrong to force matters of the heart. You must let love find its own direction."

There were so many things I wanted to say to my Mum and so many questions I wanted to ask her but as soon as my mother had passed on the guidance she had come to deliver, the rainbow began to fade and as a consequence my mother faded away with it. I woke in the morning knowing it had just been a dream but I felt I had dreamt it for a reason. It hadn't really been my mother, it was just a characterisation of my mother created by my brain but the dream seemed to be passing on an important message, I was right not to have made a move on Cathie and now it was time to let her go.

Four weeks later Cathie flew out to Australia. Bizarrely, the following morning, like Mum had predicted in the dream, my father did suggest to me that I should do my utmost to get Cathie to stay. I ignored that advice. I would be lying if I said I didn't make one last ditch attempt to keep her in Rochdale but I did back off and give her space during that last month. Importantly, when she departed, we were great friends. Cathie was well aware that I didn't think Keith Corden was 'The One' for her, but equally she knew I only ever wanted the best for her.

At first, we wrote lots of letters to each other, we spoke occasionally on the phone too, but eventually life moved on for us both. Although we continued to exchange cards at Christmas and birthdays, Cathie only really came to the forefront of my mind after I'd had a few drinks, especially during the times I felt my love life was heading down a blind alley. I wasn't really sure if there was such a thing as 'The One' or whether there were thousands of people equally compatible to you and you just had to find one of them, but if it was the former rather than the latter I felt my opportunity of finding true love had gone forever and I would have to make do with a compromise.

Andy always used to say to me that I should only approach girls that I feel are of the highest quality, 'ten out of ten' girls, as eventually one would agree to being with me and other envious males would then wonder how a guy like me had managed to capture the heart of a girl like her. In theory, this is the perfect plan but for a man who was sensitive to rejection and didn't enjoy being lonely, it didn't work out too well and I found myself abandoning this plan and dating a succession of girls who were just 'fairly pleasant' in both looks and personality. There were also a few good looking girls with average personalities and a few average looking girls with great personalities. Perhaps with the latter category I should have been wise enough to know that looks are of minor importance but unfortunately I was never that wise. By the time I reached my early thirties, I was plodding along in a very average relationship with Sandy Josephs, knowing I wasn't being fair to either of us by sticking it out, but also not having the bravery to finish it. The ideal scenario would have been if Sandy had met someone else or fallen out of love with me, but unfortunately she was too good a person to do either. I knew one day I would break her heart or I would break my own by allowing the relationship to drag on into middle age.

With regards to my Mum, despite it only having been in a dream, it felt good to have seen her again. It felt comforting to know that she could arrive in my dreams looking and acting like she used to. When I reflected on that dream, which I often did, I recalled how Mum called me 'Harry' all the time in it, rather than 'H'. The fact that she did that made it seem more real because she never really liked the name 'H' and only really used it reluctantly. For months, I went to sleep at night hoping to have that same dream again, looking out to see Mum on a rainbow but perhaps this time ask her questions that even I wouldn't know the answers to, then ask my Dad whether she was right. I kept telling myself it was just my sleeping brain in action, but I wanted to disprove my own theory and stumble across a miracle. No matter how much I wanted to see her and how often I thought of her last thing at night, my mind could just not conjure my mother back up.

Given the amount of time I devoted to thinking about that dream, I should have remembered what my mother had told me during it. 'We are only permitted to interact with the living when their minds aren't switched on'. The more I tried to think her back into my dreams, the less likely she was to appear. I hadn't really grasped that the mother I had created in my brain had now set the rules and no matter what I tried to do, she was going to adhere to them.

Chapter Thirty Seven

According to the gospel of Cosmopolitan, men reach their sexual peak at eighteen whilst women are at their sexual peak at thirty five. This may well be scientifically accurate but in real life my peak of sexual activity was reached between the ages of twenty two and twenty four, during the time I worked as a Bar Manager in the Halcyon eighties bar in Manchester. All my sexual stars seemed to align simultaneously to ensure activity reached a maximum during that two year period.

I will do my utmost to refrain from describing the regularity of my sex during those times as my 'sexual successes' because, as you will soon discover, an abundant sex life with a variety of people is not necessarily something that should be celebrated. I do think, however, that the key aspect in ensuring I was so sexually active during those two years was because the fear of rejection that I had always had previously had disappeared. I had felt so romantically drawn to Cathie Squires that when she left for Australia, I felt drained of the capacity to fall in love. After Mum had died, I reacted, for a while, by looking for fights. Once Cathie left for Australia, I responded by looking for sex. No strings attached, emotionless sex.

If you are looking for sex as a virile young male in his early twenties, there are worse places to look than in a bar that is packed to the rafters on Friday, Saturday and Monday nights and pretty damn busy for the rest of the week. The reason for the volumes on a Monday night was down to it being 'Student Night'. We would have students from the four local Universities (Manchester, Metropolitan, UMIST and Salford), queuing to get in to take advantage of our special offers, particularly Budweiser at 60p a bottle. Hooking up on a Monday night was like shooting fish in a barrel so I ended up bringing a sports bag to work on a Monday. I used to lock the bag away in a cupboard so apparently its contents became a talking point amongst my bar staff. I was told the rumours became more and more elaborate (including gimp masks and S&M gear) but all it actually contained was a pillow, a toothbrush, a fresh pair of boxer shorts and a box of condoms.

Another factor in explaining my sexual proclivity during my time at Halcyon was self-confidence. I was brimming with it. The acne that had plagued me in my teenage years had now faded. My body had also evolved from that of a skinny boy to that of a muscular, attractive young man (thankfully without the need for any effort on my part). I actually felt as though I was good looking. I knew I wasn't Johnny Depp or Leonardo di Caprio but I was aware I was attractive enough to be a magnet for drunken young women who were looking for sex. The fact that it was evident that I was one of the bosses undoubtedly also enhanced my charms.

I am not sure if I was manipulating women or I was being manipulated by them but there were very few weeks during those two years that I returned home to Dad's after every shift. I would regularly end up in student houses in Fallowfield or a divorcees home in Eccles after the Tuesday night 'Over 25s' event. The 'Over 25s' were normally well over thirty five but getting together with any of them tended to be very uncomplicated as they were largely beyond playing games. A whisper in the ear whilst paying for a Bacardi & Coke often spelt out exactly what they were intending to do to you after closing time.

On reflection, irrespective of the age, the class, the location or the looks of the lady I was escorting home, I don't think it ever made me feel overly happy. I just did it because I could. Sex was on offer and I was willing to take it. I was lonely and romantically numb. Women were coming on to me and as long as I found them moderately attractive (I must admit my standards weren't overly high) then I would have sex with them.

I am not saying I had sex with every woman I took back to their homes. There were times I found myself in bed with a woman who would end up kicking me out before anything happened due to them being overcome by guilt as they had a boyfriend or husband that they had previously failed to disclose. An even bigger proportion would throw up during the taxi journey home, on the driveway or within a minute of us arriving back. They were occupational hazards I was prepared to accept. I learnt to avoid those who appeared particularly drunk and kept a careful watch for engagement and/or wedding rings or friends 'discreetly' reminding their flirtatious friend that they had someone at home who loved them. There were times I missed the signs and ended up hiding in cupboards, under beds, climbing down drainpipes naked or fighting off an aggrieved partner but it was perhaps half a dozen occasions in hundreds of nights.

During those hundreds of nights that did actually end up with sex, I would like to say I was always sensible enough to have worn a condom but in truth I was guided by my partner for the night. I would always offer to wear one, but if I was told it was unnecessary because they were on the pill or had a coil fitted (I even slept with a few women who had had hysterectomies or had already been through the menopause) then I would happily carry on regardless.

After two years of bouncing around Manchester, lobbing my privates into women of various levels of beauty, age and class, I received a valuable lesson in life in the form of gonorrhoea.

I have to say, my trip to the GPs to report that I had a green discharge coming out the tip of my penis, swollen foreskin and a penis that felt it was being burnt at the end with a blow torch every time I needed a wee, swiftly overtook the Amy Garfunkel eye incident as the most humiliating few minutes of my life. I hadn't even heard of gonorrhoea before I was diagnosed (although I had heard of its cute nickname 'The Clap') but I could not think of a worse way to enlighten myself of the correct terminology of this disgusting sexually transmitted disease.

"So what have you been up to?" my GP asked, in a matter of fact way, as I pulled my trousers back up and pushed myself up off his medical bed. He was popping a swab, which he had just taken from my urethra, into a container as he asked.

"Having too much sex with too many people," I confessed candidly but with more than a trace of genuine shame.

"Men, women or both?" the Doctor asked, again in a tone that suggested he was not here to judge, just to do his job.

I didn't take this as an affront. I had green pus coming out of my genitalia, now was not a good time to be taking the moral high ground.

"Women. Just women."

"OK, please take a seat," my GP gestured, "the reason I ask is that you are much more likely to catch what it appears you have, which will need to be confirmed, but it appears to be gonorrhoea, through sexual activity with an infected male than an infected female. By having sex with an infected female, your chances of catching it are probably around one in four or one in five, sleeping with an infected male and the probabilities are much, much higher."

In my mind, I didn't immediately put my diseased penis down to sheer bad luck. I had slept with a lot of women, a lot of sexually liberated forward women who were, like me, probably putting their sexual parts to regular use with a variety of different people. I wasn't handpicking shy, virginal, cautious types. My penis had been a ticking time bomb. I just hoped I hadn't spread the disease around too much before my vile symptoms had reminded me it was time to stop screwing around. I must admit I had looked at it, in its leaking, shrivelled form, in the bathroom before I headed to the Doctor's and I had said,

'You're not big and you're not clever.'

It was gallows humour. I felt completely wretched and ashamed about how I had behaved.

The Doctor was beginning to type things into his computer.

"How long after you catch it do the symptoms take to show up?" I queried.

"Anything up to thirty days but generally a few days to a week. Most women who are infected, probably three in four, have no symptoms at all, which is a factor in its ability to spread."

I thought about where I had been over the last month, partially to try to identify who had given me gonorrhoea and partially to identify who I had subsequently given it to. In that four week period, I had slept with six women, four different students on Monday nights, a single mother of two in her thirties who had taken me back to her house in Prestwich and a professional woman in her late twenties from Cheadle Hulme whose boyfriend had been away in Dublin for the weekend with the lads. If luck was not on the side of the latter, there was going to be a very awkward conversation taking place in Cheadle Hulme in the next few weeks. I thought momentarily about phoning them all with an uncomfortable warning but I only ever exchanged mobile numbers when pressed (never home numbers) and would routinely just delete the number before I completed my journey back home. In my father's era, I would have been known as a cad.

"How will I get rid of it?"

I was hoping the Doctor would reveal that everything clears itself up after a couple of days but realised this was probably a little optimistic.

"We will get the results back from the lab within a few days. If it is gonorrhoea then you will be given an injection of an antibiotic called ceftriaxone and I will prescribe you a further antibiotic, which can be taken orally, which will help rid you of chlamydia if you have that too. I'm afraid gonorrhoea and chlamydia often come hand in hand."

It was no great surprise to discover a few days later that I had won the STD lottery and both numbers had come up. I did have the double whammy of 'clap' and 'chlamydia'. I subsequently had the injection, took the tablets and was told to refrain from sex for at least another seven days after I completed the course of tablets. I didn't have sex again for eighteen months and it was several years later before I had sex without a condom (twelve months into a relationship). People buy burglar alarms after their house has been robbed. The same rules apply to dignity.

I never told my Dad but I did tell Andy and I received the response I expected and deserved.

"Serves you bloody right! You can't expect to be going 'in like Flynn' with the amount of women you have without ending up catching something. I have no sympathy, in fact I'm delighted! Chuffed to bloody bits! It's about time something came along to teach you a bit of respect for women and for yourself. Just think yourself lucky that's all you caught."

Chapter Thirty Eight

During your school days it is constantly drummed into you that 'qualifications are everything', from experience I have learnt this isn't the case at all. I would imagine it probably is the case for the likes of Andy, who needed good grades as a vital stepping stone to becoming a barrister. For the likes of me though, I never really found my lack of 'A' levels or a degree to be an obstacle to getting the jobs I wanted.

For the intellectually mediocre, like myself, I have concluded whether you get a job or not is down to three factors; who you know, what you know and what you're like, in other words, contacts, experience and personality. Normally, I found at least two of these three factors come into play for most jobs. When it's a crappy job, a fourth factor comes into play which is desperation (both of employer and employee).

After two years of working at 'Halcyon', it again felt like time to move on. This time, however, it was my own decision rather than my Dad's. Gonorrhoea had played its part as the whole humiliating ordeal had made me feel dirty and I went through a few months of soul searching about the direction my life was heading in. Whilst Andy's career at that stage was progressing rapidly along his chosen path in the Law Courts, I was either working or drinking, spending all my money on wild nights out. Andy was right, I deserved no sympathy. I did feel guilty about the way I had behaved, but I was aware that plenty of people I had become involved with had no better morals than me.

I think I would have reached the decision to leave 'Halcyon' irrespective of whether or not I had caught an STD. As much as I had loved working there, Ben had always been great and I had never laughed so much, I knew it was a young man's job and I didn't like the idea of working there when I was older and hopefully had a young family. I knew I needed to change my career path but I didn't know which direction I wanted to head in. To guide me, I started buying job magazines and the Manchester Evening News on a Thursday night when it had a sixteen page job supplement.

Initially, I applied for a couple of jobs in retail, one in Woolworths as a 'Section Manager' and the other as an Assistant Manager in HMV in Manchester City centre. I was interviewed for both and although I felt I interviewed well both times, I wasn't offered either job. I put it down to a lack of experience.

The third job I applied for I didn't realistically expect to get either because I had no relevant experience, no points of contact there and was relying heavily on personality. I can only think I was given an interview for the role as 'Intermediary Account Manager' at Tyrone Building Society because of a lack of other suitable candidates (desperation).

My interview was with one of the Building Society's board members, a man in his early thirties called Sean O'Davey who had flown over from Northern Ireland to spend the day interviewing. My interview was at four o'clock, which I presumed was the last one of the day, which I saw as an opportunity to leave a lasting impression. Sean O'Davey certainly left a lasting impression on me. The interview was held in a small meeting room in The Midland Hotel. I can't remember every word of that interview, as it's sixteen years ago now, but I remember a hell of a lot of it as it was both amusing and bizarre.

I walked in wearing a shirt, trousers and a pair of new black shoes. On the morning of the interview my Dad told me that I should be wearing a suit for these interviews, but I didn't own one and decided there was no chance of me getting this job anyway so it didn't really matter. I decided I would buy one with my next wage from Halcyon as I intended to continue working there until I was offered a new job. I had invested in new shoes though. I should have had the foresight to wear them in before the interview but I was a little naïve. As a result, I must have hobbled into the interview room although my pain was forgotten when I saw Sean O'Davey was wearing a T-shirt, jeans and a pair of, what can loosely be described as, old trainers. My lack of a suit turned out to be a blessing. Sean had been sat behind a desk but came around it to greet me as I entered. He was a small, stocky, muscular man with a broken nose and cauliflower ears. I thought he was perhaps a rugby player or a boxer (turned out he was a gaelic footballer although his ears were just weird ears). He immediately spotted my uncomfortable walk.

"Holy Mother of God! What's the matter with you?"

I was stunned. I had no idea why he was greeting me in such a way. He spat out his words in a very quickly spoken Northern Irish accent. There had been a lot of Irish students that used to come in to the bar and I had already adjusted to their accent. I felt I had an advantage relative to some of the other interviewees who probably spent half their interview saying 'Pardon'. I just had to work out why I had made such a bad first impression.

"What's the matter with me?"

"Are you disabled?"

I was still stunned.

"No."

"What's with the walk then?"

Now I understood. I smiled. If he was going to take the piss out of me for the whole interview, I may as well just take it on the chin.

"New shoes, if I'd have known you were going to turn up in trainers, I wouldn't have spent fifty quid on these."

"Jesus spent his life saving cripples and you've paid fifty quid to turn into one. Take the bloody things off. We're here for a wee chat. I'm not here to torture you!"

Sean said all of this with a broad smile too so it wasn't intimidating in the slightest. I still wasn't quite relaxed enough to be interviewed in my socks though.

"It's OK, I'll be fine once I sit down."

"Fuck that, Harold! Take them off! Life's too short."

"Honestly, I'm fine."

"Listen Harold, it's been a long day. I've had to sit here listening to a load of Graduates spouting shite all day. You're the first normal lad we've had in. I don't want you to ruin your chances by grimacing your way through this. It is Harold, isn't it?"

"I prefer 'H'."

"I don't blame you, who wouldn't? Listen H, if you don't take that bastard pair of shoes off right now you'll start getting on my tits and I'll end up giving the job to one of those wee toffee nosed fuckers."

"OK."

I took my shoes off, carried them over and placed them next to my chair, sat down and the interview began in earnest. Sean told me that Tyrone Building Society had twelve branches in

Northern Ireland (which he said some, depending on their religious persuasion, called 'The Occupied Six Counties' – I wasn't politically aware enough to know what the hell he was on about but it seemed to tickle him when he said it). Following the 'Good Friday Agreement' (again I had no idea what this was either), house prices in Northern Ireland had increased significantly and the demand for mortgages had never been greater. Tyrone Building Society had been founded by Sean's great grandfather and for eighty years there had always been an O'Davey on the board. There were currently three members of the O'Davey family who were board members, Sean, his father Seamus who was Chief Executive and his sister, Siobhan. Sean explained however that Siobhan's surname was now Robinson as she had married some guy called Rodney Robinson ("and you won't believe the amount of shit that caused," Sean said with his already customary laugh). Anyway, thanks to Tyrone Building Society enjoying a period of prosperity never previously experienced in its eighty year history, they were planning to expand onto the British mainland. They had been granted permission to provide mortgages in England and Wales, so were looking for two mortgage 'reps' (Intermediary Account Managers) to travel around the country promoting their mortgage offering to mortgage brokers. One 'rep' would cover Southern England and South Wales, the other would cover Northern England and North Wales.

"Do you know anything about mortgages?" Sean asked.

"A bit."

"OK, tell me what you know. Now don't panic for a second if you don't know much. The whole idea is that we want someone from outside the industry. I don't know how much you know about the mortgage industry in England but the banks have a reputation for being full of pompous pricks. Mortgage brokers are sick and tired of being visited by arseholes who tell them how they should be doing their jobs. We want to revolutionise the market and be seen as a breath of fresh air."

"Well, I know you can have an interest only mortgage, normally backed by an endowment or other repayment vehicle or a capital and interest mortgage. Mortgages can be different loan to values based on..."

Sean had had enough.

"OK, fine, fine. My God mortgages are boring, aren't they? What music do you like?"

"Loads of different stuff."

"Like what? Give me some examples."

"James, The Stone Roses, The Eagles, Fleetwood Mac, Al Stewart, Leonard Cohen.."

"Mighty, an eclectic band of brothers. Do you like Neil Diamond?"

"Some is amazing, some is a bit cheesy."

"OK. What stuff do you like?"

"'Love on the rocks', 'Song Sung Blue', 'Forever In Blue Jeans' and 'Sweet Caroline'."

"OK, good man. I was just checking you weren't shitting me and pretending to know Neil Diamond songs when you didn't. Stand up."

I stood up without questioning why. Sean stood up too.

"Clear your throat."

I gave out a little cough. This didn't satisfy Sean's request.

"No, properly like this."

Sean gave out a hearty sequence of coughs. I copied.

"Good. Now if you can sing the whole of 'Sweet Caroline', the job's yours."

I laughed. To be fair to Sean he had made me feel totally relaxed. I knew the words and had sung it around the house or at Andy's many times. We had played it in 'Halcyon' plenty of times too although technically it was a late 60s/early 70s classic rather than an 80s one. I had never previously sung it in a job interview though.

"Do I need to sing it well?"

Sean smiled.

"No, do you fuck! Just give it your best shot. I'll provide your backing music."

So, Sean hummed the tune and I sang every line. Sean waved his arms from side to side throughout. Once we finished, he clapped joyously.

"That was fucking mighty! 'H' McCoy, you've got balls and my friend, you've got the job. When can you start?"

Chapter Thirty Nine

Working as a mortgage 'rep' for Tyrone Building Society was, as you would imagine, very different to working in an eighties bar in Manchester, but was certainly no less enjoyable. Fundamentally, at their core, the jobs had one key similarity. They were both all about building relationships with your customers. Thankfully, however, this time it was more about business relationships than sexual relationships. My basic wage was more than what I had earned at 'Halcyon', even including the tips and if I hit my business targets, I was given commission on top. They also provided me with a car, a brand new, navy blue, Peugeot 306. I felt rich, grateful, happy and fortunate beyond my wildest dreams.

As Sean had pointed out, there was nothing exciting about mortgages themselves. They were just a facility to allow people to buy homes. The proposition Tyrone Building Society were offering, however, seemed to delight mortgage brokers as it brought something new to the market. I found after I visited people, they would ring friends in the industry spreading the news on my behalf or encouraging them to set up a meeting with me. Brokers were seeking me out as much as I was seeking them. Our niche, without boring you with the intricate details, was a 95% loan to value sub-prime product that was available to people with CCJs (County Court Judgements), defaults and discharged bankrupts, their financial difficulties just had to have been more than twelve months old and they had to demonstrate, through their credit records, that they were now back on the straight and narrow. All our marketing literature had two pictures of roads, one with a sharp bend and the other a long, narrow straight road. There were various captions along the lines of helping people to deal with the bends in the roads and keeping them on the straight and narrow. It wasn't the most original piece of marketing ever used but it seemed to get our point across.

I spent huge amounts of time in the car and clocked up a ridiculous amount of miles. I traded my Peugeot in after two years and it had done 97,000 miles. I was travelling to all the major towns and cities from Birmingham upwards. Most days I did the journeys alone but occasionally someone from Head Office in Omagh would come out with me. I was directly answerable to Sean O'Davey so more often than not it was him. Days out with Sean were always fun, he had a strong belief that our key objective was to be remembered so would often turn up in outrageous clothing. He was a big Manchester United fan so one summer he came across in the full kit, he even changed from trainers to boots before going into each appointment. Some mortgage brokers liked his unique approach, others, particularly the older ones, thought he was showing a lack of respect, but we were a small enough lender to only need a few converts. Some of the brokers who were the most vocal in condemning Sean's choice of clothing ended up using us subsequently.

It was during the first year of my time at 'Tyrone' that I saw out my eighteen months of celibacy. I still went out on dates and had a few short-term girlfriends but nothing serious. If I was dating someone I tended to see them on a Friday night or on a Sunday, as on a Saturday night, Andy, Dad and I had developed a bit of a routine.

From 2001 to 2003, every Saturday, about seven o'clock, Andy would call around to our house with either a bottle of champagne or a bottle of red wine (or very often both) along with assorted crisps, nuts and a big slab of Dairy Milk chocolate (usually Fruit & Nut). The opening of the chocolate was often done ceremoniously with all three of us singing the words from the Frank Muir 'Everyone's A Fruit and Nut Case' advert. After we finished, my Dad would often say 'Poor old Frank' before tearing off the first strip. Prior to the chocolate fest, even prior to Andy's arrival, I would have nipped out to pick up a take away (usually Chinese but sometimes Indian, Italian or English). Once Andy arrived we would then have our meal and a catch up until around half past eight, from then onwards it was 'Classic Comedy Night'.

We would each take a turn, once every three weeks, to pick a certain comedian, comedy double act or team and we would devote the night to watch or listen to a carefully selected collection of their works. For example, one week Dad chose Tony Hancock, so we watched a couple of the 'Hancock Half Hour' television programmes on video (Dad had faithfully kept his old VCR and tapes) and then we listened to three of his 'Hancock Half Hour' radio programmes on cassette when he was joined by the likes of Sid James, Kenneth Williams and Hattie Jacques.

On one particularly memorable Saturday night it was my turn to choose and after a lot of thought I had chosen 'Abbott and Costello'. I thought Lou Costello was an absolute genius and my favourite comedy routine of all time is the 'Who's On First' routine. There are several versions of this but I had managed to get hold of a DVD of their film, 'The Naughty Nineties' which had a particularly good version in it. I knew my Dad had seen the film before, but not for a long time and I guessed (correctly) that Andy might not have seen it.

We watched the film and afterwards put on the Bonus DVD which was a documentary about the lives of 'Abbott and Costello'. It probably wasn't the best idea to have put that on as it dampened the mood somewhat. It hadn't been the most amicable comedy pairing in the world as the duo had plenty of fall outs but aside from their own spats, there was a lot of sadness. Lou Costello and his wife had four children but their only son had drowned as a baby in their swimming pool. Lou himself had died of a heart attack aged only 52 and his wife also succumbed to a heart attack too, within twelve months of Lou's death, aged only 47. We were just hearing about Bud Abbott's gambling and drinking problems in later life when our home phone started to ring. My Dad was struggling with his hip so I went to get it. I remember telling Andy and my Dad not to pause the DVD as I wasn't too concerned about missing any more details about Bud's tragic end. As it turned out, the phone call only added to my darkening mood.

"Hello," I said, picking up the phone in the hallway and sitting down on the lower stairs. I shivered a little as it was cold in our Hall. It was April, so Spring time, but there was always a draught in there and the small radiator could never quite conquer it.

"Is that you, 'H'?" asked a female voice that I didn't recognise straight away.

"It is. Who's that?"

"It's Cathie. How are you 'H'?"

I immediately felt guilty for not recognising her voice. I kept telling Andy that Cathie should have been the love of my life but, despite this, I still hadn't recognised her voice. I had drunk more than my fair share of the red wine and champagne that night which went some way to explaining it.

"I'm great," I lied, concluding that Cathie would not have wanted to listen to stories about Lou Costello's tragic end more than forty years earlier, "what time is it over there?"

"Seven in the morning."

"Sunday morning?"

"Yes."

I am not sure why I did it but every time I spoke to Cathie on the phone, which hadn't been very often around that time, I always ended up asking what time it was in Australia. I always forgot what the time difference was. I remember now. It is seven hours ahead of England in Perth at certain times of the year and eight hours ahead at other times.

"You're up early then."

"I am. Have you been into town, 'H'? I thought if you had been out it might be a good time to catch you."

It felt like a very mundane start to our conversation. It was straight forward and serious. No-one had laughed yet. I slapped myself on the cheeks a few times in an attempt to liven myself up. The last thing I wanted was for Cathie to think I was boring.

"No, me, Andy and Dad have stopped here. Andy'll be going soon. We've been having a few drinks and watching 'Abbott and Costello'. They're really funny."

"I thought you sounded a bit slurry."

"I'm just tired."

"Are they on Granada?"

"Who?"

"Abbott and Costello?"

"No, they're old school American comedians. They were famous in the forties and fifties. Look them up on the internet, you'd find them funny."

"Oh, ok...I will....I was actually ringing with some news."

Cathie's voice lacked its usual exuberance. Selfishly, I was hoping she was about to tell me that her and Keith had split up.

"I'm pregnant, H."

I said nothing. I didn't know what to say. I felt like that short sentence had crushed all my hopes and dreams for the future. I had never wanted things to work out for Cathie and Keith in Australia. I wanted Cathie to hate it there. This was not how I envisaged things working out, Keith and Cathie having an Australian child. Other than death this was the worst news possible.

"Hello, hello....H....are you still there?"

I would have loved to let off some steam. I could have told Cathie she was a fool, that Keith was a knob and she had ruined her own life as well as mine but what good would it have achieved? This was a massive moment in Cathie's life and a little part of me was still delighted for her.

"Sorry Cathie, I must have lost you there for a minute. It must be a bad line. Did you say something?"

"I'm pregnant, H?"

"You're pregnant! Wow! That's fantastic! Congratulations! That's wonderful news, you must be so, so pleased. Are you keeping OK? Are you far gone?"

Cathie laughed.

"Hang on, one question at a time."

"It's brilliant though, Cathie. I'm so pleased for you!"

I laid it on thick. I stayed on the phone for another five minutes asking question after question about the pregnancy. I was interested despite it not being good news for me personally.

Cathie was scared, excited, delighted and nervous. I promised I would fly over to Perth one day to see her and the baby after the birth. I had no intention of going.

After I ended the phone call, I went back into the lounge and broke the news to Andy and Dad. They could tell by my long face that it wasn't news I had been longing to hear. Andy left soon and I gave Dad a hug. He gave me my daily reminder about how much him and my mother loved me and I departed dejectedly to bed.

Chapter Forty

"I'm proud of you, Harry."

I had been sleeping but I sat up in bed when I heard those words, immediately shaking off my drowsiness. It was my mother's voice.

"Mum?"

Once again my curtains were open. Bright lights flooded into my room like petrol on water. I walked over to the window ledge and there was my mother, recreating the scene from several years earlier, perched on a rainbow.

"I didn't think you'd be back, Mum. I thought that last dream was a one-off."

"Aren't you forgetting something, Harry?"

My Mum was a firm believer in politeness, even in my dreams she was unimpressed that I hadn't greeted her in the correct manner.

"Sorry, good morning, Mum."

"Good morning to you too, Harry and what a beautiful day it is set to be. A sunny Sunday in Spring! You need to see if you can get your father up to Saddleworth."

"His hip's bad."

"Just drive up and park up then. Wind your windows down and have a breath of fresh air."

"OK. It's great seeing you again, Mum."

"It's great to be back. I'd have come sooner but you've been willing it to happen. I told you last time, my darling, I can only appear when your brain switches off to the possibility."

I looked directly at my Mum. I felt I could reach out my bedroom window and almost touch her. She was the same beautiful creature she had always been. Not only did she look radiant, she also looked content. Death was treating her well.

"I've had my ups and downs since I last saw you, Mum."

"Yes, I'm aware of that. I'm glad you've left that job in the bar. There were too many unsavoury young ladies who drank in there and you are too emotionally damaged to ignore them. It broke my heart watching you. Your father and I didn't bring you up to behave like that. Honestly Harry, it was so upsetting."

"I know, I'm sorry. The whole Cathie thing screwed me up. I thought she was going to stay and then I hoped she'd come back, now it looks like she'll be in Australia forever."

Mum looked down at my bedroom window with a sympathetic expression.

"We all get hurt in love sometimes, my gorgeous boy. I know I did. We all make mistakes sometimes too. I'm proud of how you've learnt from yours. Don't give up on love though. It will find you when you're ready to embrace it."

I knew it was just a dream but it seemed strange how I was taking advice from my Mum now she was dead. I never used to confide in her or listen to advice from her when she was alive. Was this the Mum I didn't give enough of a chance to when I was younger or was my mind just creating the Mum I wished I'd had? The Mum that I wished was still around for me now.

"I'm scared I'll end up on my own, Mum. I'm not designed to be on my own. People like Andy are good on their own, but I'm not. I want to be a husband and a father one day but it doesn't seem to be happening. I'm twenty five soon and I've never felt more alone."

"Twenty five is nothing. Your poor old Dad is almost seventy nine. He'll be eighty next year. He wasn't meant to be alone in his old age. Take good care of him."

The light that emanated from the rainbow began to fade again.

"Mum! Don't go. I need to carry on speaking to you."

"There's nothing we can do, my love. Dreams are fleeting. You just feel sad right now, Harry, because of Cathie's news. I thought you handled that very well. I'm glad you feel happy for her too. A woman receives no greater gift in life than a child. Cathie will be a wonderful mother."

"I know that, Mum. You were too."

"Your time for fatherhood will come, Harry. One day you will be an amazing father. Just be patient. Love will find you. Never forget that love will find you."

Chapter Forty One

The following Monday I had appointments booked at mortgage brokers in Manchester City Centre. I was visiting the likes of Savills and John Charcol's, so I arranged to meet Andy for lunch. He was at bar school in Manchester. I'm not exactly sure what that meant, Andy had tried to explain it but it hadn't properly sunk in. I think it was another qualification that was necessary after his Law degree to enable him to become a barrister. Andy had graduated from Hull University with a first class honours degree which was not a surprise to anyone who knew him.

Andy was in good spirits during that lunch in Manchester and was explaining to me, in gaps between eating large slices of pepperoni pizza, why he thought I should start dating a virgin.

"H, the only girl you've ever slept with, out of hundreds, who could possibly have been a virgin was Joanna Barry. You've had your fair share of slags since and it's only brought heartbreak to your door. Joanna was lovely. I think your Cinderella search this time around should be for a girl with an unbroken hymen. I don't mean a sixteen or seventeen year old, I just mean perhaps someone religious or someone socially or geographically isolated. A 'Brooke Shields' type."

I pinched a piece of pepperoni off Andy's plate. I had ordered a 'ham and mushroom' pizza but had eaten all mine whilst Andy was rabbiting on and was still hungry.

"Andy, we're in the twenty first century now, pal. You can't call a girl who has a lot of sex a slag."

Andy looked horrified.

"I can't? Why not? How many women have you slept with?"

"Quite a few."

"More or less than two hundred?"

I did a quick calculation in my head. During my time at 'Halcyon' I had probably slept with three women a week, on average, over a two year period. Over one hundred weeks averaging three women a week. An accurate figure was probably over three hundred.

"Maybe not quite that many," I lied quietly. Three hundred wasn't a good number. I genuinely wished I hadn't acted the way I had.

"OK," Andy continued, "for arguments sake let's call it one hundred and eighty. I think it's fair to say you've been a slag. Very rarely did you have any interest in seeing any of them after that first sexual encounter, very rarely did you go through a 'getting to know you' exercise before you took yours and their clothes off, the evidence in the local STD clinic suggests you weren't a regular wearer of protection...unfortunately 'slag' seems an appropriate term. Now if some of the ladies you fucked (and again unfortunately the terminology appears appropriate) behaved in exactly the same manner, then why should I not use exactly the same word?"

Once in a while Andy would irritate me rather than amuse me with his eccentricities. This was one of those times. I took another piece of pepperoni pizza off his plate. He slapped my hand but I took the pizza anyway.

"It's not a nice word to use to depict anyone."

"I'm not saying it is a nice word. My argument is that it's an appropriate one. Anyway, does it really matter what word I use? The point is you need someone that isn't that type of young lady. In fact, you need the exact opposite, a 'cock teaser'. What's the saying? 'Cock teasers don't spread diseases.'

"There is no such saying, as well you know."

"Well there should be!"

"Andy, why are we even having this conversation? I've not slept with anyone for months now. I'm already a changed man."

"I don't want any more pepperoni. It's bad for my acid reflux. Do you want it?"

I was going to ask why Andy had even ordered it in the first place but decided one weird conversation was enough.

"No thanks."

"I might ask for a doggy bag then, seems a shame to waste it. Anyway, the reason we are having this conversation is because you had been telling me about your weird recurring dream during which your angelic mother flies over a rainbow."

"I didn't say she flew over the rainbow."

"What does she do then?"

"She sits on it."

"You do know you can't sit on a rainbow, don't you, H?"

"Andy, it's a dream. Dreams don't always follow the rules of gravity."

"I'll concede to you on that one. The point is you were telling me about your rainbow dream and I was saying you dreamt it as a reaction to the revelation from Cathie that she is expecting Keith's child....so, I was saying, it's about time you had a serious girlfriend again but not a slag....sorry, not a lady who regularly enjoys the pleasure of a variety of different men and their appendages."

We had already discussed my Mum's re-appearance in my dreams in as much detail as I wanted to discuss for one day. As for discussing the potential of me dating a virginal new girlfriend, well that just seemed a ridiculous topic of conversation. My next serious relationship would not be based on that lady's historical sexual experience or lack thereof. The problem with Andy was that you couldn't just ask him to 'drop it' because that would just encourage him to mention it more. I decide the best form of defence was attack.

"What about you?" I asked.

"What about me?" Andy said, sounding somewhat surprised, as though I was asking him whether he thought he could be my next virginal partner. I guess there was an element of validity in this line of thought, but only in the virginal element.

"Isn't it about time you shook off your virginal tag?"

Andy looked uncomfortable. I rarely saw him blush but he appeared to be blushing. When he spoke, everything was spoken hurriedly,

"My virginal tag? I think you'll find the error you are making here is one of assumption. Firstly, you are assuming I am a virgin and secondly, you are assuming that if I did engage in any sexual relations that I would tell you. Just because you tell me everything does not necessarily mean I tell you everything."

Andy did tell me everything. He was definitely still a virgin.

"Andy, there is no way you could keep any sort of secret from me, especially one of this magnitude. I know you too well. If you had dated a woman you'd be keen to tell me so I could dispel all the gay rumours and if you had dated a man, I think you would confide in me because you know I'd be pleased for you and wouldn't come across as a homophobic arsehole."

"No, you see you've got it all wrong. I have no interest in dispelling any rumours. Why would it matter if people I don't care about want to presume I'm gay because I'm outrageous, theatrical and expressive? Let them presume what they want to presume. I don't care what people think, surely you should know that by now. The truth is, the real truth, is that I am a virgin and I will always be a virgin because frankly I have no interest in dating anyone."

"Seriously?"

"Yes, seriously. It has never crossed my mind."

"What do you want from life then?"

The whole subject of Andy's virginity had originally just been an attempt to deflect the conversation away from me dating virgins. Now though, I was genuinely interested in trying to get inside Andy's head for a little while. He was right, I was more candid than him and Andy's sexuality or asexuality was a subject we tended to subconsciously avoid or at least I did. If Andy was prepared to open up for a little while, I wanted to seize the moment.

"I want to be a barrister."

"Ok, so on your deathbed in sixty years' time, you'll have no-one around you as you'll never have married and never had any kids. In the obituary column, you want it to say, Andrew Corcoran sadly passed away on Friday aged 86, after a long illness. He leaves no wife, no kids, but he was a barrister."

Andy dismissed this potential future tragedy with a dramatic flick of his left hand.

"It doesn't matter what is in my obituary column. I won't be around to read it."

"That's not the point I'm trying to make and you know it. I'm not religious but I think I have a reason to exist. I want to marry, I want to have children and I want to try to be half as good a father as my father has been to me. What do you want from life if it doesn't involve anyone else but yourself?"

"I've no idea, H, I've never thought about it."

I pressed the point.

"Well, think about it now. If you lead the life you want to lead, on your deathbed, what do you want your last thought to be?"

"This morphine is strong shit."

I didn't want Andy to be his normal, dry witted, sarcastic self. Our friendship very rarely discussed anything of true meaning and if it did, it was me telling Andy about things that affected my life. A lot of male conversations tend to just skim the surface but I wanted this one to be different.

"Come on Andy, be serious for a moment. What would you want your last thoughts to be if you lived your ideal life?"

To give him his due, Andy seemed to give it some genuine thought.

"I don't know....something like, well it looks like this is the end. I've had a great life, I've never struggled for money or food. I've been a good son to my Mum, a loyal friend to 'H' McCoy, a superb barrister and..."

Andy hesitated. It seemed like this was a rare moment of true candidness and then the barriers came back up. I wanted to knock them back down.

"And what?" I asked.

"It doesn't matter."

"Yes, it does. To me it matters a lot. Go on! Say what you were going to say."

"I was going to say, a superb barrister and a bloody fine actor."

I was confused.

"Actor?"

"Well, there you go 'H' McCoy. What was it you were saying a few moments ago? I couldn't keep a secret from you? Well, I've proved you wrong straight away! My secret is out. For the last ten years' I've done amateur dramatics."

The fact that Andy did amateur dramatics seemed totally logical. The fact that he had done it for ten years and never once told me about it, seemed completely illogical.

"I don't get it. Why would you keep that from me? I'd have come and watched."

"I know you would. That's exactly why I didn't tell you."

"Nope, you've thrown me. I still don't get it."

"I have two parents who have always been more bothered about their own lives than mine. I have had hundreds of friends who have come into my life for a while and then faded back out of it. There has only ever been one person in my life who has ever genuinely cared about me and that's you, H. On that basis, your opinion is the only opinion that really matters to me. So, if you came to see me in a play, you'd tell me I was good, I know you would, but if you didn't believe it, I would know straight away. I couldn't allow that to happen. It would crush me."

Chapter Forty Two – October 2007

I was standing outside the back of Andy's mother's home with Mrs Corcoran. It was drizzling. I was just with Mrs Corcoran, which was very weird. In over twenty years of knowing Andy, I had never had a one to one conversation with Mrs Corcoran. She was smoking, which was less weird, she had a cigarette in her mouth more than Kojak had a lollipop in his. Neither Andy nor Mrs Corcoran now smoked in the house, hence the reason we were outside. Andy had been around at his Mum's too, but had left five minutes earlier for drama rehearsals. Mrs Corcoran had asked me to stay behind so she could have a word before I left, so there I was, on a damp Rochdale afternoon, watching Mrs Corcoran smoke in her slippers. After a bit of pleasant small talk, Mrs C cut to the chase.

"Your father tells me you're unhappy."

"Well, I wouldn't go as far as to say unhappy," I replied awkwardly, "just surprised."

"I understand that love," Mrs C said, taking a drag on her cigarette. She was probably twenty years younger than my father, but a lifetime of chain smoking hadn't been kind on her complexion, " I guess it takes a while to compute when your father starts dating again at eighty five."

Not just 'starts dating again', starts dating your best mate's mother. That takes some getting your head around, dating your best mate's mother who has never exactly showered your best mate with love over the last twenty years.

"I'm sure I'll get used to it," I tried to say this with a slither of genuine positivity, but I don't think I could muster even a fragment of positivity. I couldn't understand for the life of me what the silly old fool was doing and I couldn't understand what my father was doing either.

"Is it the fact that he is dating or the fact that he is dating me that is the issue, 'H'? I know I am the first since your mother died but that's a long time ago now. Do you not think your father should have some happiness in his twilight years?"

I very much wanted my Dad to find some happiness, but I couldn't understand how he could find it with Andy's mother. After Andy's Dad had left her, Mrs C had joined Dad's walking group (I think 'Rochdale Rambling Society' may have been the correct terminology) and had visited our home several times whilst he was recuperating from his hip operation. Now he was back walking again, they had started doing things together outside the group. They would regularly go to see plays together in Manchester, lunch out together and I think they had even been ballroom dancing together a couple of times. It was all very bizarre. I suppose I should have been happy for my father and I would have been if it had been anyone else. I just thought Mrs Corcoran was up to something.

"Look Mrs Corcoran..."

"Call me Maggie..."

"OK Maggie," it felt very wrong calling her by her first name, she would always be Mrs Corcoran or Mrs C to me, "if my Dad seems happy whilst he's with you, I'm sure I'll grow to be happy for him. I'm just adjusting to it all. Just don't screw him around or expect too much of him. He's eighty five. He's not going to be water skiing in the South of France or partying in Magaluf."

"We prefer San Antonio, love, the music scene's better," Maggie Corcoran cackled after she made this unfunny joke. It was a horrible, phlegm inducing cackle. How was my father even remotely attracted to this woman? I waited until she calmed herself down before I spoke again.

"I'm going to get going, Maggie. Thanks for having a quiet word. I appreciate it. As I am sure you appreciate, I just have my father's best interests at heart."

I didn't appreciate it one bit. I resented it, like I resented her.

"No problem, love. Are you going to go to our Andy's show?"

It was a 'play' not a 'show', but I was going. For the first time in sixteen years, I was being allowed to see Andy perform. I was really looking forward to it.

"Yes, I am. What night are you and Dad going?"

"Friday."

"Oh right, that's a shame, my tickets are for the Saturday."

I hadn't bought my ticket yet, but I would definitely be buying tickets for the Saturday. I was going to buy two. I had no idea who I would be going with, but buying a solitary ticket felt like I was coming to terms with my newly found sad, lonely existence.

"Never mind," Maggie said, dropping her cigarette and extinguishing it with a twist of her slipper. What a trollop!

"It'll be the first time I've ever seen him in anything," I said, without thinking, then cursed myself inwardly for engaging in further conversation.

"Really? Now that does surprise me. I know he's my son and I'm biased but he's excellent. He could make a career out of it, I'm sure, but I guess a barrister pays better."

'Stop showing off, you ridiculous woman,' I thought to myself. Andy's achievements in life have been through his own drive and ability. He had done them despite his parents not because of them.

"I can't wait to see it. Bye Maggie."

I strode off as quickly as I could without breaking into a run. The drizzle had eased and the sun had started to come out. As I walked I began thinking about Andy's forthcoming play and my father's relationship with Maggie Corcoran. The former I was genuinely excited about although I hoped I really rated Andy's performance as I would feel terrible if I thought he was hopeless. I also hoped he didn't over think my presence and give a bad performance on that particular night.

Andy was going to be in Rochdale Amateur Operatic Society's performance of 'Of Mice and Men' at the 'Gracie Fields Theatre'. Performances started a week on Wednesday and were on for four nights (five performances in total as there was a matinee performance on the Saturday afternoon). I had never seen the stage play, the film or read the book 'Of Mice and Men' so knew very little about it. Andy told me there were two main parts, 'George' and 'Lennie' and he was going to be playing the part of 'Lennie'. I asked him not to tell me anything more about it, as I wanted to go without having any awareness of the plot. Andy kept telling me what a brilliant play it was, but often when people do that, they set the bar too high and it turns out to be a disappointment.

As for the not so delectable Maggie and my father, I wasn't sure why I was so resentful about their relationship but I hated the fact that they were together. Perhaps it was just because I felt she had never been a good mother to Andy. It wasn't as though she had stubbed her cigarettes out on his arms or locked him in a cupboard, she just didn't devote much of her time to him. Andy was completely unphased by my father's courtship with his mother, even joking if our parents decided to get married that we would be 'step brothers'. That was never going to happen, as far as I was aware his mother and father were still married.

Perhaps I was just jealous that they had a relationship as at that point in my life I was single. I knew I wasn't being fair to Sandy Josephs by keeping our relationship going. I didn't love her with anywhere near the amount of passion I felt I needed to, to commit to marriage. She was a good person and deserved to have someone who cared for her far more than I did and although I knew I was breaking her heart, I also knew, further down the line of life, she would thank me for it. We had split up six weeks earlier and about ten days after that, Dad announced that he was dating Maggie.

As I walked home on that damp Autumnal Sunday afternoon, I managed a half smile as the sun's attempts to break through the clouds had been rewarded with a faint rainbow. I wondered how Mum would have felt about Dad dating Maggie. I was sure she wouldn't have liked it either. Mum would have felt Dad could have done much better.

I was daydreaming as I took a step out on to Bury Road and I swiftly stepped back when I realised a car was approaching. It would have been my fault if I'd have been run over, but the driver was driving a little too fast. I stared into the car with annoyance. I hated thoughtless driving. As I looked, I was sure I recognised the driver. It was Mussarat Miandad, a girl I'd been to school with, but even more bizarrely, I was almost certain it was Cathie Squires in the passenger seat. It didn't look like they had spotted me as they were too busy talking. I watched the car, a green Audi A4, head up to the traffic lights and stop on 'Red'. I could see there was a child seat in the back of the car. Was I going mad? Was Cathie Squires back in Rochdale?

Chapter Forty Three

"It upsets me, Mum. I can't help thinking of it as a betrayal."

I had climbed up on to my window ledge and was sprawled across it, looking out on to the rainbow for a third time. It was a bit of a child like position for a thirty one year old man to take up, but given I knew it was a dream, I wasn't too concerned about the neighbours seeing me.

"Honestly Harry, I think you have this all wrong. Who exactly do you think your father is betraying?"

"Us."

"You and me? Come off it. How long have I been dead? I don't see this as a betrayal of me at all."

It was probably a rhetorical question but I answered anyway.

"You've been dead for over fifteen years, Mum."

Mum's face, perched on top of that rainbow, wasn't looking as calm and peaceful as on the two previous occasions I had seen her. She looked more driven and passionate, as if she was determined to make her point. She had already done her utmost to make it.

"Well there you go then," she said, "he's been a widower for almost half your lifetime. Don't forget this isn't the first time he's been a widower either. Give the poor man a break, let him enjoy this time with Maggie without trying to make him feel bad about spending time with her."

I could see my mother's point but I wouldn't say I wholeheartedly agreed with her.

"He could do so much better than Maggie Corcoran though, Mum. I thought you would be the one person who would agree with me on that."

My Mum's face seemed to come closer. I suppose it was an optical illusion but then everything about rainbows and the appearance of my mother is an optical illusion.

"He's eighty five, love. Eighty five year old men are just happy having a little bit of female company. If your Dad had met someone when he was in his early seventies, he may well have been more choosy, but back then, for both our sakes, he sacrificed that opportunity. I don't begrudge him a bit of happiness now. You shouldn't either."

"She's a scrote though, Mum."

"Harry!"

"What?"

"You do know that's short for scrotum, don't you, Harry?"

"I'm thirty one years old, Mum!"

"Oh yes, sorry I forgot that. You're still sixteen to me. I don't think I have ever met the woman but I'm sure she's fine."

I had spotted a flaw in Mum's argument.

"Why have you not met her?" I queried.

"Well, when I was alive, our paths just never crossed. You would go around to Andy's house or he would come to ours."

"I know that, but you could see her now if you wanted to. You can see anything you choose to, within reason, isn't that what you told me?"

My mother's expression changed. Her determined face disappeared and it was replaced by a more vulnerable one.

"I've made the decision not to watch your father when he's with Maggie Corcoran."

"Because it upsets you."

"Yes, Harry, because it upsets me, but that doesn't mean I'm not pleased for George. I understand why you are upset and I understand why you don't want to spend a lot of time with them when they are together, but, for your Dad's sake, you need to manage your emotions. Your father, more than anyone else I know, deserves to be happy."

"I know that."

"Maybe you should start listening to some tranquil music, I think that would help. Have you heard anything by Ludovic Kennedy? 'I Gordi' is a lovely piece of music. I think you would love it. It calms the soul."

Once again, the rainbow began to fade. I started to get flustered, I couldn't remember the name of the music.

"Tell me again, Mum, what was it called?"

"Oh, Harry, you know I've never been the best with artists and titles. I think it's Ludovic Kennedy, 'I Gordi'. It's a piano piece. Give it a go."

As soon as the rainbow faded, I opened my eyes. I lifted myself up out of bed and wrote down 'Ludovic Kennedy' and 'I Gordi'. Was there really such a piece of music? I'd check it out in the morning but if there was, it was going to seriously freak me out. Music recommendations from your mother who died in 1992 are just not normal.

Chapter Forty Four

As soon as I woke up the following morning, I switched my computer on. I immediately went on to 'Google' and keyed in Ludovic Kennedy. I discovered there was indeed a Ludovic Kennedy, who was now Sir Ludovic Kennedy. He was a writer and broadcaster not a musician. I laughed at first, through relief, as I had obviously just invented this tale in my head, perhaps after seeing Sir Ludovic Kennedy on the television or in one of my Dad's newspapers. There was nothing to indicate that he also wrote tranquil piano music.

I don't know what made me key the name 'Ludovic' into my keyboard again after breakfast, before I headed out to work, but second time around I noticed another name came up. 'Ludovico Einaudi'. Images came up of a bald headed, Italian man with greying tufts at the side. When I saw some of the images were of him sat behind a piano, my heart started beating faster and my palms became sweaty. Further investigations revealed that Ludovico Einaudi had not written a piece of music called 'I Gordi', he had, however, written a piece called 'I Giorni'. After trailing through the internet for ten minutes, I managed to download it. Within ten seconds of listening to it, my eyes began filling up. By the time the six minute piece was finished, tears were streaming down my face. There were two reasons for this. Firstly, it was the most beautiful piece of music I had ever heard. Secondly, somehow, I didn't understand how, I felt something amazing was happening. This was no longer just a dream. My mother was communicating with me from beyond the grave.

Chapter Forty Five

Andy was rehearsing five times a week during the week that preceded the performances of 'Of Mice and Men' so was reluctant to drive over to Rochdale from Manchester on one of his two days off. I needed to see him though so I said I would head over to Manchester. I was desperate to hear his views on my third dream, which I was now thinking of as more of an apparition.

We arranged to meet at the strangely named 'Gorilla' bar, a trendy place underneath the railway arches on Whitworth Street West. We had one drink each sat at stools at the bar, but just as we were finishing them, a table became free by the window so we went to sit there. I felt better once we were sat away from the bar. I wouldn't have felt comfortable letting strangers and bar staff hear my apparition story. Once we were sat alone, I relayed it to Andy.

"What do you think?" I asked once I had told Andy the whole tale, "Do you think I am being haunted by my mother?"

"I doubt it. Do you want me to tell you what I think this is?"

"Go on."

"It's a coping mechanism."

It hurt me to hear Andy say that. It felt as though he was pouring scorn on my experience.

"How do you mean?"

It was unusual to see Andy looking uncomfortable but there were beer mats on the table and he started to peel off the corners of one. I presumed he was going to pick holes in my personality. He didn't mind doing it in a jokey way, but this wasn't a time for jokes. This recurring dream was starting to fascinate and concern me in equal measure.

"Well, this is the third time that your Mum has appeared to you in a dream. Think about when these times were. The first time was the night you shared your bed with Cathie. You were feeling anxious about whether you should make a move and equally anxious about Cathie moving to Australia. What happens? Your Mum appears to you in a dream.

Fast forward a few years and we're around at yours having a comedy night. I miss those comedy nights, by the way, they used to be great. I can't remember why we stopped having them. Anyway, on the Abbott & Costello night, you get a call from Cathie telling you she's pregnant. You come back into the Lounge from the Hall looking like you are about to burst into tears at any second. That night, sure enough, your mother arrives in a second dream.

Jump forward again to modern day, 2007 and my Mum starts dating your Dad. Pretty fucking weird, I'll give you that, but in the whole swing of things, as long as the old dears are happy, who gives a shit? The answer to that is you, 'H'. You hate it. It disturbs you as your old man hasn't dated anyone in the fifteen years since your Mum died. Your anxiety returns. My Mum asks if she can have a word with you which adds to your discomfort. Furthermore, during your walk home from my Mum's to yours, following this uncomfortable conversation, you think you spot the love of your life. Anxious and confused that night you go to sleep and lo and behold your mother re-appears. Are you seeing a pattern here? I certainly am."

Yeh, I get it. There's a pattern. If I'm stressing about something you're suggesting I subconsciously conjure up my Mum to help get things off my chest."

"Something along those lines."

"That doesn't explain the music though. I've never heard of Ludovico Einaudi or 'I Giorni'. If I've never heard of him, how could I store his music in my brain?"

Andy scratched his head.

"I'm sure we don't properly grasp everything our brain takes in. If you go into your kitchen and your Dad's listening to Classic FM, I'm sure not every piece of music consciously registers but it might subconsciously register. It probably wasn't quite stored correctly in your memory banks so that's why the artist and title were slightly skewed."

Andy's explanation was more logical than any explanation that I had come up with. It still seemed slightly implausible, however, that I would hear the most beautiful piece of music I've ever heard, but instead of registering it, I would just store it away in my brain for another day like a dog with a mighty fine bone. I had not just heard that piece of music once now, I had listened to it over and over again and every time I heard it I cried. If it always created this reaction within me, how could it possibly not have registered at all first time around? It still didn't quite sit right with me.

Once you have discussed something there is only a certain amount of time you can devote to it before you find yourselves going 'round and 'round in circles, so after talking through different perspectives on it for half an hour or so, over a couple more beers, I decided to let it go with a 'mystery unresolved' tag still floating around my brain. Mum might just keep appearing when I was worked up and I might never fully understand why.

I often found that conversations with Andy always seemed to revolve around my life. I tried to get him to open up to me about his, but he always just said he much preferred talking about mine. Thus, once the rainbow dreams had been exhausted, we moved on to discussing the possibility of Cathie's return to England. The more I thought about it, the more I was convinced it was Cathie in Mussarat's car. Why though, would she come back to England without letting me know? I had looked on both Mussarat's and Cathie's Facebook pages and there was no mention of a holiday or a return to England. Neither of them were prolific Facebook users though and it had been several weeks since either had written a post.

"So what happens this time?" Andy asked.

"In what way?"

"Well, there are three ways this could go. Firstly, there's the possibility that you may have been mistaken and Cathie may still be sunning that beautiful blonde hair of hers in Australia. If that's the case, it's all very simple and nothing changes. The second potential scenario is that she's back with her little lad. What's his name again?"

"Max."

"OK, she's back with Keith and Max or just Max, visiting family for a few weeks. They know it's a brief visit, they know they can't get around everyone so they're keeping it low key. From your perspective, again not much you can do. It's the third potential scenario that could bring Kitty and the rainbows to your front garden every evening for a long time."

The third scenario was the perfect scenario, that Cathie had come home because she'd split from Keith. I didn't understand why Andy was hinting that this was potentially troublesome.

"The third scenario is that Cathie and Keith are finished," I said, before Andy had the opportunity to say it.

"No, it isn't," Andy said, shaking his head, "Cathie and Keith have a child together now, they can never be finished. The third scenario is that they have split up and Cathie has come home to lick her wounds. Do you really want to become entangled in their mess? There will be emotional issues, financial issues and maintenance issues. I could go on all day with issues. Once a child is involved, a split is always going to be very messy. Also, and this is a potentially huge problem, you have no idea if Cathie has ever had or will ever have any romantic interest in you. When do you put your cards on the table? Straight away when the timing could be really bad? Two years' time and risk losing her in the interim? It just sounds like one massive head fuck. If I were you, I'd keep well clear. If Cathie and Keith have split up, I would let the asbestos-like dust of a broken relationship settle and then decide if you want to risk everything in a year or two."

I let Andy get the whole thing off his chest without commenting. I don't think he came up for air during his whole little speech. I appreciated his concerns were genuine though and I knew he was once again just seeking to protect me. He was, as he probably knew, just wasting his breath. I had already lost Cathie once and if she was single I would do whatever it took to make sure next time I was at the front of the queue.

For obvious reasons, when I arrived back home that night I played James' song 'Next Lover' on repeat until I fell asleep.

Chapter Forty Six

Cathie and Keith had split up. One evening the following week, after a busy day up in the Lake District and Carlisle, I was posting something on Facebook about tickets still being available for 'Of Mice and Men' at Gracie Fields Theatre, when I noticed Mussarat was on-line on Facebook so I poked her. A virtual conversation then took place between us and I tactfully managed to extract as much information as I could from Mussarat, about Cathie's predicament, which I subsequently felt was a little ironic, as Mussarat was a dentist.

Despite Keith becoming a father, it transpired that his adulterous days had not been put behind him and Cathie had decided he had used up his 'one last chance'. She had flown back to her parents with Max and, at this stage, didn't know whether Keith would stay in Australia or follow her back to England to be near his son. From Cathie's perspective, she was unsure how long she would remain in Rochdale for either. Cathie was, however, determined not to take Keith back.

I didn't just drop it in straight away about 'Of Mice and Men', dozens of messages went backwards and forwards between us, during which I established that Mussarat and Cathie had met up on Saturday night. Cathie and Max had slept over at Mussarat and her husband's house in Norden and I had spotted her driving them back to Cathie's Mum and Dad's on Sunday afternoon. It was only when I felt the vibe that Mussarat was about to sign off Facebook that the following interaction took place :-

ME: She's had a terrible time then, hasn't she?

MUSSARAT: Horrendous. I am so thankful that I have a good husband.

ME: Yes, sounds like you nabbed yourself one of the good ones there, Mussarat.

*Mussarat was married to an orthopaedic surgeon who seemed like a loving, family man. Andy and I had both been to their wedding. It was the first Muslim wedding I had ever been to. It was a great occasion but must have been draining for the happy couple as it felt like there had been an open invitation to the whole Muslim community. I have never seen so many people in one room.

MUSSARAT: I did!

ME: Listen, stop me if you think this is inappropriate but I have an idea I want to run past you.

MUSSARAT: Sounds interesting. Go on.

ME: On Saturday night I have two tickets to go to see 'Of Mice and Men' at Gracie Fields because Andy is in it.

MUSSARAT: Andy Corcoran ???

ME: Yes.

MUSSARAT: You never told me he did acting.

ME: Did I not? Probably because he didn't tell me for years either. This will be the first time I've ever seen him perform.

MUSSARAT: Not like Andy to keep his cards close to his chest (other than about his sexuality I suppose). Still, I can't say I'm surprised he does acting. Everything has always been a drama for Andy.

ME: Mussarat! Remember this is my best friend you are talking about.

MUSSARAT: I know! True though, isn't it?

ME: I suppose so. Anyway, what I was trying to tell you was that I bought two tickets ages ago but I've recently split with my girlfriend so I have a spare one.

MUSSARAT: Thanks 'H' it's very kind of you to offer but Imran and I have plans on Saturday night.

ME: Sorry Mussarat, I meant I was thinking of asking Cathie.

MUSSARAT: I know! Just teasing.

ME: Do you think she would come? Just as a friend, of course. It would be lovely to see her again. I do understand a little of what she's going through after my own recent split. Would you be able to ask her if she fancies coming with me?

MUSSARAT: H, I really hope you don't mind me being honest with you. I will ask but I really don't think she'll go. From what I could gauge from seeing her over the weekend, everything is very raw right now. She was with Keith for fifteen years and is understandably very hurt by his actions.

ME: I totally understand. I do think though that a night out with an old school friend might lift her spirits a bit.

MUSSARAT: I'll ask, H, but don't get your hopes up.

ME: Thanks Mussarat, I really appreciate it.

MUSSARAT: I'll message you on Facebook tomorrow and let you know what she says.

Chapter Forty Seven

I was sat in the front room in 'The Cemetery'. I have heard some people refer to that room as 'The Snug' but as far as I'm concerned every room in that pub is pretty snug, it's a snug pub. I found myself to be, temporarily, the only person in there, so took the opportunity to blow my nose. I could feel the signs of redness appearing underneath my nostrils.

Cathie came in, carefully balancing a bottle of white wine in a cooler in one hand and gripping two empty wine glasses in the other. She was wearing blue jeans and a 'Fat Face' hoody. The hood was understandably down and her hair spilled into it like a waterfall of honey. Every time I had looked at Cathie all evening part of my brain was in awe of her beauty. There was also a more level headed part of my brain that kept warning me to get a grip. I had advised myself several times that evening to 'Get A Grip'.

"It's for medicinal purposes," Cathie explained, "I believe it's excellent for runny noses, blotchy faces and watery eyes!"

We exchanged warm smiles.

"Give me a break. It's been an emotional evening."

I think Mussarat was more than a little taken aback that Cathie agreed to go to 'Of Mice and Men' with me. I pictured her asking in a 'I know you won't do this but I'm obliged to ask you' type manner. Mussarat messaged me on Facebook the evening after our previous messages to say she had asked Cathie about 'Of Mice and Men' and she was keen to go. Prior to passing over Cathie's mobile number, she felt duty bound to remind me once more that Cathie had been through a major ordeal recently and I must tread very carefully around her. My initial thoughts were that women have a tendency to put a protective arm around those closest to them but when I thought about it, I could imagine Andy doing the same for me.

As soon as I was given Cathie's number I phoned it. I was in my thirties. I didn't want to find myself reverting back to my procrastinating former self. I had no idea where this would head, if anywhere at all, but I wanted to see Andy's play and I wanted Cathie to be with me when I did.

I wouldn't go as far as to say that our initial conversation was awkward but it was pretty clinical and business like. Cathie's relationship break-up was not discussed. We just agreed that I would pick her up from her parents' house at half past six on Saturday evening.

Saturday couldn't have come fast enough nor could half past six when Saturday did eventually arrive. By twenty past six I was already on Cathie's parents' road, but didn't want to appear as over eager as I actually was, so I pulled up a few doors down and listened to Leonard Cohen's 'Hey That's No Way To Say Goodbye'. The first few lines of that song had, for several years, been used to stimulate a fantasy image in my head of me waking up each morning in a bed next to Cathie. The rest of the song, however, was more of a reality check, given it was about being apart.

Once the song finished I drove the extra few yards down to Cathie's Mum and Dad's house and parked up outside their home. Cathie greeted me at the door with a gentle hug and a kiss on the cheek before inviting me inside. She showed me through to the lounge where her parents were sat on the sofa watching a young boy kick a balloon around the room. Cathie's parents looked considerably older and frailer than the previous time I had seen them around six years earlier. I immediately felt guilty that they were being given the responsibility of looking after their lively grandson for the evening. Max was a miniature, boyish version of his mother with ringlets of long blond hair.

"This is Max," Cathie said, providing an explanation that I didn't need.

"Hi Max," I said cheerily but Max was too busy chasing his balloon around the room to hear my greeting.

Cathie walked over and grabbed the balloon into her stomach. Max looked at her with a protruded bottom lip.

"Can I have it back please, Mummy?"

"Not until you say hello to 'H'. He's an old friend from when I was a little girl and went to school."

"Hi H," Max said without even looking in my direction, "Mummy, can I have my balloon back now please?" Max asked again in his very strong, very cute Australian accent.

After a more genuine greeting from Max he was allowed his balloon back. I then briefly spoke to Cathie's Mum and Dad but I formed the impression that they weren't overly comfortable with Cathie heading out with me and Cathie also seemed keen to get going.

"Were your Mum and Dad not happy about you coming out with me tonight?" I asked in the car.

"It isn't you 'H', it's me. They're disappointed in me. They are very much of the generation that believes you work hard to resolve your differences no matter how difficult that might be. They have no idea how bad things got."

During the rest of the short car journey and subsequently in the bar in the theatre Cathie spoke candidly about her break up with Keith. There had been several affairs, probably several others that Cathie had been unaware of. Trust broke down. Cathie said she hated herself for doing it but she found herself checking his phone, trailing through his browser history on his Laptop and checking out who his female friends were on Facebook. She said her heightened levels of anxiety probably drove them even further apart and they just found themselves spiralling out of love. She had wanted to maintain the family unit for Max's sake but eventually it became fairer to Max to leave it. At this stage, she didn't know whether they were going to stay in England. She also didn't know whether Keith would follow them over because, despite everything that had gone on between them as a couple, he had always been a good Dad to Max. Cathie said she was just living day to day but could say with utter conviction that she would never go back to Keith. She said both her and Max deserved more than that.

After a glass of white wine for Cathie and a diet coke for me, we headed into the theatre. 'Gracie Fields' is a modern looking theatre which to me looked like one of those big lecture halls you see in American films. The rows are steep to ensure if you were ever stuck behind a giant like Andy your view would not be obscured. There is also plenty of room to stretch your legs out which I was pleased about when I sat down as I knew my legs would get twitchy if I got bored. Thankfully boredom was not an emotion I experienced.

Andy had arranged for us to have seats six rows back, dead centre of the front stalls as he felt this was the best vantage point in the theatre. Prior to 'Of Mice and Men' beginning, I must admit it felt like a necessary inconvenience to enable me to have an evening out with Cathie. On reflection, I feel awful that I had such low expectations. Once it started, I very quickly allowed my mind to be transformed to America during the Great Depression. The next two hours were magical.

'Of Mice and Men' is a twentieth century classic by John Steinbeck which seemingly most people have seen or read in one form or another over the years but I hadn't. It is a story of the special friendship between George Milton and Lennie Small, two ranch workers who are moving around looking for work during the Depression. George is the smaller, more intelligent one whilst Andy's character, Lennie, is meant to be tall, strong but mentally slow and he relies heavily on George. They have a shared dream of owning their own piece of land one day and having animals on it that Lennie can pet. The underlying problem there, however, is that Lennie has a tendency to pet animals too heavily and inadvertently kill them.

From the first minute to the last, 'Of Mice and Men' is funny and clever with a gathering sense of doom. Andy had the ideal build for his character but it was also intriguing watching a highly intelligent man act out the role of someone with such limited intelligence. Andy had been worried that I may have to pretend to think he was a good actor, but I hadn't anticipated that he would be so good. He was simply sensational.

I have always worn my heart on my sleeve but I can't remember being quite so emotional about anything ever as I was about that performance of 'Of Mice and Men'. I was laughing through tears in the opening scene, I intermittently cried throughout, the dramatic ending had me in floods of tears and when Andy walked into the bar afterwards I cried again. I think it was all down to three factors, the show itself, my pride in Andy and the fact that Cathie was with me to witness it. I am not sure how prepared Cathie was, though, for me to spend half the evening apologising whilst wiping away a tear or blowing my nose.

"I'm so sorry for all the tears," I said as I drove Cathie home, "it was brilliant though, wasn't it?"

"It was. Who knew Andy would be that good?"

"I know. He was a superstar. Having you with me was the cherry on the cake."

Was the expression 'the cherry on the cake' or the 'icing on the cake', I think I probably got it wrong but the sentiment was right. I thought of Mussarat's warning about 'treading carefully', I wasn't sure I was exactly doing that. I just felt everything about the night had been magical and I didn't want it to end.

"Do you need to get back for Max?" I asked.

"Not particularly, he'll be fast asleep by now, so will Mum and Dad. Why?"

"I just wondered if you fancied having a drink at 'The Cemetery'? I could leave my car there and then walk you back. I fancy having a drink."

And I fancy you, Cathie. In a big way, I fancy you.

Cathie's face seemed to light up in the semi-darkness of my car.

"Sounds like a great idea. There's one condition though."

"Go on."

"You let me pay 'H'! You've been paying for everything all night and you've been driving. You wouldn't even let me pay for the vanilla tubs in the interval."

"I'm working."

This was a discreet way of saying Cathie wasn't working without actually spelling it out. She had told me she had worked in a designer clothes store for ladies in Perth for a number of years but only on a part time basis since Max's arrival. Keith was apparently earning big money as an architect though and was regularly being flown all around Australia and several Asian countries too (his time away from home was probably a contributory factor regarding his sexual shenanigans but I surmised this rather than being told it directly by Cathie). I wouldn't have imagined Cathie would have struggled financially whilst in Perth, but wasn't sure how she was financially managing since the split. I decided the safest option was just to pay for everything, Cathie had obviously noticed.

"That doesn't matter," Cathie replied, "I like to stand on my own feet."

"OK, if you're sure."

"I am."

I didn't care too much about who was paying, the main thing was that I had managed to get Cathie to stay a bit longer.

We probably only stayed in 'The Cemetery' for not much more than an hour but by the time I walked Cathie home I could tell she was pretty drunk. I had had a lager shandy at 'Gracie Fields' and only a couple of glasses of wine in the pub but Cathie had been drinking both before and after the play so I guess the half bottle of white wine had tipped her over the edge. She wasn't smashed off her face just a little merry. Merry and confessional.

"I slept with someone else in Perth," Cathie said as we walked along, "does that make me a terrible person, H?"

I have to admit I was really shocked to hear this. Since the day of my pizza delivery to her door, I had always thought Cathie was flawless.

"No, of course not, I'm sure you had good reason."

"I thought so at the time. I had lost some of my self-worth. I wasn't happy at home. I needed to feel loved again and my boss at work started paying me some attention. I suppose I really should have kept him at bay, he was older and married, but I felt flattered and I didn't."

I was uncomfortable hearing this. It wasn't as though it was me that Cathie had cheated on but somehow it felt like it was or perhaps it felt that if Cathie was going to cheat on Keith, it should have been with me. Nevertheless, I was intrigued and kept asking questions. His name was Leyton, he was fifty and the affair lasted two months. It had been Leyton that had ended it too which I hadn't anticipated.

"What about you?" Cathie asked, "Any skeletons in your closet?"

"Not really," I answered, which was true, there wasn't enough room for skeletons in my closet. They were stuffed in the loft, the shed and buried under the patio.

"Come on," Cathie coaxed good humouredly, giving me a gentle prod, "you're thirty one. There must be something. How many have women have you slept with?"

"Nine," I answered immediately.

Cathie seemed to stare at me for a few uncomfortable seconds after I said it. I thought she could tell this was an outright lie. Turns out she was anticipating a number that could be counted on one hand. Lucky she didn't know that in reality fingers and toes didn't cover it but an abacus could just about manage.

"Wow, nine? Really? I'm a little shocked, H, I wasn't anticipating it to be that many."

I wasn't anticipating that she would have had an affair with some fifty year old Australian bloke called Leyton either but I let that go. I was hoping she wasn't going to go all precious about nine women. I'm not sure how Cathie would have reacted if I'd mentioned the three hundred and twenty odd others, but I'm guessing not well.

"Nine isn't many, I worked in a bar in Manchester for two years and I had girls throwing themselves at me."

And I slept with every one (unfortunately).

"I suppose not. I guess after the letter you sent me before I went to Australia, I just liked to imagine you sat in with your Dad and Andy pining for me."

The letter. I suppose the letter was always going to have to be discussed again at some stage although I hadn't anticipated it would happen quite so quickly. A few days before Cathie went to Perth, desperate for her not to go, I had posted a letter to Cathie, telling her exactly how I felt about her. I told her that I didn't think Keith was right for her, that I was in love with her and that it would break my heart if she left. It was one of those situations when you pop an envelope into a post box and then your heart starts pounding and you wonder whether you have just made a terrible mistake.

The following day, Cathie phoned me to say she had read my letter and that we needed to speak. Literally within ten minutes she was around at our house. Without a hint of awkwardness or emotion, Cathie explained that she thought I had mistaken friendship for love. She went on to say that we were never destined to be together romantically and for the sake of our friendship she wanted me to do her a huge favour. Realising my error of judgement and feeling pretty humiliated by my own actions, I agreed to do whatever she wanted me to. Cathie handed me the letter back, told me to put it in a pan, set it alight and then we could both completely forget that it had ever been sent. I did as requested and for the next few days we acted like my declaration of love had never happened.

"What letter?" I responded, "as far as I'm concerned there has never been a letter."

Cathie stopped walking and turned to face me, she put her arm in front of me, forcing me to stop too.

"We can stop playing that game now, H. There is no Keith any more. It was just that your timing was terrible. I was about to fly to Perth three days later. My bags were already packed, what did you expect me to do? Maybe if you'd have kissed me that night when we were in the single bed at yours it might have been different."

This confession excited me. I had always felt there was a certain chemistry between us, always felt I had some sort of chance and now I felt like I was being told I had always been right.

"Would it? Really?"

Cathie shrugged, looking a little embarrassed about this confession.

"I don't know, maybe."

"What about now?" I asked.

"What about now?"

"We have already established I'm shit at reading signals. Is now a good time to kiss you?"

"Now would be a very good time to kiss me but anything more…"

I didn't want to listen to the 'anything more' bit. After ten years of waiting, I had finally been given the green light. I wasn't going to wait any longer. I put Cathie's face in my hands and we exchanged a slow, caring kiss. Now wasn't the time for a mad passionate kiss with tongues and sexual undertones.

"Bloody hell! Missing my chance in the single bed is going to bug the hell out of me," was the first thing I said after we stopped kissing. Cathie laughed.

"I only said 'maybe'. It probably would have still become too complicated for it to work."

"It's still complicated now. You have a lasting memento of your relationship with Keith."

I cringed as soon as the words left my lips. Cathie reacted immediately. I knew I was in trouble straight away.

"H, if you ever call my son a memento again, I'm telling you now this will never work."

"Fuck. I'm so sorry. I didn't mean it to come out like that. I've only ever wanted you, Cathie, I'm desperate not to screw this up and here I am screwing it up already."

Cathie gripped my arm by the elbow in an act of re-assurance.

"No, you aren't. You said something daft and I just did the protective mother thing for a second. It's no biggy. I'm sorry too."

"No need. My fault entirely."

"Look 'H', it's taken us ten years to get to this point. We've both made massive mistakes in the last ten years and no doubts we'll make heaps in the next ten. Let's not start worrying about the little ones. I don't know if we'll end up as a couple, I think I'll need to take some little baby steps for quite some time but I'm single, you're single, let's just see how it goes. Now hold my hand and walk me home."

We interlocked fingers and kept that way for the rest of the walk. I was happy. I was very, very happy, but I was also terrified. I was in my thirties and for the first time ever I could get to be with the person I wanted. When we reached Cathie's house, we shared another gentle kiss and a hug on the front drive.

"Do you want to come in?" Cathie softly asked.

"No, no, I'll get going. I don't want to wake anyone up," I whispered back.

"OK, thanks for a lovely evening. I've had a lovely evening."

"No, thank you."

I was just about to head home. I just wanted to watch Cathie go through the door but she stopped looking in her handbag for her keys and turned away from the door towards me.

"H, what's your favourite song."

I didn't have one prepared. I don't really have one.

"Why?"

"I was going to listen to my favourite song before going to sleep. I thought I might listen to yours too."

I wanted to think of a song that would particularly impress her but with not having much time to think, I answered honestly.

"REM, Country Feedback."

I instantly regretted owning up to that. I suspected as soon as Cathie listened to it, she would realise I would have been thinking of her every time I played it.

"OK, I'll give it a listen. Goodnight!"

As she put the key in the door and pushed the door opened, I gave out a muted shout,

"Cathie! Cathie!"

"What?"

"What's your favourite song?"

"Anna Nalick's Breathe (2am). One day, maybe, I'll tell you why."

Cathie headed into the house leaving the scent of mystery behind. I had never heard of Anna Nalick and wondered whether I would still remember her name by the time I arrived home. I walked home briskly, upright and with a skip in my step, occasionally mumbling the lyrics of 'Country Feedback' to myself.

"Please God," I said as I reached our road, "don't let me fuck this up."

Chapter Forty Eight

Given my father had always had a soft spot for Cathie, I expected him to be delighted to hear that she had come back from Australia, but his initial response was subdued which tipped over to concern once I began to spend more time with her. My Dad was worried, like Andy had been, that I would end up getting hurt. He also expressed concerns about Max, stating a very strong case over tea one night of the importance to a child of having both a mother and father figure in the home.

After a couple of months in England, Cathie made the decision that she wanted to remain here for the foreseeable future and began looking into primary schools for Max. Whether Cathie's decision to stay was anything to do with our blossoming relationship I'm not sure, but I certainly didn't exert any pressure on her to stay.

In those formative days of our relationship I actually surprised myself by how relaxed I was. I let her take the lead, see me when she wanted to see me and stay home with Max and her parents when she needed to. I tended to see her once during the working week and one evening at the weekend. There was no sex and there was certainly no pressure to have sex. We were tactile though. I enjoyed holding hands or just curling up on the settee or on the top of my bed and watching TV.

We watched a lot of films during the months leading up to Christmas. Cinema Paradiso was our favourite. Having enjoyed books by European writers from my late teens, I had developed an interest in foreign films too and was delighted to discover Cathie enjoyed them as well. We watched a lot of European films like 'Il Postino', 'Betty Blue' and 'Life is Beautiful'. Around this time Dad and I went halves on a second hand piano (I think his first wife could play and he liked the idea of a piano being back in the house) and the first thing I learned to play was 'C'est le vent, Betty', the music Zorg plays on the piano in 'Betty Blue'. I did it to impress Cathie and it worked.

As Christmas approached, Cathie wanted to watch some feel good Christmas movies too, so we watched the likes of 'Home Alone' (we watched that one with Max and he thought it was hilarious), 'National Lampoon's Christmas Vacation' but without doubt our favourite was 'Elf'. We cried laughing watching that. I think we must have watched 'Elf' half a dozen times that Christmas. I took some gentle ribbing off Cathie though as she could tell I had a bit of a thing for Zooey Deschanel.

During December 2007, I made a significant decision with regards to my job. The housing market had continued to boom and throughout 2007 I had received almost daily calls from recruitment consultants saying new lenders, often American, were entering the British mortgage market and they were looking for experienced Intermediary Account Managers (often known as Business Development Managers) like myself. By this point my basic had risen to over £30,000 a year but the recruitment consultants were suggesting I could double my salary if I moved to pastures new.

I know it probably shouldn't have been an influence but the fact that I had started dating Cathie had played a part in my decision to leave Tyrone Building Society. Keith had always been an ambitious sod and I didn't want Cathie to start thinking I wasn't in his financial league or that I lacked his ambition. Everyone at 'Tyrone' had always treated me like one of the family but there were no opportunities for me to be promoted unless I moved to Northern Ireland. Cathie had two parents of pensionable age and I had one, there was no chance they would all move. I was the solitary staff member in Northern England and although Sean O'Davey spoke of possibilities of us expanding our sales force in England and me becoming a Sales Manager, I knew it was unlikely to ever happen.

In November 2007, the 'Avon & Severn Bank', one of the countries 'Big Six' banks approached me with the suggestion of joining them. They were an established British bank not a new American entrant to the market, so wouldn't be paying the wild sums of money the American banks were paying, but would still pay significantly more than Tyrone Building Society did. They said they had heard a lot of good things about me from mortgage brokers and I was the man they wanted to replace Dani Wharton as their Business Development Manager in Manchester. Dani had been with them for six years but she had succumbed to financial temptation and agreed to join one of the big US firms. I was told I would have to go through a two stage interview to placate the Human Resources department but the job was as good as mine.

I was really undecided whether I should leave 'Tyrone' or not so I chatted it through, on separate occasions, with my Dad, Andy and Cathie. My Dad and Cathie were encouraging me to make the jump whilst Andy was more cautious, suggesting that happiness in a job was more important than money. This was easy for him to say, he was earning bucketloads! After a lot of thought, I ended up going through the process and after two fairly relaxed interviews I was offered the job, with a basic wage of £36,000 per annum, a bigger annual holiday entitlement, private health care and an impressive pension scheme.

In mid-December I flew over to Belfast to have my annual review meeting with Sean O'Davey in Omagh. I didn't want to go through the whole meeting discussing aspirations and intentions for 2008, then announce I was leaving, so explained my situation at the outset. I felt I owed it to Sean to break it to him face to face. Sean was really understanding and asked if I had signed any contracts with Avon & Severn. When I said I hadn't, he asked me if I could give him a few hours to see what package he could come up with after speaking to his fellow board members. I felt I owed him that much. 'Tyrone' had been a fantastic place to work but I explained I was thinking of career progression, as well as the immediate package, so it was very unlikely they could say anything that would change my mind.

After two hours, Sean came back into the meeting room to say they would be prepared to match Avon & Severn's offer of £36,000. I was flattered that such a relatively small Building Society were prepared to do that for me, but I couldn't accept. Avon & Severn employed over 100,000 staff and there were loads of different career paths I could follow. I thanked Sean for everything but explained I still wanted to hand my notice in.

"No bother 'H', I'd do exactly that same if I was in your shoes. I just had to give it our best shot. Can you do me one last thing for me though?"

"Of course I can."

"Can you let me join you for a meal in Belfast tonight as a way of thanking you for all your hard work over the last few years? After the pair of us have eaten we can go out and get pissed!"

We had a brilliant night out. We spent most of it drinking Guinness in 'The Crown Liquor Saloon' and stumbled into a couple of clubs after that but I don't remember much about them. Cathie said I woke her up at three o'clock in the morning, as I rang her on my mobile declaring my undying love when I was smashed but I have no recollection of this. Apparently Sean and I also sang Joe Jackson's 'Slow Song' down the phone to her until she hung up.

The following morning, armed with a small suitcase and a hangover, I headed home. I was a little nervous about what lay ahead in the New Year but I was convinced I was doing the right thing. Avon & Severn were massive and I knew I would be well looked after working for one of the biggest mortgage lenders in the UK. I was in love and I had a great new job. Everything was working out perfectly.

Chapter Forty Nine

2008 could not have started better. Jenny Trescothick, aka 'Waddy', the girl who had exposed her Showaddywaddy knickers back at primary school, had got married a couple of years earlier and in late 2007 moved into a new build property over in Bury. To celebrate, she decided she wanted to throw a housewarming party on New Year's Eve. I hadn't really kept in touch with many of the people from school until the whole social media phenomenon had properly kicked in but Cathie had and as we were now officially 'dating', this gained me an invite too. I think out of sympathy, 'Waddy' decided to invite Andy too (rumours had circulated on Facebook that he was a bit of a loner). Cathie said she would make her way over to Bury with Mussarat and some of the other girls, so I said I'd get a taxi over from ours with Andy.

On New Year's Eve, Andy arrived at ours with his mother. Andy was gripping the top of a champagne bottle in one hand and a bottle of vodka in the other. Maggie looked like she had brought a bottle of red wine for her and my father. I dutifully gave her a kiss and took her coat. Both Maggie's coat and lips smelt of burnt toast. I gave Andy a hug before showing them both through to the lounge.

Having noticed that Cathie's parents were hurtling towards rigor mortis at great pace, I had started to become more aware of my father's frailties too. I had spent my whole life worrying about his mortality but once he had passed eighty, I tried to approach the whole matter with a 'he's had a good innings' perspective and tried just to be grateful for every additional day. Over the last twelve months he seemed to have developed a persistent shake, his walked had slowed, he complained regularly about his tinnitus and he was given a hearing aid for his right ear that he seldom wore, especially if he was due to meet up with Maggie Corcoran.

Andy and I had a glass of champagne each (not Andy's bottle, a bottle Dad had chilled in the fridge) with Dad and Mrs C before a taxi beeped its horn outside, indicating it was time for us to go.

"Right," Andy said, "that'll be our taxi. You two behave yourselves. George, don't you be pulling my mother's knickers off the moment we're out of here and if you do get up to anything later on, please wear a condom, I couldn't vouch for where my Mum has been."

"Andrew!" Maggie called out in mock indignation.

Andy was always wanting to know about the trials and tribulations of my life so once we were on our way, I made a conscious effort to ask about his first. He had climbed into the passenger seat next to the driver so I was sat in the back. My Dad had already been asking Andy about his job so I took a different tact.

"How's the acting going mate? Anything else on the agenda now?"

"It's pantomime season at the moment, H and I'm not really into all that."

I was initially surprised by this because Andy had always been quick witted and had the ability to make people laugh.

"How come? I thought you'd be good at pantomimes."

"I don't know really. I've always just avoided farces and pantomimes. I probably take it all a bit too seriously. Basing my performance on entertaining five year old kids, with the odd innuendo thrown in for Mum and Dad, isn't really for me."

"Makes sense."

"How about you 'H'? Still smitten?"

I was still smitten with Cathie. I had always been smitten and felt I always would be but I didn't think Cathie had all the power in the relationship. We were very much on a level. I'd like to think at that point Cathie was smitten too. I think it probably helped me that Keith had decided to stay in Australia for now. I would have felt a lot more uncertain if he was around. Although their break up hadn't exactly been amicable, they were making the best of a bad situation for Max's sake. Every Sunday morning, at 8am, Keith would ring and have a brief chat with Cathie before having a longer one with Max. He had said he would start looking for work in the UK later in 2008, once his current project was completed, but whenever he left, he would have to give three months' notice, so I would have time to mentally prepare for his arrival. Cathie had decided not to tell him she was seeing anyone else just yet, which I agreed was for the best too. I had started spending a bit more time with Max though and I knew if that continued Cathie would have to tell Keith about me. It wouldn't be fair on Keith (or Max) if the truth was revealed in one of their Sunday morning conversations.

"Yes, mate, still smitten."

The party at Waddy's was absolutely brilliant. It was great catching up with old friends, male and female, that I hadn't seen for years although I did receive more than my fair share of,

"Are you seeing Cathie Squires? Bloody hell, you're punching above your weight there mate!"

The comment was normally followed by a pat on the back if the comment was made by a lad or a warning to look after her if the comment was made by a woman.

"Tell them to piss off," Andy commented later when I told him, "She's punching above her weight, as well she knows. Just because you never did sport, don't work out in the gym every night and aren't a 'Man's Man', doesn't mean you're not about as good a man as any woman could have. Don't start doubting yourself mate. You're one in a million."

Some people can be told ten things about themselves, nine positive and one negative, and only hear the good. In that same situation, I only hear the one negative. I'm sure Andy didn't mean it as a negative either, but I picked up on the 'Not a Man's Man' comment."

"What do you mean I'm not a 'Man's Man'?"

Andy smiled and then laughed a little to himself.

"See, I knew you'd pick up on the negative! I meant you're thoughtful, sensitive, romantic, deep thinking and sport hating. You're not a football loving lager lout who shags lots of women."

"I have in my time," I said defensively, referring to the last point and trying to sound proud about a sexual record I was actually ashamed of.

"They approached you though, H, not the other way around. You just didn't have the balls to say 'No'."

I had never thought about it like that before but Andy was probably right. I was going to explore this line of thinking but Cathie came into the room. After a bit of pleasant chatter between the three of us, Andy slipped away. Cathie was wearing a long, peach, chiffon dress that to me looked like something a bridesmaid would wear at a wedding, but Cathie still managed to look stunning rather than overdressed. Other than the two straps over her shoulders, most of Cathie's back was exposed, which was a turn on for me, as I found her back to be incredibly sexy. Let's face it, I just found everything about Cathie a massive turn on.

Our conversation stopped for a moment after Andy left the two of us alone together but then I remembered something I had been meaning to discuss.

"I forgot to tell you I listened to that song you mentioned when I first walked you home."

"Which one?"

"By Anna Nalick."

"Oh right, yes. Breathe."

"Yeh, I saw an acoustic version on 'You Tube'. Lovely song and she's a bit gorgeous too, isn't she? Top choice."

"Thanks, it helped me through a tough time when I was in Australia. Talking about beautiful women, I've just been talking to Joanna Barry in the kitchen. She did the whole ugly duckling thing, didn't she? No wonder you went out with her. She seems a lovely person too."

"Yeh, she was nice Joanna was, obviously not as nice as you though, honey. Once I've had a few more drinks I'll have to summon up the courage to speak to her. I was an arse to her back in the day and need to apologise."

"I think you should."

Cathie didn't seem to do jealousy. She knew I was crazy about her so didn't worry about anyone from my past. Joanna was now married with a couple of little ones anyway, which I guess diminished any romantic threat even further. Cathie's confidence was well placed though, if Megan Fox had come into the party naked and tried to lead me up the stairs to the bedroom, I would have clung on to the bannister. I wouldn't have swopped Cathie for anyone.

When Cathie had entered the room, as Andy and I had been chatting, I had watched in awe as she came towards us. She moved in an almost regal way. I had a tendency to 'hunch', Andy did too, so I always had to consciously tell myself to stand straight, but Cathie moved in a very natural, upright way, like a swan. I found it alluring. I remember Amy Garfunkel having a similar confidence when I was a teenager.

Midnight and the New Year soon arrived. After sharing my first kiss of 2008 with Cathie, we both hugged Andy and then did the rounds shaking hands and giving out a few polite kisses. Once the circulating was done with, I phoned my Dad. He was enjoying his night in and told me that he'd just been outside with Maggie to 'Let the New Year in' and watch the fireworks. He asked me if I could put Cathie on so he could wish her a 'Happy New Year' and I said once they were done, he needed to let me and Andy speak to Maggie. Bless her despite my initial concerns she seemed to have put a spring back in his step. After we all finished speaking to my Dad and Maggie, Andy made himself scarce once more and Cathie led me to a dark corner of Waddy's dimly lit dining room and gave me a really passionate kiss.

"2008 is going to be our year, H, I can sense it," Cathie said in an interlude between two kisses. In previous years, I had rarely had cause for optimism, but this time it all felt very different. I really felt Cathie was going to be right.

Chapter Fifty

"I can't believe we are in Lanzarote for our National Sales Meeting!"

It was mid-January and I was sat drinking cocktails in the late afternoon sunshine in Playa Blanca. We were staying at a hotel called Volcan, which was a stone's throw from the marina and, as the name suggested, was built inside a huge, fake volcano. Tyrone Building Society had our Sales Meetings in Omagh or, if pushing the boat out, in Belfast and although I loved both places, neither was the warmest place to be in mid-January. I was quickly learning that Avon & Severn Bank was a monster of an organisation and liked to do everything with a bit of panache.

My new job had started brilliantly. My new boss, Martin Sunderland, seemed like a good bloke. He took life a lot more seriously than Sean O'Davey but was keen to integrate me into his team of twenty Business Development Managers as soon as possible. He insisted I came on the four day trip to Lanzarote despite still being on my first month's induction programme. I was apprehensive because I didn't like the idea of leaving Dad, in his frail state, on his own for that long. Cathie encouraged me to go, saying she would call around every evening to make sure my Dad and Maggie were alright, but I still felt guilty as Cathie had Max to look after. I didn't like the idea of Maggie leaving my Dad alone, but equally wasn't comfortable with her staying overnight, something she never tended to do when I was around.

I had been sat with several other Business Development Managers by the pool but Martin had come over to us and asked if he could have ten minutes with me. We had arrived at lunchtime after an early morning flight and were allowed a few hours to chill out. There was a formal meal arranged for the evening with a full programme of events scheduled for the following two days.

"Settling in?" Martin asked.

"Yes, I'm loving it so far," I replied genuinely, although it had quickly become apparent that there was an expectation for Business Development Managers' to enthuse about everything related to Avon & Severn.

"Good. How did you feel the training course went down in Bristol?"

"Very well, all the training guys were great."

The training course in Bristol had been for two days with an overnight stop in the middle. Cathie had helped me out then too.

"The trainers were impressed with you too, Harry. They said you knew your stuff. I still don't want you out on the road and answering calls from brokers though until you know our criteria inside out. Once we switch that phone on, there's no going back."

"OK. The product and lending criteria guidelines are bedtime reading at the moment."

"Good lad. Take it easy whilst you're here though. I'll introduce you to some of the bosses at dinner tonight. It's always important to know who they are. I'll just warn you though you'll need to know how to party to fit into this team. The Sales guys at Avon & Severn are expected to party hard."

"Thanks Martin."

I wasn't worried about being able to party. I was aware that I wasn't the best dancer in the world or the biggest drinker but I would happily give both a good go if it meant fitting into a corporation like this.

"Listen H, before you go back to the lads and ladies," Martin said in conspiratorial tones, "there's something I wanted to mention to you. You did the right thing leaving Tyrone Building Society. I didn't say this to you in your interview as I didn't want you to think I was scaremongering but I think your best off away from the sub-prime mortgage market currently. The talk is it won't be long before the whole market implodes?"

"Really?"

"Yes. The shit is really hitting the fan in the sub-prime market in the States and trouble is expected to spread to the market here too. It'll definitely hit the sub-prime market and could even cause trouble in the whole banking industry. When waters get rough you're always better on a big boat that can ride the storm, 'H 'and there aren't many bigger than Avon & Severn."

That night, I thought more about what Martin had said about being able to party than I did about his forecasts of doom for the sub-prime mortgage market. Despite having worked at 'Halcyon' for two years, nothing had prepared me for a night like this. There was a free bar throughout the evening and as far as I could work out everyone was acting like prohibition was about to be introduced in Lanzarote. No-one had a single measure when they could have a double and as the night progressed no-one had a glass when they could have a bottle. In the early stages there was also a lot of flirtation between the sexes, later on there was a lot of kissing, hugging, touching, feeling, straddling and god knows what else went on in the privacy of the hotel bedrooms. I was not involved in the late night mischief though. I was happy in my relationship with Cathie so was never going to revert back to my Halcyon behaviour. The shenanigans didn't totally pass me by though.

The meal went well. I was on a boisterous table of ten but, given Martin was on my table, I felt a little on my guard. After the meal finished, the Head of Sales, Ian Hornby, compered the '2007 Avon & Severn Mortgage Sales Awards' which involved a lot of mickey taking of some existing and some former staff members. I wasn't sure if I was becoming prudish in my thirties, but I found some of the jokes about ugliness, large breasts, anal sex and bucket vaginas to be distasteful. I seemed to be in the minority though, as most of my colleagues roared with laughter. The other thing I found strange was not only did they reward the best performing Business Development Managers they ridiculed and shamed the worst performers. As a sensitive soul myself I felt for the 'BDMs' who had been highlighted as having a bad year but they seemed to be trying to laugh off their shame.

As I had felt a little uncomfortable, I had probably resorted to the security of the champagne and white wine on the table a little too often. Once the disco began, after the Awards and speeches were concluded, I was ready to strut my stuff as best I could. I spent about half an hour on the dance floor but I remember a song came on that I didn't like so I decided to head to the bar. I grabbed a bottle of San Miguel, which surprised the bar tender as the two people he served before me took a bottle of Baileys and a bottle of Southern Comfort off him, then returned to the seat I had occupied during the meal. It had been a black tie evening, but my jacket and bow tie had already been dispensed with. As I enjoyed my San Miguel, I also undid a further button on my shirt as I could feel my face and body burning through the heady mixture of sunshine, alcohol and disco dancing.

I was watching and smiling at how different people on the dance floor were dancing (I wasn't the only poor dancer) so failed to spot that someone was approaching me.

"Do you fuck like you dance?"

The dance floor was to my right and my head shot around to the left to see who had asked me this question. An immaculately dressed woman in her forties had taken a seat next to me. She had a shoulder length blonde bob and reminded me of the type of woman who would sit on a Miss World judging panel after having formerly won it several years earlier. She was wearing a navy blue dress that accentuated her curves but in a glamorous rather than tacky way. For her age she was hotter than a Bhut Naga Jolokia chilli served on a bed of hot coals.

"I beg your pardon!"

"You heard what I said, hun. Are you the new boy?"

"I am. 'H' McCoy."

I offered my hand for her to shake. Given her greeting I felt a polite hug and kiss would have been giving out the wrong signals.

"Liz Victory. I'm not shaking hands, hun. I'm a lady, kiss my cheeks."

This was beginning to feel very awkward. I didn't know what to say or do so just looked at her blankly.

"Come on 'H'," she ordered, "we're in Lanzarote, give me a kiss on both cheeks like the locals do. It's tradition."

I did as I was told. She smelt like she had showered in expensive perfume. I had the uncomfortable feeling that this cougar had me trapped.

"Are you a 'BDM' at Avon & Severn too?" I asked, trying to keep the conversation business related.

"Not just a 'BDM', hun. Number one 'BDM'. I've been Business Development Manager of the Year for the last three years. I'll be getting my trophy back again tomorrow night at the Awards Ceremony. I think I might get to keep it now I've won it three times. I'll win it this year too. Anyway, you didn't answer my question, 'H', do you fuck like you dance?"

"How did I dance?"

"Like someone who knows how to please the ladies."

I couldn't help but laugh.

"In what way?"

"You know what you're doing, you let the women take centre stage, express themselves, have fun and you get off just at the right point."

"And I thought I was just dancing. I didn't appreciate the sexual connotations "

"Well maybe you should. You seem like you have the tongue to match."

"As far as I can see, I am one of the quieter ones here."

"No, literally I mean you have the tongue to match. Stick it out."

I don't really know why I was playing along. Excess alcohol undoubtedly played its part. I stuck my tongue out.

"Wow! Take a look at that! I bet that's done its fair share of tasting, licking and slithering its way into some tight spots. I know how much I like tasting, licking and swallowing with mine."

Liz Victory thrust her tongue in and out rapidly and violently like a Maori doing the Haka. I was equally intimidated. I felt like a rat in a cage with a hungry python.

"My tongue, along with the rest of me, is fully domesticated these days, Liz. My wild days are behind me."

Liz gently rubbed a finger up and down my empty ring finger.

"You're not married though, H. Whatever happens in Playa Blanca, stays in Playa Blanca."

I was a little annoyed for allowing myself to be party to Liz's games even for this long. Nothing was ever going to happen.

"You're married though," I pointed at Liz's finger, which had three rings on it, which were presumably an engagement ring, a wedding ring and an eternity ring. The diamond on the engagement ring was almost the size of a pebble. Mr Victory had expensive tastes.

"My husband understands me, 'H'. He knows there are times I need fresh meat to sustain me. Enjoy the rest of your evening. I see you're sharing with Jimmy Swain. He won't be back tonight. If you think you'll be lonely all it takes to resolve the problem is a word in my ear."

Liz glided away from me, just leaving her expensive scent behind. She took a seat at a stool at the bar and I watched as she summoned a bar tender over with her finger then whispered her order in his ear. I found her sexy and fascinating to watch but not for one second did I consider the possibility of going anywhere near her. I was in love with Cathie, I had no inclination to jeopardise that.

I was enjoying people watching and as I took another swig from my San Miguel, a tall, stocky man with a full head of grey hair and a large stomach approached me.

"Do you mind if I sit down, pal?" he asked with a strong Glaswegian accent.

"No, of course not, grab a seat."

"Cheers man, I'm Michael Moriarty, by the way. I cover the North East of Scotland but I'm originally from Milngavie. My wife's from Dundee."

My geographical knowledge of Scotland isn't the best so this explanation was wasted on me until I got back home to Rochdale and had a look at a Road Atlas. At the time, I just smiled as if what Michael was saying made perfect sense.

"Harry McCoy, but people tend to call me 'H'."

I stood up to enable us to shake hands and then we both sat down.

"I see you've met the delectable Elizabeth. Has she offered to fuck you yet?"

I laughed.

"Indirectly."

"She's consistent, I'll give her that. She's our Newcastle BDM. She's not from there though, she's from Hertfordshire or Buckinghamshire or somewhere, but she's lived up in Newcastle for years, not sure why. Maybe her first husband was a Geordie. She was in the Scotland & North East England team for years but she got moved out. The powers that be found out she was shagging our boss, Benny. They were both married at the time, and not to each other, so they moved her into the Yorkshire team. Pity they didn't move Benny over, he's a right evil bastard."

"Is he here?" I asked, wondering if her flirtation with me was perhaps an act to make an old friend jealous.

"No, he's had to stay home to attend some Scottish Mortgage Awards night in Edinburgh. The lucky bastard avoided this shindig. He's married to Lizzie now by the way. They both ended their marriages so they could be together and left their kids with their exes. A dirty bitch and a bastard, they belong together."

I sat and chatted with Michael for some time. He was very different to all the other Business Development Managers at Avon & Severn. He was self-deprecating with a dry wit. Whilst everyone else had been telling me it was a wonderful place to work and everyone was marvellous (but not quite as marvellous as them), Michael was more cynical.

"Do you know what Avon & Severn Bank is 'H'? It's a shit rolled in glitter. It looks all sparkly and extravagant from the outside, but once you get inside it's all just shite. Bosses who are arseholes and BDMs who think every day is rimming season. Make you own mind up, pal, it might be different down your way but in Scotland it's a scramble to the top of the shit heap and everyone is gauging each other's eyes out to get there."

"Do they put you on the stand at the careers fair?" I asked, trying to lighten the mood a little but Michael didn't laugh.

"To be fair, your boss, Martin, seems like a decent bloke, but be on your guard all the time, H, because everyone is just looking after 'numero uno' at this place."

"Thanks Michael, I appreciate the warning. How come you haven't left if you hate it so much?"

"Oh, I will. I'll jump or be pushed soon enough. I worked for 'Smart Money Mortgages'. We did offset mortgages for high net worth clients. That was a brilliant place to work. I can't tell you how much I enjoyed it. It was one small team with a common goal. Two years ago, Avon & Severn Bank took us over. We had eight sales staff. One by one they've got rid of the other seven 'Smart Money' BDMs so I'm the last man standing. God knows why I'm still here but I'm sure they'll find a way to get me out soon too. It has an air of inevitably about it. They're already shafting me on my targets. I've had plenty of job offers. I just want to pick up some sort of severance package before I go. Benny is a scheming twat though so I don't know whether he'll find some way to do me over. Anyway, H, I'm sorry I've pissed on your parade. Judge for yourself, who knows, your experiences may be very different to mine. In my opinion though, it's places like this that make the general public think bankers are wankers. If you're a good guy and from initial impressions it seems like you are, I think you'll end up hating this place just as much as I do."

Chapter Fifty One

My relationship with Cathie gathered pace quicker than I think either of us had intended. By February 2008 we were seeing each other four or five times a week and by the Spring it was every day unless I was away for a work meeting or Cathie was on a late shift at work. She had started working at JEM, a clothes shop in the Trafford Centre, a massive indoor shopping centre on the outskirts of Manchester. Her normal shift was ten until six but sometimes, due to staff shortgages, she had to do the one until nine shift. Max had started at my old primary school in Bamford so he would go into after school club on the three days in the working week that Cathie worked and I would pick him up around five and take him back to ours for his tea. I think we all felt settled and happy as we adapted to our new routine.

I don't remember exactly when it was, but I remember arriving back home one Saturday night in the Spring. It was about eleven o'clock and unusually Dad was still awake. He was carrying a cup and saucer in either hand from the lounge to the kitchen and due to the slight shake he now had, they looked very precarious.

"Dad, you should have left them. I'd have cleaned things up."

"I might be nearly eighty six, son, but I'm still capable of looking after myself. I can manage just fine thank you."

He said this a little defensively. I think he knew his ability to manage for himself would not last long and he wanted to be a burden for as limited a time as possible.

"OK, Dad, no problem. How come you're still up?"

"Maggie's only just left. We were watching some De Niro film from a few years ago. It was very good."

"Which one was it?"

"I can't remember the name of it now. It had some actor called Charles somebody in it."

"Not the best of clues that, Dad!"

"De Niro was a bounty hunter."

"Oh, 'Midnight Run'. It's brilliant that one."

"Yes, it really was good. Maggie managed to sit through the whole film without going to the back door for a cigarette which is always a good sign."

"How did she get home? She didn't drive, did she?"

Although she lived less than a mile away, as would be expected of a lady in later life, Maggie didn't like walking in the dark, so tended to drive around to ours. She was a terrible driver, particularly in the dark, as she was short sighted but was too vain to wear glasses. She had had a few bumps into stationary objects like walls and gate posts but that Spring she had reversed into one of her neighbours cars one evening and it had put her off driving at night. My Dad and I had started referring to her as Mrs Magoo but only when she wasn't around as we were both a little scared of her.

"No, Andy came to collect her. He walked around and then walked her back. He's staying at hers for the weekend as he's working on some case that's about to go to trial and he said he felt like getting out of Manchester for the weekend."

I had only seen Andy a couple of times since New Year. With my new job and blossoming relationship, I hadn't had much time to head over to Manchester and Andy was always busy too. We exchanged texts on a fairly regular basis and messaged each other on Facebook from time to time too.

"Things going well with Maggie then?" I asked as I started to wash the cups and saucers Dad had brought through.

Dad had taken a seat in the kitchen. The journey from lounge to kitchen had seemingly tired him out and I think he was summoning up the energy to get upstairs. It was around that time that I began to think about converting the dining room into his bedroom to save him from having to struggle up and down the stairs.

"She's good company, 'H'. She's not your mother but she's a nice lady with a good heart and I enjoy spending time with her. I know I should be very grateful for having reached this grand old age, don't get me wrong most of the time I am, but it's not a bundle of laughs being old. Maggie makes life feel better. I feel less of a burden on you now too."

"Don't be daft, Dad. You're not a burden."

I was thirty two that summer and had never lived anywhere other than in Bamford with my father, so I suppose, to some extent, he had been a burden but it never felt that way.

"I know it's easier to appreciate youth when you've lost it but you need to enjoy everything you have in your life right now as it won't always be there for you. Enjoy being young, fit, handsome, able to run, able to drive and especially the freedom you have because once you get to my age you just become grateful for not having died in your sleep."

My Dad had definitely become more prone to bouts of misery as he had grown older but I understood why. Lots of the pleasures of life that he used to enjoy like walking over at Saddleworth or driving his car to wherever he wanted to go had been taken away from him with age. He was an independent soul who was now dependent on others and he didn't like that one bit.

"What about you, H? How are things with you? You don't seem to tell me as much these days about what's going on in your life? Is the job good?"

"It's a crazy job, Dad. From six in the morning until seven at night it's non-stop with emails, phone calls and appointments. Tyrone Building Society was very chilled but every mortgage broker in the country uses Avon & Severn Bank, so there is always a question to answer or a problem to sort out."

"Do you like it though?"

"Yes. I've never earned as much money so I'm particularly enjoying pay day. I get paid commission on top of my basic wage so it's definitely in my interest to put in the hours and make it work."

"I think the neighbours must think we've won the Lottery with us having a Mercedes on the drive now. I'm proud of you, son. Look how far you've come from delivering pizzas!"

"I know. I loved that job though."

"And what about Cathie? Things seem to be going very well with her."

"Yes, I just worry one day she'll come to her senses and realise she could do a whole lot better than me."

This seemed like a preposterous statement to my father. He pulled a face.

"Whatever gives you that idea? You're as fine a person as I've ever met, H."

I understood why he would think this. I had always tried to please him. It wasn't the full picture though. Truth was, I was run of the mill with a history of moments that I was ashamed of.

"Not in Cathie's league though."

"What are you on about, H? How can you get any finer than the finest?"

I thought about what Michael Moriarty had said about Avon & Severn being a shit rolled in glitter, perhaps that's all I was too.

"I don't know. I just worry sometimes that I'm not as fine as you think I am. I worry that Cathie will see through to my soul and not like what she sees."

"For goodness sake, H, stop being so harsh on yourself! You need to start looking for reasons to be happy rather than searching for reasons to be sad. We go through life worrying about what others think of us and our defects. As a teenager you worried about spots, in ten years' time you will be worrying about wrinkles, greying and balding. Then one day you'll get to my age, realise you're almost done and wish you'd never worried about all that trivial nonsense and just embraced happiness until the real issues came your way. Embrace your happiness now, H. Cathie loves you but don't sully it by inventing misery."

"You're right, I know that. Don't get me wrong, I'm really, really happy at the moment."

Dad slowly and with what seemed like an inordinate amount of effort, pulled himself up off his chair. Once the realisation dawned that he was in his late eighties, I momentarily went towards him but then stopped myself. He was a proud man and wanted to do as much as he could without my interference.

"Right son, I'm off to bed. I was just waiting up to see you come in. Sleep well and if I die in my sleep never forget how much your Mum and I loved you."

Despite his friendship with Maggie, Dad continued to say the same farewell each night before he went to bed. I know he wanted to imprint it into my brain so I would never forget it. I never have.

I remember that particular conversation with such clarity because, on reflection, I would say that period of time was probably the happiest in my life yet I still had worries and concerns. I still had my father around me, I was earning more money than I had ever earned before in a job I was enjoying and I had a blossoming relationship with the love of my life and yet I still worried, still found something to make me anxious.

When I look back, I wonder if I could have acted differently to avoid the mental mess that subsequently invaded my brain. I certainly made a lot of bad choices from then onwards but I think that perhaps I was just susceptible to mental illness. It is possible that the more sensitive you are as an individual, the deeper you care and, as a consequence, the more vulnerable you are to becoming mentally ill. As far as I'm aware, people who don't give a shit about others don't tend to get mentally ill and as a consequence it is those particular individuals who lead the 'Pull Yourself Together' campaign. Maybe if society treated people with depression or anxiety as 'those who care too much' rather than 'those with an inability to deal with day to day life' then the path to mental wellbeing would be strewn with fewer thorns.

There were still a lot of good times ahead after that chat with Dad but the dark clouds that were needed to make a rainbow were now being blown by a gale force wind right into my path.

Chapter Fifty Two

Avon & Severn Bank's Chief Executive, Nicholas Morrison-Adshead was on the rostrum speaking to two thousand sales staff and branch managers in a lecture theatre within the Birmingham NEC. After thirty minutes of eloquent positivity he was bringing his speech to a close.

"So, ladies and gentleman, I can assure you all that the negativity and scaremongering in the national press about the financial plight of our organisation is misplaced. There are tough times ahead for the banking sector, of that I have no doubt, but you have my word that we are better positioned than every organisation in our industry to ride the waves. If you are confronted by a tidal wave you want to be on board a 'Freedom Of The Seas' type cruise liner and not a pedalo. We will sail through to calmer waters and in doing so, we will only enhance our reputation as the best bank on the British high street and the one that held the hands of our customers and led them safely through these dark times.

Thank you all for attending today at such short notice. Please take the positive message back to your branches and your territories. Our customers have relied upon 'Avon & Severn' for over two hundred years and will be able to rely on us for two hundred more."

The 'Chief Exec' was given a polite round of applause and as he left the stage his audience filtered out. Several of the Business Development Managers in the North West and Scotland/North East team had agreed to reconvene in one of the bar areas around the auditorium to share our feelings about whatever the breaking news turned out to be. I must admit a lot of us were nervously anticipating news of mass redundancies so Nicholas Morrison-Adshead's speech had been somewhat of a relief. I had several positive chats with some upbeat colleagues who were feeling as relieved as I was but it was my subsequent conversation with Michael Moriarty that stood out.

I had got to know Michael a fair bit better in the months that had passed since our trip to Playa Blanca. I wouldn't go as far as to say he had become a mate but if I ever needed help with a mortgage criteria question or some guidance about who I needed to contact within the company about a specific issue, Michael was always on hand to guide me. He was in his early forties, was passionate and enthusiastic about the job he did but detested the bosses at Avon & Severn. He hated no-one more than his own boss, the notorious Benny Victory.

"Wanker!" was the first word Michael uttered as we came head to head.

"Great to see you too, Michael."

"Not you, you knob. Nick-Morrison-Shithead. Did he really think we'd believe all that crap?"

I had believed 'all that crap'. I had taken it at face value. The press had been highlighting, for a number of weeks, how Avon & Severn were particularly exposed by the banking crisis as our commercial arm had invested heavily in the North American sub-prime markets. Nicholas Morrison-Adshead had conceded our commercial business arm had indeed invested in these markets but insisted this was a miniscule percentage of our total business and its impact would be minimal.

"I thought he spoke well," I admitted, "I got engaged a few weeks ago and I was worried that I might not have a job after today but I feel much better now."

"Congratulations on your engagement, I hope you and your boyfriend have a long, happy life together but you have no reason to feel relieved, you…"

"Hang on," I interrupted, "my fiancée is female, thank you very much. Why did you presume I was gay?"

This felt like being back at Primary school. The whole school disco thing felt like it was happening again. I must admit I was offended.

"I don't know. No offence but you act gay so I just presumed you must be."

"I don't act gay!"

"Yes, you do," Michael stated firmly and insistently, "anyway, it's 2008 so who gives a flying fuck? The main issue is Nick Morrison-Shithead gathering us all together in a desperate attempt to stop our share price plummeting. He knows we're in the shit. He just doesn't want us to know. He'll be planning his escape to a thriving PLC as we speak. Sorry, no pun intended with the 'in the shit' comment."

"How come no-one else is reading into it the same way as you?"

"Because it suits them to ignore it. If someone tells you you're beautiful enough times you start to believe it even if you're a minger. The same principles apply here. No-one wants us to be the next Northern Rock but I reckon our commercial arm have us up to our eyeballs in it and that's why we've had this hastily arranged 'Don't Panic' meeting."

Northern Rock had been nationalised that February as they had borrowed heavily through international money markets. The growing mortgage and banking crisis had ensured they could no longer repay those debts. The government had had to step in to protect Northern Rock's customers. Avon & Severn were about five times the size of Northern Rock and although I thought Michael was unlikely to be right if he was the fallout would be on an unprecedented scale.

"Well, thanks for being your usual ray of sunshine, Michael. You've just ensured my three hour drive home is going to be a miserable one. I'll put a Leonard Cohen CD on and maybe stop at a service station and see if I can get hold of a noose or some razors."

"They're flying us back, thank God. Just think for a minute how much today will have cost them to bring two thousand people together from all over the country and hire out this place. Do you really think they'd do all this if it really was 'business as usual'? The boat's sinking, H, if I were you, I wouldn't be booking your wedding just yet."

I didn't say a word. Truth was, I already had.

Chapter Fifty Three

It was a bright, sunny, Spring Saturday afternoon. I was on one knee, on the banks of Dovestone reservoir on Saddleworth Moor, the most romantic spot I could think of that meant something to me. The little navy blue box Cathie's father had given me had opened to reveal Cathie's grandmother's engagement ring. When I asked Cathie's Dad's permission to marry his daughter, he had stood up, slowly shuffled out the room to his bedroom and then returned with the ring. He said it would make the moment extra special.

"Cathie, will you marry me?"

When I had run through this scenario a thousand times in the mirror at home and in my head, I had toyed with using the words, 'Will you do me the great honour of being my bride?' but it hadn't felt right saying that during my practice runs so I had opted for the straight forward option. Once I had said it though, it immediately didn't seem right, not because of the words I'd chosen but when I looked up into Cathie's eyes I didn't see excitement and elation, I saw upset and fear.

"No, H, I'm so sorry I can't do this now."

Cathie let go of my hand and made a feeble attempt to run away. I had driven us both there in my car so it wasn't as though there was anywhere for her to go. Nevertheless, with a horrible sense of dejection about reading all the signals wrongly, I pursued her as I was desperate for an explanation.

"Cathie, wait, just talk to me. How have I managed to balls this up?"

I could hear Cathie was crying. She stopped running though and just covered her face in her hands. I walked over and put my hands around her waist. She didn't flinch or try to push me away which I found encouraging. I was convinced Cathie was in love with me and that she would one day want to be married to me but it just seemed my timing was all wrong.

"Cathie, don't get upset. It's me who's made a mess of this. I've rushed this, I know I have. It's all too soon after Keith, isn't it?"

Cathie looked at me all teary eyed. At that point, I wasn't concerned about what the fallout from the rejection could be, I was just worried I'd upset her.

"Honestly 'H' that's not it at all. My relationship with Keith lost all value a long time ago."

"Is it the ring?"

"Of course not."

"Is it me then? Do you just not want to marry me?"

"You don't know me, 'H'."

"Of course I know you. I've known you nearly all my life, Cathie."

"No, you don't understand 'H'. You don't know what I'm capable of."

I think I did know. I think I had worked out what Cathie had done. It had been on my mind for a little while and admittedly it had bothered me when I thought I had figured it out but it didn't stop me loving her. I don't think anything could stop me loving her. All I worried about was that Cathie could stop loving me.

"I don't care what you've done, Cathie. Whatever it is, it's in the past."

Cathie really started crying then. I don't think I've ever seen one person cry so hard. They were tears of guilt about something and as I said I was convinced I knew what. It was heart breaking to witness.

"No, it isn't in the past," Cathie said through a torrent of tears, "it will always be with me, H. I've done a terrible, selfish, horrible thing. I feel so ashamed. I try to tell myself I was pushed into it but I really don't think I was. I just took the easy way out."

It was time for me to come clean. Time to explain that I knew exactly what it was that had happened and although I didn't really understand why Cathie would make a decision like that, it was her decision and I would support her through it as best as I could.

"Cathie, I think I know why you're upset. When you were in Australia, did you have an abortion?"

Cathie momentarily stopped crying and looked at me.

"An abortion?"

"Yes, I've listened to that Anna Nalick song you said you loved. That 'Breathe' one. It sounds like it's about someone who got pregnant by someone they didn't love and then had an abortion. Did the married man you were seeing get you pregnant and did you abort it?"

Cathie made a bizarre sound which was a mixture of a cry, a snort and a laugh.

"No, I've never had an abortion. I understand why some people do but I'm not sure I ever could. Hopefully it'll be something I never have to consider. I didn't realise that was what the song was about. I just thought it was about making mistakes and just having to put them behind us because we can't make time go backwards. That's why I liked it because I've made so many. It felt like a personal message."

"Do you think marrying me would be another one?"

"No. Marrying you would be the best thing I could ever possibly do, 'H'. I love you but things are really difficult for me right now and I just think it's the wrong time."

"Why? I don't understand what's going on."

"I've started to make plans for my parents to go into a care home. It's not something I've wanted to talk to you about but since I've come back from Australia I've just watched them steadily go downhill. Mum has started to have incontinence problems and Dad is starting to get very muddled and they are both very frail. I'm not talking about taking them tomorrow but if the steady decline continues over the next six months like it has in the last six months, I don't think I'll be able to cope with them, not with having Max too."

"Cathie, you're not doing anything wrong by making plans. You're just being prepared."

"It feels like such a betrayal though. It feels like I've come home, used them to provide Max and me with a place to run, to support me emotionally and babysit Max but now as they are getting frailer, it feels like I am stabbing them in the back. I just don't think they'll be safe in their own home much longer unless I'm there twenty four hours a day which is just impossible. They need to move somewhere safe. A warden controlled place maybe, I don't know, it just breaks my heart looking into all this."

I seem to be able to stir up internal feelings of guilt in a whole host of circumstances. I had just asked Cathie, the lady I loved more than I had ever loved anyone, to marry me but instead of feeling dejected or annoyed, all I felt was guilt. There was no real reason for me to have felt guilty. It wasn't as though I had known of Cathie's ordeal but guilt washed over me from head to toe like water from a shower. As my father was of a similar age to her parents, I also felt particularly able to empathise with her predicament.

"I understand, Cathie. If and when the time comes for me to put Dad into a home, I would feel the same."

"Look 'H', please don't think this is a 'No'. It's a 'not now'. I just want the timing to be right. Does that make sense?"

Of course it made sense. We walked back to the car with our arms around each other. It felt a bit like the scenario after you have had a blazing row and then patched things up. Still in love but aware of a fault line running through your relationship that you had previously been oblivious too. We drove back to my house to pick Max up. I had told Andy my plans to propose so he'd offered to look after Max at mine for a few hours as Cathie was understandably no longer happy leaving him with her parents. Max thought Andy was the funniest man on earth and loved spending time with him.

I slept well that night. Sometimes I find an overdose of emotions draining so went to bed at the same time as Dad did and slept soundly. My body clock gets confused by early nights though so I was stirring from 5 a.m and when there was a knock at the door at seven, I was already in the kitchen in my dressing gown making spreading jam on a couple of pieces of toast.

When I opened the door, Cathie was there on bended knee with Max standing beside her. Cathie was all choked up so couldn't get her words out so Max said it for her.

"Hi 'H'. Mummy wants to know whether you'll marry us?"

I scooped Max up and gave him a kiss on the cheek.

"How could anyone not want to marry you, chubby chops? Are you sure your Mummy wants to marry me?"

"She said she does."

"Does that mean I'd have to live with you Maxy and your trumpy bottom?"

"I don't have a trumpy bottom. You have a pooey face!"

"I do not!"

I tickled Max under his arms and he gave out a delighted giggle.

"Is that a 'Yes'?" Cathie asked as she got back on to two feet.

"There's no way I'm ever going to say no to you two. Of course it's a 'Yes'."

Cathie and Max came in and as Max played with some toys on the lounge carpet, Cathie and I sat down and talked things through.

"I thought this whole idea needed to be postponed," I said as I drank my tea.

Prior to answering Cathie had made an observation that she wanted to question me about.

"How can you drink that tea when it's that hot?"

"I don't know. I just do."

"You must have an asbestos mouth."

"Must do. Anyway, why the change of heart?"

"I didn't sleep well last night thinking about it. Our Dads are in their eighties, my Mum's late seventies, but she's not in much better shape than them. Their energy and their vitality is ebbing away from them day by day. All three of them have been wonderful parents to us. I would feel so guilty if one of them didn't live long enough to see us getting married. I want them to be there whilst they are mentally and physically fit enough to enjoy it too. Mum and Dad not being in great health isn't a reason to put things off, I mean it's not as if they are going to get better, so I said to myself 'Let's just do this'. I can't imagine my life without you so why wait? Let's just do it. I've always wanted a big white wedding and I've always wanted my father to walk me down the aisle. He would be so proud. Let's speak to people today and see if we can get something booked for as soon as possible."

"Are you sure?"

"I've never been more certain of anything in my entire life."

This was fantastic news. In fact 'fantastic news' was underplaying it. It was the best news I had ever had. From that point onwards, things fell into place very quickly. Later that day, Cathie managed to book Crimble Hall in Bamford for a September wedding. There had apparently been several cancellations due to couples panicking about money and employment due to what was to become known as 'the credit crunch'. Once everything was booked and we started having to pay out deposits left, right and centre, Cathie started to worry about costs too. She determinedly resisted any attempts by her Dad to contribute to our Wedding and I did the same with my Dad but having done so, Cathie started to get edgy about how we would find the money ourselves. I told her not to panic. I told Cathie I had sufficient savings and I would sort everything out. I had saved £20,000 over the years and that would have been fine to cover the wedding costs, the thing I hadn't really factored in was where we were going to live once we were married. I sort of (wrongly) just assumed Cathie and Max would move in with me and my Dad. Cathie would have been fine with it too it was my Dad who had other plans. Two weeks after we announced our engagement, Dad announced Maggie Corcoran couldn't afford the upkeep on her property and that she would be putting it up for sale and moving in with him. In no time at all, I went from having no debts and £20,000 savings to no savings, a relatively large mortgage and several credit cards maxed up to the limit. Given the financial crisis I should have been far, far more cautious but I just wanted to do anything and everything to keep Cathie happy. Nothing was more important than that.

Chapter Fifty Four

The atmosphere was tense. About one hundred Branch Managers, Area Managers and Sales staff of 'Avon & Severn Bank' were gathered together, in universal trepidation, in a meeting room in Bewleys Hotel at Manchester Airport waiting for a midday announcement. The previous day we had received text messages, emails and phone calls telling us to cancel all plans for the following day. We needed to be at one of eight designated meeting rooms across the length and breadth of the UK for an 'important announcement'.

At one minute to midday, a man called Graham Cunliffe, North West Regional Manager for the bank, got to his feet and flanked by bodyguards from Human Resources walked to the front of the room. Clutching a piece of paper he turned to address his audience.

"Thank you all for re-scheduling your day at such short notice. I have a set script that I need to read from. I am not in a position, at this stage, to answer any questions, but I am sure in the fullness of time there will be further briefings. Right, it's midday so I will crack on with the announcement."

Graham took a glasses case from the inner pocket of his jacket, gave his glasses a quick polish with a cloth, popped them on and began to read.

"Ladies & Gentleman, as I am sure you are all aware, we are currently in the midst of a global financial crisis. Due to liquidity issues, 'Avon & Severn' is one of several Banks that have approached the UK government for help during these troubled times. The government has agreed to step in to provide some security to the UK public and ensure our banking industry is not under threat. Several UK banks, including 'Avon & Severn' will be nationalised or partially nationalised to adequately manage the ramifications of this global crisis.

Internally, here at 'Avon & Severn' to comply with the terms of the agreement made with the UK government, there will be a process of streamlining the company. As yet, we are not fully aware of how significant this streamlining will be. You will all, however, receive formal notification within the next seven days that your current role may not exist in the newly re-structured company. As a result, I regret to inform you, that you are all 'potentially redundant'. Once we are fully aware of the measures necessary to streamline our newly nationalised company, we will formally advertise every position. We thank you again for your attendance today and ask you all to continue to work with the passion and dedication you always have during this transformation. Thank you."

At this point Graham Cunliffe took off his glasses, put them back in their case, popped them back in his jacket pocket and hurriedly left the room. It was left to one of the Human Resources ladies to bring the meeting to a close. There was a general murmuring on every table as everyone sought clarification from their colleagues about what exactly this announcement had meant.

"Can I have a bit of quiet, please?" the lady from Human Resources pleaded.

No-one took much notice originally, as they were too engaged in conversation but after a further minute or so of pleading and shushing, there was finally silence in the room.

"Thank you," HR lady said in a tone that didn't sound genuine, "As Graham has just said, there is a limited amount of information available at this stage. Your line managers will receive further briefings over the next few days and they will relay this information to you all. You are all now free to leave but may I re-iterate it is 'business as usual'.

I didn't leave straight away. As far as I was concerned they could shove their 'business as usual' up their backsides, at least for the rest of the day. I had paid for two hours parking and had cancelled all my appointments so I went for a coffee, sat on my own and let the panic slowly sink in.

Cathie and I had just bought a three bedroomed, three storey terraced house in Coal Bank Fold, Norden for £150,000 with a mortgage of £135,000. It had a massive kitchen dining area and three double bedrooms and as soon as Cathie set eyes on it she knew this was her dream starter home. With the wedding coming up, I was hoping to just put down a 5% deposit to keep some money back but 95% loan to value mortgages had disappeared and there were very few lenders even offering 90% deals. I put the majority of the £20,000 I had saved into the house with the rest soon eaten up by moving costs and a few of the wedding costs. The remaining costs went on to credit cards. Those in the know were predicting the financial crisis would last a couple of years so if I could keep my job and get back to being paid bonuses then I could chip away at the balances then. In the meantime, I intended just to make the minimum payments each month. If I lost my job it wouldn't just be the credit cards I would have to worry about. I would also have to find a way to pay the mortgage. I could feel my hands trembling. If Avon & Severn operated a 'last in, first out' attitude then I was in serious trouble. I couldn't bear the thought of breaking Cathie's heart but without a job there was just no way I'd be able to keep her dreams alive.

Chapter Fifty Five

My mother returned. I hadn't slept well during the run up to the wedding. After the news about having to re-apply for the jobs that remained at 'Avon & Severn', I never seemed to be able to settle at night time and spent several frustrating hours every night tossing and turning. To try to help me relax on the eve of our Wedding, I had drunk a few bottles of Whitbread's Celebration Ale. Dad had bought them back in 1992 to celebrate two hundred and fifty years of the brewery and had saved them in the garage for a special occasion.

"No occasion could be more special," Dad had said as Andy came out of the garage carrying half a dozen of the twelve bottles that Dad had bought. By the time Andy left, all twelve were empty. I was probably responsible for half a dozen of them. I didn't realise they were 11.5% alcohol until I woke up on the morning of our Wedding Day with a stinking hangover and checked the label on one of them in an attempt to fathom out why I felt so bad. People who look at our Wedding photos often ask if Dad and I had a stomach bug or flu that day as we both looked so pale.

The beers weren't solely responsible for my pale complexion. A lack of sleep once again played its part. I had a lot on my mind and despite the beers (or perhaps partly because of them) my mind wouldn't settle. I became increasingly frustrated with my inability to sleep and the more I thought about it, the more difficult it became. At about four in the morning I must have finally drifted off. It felt like I had barely snatched a moment of sleep when I became aware that bright lights had filled my room. I opened my eyes to discover the brightness from a rainbow pouring through the window. I was just about to climb out of bed and walk towards the light when I spotted, out the corner of my eye, that there was a figure sitting bolt upright next to me, propped up by several pillows. I turned my head so quickly it jolted. The figure was my mother.

"Shit Mum! You scared me to death!"

My mother frowned. She was looking older. She was definitely greyer and more lined than I had ever seen her before. Somehow she was losing her youthfulness.

"Harry, you should be well aware that cursory words and references to death are entirely inappropriate in my presence. Nevertheless, given the circumstances, I'll forgive you. I know there's a lot going on in your life at the moment. When did you get this double bed? It's very comfy."

"I've had it a few years now. Mum can we hurry this along in case I wake up. I'm getting married in the morning."

I sensed Mum's purpose in visiting was more important than discussing how comfy my mattress was.

"I know you're getting married my love. I will be very proud watching over you."

"I wish you could be there."

"I wish that too, Harry and I will be there, in spirit."

"It's not the same."

"I know. It doesn't seem fair, does it? I only have one child and you only have one mother and we can't share this significant day in your life. If there was something I could do to be there with you, I'd do it but unfortunately it's impossible. At least your father will be there. I am so pleased about that."

My Mum had always thought about everyone else before herself. Sadly, that was the very reason she would be missing my Wedding Day. What a fool I had been not to treasure her.

"Can I give you a hug, Mum?"

"Now wouldn't that be lovely? I don't think it could possibly work though, Harry. You're in a dreamlike state, if you reach over to hug me, grasping at thin air or maybe even a pillow, it would just wake you up and I'd be gone."

"How come you're here beside me anyway rather than on the rainbow?"

My Mum smiled like she was proud that I'd figured that out. It wasn't rocket science normally she was up on a rainbow now she was on my bed. I realised Mum's are just proud of everything their children do.

"You're more anxious than you've been previously, Harry, so you've drawn me closer to you. I believe that can only ever happen once, if I ever come back I will be back on the rainbow. What is it that's making you so anxious? Tomorrow should be the best day of your life. You should be excited not apprehensive."

"Mum, I couldn't be more excited about marrying Cathie, I really couldn't. I'm not compromising or settling in any way. If every single woman in the world stood side by side in one long line and I got to take my pick, I'd pick Cathie. Not based on looks based on the whole combination of factors that make Cathie who she is. She's not perfect, nobody is, especially not me, but she's wonderful and to think I am going to be able to spend my life with her is fantastic beyond words."

"So what's the matter?"

"Money. I'm not sure how I'm ever going to repay all these debts from the wedding and from buying the new house. My savings paid for half of it but the rest has gone on to credit cards."

"Could your Dad not have helped?"

"We didn't want to ask Dad or Cathie's parents. None of them have much and none of them are in the best of health so it didn't seem right asking."

"What about Cathie?"

"She's helped as much as she can but she doesn't have much to give."

"So it's all been down to you."

"Pretty much, which is fine as long as I'm still in a job but everyone at work is being interviewed for the jobs that are left at the moment and I won't find out whether or not I've got one until I get back from my honeymoon."

My Mum gave me another familiar look. This time it reminded me of a look she used to give me as a teenager when I was acting in a self-deprecating manner and Mum would just say a few words but they were enough to get the message across that she believed in me.

"You'll be fine. People like you aren't ten a penny, Harry. Your company wouldn't want to lose someone like you."

"I hope you're right."
"I will be. Just concentrate on enjoying every moment of your wedding and honeymoon. You can concentrate on your job once that's all out the way. If it doesn't work out with the job, there will be other jobs. There will only ever be one wedding and one honeymoon. Don't let insignificant concerns spoil such significant occasions."

I understood this was just a dream even whilst dreaming I understood that's exactly what it was. My Mum had been a fine woman but the Mum I had created was chattier, smarter and closer to me than the Mum I had as a child. Perhaps our relationship would have become like this if she hadn't died but I understood I only conjured up images of my Mum when I needed her most. Once my mind started working overtime with my fears and concerns it would create a scenario where my Mum would arrive to provide me with some sort of re-assurance. The fact that she was here talking to me soothingly about the need for me to put my fears to the back of my mind was, in reality, an indication that I was failing to do just that.

Chapter Fifty Six

If I could have paused my life at any point up until now, allowing me to savour the moment or had the ability to rewind my life back to a certain instance to relive it all over again, looking over my left shoulder as Cathie and her father walked slowly up the aisle on our Wedding Day, in the function room at Crimble Hall in Bamford, would undoubtedly be the moment I would select.

It goes without saying that if I could have changed a moment and allowed my life to change direction then I would change the Sunday morning walk that killed my mother. I would have pushed her out the way before she even contemplated sacrificing her life for my father and me.

If I could only relive rather than change my life though, our Wedding Day would be the day I would want to return to. Not only was it incredible to see the most beautiful woman that has ever graced this earth, looking more astonishing than she had ever looked before, heading up the aisle arm in arm with her father to become my wife but I was surrounded by very special people too. To my right stood my 'Best Man', Andy and in the row behind, beaming with pride, was my father. Across the aisle, sobbing heartily, supported by one of Cathie's sister's, was Cathie's Mum. Eight years on, my Dad and both Cathie's parents are no longer with us, but nothing will ever take away the memories of that amazing day.

I am obviously aware that life has no rewind button nor does it have a pause button. I am aware that we are all mortal beings and no matter how much anyone tries to convince themselves that they will live forever in their own idea of paradise, it simply isn't so. For me, religions are just a blindfold to protect us from seeing the truth. From the beginning of time to its inevitable end, we are all just here for the blink of an eye. We just need to treasure the special people we have been fortunate enough to share our brief moments with. Reality dictates that I won't ever see those I've lost again. I just sometimes like to dream that I can. To travel back to our Wedding Day, surrounded by all the people that loved us most on our special day would be almost perfect. If my Mum had been there to share it too, it would have been beyond compare. No-one has the same unconditional love that a parent has for a child and no child appreciates exactly how much they are loved until that love is taken away.

I'm not the best at describing clothes so if you want to know what Cathie's wedding dress was like, you're probably best asking one of the women who attended, they generally have a far better eye for detail than me. On a basic level, I can tell you it was white, it was stunning, Cathie had bare shoulders so it appeared to have magical qualities that kept it from falling down and it was designed by someone called Maggie Sottero. I remember the back of the dress was just as mindblowingly gorgeous as the front, which I think is unusual. Admittedly Cathie is one of those women who could wear a sack and still look beautiful but her wedding dress definitely enhanced all her charms. It was tight to the skin in all the right places but then flowed outwards below the knee. Cathie's Dad kept saying she looked like a princess and she truly did. Max followed Cathie down the aisle, in front of the bridesmaids, wearing navy blue trousers, a white shirt with a grey waistcoat, a navy blue bow tie and a very sophisticated navy blue flat cap. I kept expecting him to get fed up of the flat cap and throw it off but I think he liked all the female attention it was bringing him as he kept it on pretty much all day and into the evening.

Andy's speech was as funny, sentimental and clever as I had anticipated it would be. He avoided the stereotypical 'Best Man' routine of taking the mickey out of me but still managed to get everyone roaring with laughter in his fifteen minute speech. At one stage, to illustrate that we were both really into our music, he told a story and would pause from time to time and hold up a cover of an LP and I would have to say what the album title was. It started with him saying,

" I first became friends with H when we were....(and Andy held up the James album cover with the embryonic child on – at which point I said 'Seven'), when I heard (he held up the Fleetwood

Mac album with Stevie Nicks' calf over Mick Fleetwood's knee – at which point I said 'Rumours') that he wasn't very good at football. As I was hopeless myself this was great news for me. The other kids at school had tried us both in (Andy held up the LP with the close up facial shot of Leonard Cohen and I said 'Various Positions') but no matter where we played we were always a (Andy held up a Talk Talk album with a bare tree full of exotic birds and I said 'Laughing Stock')."

Without boring you with the whole routine he deliberately made the stories more elaborate and the titles longer so towards the end I was being linked in to say things like 'Whatever People Say I Am, That's What I'm Not' and finished with the Fiona Apple album cover with one of the longest titles ever, which is 'When The Pawn Hits the Conflicts He Thinks like a King What He Knows Throws the Blows When He Goes to the Fight and He'll Win the Whole Thing 'fore He Enters The Ring There's No Body to Batter When Your Mind Is Your Might so When You Go Solo, You Hold Your Own Hand and Remember That Depth is the Greatest of Heights and If You Know Where You Stand, Then You Know Where to Land and If You Fall It Won't Matter, Cuz You'll Know That You're Right."

I received a standing ovation from everyone at the Wedding, including Cathie, for remembering that Fiona Apple album title and that was my point, in Andy's speech he avoided ridiculing me for easy laughs but set out to portray me in the best light possible. Andy loves attention and he could have made it all about him but it takes a special person to make people laugh by making someone look clever rather than making them look stupid.

The other two speeches that preceded Andy's were well received but I'm guessing more forgettable for our guests on the day. Cathie's Dad's speech was brief but heartfelt and mine was hopefully the right combination of appreciation (of what a lucky man I was) and thank yous (to everyone who had ensured our day was a continuous joy).

In the evening, Cathie had arranged, prior to the disco, for us to have ninety minutes of karaoke. If this matter had been discussed with me, I would have advised against it as the stage can be hogged by a couple of idiots or it can create an atmosphere of universal reluctance amongst the guests but on this occasion I would have been spectacularly wrong. Everyone loved it. Pretty much everyone took a single turn with the microphone and the highlight of the whole evening for me was when my Dad got up to sing 'Mr Bojangles'. He may not have been able to skip around the dancefloor like Sammy Davis Jnr or Robbie Williams but boy did he sing it well. He must have known he was going to sing it, as he'd even brought a top hat with him. I don't think there's a month that goes by that I don't still watch that three minute clip from our wedding video of him belting it out. One day I'll get past the first minute without crumbling in a flood of tears but I think that may still be a while off.

Not long after Dad sang Mr Bojangles, the karaoke came to an end and it was time for Cathie and me to have our first dance. Andy had fallen in love with the music of an Australian brother and sister duo called Angus & Julia Stone and had urged us to listen to one of their songs which he felt would be great for our first dance. It was (fairly unoriginally) called 'The Wedding Song'. I reluctantly agreed to give it a listen as I was anticipating it to be cheesy and completely inappropriate, but a few weeks before our wedding Andy sat us both down and played it to us. Everything about it was ideal; the pace, the voice, the lyrics and the simplicity. Sometimes Andy just seems to know me better than I know myself. When we danced that night it didn't feel like anyone else was in the room. I'm a man not afraid to cry but it was Cathie who cried her way through our first dance. It seemed to round off a wonderful day perfectly and we felt so privileged to have found each other.

Cathie and I left the evening 'do' just before midnight. My Dad and Maggie, as well as Cathie's parents, had long since said their goodbyes but the younger members of the Wedding Party were still in full swing and apparently many of them partied through the night. One or two of Cathie's friends from work ended up getting it together with a couple of the Irish guys from Tyrone

Building Society who had travelled over. I'd say the two lads were both punching well above their weight but English women seem to swoon over the Irish lilt and perhaps the free flowing Prosecco may have impaired their judgement too. Anyway, as a fellow male who was so obviously punching above his weight, I was delighted for them.

As we left, the DJ played Gracie Fields 'Wish Me Luck (As You Wave Me Goodbye)' and everyone formed a large archway to the door. Outside there was a taxi waiting with the anticipated 'Just Married' sign on the back window and a load of cans dangling on the floor at the back having been tied to around the bumper with string. It took us over to the 'Village Hotel' in Bury. We could have stayed in Rochdale but Cathie was worried that some of the lads may have found it funny to trash our room so we headed over to the 'Village', only telling our parents (and the taxi driver) where we were staying.

Our honeymoon was a little unconventional. We could have gone for the beachside location and just chilled out for a fortnight after the manic build up to the wedding and I'm sure we would have enjoyed it but we decided to hire a camper van and we toured around Germany, Austria and Switzerland in it. I always got a perverse kick out of seeing the reaction on people's faces when I told them what we were doing for our honeymoon. I guess it's a bit like calling your son 'Harold', people pretend to like it but you can see it written all over their face that they think it's a dreadful idea.

Despite the misgivings of others our honeymoon turned out great. We were blessed with bright blue skies and starry evenings pretty much throughout our trip. All three countries are filled with gorgeous places and we pledged to go back as there is only so much you can do within a two week trip. We also wanted to build in an element of relaxation so we had a rule that other than the first and last day, I could only drive between breakfast and lunch. We tended to map out routes of an evening that ensured I rarely did more than ninety minutes driving. I'd do it all again in a heartbeat.

I spoke to my Dad every couple of days whilst we were away. Cathie was ringing home at about five every day to speak to Max as Andy and Maggie were looking after him, so I would often grab the phone off her to speak to them all. They would often ring us too, to ask if Max was OK with certain foods so it didn't seem in any way unusual when my phone rang on our final morning and my Dad's name came up. We were just eating breakfast at the table in the motorhome before driving down to Geneva to hand the vehicle back in and fly back to Manchester.

"Hi Dad."

"Hello 'H'. It's Maggie, not your Dad. Now I've got something I need to tell you but I don't want you to panic...."

I immediately started to panic. If Maggie was phoning and Dad wasn't able to, that meant something had happened to him, something serious. Was he dead?

"...it's your father."

I knew it.

"...he's had a heart attack."

Chapter Fifty Seven

I felt nauseous. I had spent my whole life living with the fear of losing my Dad but nothing major had ever happened to him – until now.

"Is he OK?"

"He's as OK as an 87 year old who's had a heart attack can be. He's back home now. They've done all the tests at the hospital and they said it was a mild one."

"Hang on. He's back home? When did he have a heart attack, Maggie?"

"On Tuesday," she replied sheepishly.

We had spoken to Andy and Maggie since Tuesday and there had been no mention that my Dad had been ill. I had even asked to speak to him on Wednesday and Maggie said she had run him up to the 'Cemetery' in her car as he fancied a pint. That now seemed like a bit of a sick joke.

"Tuesday! Tuesday? We spoke to you yesterday and on Wednesday. It's Friday morning, Maggie. Did you not think to tell me before now?"

Cathie was looking over at me from the other side of the table. I had mentioned Dad's heart attack so she was partially aware of the situation but I could tell she wanted the conversation to end so I could properly update her as to what was going on.

"Your Dad wouldn't let me, love. He said the moment you found out you would cancel your honeymoon and come rushing straight back home."

"That's exactly what I would have done, Maggie, because my father had a heart attack."

"He didn't want to spoil things for you, love. If he'd have been on death's door then of course I would have told you, but he isn't. He's doing very well."

"You still shouldn't have taken any notice of him, Maggie. Can I speak to him?"

"Of course you can love. I just wanted to have a word first. I knew you'd be mad with us and I wanted you to get your anger out on me before you spoke to your Dad. Anyway, I'll pass you over now."

I didn't think I was angry just annoyed that I hadn't been made aware that my father had suffered a heart attack 72 hours earlier. I took a deep breath though as I didn't want my irritation to come over when I spoke to Dad. I heard the muffled sounds of the phone being passed over and then the frail voice of my father.

"Hello 'H'."

"Hi Dad. What have you been up to you daft old sod? Have you been watching those re-runs of Baywatch again? I've told you it's not good for you watching C.J bounding along that beach."

"I wish I had son. I just went to get the milk off the step on Tuesday morning and as I bent down to pick it up it felt like someone had put my left arm and chest into a vice. Luckily Maggie was watching me from the bedroom window so she ran down, sat me on the doorstep and rang an ambulance. I thought it was curtains for me and do you know what, I felt ready. I've had a long life, I've been lucky enough to see you grow into a wonderful man and marry a beautiful woman. If it had been my time, I could have had no complaints. Anyway, turns out, as heart attacks go, it wasn't a bad one. Looks like I may be hanging around for a little while yet."

"How long were you in hospital for?"

"Just a couple of nights, Tuesday and Wednesday. I don't want you being cross with Maggie for not phoning, 'H'. I insisted that she kept it from you. What good would it have done you cutting short your honeymoon? It wouldn't have helped to mend my heart, it would have broken it."

"I don't know. It just doesn't seem right us having the time of our lives whilst you were in hospital."

"Don't be daft. I'm absolutely fine. When I do eventually die, I don't want you to be moping around then either. Have a bloody big party. Your mother's funeral was the sad one. Mine needs to be a celebration. No black clothes, no false announcements about me finding God at the last minute so Christian friends can persuade themselves I'm going to their heaven, all I want is everyone who goes to have some good old fashioned fun. I think I'll make a list of what songs I want playing. I've decided I don't want a church service either just an hour at the crematorium will suit me fine and a reception at 'The Cemetery'. I don't think there'll be many people there, you, Cathie and Max are the only family I've got and, other than Maggie and Andy, I can only imagine one or two neighbours and a few of the regulars from the pub coming along."

It seemed wrong Dad talking about his funeral and equally wrong that a gentleman as fine as him wouldn't pack out the crematorium.

"Dad, let's not talk about your funeral."

"Why? It's going to happen soon enough. If you don't want to talk about it, I'll write up some instructions and leave them in the bottom drawer next to my bed. Don't forget that's where they will be. I started paying into a funeral plan when I was seventy so it's all paid for."

Given my financial issues I must admit that I was a little relieved that I wouldn't have to magic up some additional money when Dad did pass away.

"Dad, you just concentrate on enjoying life for now. How's Max doing?"

You could hear the joy in Dad's voice when he spoke about Max.

"He's great. I don't think Andy will want to give him back to you. They've been up to Blackpool Pleasure Beach, to the cinema, over at Gracie Fields to see the children's play and been on the train into Manchester as Max wanted to see where Andy lives. He's had a whale of a time"

We pretty much knew all this from our conversations with Andy, Max and Maggie but it was great to hear Dad enthuse about Andy's time with Max.

"Away from work Andy's still a big kid. He's probably enjoying himself more than Max."

My Dad's voice suddenly took on a conspiratorial tone.

"H, there's something I want to ask you. Just wait a second, I think Maggie's gone upstairs to do her hair…"

I pulled a confused face to Cathie.

"What's the matter?" she asked.

"Dad's up to something, I'm not sure what."

There was silence for thirty seconds other than the sound of Dad putting the phone down. He came back sounding a little out of breath.

"It's fine. She's got the hairdryer on. H, how would you feel if I asked Maggie to marry me?"

I was taken aback by the question. It wasn't as though I hadn't previously considered the possibility of Dad marrying Maggie, but as time had gone, I had stopped thinking about it. I had grown to like Maggie, over the years I don't think she had been the best mother in the world to Andy but she was definitely good for my Dad and took good care of him. As my mother had pointed out in one of my dreams, Dad probably wouldn't have been interested in Maggie in his younger days but these days they both filled a void in each other's lives. I had no reason to object.

"Dad, if you think it would enhance your life by marrying Maggie, just go and do it. You don't need my permission and as long as you would be happy, I would be delighted for the pair of you."

"It wouldn't affect your inheritance, H, I would see to that."

"Dad, I couldn't care less about your inheritance money. I'd rather you spent all your money enjoying your life whilst you're here."

"I care though. I haven't got much, other than the house, but if it helps you and Cathie a bit, I'd like to make sure you have it."

"Dad, just go with your heart. If it makes you happy then I'm happy too just don't do anything until we get home. You've just had one heart attack, I don't want you to give yourself another one."

"OK. Thanks son. I'm really pleased to know you wouldn't think I've lost my marbles."

"Of course not."
"Give my love to Cathie and if anything does happen to me, son, never forget how much your Mum and I loved you."

Chapter Fifty Eight

I was sat outside a meeting room in one of 'Avon & Severn's' office buildings in Bristol. I had just been for a wee but felt like I needed to go again. I put it down to nerves. I'd been into the cubicle to avoid the splash back off the urinal. If I was made redundant I was thinking I was going to patent a urinal that didn't leave a gentle spatter of urine all over the crotch area. It wasn't a serious thought.

Why the powers that be had decided to make everyone in the junior management and sales teams, from across the UK, drive down to Bristol to hear news on their fate seemed very strange to me. We all had work mobile phones so it would have saved the government a tidy sum if we had just received a call but I had long since stopped trying to work out the thought process of the senior management, perhaps if they had worked logically and responsibly 'Avon & Severn' may not have been one of the British banks being nationalised.

I had received an email to say I was to be at 'Meeting Room 117' in the Sir Stanley Booth building, named after one of the company's founders, but it was just an automated Human Resources email which didn't indicate who my meeting was with. I presumed it was my boss, Martin or someone from Human Resources but when the door opened it was Graham Cunliffe, the North West Regional Manager who ushered me in.

I remember my heart really started pounding at that point, so much so I wondered if there was some sort of hereditary defect as I'd never been so aware of it bouncing around in my chest like a rubber ball. My whole career felt like it was on the line and I wasn't sure if Martin Sunderland's absence was a good sign or a bad one for me. Did 'Avon & Severn' want someone that wasn't close to you to act as the executioner?

Graham shook me warmly by the hand. I wondered whether this was to calculate my weight for the hanging.

"Come in, Harry, good to see you again, please take a seat."

I had been in previous group meetings when Graham Cunliffe had been in attendance but had never spoken to him on a one to one basis before. I'm pretty sure if I'd have said I wasn't Harry McCoy and had just got lost searching for the restaurant he'd have apologised and sent me on my way. I was just a name on a list to him. I just wanted to find out if it was the list of those staying or the list of those leaving.

It was a small room with two chairs either side of a desk. The comfy leather seat and all Graham's paperwork were on one side of the desk so I correctly assumed I needed to sit on the opposite side. Graham walked around the desk and sat down to face me.

"Difficult times, Harry, aren't they? It's beyond everyone's worst nightmares to see a fine institution like ours on its knees. The Americans have triggered all this off with their reckless internal lending. They say when America sneezes the rest of the world catches their cold, well this time the States have caught a stomach bug in a world without toilet roll and they're just crapping all over the rest of us."

I refrained from mentioning we might not have caught the bug off them if we hadn't spent so much time kissing their arse. I don't know much about politics other than knowing it's best not to mention it especially if you're going to contradict what someone else has just said. I kept my mouth shut other than stating my agreement.

"Yes, it's awful."

"Anyway, Harry, like everyone else you've had to sit and suffer since the first announcement so I'm not going to beat around the bush. I'm pleased to tell you that we would like to offer you a Business Development Manager's role in our new mortgage sales force."

Relief swept over me.

"That's fantastic! Thank you!"

"No problem, nobody gets offered the roles down to sentiment, Harry. We think you are perfectly suited to the job that you're doing, that's why we want to keep you on. You have the earned the offer through you hard work since you joined 'Avon & Severn'. Keep it going."

I felt a little flattered. The Business Development Managers had a tendency to tell you themselves how good they are, so it was great to have a compliment from someone else. A senior figure, as well. As I now knew my job was safe and, at least in the short term, my finances were too, I wanted to know what, if anything, had changed.

"Will I have the same territory that I had before?"

"No, I'm afraid not. As you can imagine, the logistics have been incredibly complicated. We have a smaller sales force now and some of our new guys have been brought in from other areas of the business so we have had to consider where they live. Let me check where you will be covering. All I know off the top of my head is that it's changed."
Graham put his glasses on and inspected his list.

"Where is it you live again, Harry?"

"Rochdale."

"OK. Well your new territory is going to be from Wigan upwards all the way to Carlisle. Your territory stretches eastwards as far as Colne, so you'll have all the M65 brokers too, the Blackburn, Burnley, Accrington and Clitheroe guys. You'll be clocking up the miles but there aren't many mortgage brokers between Blackpool and Carlisle so if you cover the Lake District a couple of days a month, Carlisle once a month and do all your other major towns on rotation, you should be fine."

I knew how to work a territory. I was incredibly analytical so wasn't worried about the logistics at all. People in power like to have their say on everything though. It's the way of the world. Good bosses like to help you. Bad bosses only ever want to tell you. I wasn't presuming he was a bad boss, just because he was telling me how to manage my territory but it made me smile a little inside that he thought he needed to tell me.

"Thanks Graham, you're right it should be fine. Do you know if Martin Sunderland will still be my boss?"

"Did you get on with Martin?"

I gathered immediately that the answer was obviously 'No' but Graham wanted to do a bit of prying.

"Yes, I liked him. I thought he was a good bloke."

"Yes, he was. Not quite as good a manager but that's immaterial now. Martin has decided to take the redundancy package that was on offer."

I presumed this was his only choice. I knew from the conversations I had had with Martin that he was very keen to stick around.

"That's a shame. Do you know who my new boss will be?"

'Avon & Severn' had already taught me that my only priority was to look after number one. There was no room for sentiment at this place. Three seconds after discovering my boss had been ousted my thoughts were more about who his successor would be.

"Well, the new North West Regional Sales Manager, who reports in to me, will be Maria Pilkington…"

I knew Maria Pilkington very well. She had been in the commercial division but had a reputation for being a young, strong and motivational manager. Every time I had met her she had seemed to have an in depth knowledge of the mortgage industry but also, more importantly, seemed to be the type of person who was genuinely interested in people. She would ask about you rather than tell you about her. This was exciting news. My excitement didn't last long.

"….it was a necessity, however," Graham continued, "to place one of the North West team into the Scotland and North East team to balance out the numbers. As you are going to be geographically closest to Scotland, it seemed to make sense for you to be the one that we transferred across to that team. How do you feel about that?"

It was happening. No matter how I answered the question it had already been decided. I decided to play the game.

"It's great news. I don't have any experience of the Scottish market so hopefully I will learn more about it whilst I'm in that team. I always enjoy going to Edinburgh and Glasgow too."

"Excellent. Just the sort of reaction we were hoping for."

"Who will my boss be?"

"Benny Victory. Benny's been with us for donkeys' years. Do you know him?"

"I know who he is but I've never met him."

"You'll enjoy working for Benny. He'll teach you a lot. He doesn't suffer fools gladly but he most certainly gets the best out of those who want to learn."

That wasn't the reputation I'd heard at the coal front. I didn't know anyone that liked Benny Victory. From what I had witnessed first hand even his wife didn't appear overly keen. I would just have to judge for myself though. If I continued to work hard and hit my targets I told myself there would be no reason for Benny Victory to dislike me.

"I shall look forward to meeting him," I lied.

"Any further questions, Harry?"

"No, thank you for giving me this opportunity. I'm delighted to still be working for 'Avon & Severn'."

That bit was true. I felt incredibly relieved. I somehow had to find the money to pay off my credit card debts from the house move, the wedding and the honeymoon, if I hadn't kept my job that task would have been impossible. I stood up and shook hands with Graham.

"Oh, one last thing before you go, Harry. Keep your diary free on 25th and 26th August, three weeks on Tuesday and Wednesday."

"OK, I will do. How come?"

"We're going to have a re-launch party for the new Sales team at Peckforton Castle. It's a great spot up in Cheshire. It's all booked under my name as I don't think the Government would take too kindly to knowing that the nation's taxpayers are forking out for a good old fashioned 'Avon & Severn' knees up. I'll just claim it all back through my expenses. We'll have a brief informal meeting but the main intention is to let our hair down a bit after a stressful few months. Bring your beer goggles."

I thought about that final sentence on my way home. Did he really mean 'bring my beer goggles'? As far as I was aware that meant to drink enough to get together with someone you wouldn't find attractive when you were sober. Was that what he was encouraging a recently married member of his staff to be doing? I decided he probably meant 'have your drinking head on' or something similar but had just mistakenly chosen the wrong phrase. I wasn't looking forward to it. I hated events like this and had no doubt this one would be particularly uncomfortable with some of the bosses telling their surviving staff how wonderful they were and a few of the more arrogant Business Development Managers basking in the adulation.

During my drive home Benny Victory called me. He sounded firm but upbeat and friendly. He explained that due to his diary being chaotic before the Peckforton Castle meeting, he wouldn't be able to spend a day on the road with me but he suggested we meet up in Carlisle for an hour just to run through his expectations of me now I was one of his team. I must admit I found myself warming to him almost immediately during that call and put the phone down thinking that perhaps colleagues didn't like him because he pointed out their inadequacies. Everyone at 'Avon & Severn' seemed to like to tell you how good they were so perhaps Benny pointing out their faults had not gone down well. I re-iterated the message to myself that I would judge Benny by how I found him not by what others said about him behind his back.

Chapter Fifty Nine

Cathie and I were naked in bed. We had finished what was, at that time, our nightly routine of making love and had both subsequently ventured to the bathroom to clean ourselves off. I was lying on my back with my eyes closed, empty of desire and with a brain full of nothing when I felt Cathie's hair stroking my face and her warm breasts smothering my chest. I opened my eyes to see her curly hair spilling out in front of me like a blonde weeping willow and her eyes quizzing the lines on my face with concern.

"Are you OK?" she asked with concern.

"I'm great."

"You seem a bit distant."

"Do I? I'm sorry. I'm just throwing myself back into work. My new boss has a reputation for being a bit of a bastard so I want to keep on his right side from the start."

"How can he not love you?" Cathie kissed my forehead and there was silence momentarily before she added, "They get their pound of flesh from you, don't they? From the moment you wake up you're on that laptop and from eight in the morning until nine at night your phone hardly stops. Can't you turn it off?"

"It wouldn't solve anything if I did. The brokers would just leave messages so I'd have to ring them back. They often go to see clients of an evening when the clients have finished work, that's why phone is still red hot when I get home."

"I thought there was supposed to be a credit crunch? In the papers and on the news they keeping saying the housing market is on its knees."

"I know but 'Avon & Severn' are one of the few lenders still out there lending as we're being propped up by the government so that's why everyone is ringing me. All the Irish and American lenders have stopped lending over here as they have enough problems back home. If I was still at my old firm, Tyrone Building Society, I'd probably have been out of a job."

"So it's just work stuff?"

Mortgages could only hold Cathie's attention for so long. I understood for the uninitiated it wasn't the most enthralling of topics.

"What else would it be?"

"I just thought you might not be too happy about your Dad and Maggie getting married."

I made a dismissive gesture with my hand.

"No, that's fine, if it keeps the romantic old buggers happy then good luck to them!"

"Honestly, that's how you feel? You don't feel like he's betraying the memory of your mother in any way?"

"Of course not. My Mum's been dead a long time, Cathie."

"I know honey, but she's still your Mum."

"No honestly, I'm pleased for my Dad. If anyone deserves a bit of happiness in his final days on this planet then it's my Dad."

Cathie kissed my lips.

"I agree. And you and Andy'll be step brothers."

"I know. Weird, hey?"

"Yes, but somehow fitting."

Chapter Sixty

Peckforton Castle is a wonderful building set amongst the Peckforton hills in Cheshire. It looked like an immaculately maintained medieval castle but it transpired that it was actually a country house built for a rich nineteenth century landowner, John Tollemache. It may not have been medieval but it was still a stunning building. The sort of place you would want to get married if you were a millionaire celebrity. I heard someone say Wes Brown recently got married there but didn't like to ask who Wes Brown is. I would imagine he's either a rapper or a footballer.

"How much for the bottle of Southern Comfort?" a small, thin, dark haired man with a hint of a Liverpool accent enquired of the barman as I stood next to him in a small function room at the back of the castle which was being used as the bar area.

"The whole bottle? Not a glass?" a confused barman asked seeking clarification.

"No, the bottle. How much?" the man confirmed firmly.

The bar tender looked uncomfortable.

"I've no idea. Let me go and check for you."

The barman headed across to another member of staff, who I presumed to be the manager, to check the price out.

"You can't get the fucking staff these days, can you?" the man muttered, half to me, half to himself.

"Not a standard request, I suppose" I said, in the bartender's defence.

"Fucking will be tonight," the man replied.

I decided from his accent he must have been from somewhere like Southport, Ormskirk or the Wirral, where they tend to have the Liverpool accent but in softer tones. His accent was soft but his actions were aggressive. He tapped his fingers on the bar as I watched the young barman whisper in the ear of his older boss, then nod and return to the man at the bar.

"The bottle will cost you £150."

"OK. Get it down and put it on our bill."

The optic was removed from the full bottle. It was turned over and passed to the man who left triumphantly nursing his booty. I should have been next in line to be served but the barman was a little out of sorts following the previous order so he served a woman who had arrived a few minutes after me and several others but had kept repeating her order to the barman every time she caught his eye.

Michael Moriarty came over to stand next to me.

"Have you still not been served? Are some of these bastards jumping the queue, pal?"

"Don't worry about it. We'll get served soon enough."

"No bother. I wasn't having a go, I'm just pissed off."

I had only run into a Michael few minutes before and had offered to get him a drink from the bar. It wasn't an overly generous offer as it was a free bar but I thought it would save him queuing up. Turns out it hadn't. I was surprised he had survived the cull given he seemed to hate the company and intended to ask him why he was still here once I eventually got served.

"How come?"

"Our arsehole of a boss has put me on report. How can he do that? He's just given me a job and within a fortnight he's putting me on report. Explain that one."

"It does seem odd."

"Odd? It's fucking lunacy. If he doesn't watch out one day I'm going to crack and I'll end up grabbing the bastard by the throat and choking the life out the fat little fucker."

I empathised with Michael but avoided telling him that I had been impressed with my initial dealings with Benny Victory. Following our telephone conversation, I had met up with Benny in Carlisle for an excellent sixty minute meeting. He was really welcoming, had done a huge amount of research into my new area and provided me with a load of useful data on various mortgage brokers in my new patch, where they were located, how much business they did, what network they were linked to and various contact numbers. He said he would be doing everything in his power to ensure I made my territory a success and purely saw himself as a facilitator. As we had headed back to our cars after the meeting he had commented on how he saw things going,

"I've a feeling you and I are going to work brilliantly together. I really need a second in command for this team and think you could be perfect for that role. When I go on holiday, I'll pass some of my day to day duties to you. It'll look good on your c.v if you are ever looking for a promotion. All I ask of the people that work for me is that they can look themselves in the mirror at the end of the working day and know they have given their all. Martin Sunderland told me you're that sort of guy, a hard worker. There are unfortunately still one or two members of the team who don't have your work ethic. I would have liked to have waved them goodbye in this round of redundancies but sometimes internal politics gets in the way of common sense."

It wasn't difficult to deduce that Michael Moriarty and Benny Victory didn't see eye to eye and I concluded as the evening progressed that Michael was probably one of the BDMs Benny had wanted rid of. He had been with 'Avon & Severn' for over two years but just kept going on how much better 'Smart Money Mortgages' had been.

"Why didn't you just grab the money and go when the redundancy was on offer?" I asked after a couple of pints and an earful of moaning.

"I wanted to but Graham 'Cunt-liffe' wouldn't sign off my redundancy. He said there were a shortage of BDMs in Scotland and they weren't permitted by the government to recruit externally. I could have left with statutory redundancy but I wasn't doing that. I reckon Victory is massively pissed off I'm still here and he's going to try to force me out. He likes to have someone to bully and he's just seen off Gordon Cherry who he's been victimising for the last six months. I'm ready for him Harry and if he tries to treat me like he treated Gordon, he'll be changing his name to Benny Defeated."

Perhaps Gordon Cherry was lazy or perhaps he wasn't great at his job, I was pretty sure Benny wouldn't have tried to get rid of him just for the pleasure of being horrible. I didn't feel a great deal of sympathy for him or, if I'm honest, for Michael Moriarty, who seemed to have a chip on both of his shoulders. I knew Benny didn't suffer fools gladly, that's what everyone kept saying and perhaps Gordon and Michael were just fools. I imagine Gordon Cherry had probably just been a bang average Business Development Manager and Benny hadn't been prepared to accept someone like that in his team, if I was the boss, I wouldn't either. I would bear Michael's warnings in mind and would continue to tread carefully but would keep an open mind. Michael liked to slag Benny off but if he had hated the man and the job as much as he made out, he would have just taken the statutory redundancy and found a job elsewhere. I concluded Michael was just someone who liked a good moan.

I eventually managed to order a couple of pints of lager.

"Sod it," Michael said with a smile, "let's just get slaughtered."

As the barman was filling our glasses a genial man in his sixties who was wearing circular John Lennon glasses and had a smooth, bald head came over to join us at the bar.

"How's it going guys?" he asked addressing Michael and me, "I believe you gentlemen are going to be my colleagues. I'm Wilbur Kennedy. I used to manage the car leasing division in Northern Ireland but sadly they've closed it down and are managing the whole leasing process from Bristol so they've moved me across into the mortgage sales team.

"You don't sound Irish," I observed, he had a strange accent that was half Lancastrian and half Geordie.

"No, I'm not. My wife is a Belfast girl and I've lived over there for thirty seven years now but I'm originally from Whitehaven in Cumbria."

That explained the accent.

"What do you know about mortgages then?" Michael asked.

"Well, I've got one, but other than that diddly squat. Bit of a new challenge at sixty five but my daughter and my three year old grandson have just moved back into our house and I've only got five years' service so I couldn't afford to retire. I believe the young lady in Belfast was made redundant so they were looking for an Irish based staff member to take over and here I am. Probably not the ideal job for me at my time of life but I'm probably not their ideal candidate either just someone to plug a gap. Funny story..."

I can't tell you what the funny story was. I just remember it took a long time to tell. Wilbur was one of the loveliest, but at the same time one of the most boring, men I have ever met. He talked and talked and talked. Despite it being a free bar, he only drank tap water all evening as he wasn't a drinker but he took a shine to Michael and me and remained with us until he retired to bed at about half past ten. I remember the more Michael and I drank, the funnier we found Wilbur. He was funny because he wasn't in the slightest bit funny.

By the time Wilbur went to bed, the mission Michael and I were on to get slaughtered was on the way to being achieved. I remember begging Wilbur to stay with us, as it seemed the whole night was still ahead of us, but six hours later I recall slumping face first on to my double bed wondering where the hell the rest of the night had gone.

Other than my time spent with Wilbur and Michael, the most memorable segment of the evening that I could subsequently recall with any clarity was one of my many trips to the bar. Corks were popping off expensive bottles of champagne, left, right and centre. Women were ordering ridiculous cocktails with equally ridiculous names and men, especially men in the Senior Management team, seemed to be competing to order the most expensive round. Stupidly, somewhere in the course of the evening, Michael and I made the stupid decision to move from lager to 'Scotch On The Rocks'.

At about one o'clock in the morning, I was slumped over the bar, listening to Graham Cunliffe offering to pay the bar staff 'whatever money they liked' if the bar was kept open until four instead of closing at two. A compromise deal was eventually struck whereby last orders would be served at three. Whilst listening in and using the bar as a crutch, I felt someone pinch my bottom. As I turned around carefully to apprehend the culprit, I remember thinking there were only a limited number of suspects. Wilbur Kennedy was tucked up in bed so I could only imagine it was an inebriated Michael Moriarty playing silly beggars. I wish it had been. When I turned around I discovered it was Liz Victory.

When you are very drunk yourself, others have to be several degrees more drunk than you for you to appreciate their drunkenness. As I turned around, I knew from Liz's vacant stare that she had consumed far more than her body could manage. I really didn't want to speak to her. I seemed to be off to a good start with Benny, her husband and he seemed to like me a lot. I was bucking the trend by thinking he was OK too.

"You ignored me, Harry McCoy," Liz said in an exaggerated childish voice. She was wearing a very elegant black dress and I'm she would have looked a million dollars earlier in the evening before alcohol took hold. I doubted that she would ever remember the conversation we were about to have but for the sake of my career, I needed to remain tactful. I decided not to even bother mention the pinch of my backside.

"Liz, one thing I already know about you is that you are impossible to ignore. Good to see you. Have you had a good night?"

I moved towards her to politely kiss her cheek but she pulled her head away from my puckered lips.

"Don't try to sweet talk me, 'H'. You ignored me."

"When?"

"In Playa Blanca."

"No, I didn't! We chatted in Playa Blanca."

"Talk smork. I'm not talking about chatting. I offered you my foo foo in Playa Blanca and you ignored me. When I was younger, men were queuing down my street just to get a glimpse of me and now an average looking man like you, turns me down. You have no idea how upsetting that is."

"Liz, it was nothing personal, I'm in love with someone else."

It was noisy in there as the vast majority of people in the room were drunk and shouting over each other to be heard. I don't think Liz heard what I had said so just tried to lay things on thicker.

"You made me feel like a wrinkly old has been. I was very sad. Men like you shouldn't be turning women like me down."

I think I really should have been the one that was offended.

"Liz, it's nothing personal," I stated again, "if Miss World had been interested in me in Playa Blanca I wouldn't have wanted to know. I'm in love with my wife."

Liz stared down at the wedding band on my finger.

"Why didn't you wear that wedding band in Playa Blanca?"

"I wasn't married then."

"Really?"

"Yes."

"So you're saying it wasn't to do with me. You're married, you love your wife and Miss World would have been turned down too."

"Exactly! That's exactly what I'm saying."

For a brief period Liz's face seemed to brighten up but then she scowled once more.

"I don't believe you."

"You don't believe I love my wife?"

I let out a brief laugh.

"Oh, I believe that, I just don't believe you'd turn Miss World down."

"Why?"

"You're a man. Men don't believe in monogamy. Your lives just go around in circles….thinking about sex, having sex, recovery, thinking about sex, having sex, recovery…. If you could have sex with me tonight and no-one would ever know, why would you wait until tomorrow night?"

"That's not how it works."

"Yes it is."

I was too drunk to be arguing my point with Liz Victory. I should have just made a polite excuse and walked away but because my stomach lining was soaked in Scotch, I wanted to get my point across.

"Liz, you're undoubtedly a very beautiful woman, Benny is a very fortunate man but I'm married to an equally beautiful woman. I'd like to think the beautiful woman I'm married to doesn't want to sleep with anyone else. She's faithful to me and I'm faithful to her and that keeps us both happy. Why would I ever want to jeopardise that?"

"You will. One day you will and so will your wife and when that happens you will wish you had slept with me when you had your chance. If I still looked like I did when I was in my twenties you wouldn't have been able to resist me. No-one could."

I should have just said agreed with her. There may have been no repercussions if I'd have kept my mouth shut but I was drunk and didn't want to agree with her that I would have betrayed Cathie's trust.

"I would. I am 100% sure we'd have been having exactly the same conversation we are having now. You're married, I'm married, let's just leave it at that."

Liz's eyes were full of sorrow. She had probably spent thirty years of getting everything she wanted when she wanted and had never grown accustomed to rejection.

"You only hate me because I'm old."

"I don't hate you, Liz, I just love my wife."

"You hate me."

Liz moved away from the bar and disappeared into the night. It was a brief two minute conversation that had taken place when I was very drunk but it still made me feel uncomfortable. Liz was the wife of my boss and there was something dangerous about her. I just hoped everything would be forgotten by the morning.

Chapter Sixty One

My alarm went off at nine o'clock the following morning but I was still tired and hungover so just switched it off and went back to sleep. By the time I woke up again, at ten to twelve, I could hear that there was a gathering of cleaners outside my door, so hurriedly showered, dressed and departed. Thankfully, the Senior Managers at 'Avon & Severn' were well aware of the partying tendencies of the staff and a clear day had been arranged just to allow people to make their way home safely.

I had been half-expecting some sort of drama to materialise with Liz Victory but thankfully no news was good news. As the days, weeks and months passed, I increasingly grew accustomed to the way in which Benny managed and my initial positive impressions appeared to be well placed. Every month he would spend a day on the road with me for an 'Assessment Day' and each month, without fail, he would sign me off as excellent. When he went on holiday, as promised, I was placed temporarily in charge of our team. 2009 passed into 2010 and despite the credit crunch showing no signs of abating, Avon & Severn remained at the forefront of the UK mortgage market.

Closer to home, following on from their engagement, my Dad and Maggie booked their Wedding for Sunday 14th February 2010 (Valentine's Day) in the Mayor's Dining Room at Rochdale Town Hall. It was only going to be a small, intimate wedding with a few of Maggie's friends joining both families. Including the bride and groom, there were eighteen invited to attend.

Maggie wanted to do things in the traditional manner so, despite having lived with Dad for some time, decided she would stay at her sister, Audrey's house, in Failsworth, the night before the Wedding. I was 'Best Man' so I said I would stay with my Dad the night before and, not wanting to miss out, Andy asked if he could too.

Andy arrived at Dad's house about seven o'clock on the Saturday evening in an expensive work suit as he had been snowed under with legal cases and had to go in to the office to do a Saturday nine to five. He was driving a new silver grey Mazda MX-5 Miata which he'd had since September. It always looked more than a little out of place in Rochdale in the winter.

"Have you come to do my hair, Tootsie?" Dad asked after he opened the door to let Andy in. Dad was continually teasing Andy about his choice of car saying it looked like the sort of car a mobile hairdresser would drive.

"Sod off, George! You're just jealous," Andy countered, "Anyway, what's the plans before you make an honest woman of my mother. A quiet night in or a proper Stag Do?"

"May I remind you, Mr Corcoran, that I am eighty eight years old."

"Exactly, so you should know how to party better than anyone. Bet there must have been a right old knees up when you won the War."

"Not for me, I had to find my way back across Europe from a prisoner of war camp."

"Oh right," Andy said and pulled his 'I just put my foot right in it' face.

"I've never been the partying type, if I'm honest. I wouldn't mind going up to 'The Cemetery' for a couple of pints though."

Andy smiled broadly at Dad. I think Andy wanted to get out himself rather than spend the whole evening in Dad's lounge.

"George, it's your night, whatever you want to do tonight, that's what we're doing."

We didn't rush out though. As 'Best Man' I was responsible for getting my Dad to the Town Hall in one piece so I wanted him to take it easy. I knew Andy could potentially be a bad influence. I suggested, for old time's sake, that we watch a classic comedy episode of 'Laurel & Hardy' or 'The Three Stooges'.

"Do you know what I'd like to watch?" my Dad declared, "Only Fools and Horses."

"Good shout, George!" Andy replied cheerily, as he uncorked a bottle of red wine.

"'H' obviously knows this but Andy, you may not. 'Only Fools and Horses' was the only programme we used to watch as a family when 'H's mother was alive. I'm honoured to be marrying your mother tomorrow, Andrew, but a little bit of me will always belong to Kitty so I think it'd be fitting if we watched that."

I could feel myself welling up when Dad said that, but I kept my emotions in check. It was a night of celebrations and I didn't want it to be marred by sadness. It was right to remember Mum fondly but it wasn't the right time to cry for our loss.

"Which episode do you fancy watching, Dad?" I asked as I got down on my hands and knees amongst his video collection. After the wedding, I might suggest he started getting his videos converted on to DVDs.

"The one with Grandad and the chandeliers. That was your mother's favourite, 'H'".

So, we sat and had a beer (well, I did, Andy and my Dad had a glass of red wine) and watched 'Only Fools and Horses' before Andy drove us up to 'The Cemetery'. He had to make two journeys as his car was only a two seater. He took me first and I got a round in whilst Andy went back for my Dad. Once he came in with my Dad, the plan was that he would leave his car at the pub and we would get a taxi back to Dad's. It was only a short walk but, despite him arguing to the contrary, we felt it was too far for my Dad.

I bought a bottle of red wine for my Dad and Andy, whilst I had a couple of bottles of beer. We spent a couple of hours in the front room of the pub merrily chatting about all and sundry. Dad was particularly talkative. The wine probably played its part as I don't think he drank much at home other than tea and coffee.

"Do you know what I don't understand about young men these days?"

"Go on, George, tell us."

"I don't understand why you've all stopped appreciating a woman's legs. In my day, face and legs were the most important features on a woman. These days it's just tits and arse. That's all young lads seem to be interested in, tits and arse."

I was a little taken aback. The words 'tits' and 'arse' were about as close as I remember my Dad ever coming to swearing in my presence.

"I don't remember ever having had a conversation with you about Cathie's tits or arse, Dad!"

"Speak for yourself mate," Andy joined in, "me and your Dad often have conversations about Cathie's tits and arse, don't we George? Well, I talk about her tits and arse, your Dad talks about her face and legs!"

My Dad had just taken a sip of his red wine which he still had in his mouth so he just shrugged and smiled. He looked at one point like he was going to laugh it all back up.

"You better not have done!" I joked, pointing a finger accusingly at both Andy and my Dad.

"Given I'm as close to being a eunuch as a man with a full package can be, I think you're pretty safe, mate."

"No, I don't mean you pair," Dad continued now his mouth was empty, "I mean young men on the television. Since your mother moved in, Andy, I have had to watch a whole load of rubbish on the television just to keep the peace. Soap operas, Big Brother and these fly on the wall documentaries tracking young lads and girls on holiday in Greece. I tell you what, I'm glad I'm not young but the point is, when referring to young ladies, they hardly ever mention how pretty their faces are or how beautiful their legs are, just tits and arse, tits and arse. I didn't realise it until Maggie moved in but young men have turned into monsters."

Andy and I looked at each other and laughed.

"Present company excepted," Dad added.

I loved the time we spent at 'The Cemetery' that evening, just the three of us. We had a special bond and hadn't spent anywhere near enough time together recently, for a whole host of reasons and I suspected, due to a change I knew was coming, that there wouldn't be many more nights like this in the near future.

"Dad, Andy, before we go back there's something I want to tell you both. Now at this stage, it's still a bit of a secret, so I don't want either of you mentioning it tomorrow but Cathie's pregnant."

They both looked at me with stunned delight. Dad spoke first. He stood up and patted me on the back, then sat back down and shook my hand.

"Marvellous, that's just marvellous. That's about the best news I've ever had. I'm going to be a Granddad! Is Cathie OK? How far along is she?"

"She's six weeks Dad and she's feeling pretty grotty but she's very excited about it. We haven't told Max yet though. He's too young to handle the wait. We'll tell him when he notices his Mum's tummy is expanding."

"Brilliant," Dad said, "I can't tell you how pleased I am right now. I'm bursting with pride."

"Me too," Andy added, "Congratulations pal. I think this calls for champagne. Let me go and get a bottle."

"Should we not be getting going?" I asked with concern in my voice, "I just wanted to tell you my news before we ordered a taxi."

"What do you reckon, George? Shall I buy a bottle of champagne to celebrate 'H' becoming a father for the second time or shall we just go home?"

"I don't even think there's a decision to be made," Dad answered.

"Champagne it is."

Andy had won me around a little by saying about becoming a father for a 'second time'. Technically (and biologically) it was my first time. I liked to think I treated Max like a son but he had his own father. His Dad still didn't seem in any rush to come back from Australia and his weekly calls now seemed to be fortnightly, but he was still Max's real Dad.

Partially because I was keeping an eye on him and partially because he was, on the whole, a sensible soul, my Dad only drank half a glass of champagne. It was left to me and primarily to Andy, to drink the rest of the bottle. Once it was polished off we were both feeling the effects and the time now seemed right to head back to Dad's.

"Shall we get you back home, George? Big day tomorrow."

"What time is it?" Dad asked.

"Quarter past ten," I said after checking on my phone. I had long since stopped wearing a watch.

"Do you know what I think would be really funny?" Dad said with a twinkle in his eye.

"Go on," Andy said.

"If we went back home, put our wedding suits on, got a taxi into Rochdale and went to a nightclub. I mentioned before that I've never been the partying type but I think it'd be so funny if we turned up at some teenage nightclub in our wedding clobber and just acted like it was perfectly normal for an eighty eight year old bloke to be in there."

It seemed wrong to keep my father in check, but I felt under an obligation to Maggie to do it.

"Dad, it would be funny, but as Andy said, you've got a big day tomorrow. You need your sleep."

"Come on! You two said before it was my night and I could do what I wanted. I want to go to a nightclub."

"Dad, I'll think you'll find it was just Andy that said that."

"Come on 'H', please. I only want to go for an hour. I just want to see the looks on all the kids faces if I go on the dance floor in my wedding outfit. I'm sure there aren't many old blokes like me boogying away on a Saturday night."

"If you're trying to pass for under eighty, I wouldn't call it boogying again, if I were you. Gives the game away," Andy said, with a straight face.

Part of me was starting to be tempted by the idea of taking him but common sense was still winning me over.

"No, I'm sorry, Dad. I said to Maggie I'd get you to the altar in one piece. You can't turn up pie eyed."

"'H', I've hardly been drinking. I had half a glass of red wine at our house, a glass of red here and less than half a glass of champagne. It's you and Andy who have been knocking them back. I'm probably under the limit. I could even drive us over in Andy's car. It's only a couple of miles. Come on son, live a little."

It was Andy's turn to weigh in and unfortunately not on the side of caution.

"You'd have to make two journeys, George, unless one of us squeezed into the boot."

"Get a grip, Andy! He's eighty eight and borderline drunk. There's no way he's driving us. He's probably not even insured for your car."

"He is. It's insured for any driver."

"Dad, I can't believe I'm even asking this but do you still have a drivers licence?"

"No, but I still know how to drive."

"No chance! That's it settled, come on, let's just go home."

"Come on 'H'! Please," Dad begged with sad eyes and a protruding bottom lip.

"Yeh, come on 'H'," Andy said, clasping his hands in begging mode, "it'll be a great story to tell in your speech."

I'd already finished writing my speech but I just thought 'what the hell', if my Dad wants to do one last wild, impulsive thing before he gets married (which at eighty eight was pretty wild and impulsive in itself) then why should I be the one to stop him.

"Promise me you'll only drink Diet Cokes, Dad?"

"I promise."

"And we'll only stay for an hour?"

"Fine, I only want to stay for an hour."

"Right, let's go clubbing. Andy, ring us a taxi."

Chapter Sixty Two

I think if David Beckham and Victoria had gone for a night out at the Darli Bar in Packer Street, opposite Rochdale Town Hall and brought a few celebrity mates with them, the clubbers would have made less of a fuss of them that night than they did of my Dad. It was as though someone had dipped him from head to toe in pheromones.

The taxi picked us up at 'The Cemetery', left its engine running whilst we literally carried Dad into his house, put our wedding garb on and then came running back out like we were contestants on 'Stars In Their Eyes' ("Tonight, Matthew, we are going to be three members of 'The Rat Pack'!") Dad was obviously unable to run so Andy gave him a piggy back to the taxi. We laughed all the way to the nightclub and it didn't get any less funny once we had arrived.

I know only too well that there are some characters out and about in Rochdale on a Saturday night but I would imagine it is very rare to have an eighty eight year old in a tuxedo queuing outside the 'Darli Bar'. Several girls took pity on Dad as it wasn't the warmest of nights and although he declined plenty of offers of chunky coats from males and females alike, the bouncers were soon aware that there was a bit of commotion and strutted out to investigate.

"Are you sure you're over eighteen, pal?" a particularly muscle clad bouncer asked my father.

"Pardon?" Dad asked, looking a bit muddled. He was very good at hearing what Andy and I had to say but new voices tended to confuse him.

"I said 'Are you over eighteen, sir?'" the bouncer repeated, this time almost shouting into one of Dad's ears.

"I'm seventy years over," Dad replied.

"Any ID?"

"I've probably got my ration book somewhere."

"Seriously?"

"No, but I reckon I've got my Senior Citizen's bus pass somewhere," Dad said and began fumbling for his wallet.

"Don't worry, pal, we'll take your word for it. Come on, the three of you in penguin suits, this way," the bouncer said leading us through the crowds and straight into the club.

"Who the bloody hell are they?" one woman in the queue asked another.

"I reckon it's Morgan Freeman's Dad," was the reply.

The most bizarre night of my life was well under way. Once we were in the 'Good Samaritan' bouncer found us a table and once Dad was sat down and comfortable, Andy went off to buy another bottle of champagne and a glass of Diet Coke for my Dad.

"It's very noisy in here," Dad shouted in my ear.

"I know, it's terrible, isn't it?"

"Awful. Do you reckon they'd play a bit of Sinatra if I asked nicely?"

"Dad, if you asked they probably would."

"Thanks son."

"What for?"

"Bringing me out. I just wanted to do something different. I know I'll never be back."

"Never say never, Dad. Who knows what Maggie has lined up for you tomorrow?"

Give the people of Rochdale their due, they could not have been nicer to Dad in the time we were there. All the young ladies kept coming over and telling Dad how handsome he looked or they asked him why he was dressed so smartly. I think pretty much every lady in the place kissed him on the cheek (and the others on the lips) once they discovered he was getting married the next day. Half the blokes in there also came over to shake his hand. When we decided to hit the dancefloor (for House of Pain's 'Jump Around') everyone took a step or two backwards to give Dad space. It was surreal watching him jump to the beat of the music, Andy was crying with laughter, a few people were recording him on their phones, others were cheering along but I was just worried he'd slip and break his hip or have a heart attack so I was relieved when the song finished. The whole place broke into heartfelt applause whilst I whisked him off the dancefloor.

"Come on Dad, we've been here an hour. It's time to go."

"OK 'H', just let me have a sit down for five minutes to catch my breath and then we'll head off. It's a long, long time since I've had that much fun. I don't think Maggie will like it here but maybe the three of us could come back every other Saturday."

"I tell you what, Dad, if you can persuade Cathie tomorrow, I'm in."

When Andy came to join us, I just told them I would nip for a wee and then we'd go outside and hope Dad's charms could help us jump the queue for the taxi.

The toilets weren't the greatest. They had the rebounding boomerang urinals so I tried to opt for a cubicle. There were only two and when I pushed the door open on the first someone had vomited all over the floor and the rim of the toilet. The ugly stench was like a magnetic field around the porcelain forcing me back out. I moved along and pushed the second door open. To my horror, there was a woman in there, knickers around her ankles, fag in one hand, toilet roll in the other.

"I'm so sorry," I said as I went to close the door but missed as I tried to grab it. If the first cubicle had a magnetic field driving me away, this one seemed to have a force field keeping me there as I was stunned into a confused, prolonged stare.

"It's alright love," the gap toothed raider slurred back at me, "the queue was massive for the women's and I'd have pissed myself if I'd have waited. If you're bursting I'll shuffle forward and you can pee behind. Just make sure you don't spray my back."

The power of the force field was relinquished as panic set in.

"You're alright thanks," I said as I backed away, "I'll just wait until I get home."

"Don't say I didn't offer."

In the taxi on the way back, Andy was in the front and I was in the back with Dad.

"This time tomorrow you'll be a married man again, Dad."

"I know. Tomorrow is going to be a wonderful, wonderful day. Maggie is a lovely lady."

I squeezed Dad's hand, "I know she is."

"But not as lovely as your Mum," Dad whispered quietly.

Moments later Andy turned his head around from the front seat,

"Have you enjoyed your Stag Do, George?"

"It's been great fun. I think I can still out party the pair of you!"

"I think you can, George. Me and 'H' are knackered!"

We all laughed, like we had almost non-stop throughout the evening. Once we got back to Dad's, Andy had a glass of red wine from the half full bottle that was sat on the table in the kitchen whilst Dad and I had a cup of tea. It still wasn't exceptionally late, we were back before one.

"Andy, your Mum's put an extra mattress down on the floor in H's old room. You can either sleep on that or get in the double bed with 'H'."

"I'll probably just jump in the double bed with H. I've known him for twenty five years and I'm well aware there's no sexual chemistry."

"That's fine," I said, "but if there's any snoring or farting you're out."

"Same rules apply to you, mister. It's not your room any more. I sleep in there more often than you do."

My Dad lifted himself up from his chair at the kitchen table, put his mug in the sink and then said his farewells,

"It's been a fantastic night, lads, but I'm going to head off to bed now. See you in the morning."

Andy stood up too and went over and gave Dad a hug.

"It's been brilliant, George. Sleep well and good luck tomorrow!"

"Thanks Andy but there's no luck needed. Your Mum's a good woman."

"I know but you've made her into a better one."

It was my turn to stand up and hug my father.

"Good night Dad! I'll be a very proud 'Best Man' tomorrow."

"Maggie and I are proud to have you. I'm so pleased for you and Cathie too. Sleep well. Remember if I die in my sleep never forget how much your mother and I loved you."

"I know Dad. I love you too. Goodnight."

My Dad headed off to his bedroom which was now downstairs, the dining room having been converted to a bedroom.

"What's that all about?" Andy said when he knew Dad was out of earshot.

"What?"

"The 'if I die in my sleep tonight never forget how much your mother and I loved you'?"

"Oh right, that! I'm sure I must have told you about that. He used to say it to me every night when I lived here. Now he says it every time he sees me. Mum died without having had the chance to say her goodbyes so Dad has made more than sure he has said his."

"Bless him. He's a lovely man, your Dad, isn't he?"

"He is. Can you believe we've just been to 'Darli' with him?"

"I know. My Mum's going to kill me when she finds out."

"I suspect Maggie's going to kill us both!"

"It was worth it though, wasn't it?"

"Without a doubt. Are you heading up to bed?"

"Yes, big day tomorrow."

"I can't wait."

Chapter Sixty Three

I have no recollection of Andy snoring when we were kids but unfortunately, these days, he snores like a warthog with a megaphone. Perhaps it was the drink that made it so bad. By the middle of the night it was irritating me so much that I decided remaining in the same room was a torture I could no longer tolerate. I grabbed a pillow and made my escape. I was going to head downstairs and sleep on the sofa in the lounge but then realised Mum and Dad's old room was empty. I nipped into the bathroom for a wee, was relieved to find no gummy drunks in there and then headed downstairs for a glass of water as it felt like someone had removed all moisture from my throat with a suction pump. As I passed the lounge I noticed my Dad was up and the TV was on.

"What time is it, Dad?" I asked as I stumbled through.

"About four, I think."

"How come you're up?"

"I've a lot to think about. I'm about to spend the rest of my days with the woman I love."

"Well don't stay up too long or you'll feel it tomorrow."

"I'll be fine. I love you very much, 'H'."

"Love you too, Dad."

I poured myself a glass of water and carried it upstairs to my Mum and Dad's old room. I climbed onto my Dad's old bed. The mattress was far too soft and it smelt musty which was no doubt why Maggie didn't want us sleeping in there. At least no-one was snoring. I could still hear Andy from across the landing but I was far enough away to be able to ignore it. Given I was in her old room, I prepared myself for a visit from my mother but it didn't materialise. I soon drifted off into a heavy and much needed sleep. I didn't hear another sound until the morning.

Chapter Sixty Four

I don't think I had slept in Mum and Dad's room for a quarter of a century but aided by the champagne, lager and snore-induced weariness, I ended up sleeping in far later than normal and would have been even later if a familiar voice hadn't disturbed me.

"What are you doing in here?" Andy asked, confused.

"You snore."

"No, I don't! No-one has ever told me that I snore."

"Who has ever been close enough to tell?" I replied.

"Fair point," Andy conceded.

"Take it from me you do. What time is it?"

"Nine o'clock."

"Shit! Is it nine already? We need to get cracking. How long have you been up?"

"Thirty seconds."

"Is my Dad up?"

"'H', I've just said I've been up for thirty seconds! How much do you expect me to achieve in half a minute?"

"He will be up. He rarely sleeps in past seven. Go and put the kettle on and make us all a nice cup of tea."

"May I remind you who you are speaking to. I am a barrister, 'H'. I don't lower myself to make tea. I have my tea made for me," Andy said with his tongue firmly in his cheek.

"They probably spit in it and call you a pompous prick behind your back."

"I don't care. You go and make it. Feel free to spit in it and call me a pompous prick as well if you like whilst you're at it."

I pulled myself out of bed. I looked down at my stomach. I wasn't proud of the gut that had steadily grown over the previous couple of years. I needed to start doing some exercise. I took my frustrations out on Andy in a fairly jovial manner.

"Pompous prick."

"I think I'm supposed to be out of earshot when you say it, 'H'."

"Tough titty. I'm going to spit in it in front of you too."

"Charming! That's hospitality for you."

"It's just as much your house as mine now remember?"

It was schoolboy banter but it was fun. It was the type of stupid conversation I would never have with Cathie. I still felt at the stage that I was trying to impress her mentally despite letting my physical form literally go a bit pear shaped. Andy wasn't in a position to have a childish conversation first thing in the morning either as he lived alone. I did wonder if anyone ever did sleep over at his place, male or female, but I suspected I would never find out.

I went downstairs to put the kettle on and threw three teabags into mugs. All the mugs could have done with bleaching but I didn't have the time or inclination to carry out the task on Dad's Wedding Day. There was no sign of Dad in the kitchen or the lounge. I presumed he was either in the bathroom or his bedroom. I saw from underneath the closed bathroom door that there was no light shining through so I moved across to his bedroom. I knocked and immediately entered.

"Tea's brewing, Dad, I take it you want one?"

Dad's curtains were still closed. I didn't want to dazzle him by switching the big light on, so walked across to the curtains and pulled them open.

"What time do you call this, Dad? Has all that jumping around worn you out?" I said as I opened them.

My Dad was lying on his right shoulder facing towards the window. He had light blue Marks & Spencer pyjamas on. He looked very peaceful, too peaceful, it was nine o'clock.

"Dad, come on sleepy head, time to get up!"

There was no response.

"Dad....Dad....DAD!"

My voice was getting louder and more anxious. I put the back of the fingers on my right hand on to his cheek. It was cold. I stroked his face. I knew there and then, but I kept talking.

"Come on Dad, please wake up one last time. Maggie's so excited about today. We all are. I need you to hear my speech, Dad. It says how much I love you and how you're the best Dad in the world. 'The Greatest Man That Ever Lived' to be exact and I'm going to list the ten reasons why. You really do need to hear it, Dad. Please..."

Still nothing.

"ANDY! ANDY!"

Andy could hear the desperation in my shout. I heard the staircase shudder as the uncoordinated giant stumbled down. He burst into the room. He had already correctly assumed the worst. I was kneeling next to the bed, sobbing.

"He's gone, Andy."

"Oh shit! I'm so sorry 'H'."

Andy was probably half thinking about his poor mother and having to break the terrible news on her Wedding Day but in those initial moments though he just focused on my grief.

"I've always dreaded this day, Andy. I've always been so scared of this happening. I knew it was coming though especially after the heart attack. He did too. I've tried to prepare for it, but nothing prepares you for losing your father, especially a father like mine."

"I know 'H'."

"Poor Maggie too. Why could he not just have stuck around until tomorrow?"

"No matter when he left us you would have always been wanting one more day, 'H'."

"I know but it's his Wedding Day. He would have loved it. You would have been his stepson, Andy. He'd have got a real kick out of that."

"So would I, 'H'. He's a million times better man than my real father. He's had a fantastic life though. Let's not lose sight of that."

"I know. I know. He knew we all loved him, didn't he?"

"Of course he did, 'H'. We all idolised him and George was totally aware that we did."

"He looks peaceful, doesn't he?"

"Very."

We stayed in my Dad's room chatting for several minutes. There were rivers of tears, nearly exclusively belonging to me, but I knew I was never going to be able to react in a composed manner when it was my Dad's time to leave us. Eventually though, Andy told me that he was going to have to head over to his Auntie Audrey's to break it to his Mum, face to face, that George had left us. Neither of us knew what the correct procedure was for reporting a death but Andy suggested I phoned the ambulance service.

That evening, Andy rang me to see how I was bearing up. He confessed that he had managed to keep his composure whilst he was at the house, as he knew I needed him to be strong, but once he drove a hundred yards down the road, he pulled into a lay by, switched his engine off and let all his emotions flood out. He said he cried for my father, he cried for his mother but most of all he cried for me.

George McCoy died in the peaceful manner he had lived his whole life. I would never recover from my loss but eventually I would adjust and accept. For thirty four years I was given the opportunity to share my life with 'The Greatest Man That Ever Lived' – how could I be anything but happy about that?

Chapter Sixty Five

The day Dad died, 14th February 2010, Valentine's Day, will be one of only a handful of days that will stay with me forever. On a Monday morning, I can often go into work and when people ask whether I had a good weekend, I can honestly not remember a single thing I did, but that day has managed to lodge itself in my brain.

I rang for an ambulance but the emergency services operator explained that as my Dad had already passed away, in normal circumstances, I would be expected to contact my local GP. As it was a Sunday though, she suggested I contact the 'Out Of Hours' surgery and also a Funeral Directors. A very compassionate Asian lady Doctor came around late in the morning and then at lunchtime the Funeral Directors took Dad's body away.

By midday, Cathie had come around to join me and Andy had phoned me on my mobile to say his Mum was 'in bits' and that she couldn't face seeing my father's body. Despite being well into her sixties Maggie had never seen a dead body and wanted to remember Dad as the cheerful, lovely old man she had fallen in love with rather than have memories of his corpse. Andy said they would stay at his Auntie Audrey's until after tea and he would drive his Mum back then. He said he would stay with her for a couple of nights. Andy said he had already made contact with everyone that was due to attend the wedding, which had only involved a handful of calls, to let them know what had happened.

I completely understood why Maggie might not have wanted to see Dad's body but I think it helped my grieving process to be with him for a few hours after his death. He didn't look troubled or that he had suffered in any way. He just looked like he had slipped away peacefully. In the whole scheme of things it wasn't a tragedy, he had lived a long, eventful life and it had reached a natural end.

That afternoon, I remembered about the note Dad said he would leave in his bedside drawer with funeral instructions. I couldn't recall which drawer he said it would be in, but it turned out there was a white envelope, in the bottom drawer, with just a capital 'H' on the front. I hesitated before opening it, then carefully ran my finger under the sealed part and pulled out the piece of white paper inside. Through watery eyes, I read the following message :-

Dear H,

If you are reading this, it can only mean my time has finally come to leave you and move on to whatever comes next. I hope more than anything that I haven't been a burden to you in my final days.

I am sure you recall our conversations about my funeral. I have had some very sad times in my life but, on the whole, it has been marvellous. Please use my funeral as an opportunity to celebrate my long life rather than to mourn my passing. I have left you now so I don't want to burden you with an extravagant send off. As we have discussed, I have already paid for my funeral, which will just be an hour at the crematorium and a reception at 'The Cemetery'. I have just asked for a couple of hearses, one for my coffin and the other one for you, Cathie, Max, Maggie and Andy.

I have given a lot of thought to the music I would like to be played. Once you get back to 'The Cemetery' it's party time so just play a lot of up tempo stuff but none of the modern stuff that you know I'd hate. If I hate it, most of the older guests will probably hate it to. As for the music at the crematorium, I think some people, including Maggie, would find it inappropriate if you played celebratory music so I have decided on the following :-

Pre-Service

Sir Edward Elgar – Nimrod from 'Enigma Variations'.

Samuel Barber – Adagio for Strings.

<u>During Interlude In Main Service</u>

Laurel & Hardy – Blue Ridge Mountains of Virginia (to stop things getting too sad).

Once the service finishes, the curtains will open and my coffin will travel away from the congregation. At that point, I would like you to ask them to play a version of Leonard Cohen's 'If It Be Your Will' performed by Antony Hegarty. We have both always enjoyed Leonard Cohen's music and I think that's a powerful version to bid me farewell. As for a reading, 'Remember' by Christina Rossetti would be perfect. As you all leave, could you ask them to play Sarah McLachlan's 'Angel'. Thank you.

I have a few last instructions and things I would like to say. First of all, between you and Andy, make sure Maggie is looked after. She has made the last years of my life very special so make sure she knows how grateful I am.

As for you son, I cannot begin to tell you how much you have enriched my life. I have tried to express as often as possible how proud your mother and I always were to have a son as fine as you. I only wish she had lived long enough to see the man you have become. You have made the occasional mistake in your journey through life, like we all have, but you are a very fine human being. I hope Max grows up to be as fine a son to you and Cathie as you have been to me.

Now I have left, you may discover certain things about me and also about yourself that you never knew. Please always remember, no matter what, that everything your mother and I did, we did it out of love for you and in what we thought were your best interests.

Thank you again for everything. Your mother saved both our lives on the day she died and in so many ways you have saved mine since.

Dad xx

It was an emotional letter for me to read but also a mysterious one. I had no idea what Dad meant by discovering 'certain things about me and also about yourself that you never knew'. I passed the letter to Cathie after I had read and re-read it several times.

"Read this letter, Cathie. What do you think he means?"

Cathie pulled a few weird expressions with her face to enable her to focus. She needed reading glasses but for reasons of vanity she refused to go to the opticians. She read it without commenting for a couple of minutes.

"It's a bit cryptic, isn't it?" she said as she passed the letter back to me.

"It is. If you were guessing, what would you think?"

"I don't know. Could your Dad have had money issues you didn't know about?"

"Possibly," I said, trying not to look sheepish and guilty myself as I had money issues of my own that I had been keeping from Cathie, "but that wouldn't mean I would be finding something out about myself that I never knew. It makes no sense."

"It might one day."

"I hope so. I don't want to go through the rest of my life wondering what he was on about. Do you think Maggie might know?"

"Ask her. I'm sure she'll tell you if she does."

Chapter Sixty Six

We didn't have a Vicar at Dad's funeral. We had a man who had the title of 'celebrant' – someone who ran the funeral proceedings, spoke about the person who died and made sure the funeral would have been exactly what the deceased would have wanted. Co-incidentally, the 'celebrant' was mixed race like my father. It was very rare for me to think about Dad's skin colour or my own for that matter but it felt appropriate, in a certain sense, to have someone of mixed heritage conducting the service. His name was Ray, he was in his fifties and he had a deep, rich voice that would have been perfect for reading the news on BBC Radio Four.

The crematorium wasn't full but the congregation was larger than at Mum's funeral. There were probably sixty people in attendance, most of whom were pensioners. I recognised the vast majority of them. They were friends of Dad's from the pub or the rambling society, but there were a dozen or so I didn't know. I imagined they were mainly former work colleagues of Dad's. The funeral brochure detailed that everyone was invited back to a reception at 'The Cemetery' afterwards so I was hoping to establish who some of them were later on.

One of Cathie's sisters, Sarah, had come over to Cathie's Mum and Dad's to look after them and Max for the day. Cathie had had a meeting with her sisters a few months earlier about her parents worsening conditions. They were all reluctant to make the next step of putting them both into care so had agreed to share caring responsibilities for six months before reviewing the situation. Cathie, understandably, didn't want Max to come to the funeral, so asked Sarah if she wouldn't mind looking after him for the day too. Sarah agreed without hesitation. No-one wants to see their parents cry and no-one wants to cry in front of their children.

Prior to the coffin being brought through the first classical piece Dad wanted playing Sir Edward Elgar's Nimrod from 'Enigma Variations' was played. I don't think I could name any piece of classical music (other than 'I Giorni' thanks to Mum) but I recognised this piece and understood why Dad had chosen it. It had a powerful British feel to it and although Dad wasn't a flag waving Royalist, he was proud of the fact that he had served his country in war.

A few minutes later, as the undertakers carried Dad's coffin through, it was the turn of Samuel Barber's 'Adagio For Strings', a more melancholy piece of music but no less beautiful. Andy told me later it had been in the film 'Platoon' but I've never seen it and presume my Dad hadn't either.

The funeral directors had asked me whether I had wanted to carry Dad's coffin either with a group of close family and friends or alongside them. I thanked them for asking but told them I would rather not. If I had carried the coffin with Andy, I thought it would have looked very odd because of his immense height and my very average height. I had visions of the coffin sloping diagonally rather than being carried horizontally. I suppose I could have carried Dad with the funeral directors but I don't like being in a situation where everyone knows what they are doing except me (it brought back memories of both country dancing and football at primary school) so I politely declined that option too.

Once the coffin was set down in front of the congregation, with a picture of my father on the table in which it rested (Maggie's idea), Ray asked us all to sit down and then, for ten minutes, he talked about Dad's life. He had met up, separately, with Maggie and myself to learn as much as he could about Dad and he spoke very eloquently about Dad's childhood in London, his experiences in World War Two, his two happy marriages, his work life, his close relationship with me and finally his time spent with Maggie in his final years.

When Ray had finished running through Dad's life chronologically, he explained that Dad had chosen all the music for the funeral and whilst we all took a few moments to reflect on the life of

George McCoy, he would play one of his favourite songs. Having played a couple of serious classical pieces I imagine the congregation were expecting another serious piece so when Laurel & Hardy's 'Blue Ridge Mountains Of Virginia' started playing I looked around at everyone's faces and it was lovely to see them laughing through their tears. Once the ladies voice kicked in at the end, I swallowed hard. I was up next.

As the music faded out, Ray took a central position again to introduce me,

"Harry McCoy, George's son, would now like to say a few words about his father."

I moved out from my seat in the front row and Ray stepped aside to allow me to turn and take centre stage. I had no notes, I didn't want to say a lot, I just wanted to say whatever came into my mind about my father.

"Thank you Ray and thank you everyone for joining us in celebrating the life of my father. Dad passed away suddenly but after his heart attack last year he started to think about his funeral and he was very keen for it to be a simple celebration of his life. I hope you will all join me after the service has finished, at 'The Cemetery' public house to raise a glass to Dad and share memories of his long, happy life.

I have inherited my father's love of walking. Several times a week, Cathie, my wife and I will go out for a long walk. In the summer, when the paths aren't muddy, we often head into the countryside, along public footpaths that border farmer's fields. Last summer, every evening we would walk the same route, passing alongside a particular field. One day, an inquisitive young cow spotted us and decided to come over to say hello. Pretty soon, emboldened by their sister, the whole herd of about thirty followed. Cathie and I pulled some long grass from the floor, put our hands flat and watched as these friendly creatures licked our hands and munched on the fresh grass. For two or three weeks after that, each evening as we passed through that field the cows would wander over and we would take great delight in feeding and patting them.

One day as we walked past, the farmer was in the field with the cows. As they moved across to greet us, the farmer followed.

"We look forward to our evenings now. We say hello to your cows every night about this time. They're such friendly creatures," Cathie said to the farmer with a smile.

Without emotion, he just said,

"Make the most of it then. They're off to be slaughtered next week."

Now, as upsetting as that was to Cathie and me, we understood that farmer was just doing his job, neither of us are vegetarians. It made me think about the human species though, particularly men and what a cruel race we are. We kill other creatures not only for food but often for selfish amusement. We are responsible for wiping many species from the planet. We don't just kill other species either. We are forever inventing more ingenious ways to kill other men, women and children who don't agree with our ideologies. The conclusion I came to, when I was thinking about all this, was how the world would be a much better place if every man had a personality like that of my father. Instead of being aggressive, deceitful and selfish, everyone would be peaceful, honest and altruistic. When John Lennon wrote 'Imagine', all he was doing was imagining a world full of people like my Dad. He was the embodiment of everything that is right in the world and this planet is going to be a significantly darker place without him here.

As Ray mentioned, there were sad times in my Dad's life. He lost many friends during the War and spent four years in a prisoner of war camp. His happy marriages were both cut short by tragedy. He lost his first wife, Irene, to cancer and his second, Kitty, my Mum, to a terrible accident involving a loose horse. Despite all of this, he bounced back, time after time, remaining positive and cheerful until the end. I remember a couple of years ago I was discussing with Dad what the first thing that crossed our mind in the morning was. Dad said, once he passed seventy, without fail the first words that came into his head each morning were,

"I've won again! I get to spend another day on this wonderful planet."

It's very hard in a short speech to even begin to tell you how proud I was of Dad and how much I admired him. A lot of men of his generation hide their feelings but Dad was never afraid to tell you how much you meant to him or to show you by giving you a big hug.

As Ray also mentioned, in the last few years, Dad found happiness again with Maggie. I know after many years as a single man, he had never anticipated finding love again so late in life but I also know how grateful he was that he did. Maggie should have married Dad last week but she has dealt with his passing in a courageous and accepting manner. Dad and Maggie didn't quite make it to the altar but she will always be my stepmother now.

I don't really have to say much more. If you are here today, it means you have been lucky enough to know George McCoy, so you don't need me to tell you too much about what sort of man he was. He wasn't just my father, he was my best friend and my hero and for the rest of my life I will celebrate how lucky I was to have him for so long. Thank you all, again, for being here to today."

After I sat down, Cathie gave me a consoling kiss and from the row behind Andy patted my back. It was an ordeal and I was just glad I managed it without tears. The rest of the service seemed to pass very quickly. Ray introduced Maggie to give the reading Dad had chosen. Andy had been right about Dad improving her. She looked far more confident, caring and composed than she ever used to and walk to the front with an air of calm. Her voice faltered a few times during the reading but I think that added to the power of it rather than detracted from it.

"Remember by Christina Georgina Rossetti.

Remember me when I am gone away,

Gone far away into the silent land;

When you can no more hold me by the hand,

Nor I half turn to go yet turning stay.

Remember me when no more day by day

You tell me of our future that you planned:

Only remember me; you understand

It will be late to counsel then or pray.

Yet if you should forget me for a while

And afterwards remember, do not grieve:

For if the darkness and corruption leave

A vestige of the thoughts that once I had,

Better by far you should forget and smile

Than that you should remember and be sad."

I wiped a tear from my eye as Maggie spoke Christina Rossetti's words. It was so typical of my father to choose a message that encouraged us to smile rather than be sad, even in death he was still teaching me how to live. After Maggie's reading, Antony Hegarty's 'If It Be Your Will' played as Dad's coffin moved slowly behind the curtain. I gripped Cathie's hand tightly as his body departed from our lives forever, leaving only memories.

Before we left, Ray thanked us all for our attendance and as everyone filtered out, a surprisingly modern choice, Sarah McLachlan's 'Angel' played. It was a delightful way to conclude the service. We all gathered outside for a while and I cried, hugged, laughed and chatted with the people I knew. We then headed on to 'The Cemetery' for the reception. As we drove across in the hearse, I spotted a rainbow over the hills. I knew it wasn't a sign, it was just nature playing her tricks but it was a stunning display of the earth's wonders and perhaps, if it hadn't been for my father, I would never have fully appreciated how wonderful life was.

Chapter Sixty Seven

I was at the bar discovering we had gone over Dad's allocated drinks budget, paying off the extra and deciding whether or not to get another drink when I felt an arm around my waist. The stubbly kiss on my cheek revealed it was either Andy or some weird hormones were kicking in during Cathie's pregnancy.

"As far as funerals go, it's been a great one, 'H'. You've done your Dad proud."

"Cheers. Can I get you a drink? I've just closed down my Dad's tab but I was thinking of getting myself one. What are you having?"

"Don't be daft mate, I'll get them. Champagne? Bit of bubbly for old time's sake?"

"No, just a bitter for me, please."

Andy avoided the champagne too and bought himself a glass of red wine. We wandered through into the front room. A couple of people said thanks and goodbye as we did so. We'd probably been in there for a couple of hours by this point and people were starting to drift away. Only a few stray sandwiches and chicken drumsticks had survived the buffet. Cathie and Maggie were sat nattering to an old couple who I didn't recognise so rather than join them, we grabbed of seats in the corner away from everyone.

"How's your Mum doing?" I asked as I took my first sip of bitter. I knew Cathie would be driving home but given she was feeling constantly nauseous I had told her she could head home whenever she wanted and I could always follow on in a taxi. Her sister had already text to say she would have Max overnight.

"Up and down to be honest."

"I suppose that can only be expected. It's no fun losing those you love."

"It's funny the things that bother her. I can empathise with her missing your Dad and feeling lonely, but it's the other things I can't get my head around."

"Like what?"

"Like at the moment she keeps worrying about being eternally lonely. I mean she's divorced from my Dad now and thankfully has no intention of trying to track him down but she's been saying your Dad will already have an orderly queue waiting for him up there, so she's certain he'll be all sorted by the time she gets there. She thinks she is all set for billions upon billions of years on her own."

"Do you believe there's a heaven, Andy?"

I knew what Andy had always said in the past but sometimes a death can jolt people away from the viewpoint they have always maintained.

"No. You?"

"No. If there was though, who do you think my Dad would be with now then? My Mum or Irene?"

"Ooh, good question!"

Andy scratched his stubbly beard. He had decided to take a couple of weeks off work. He wasn't due in court for a month or so, so decided to help his Mum through Dad's death by living with her for a while. It was a rare opportunity not to worry about his appearance, so for the first time ever, he had grown a beard. I was so used to his clean shaven, immaculate appearance that it looked very odd to me.

"Tough one," Andy continued after a pause for reflection, "He didn't half love your Mum but then Irene had first dibs. They may have to fight for him like Christina Aguilera did in the 'Dirrty' video."

Andy could still make me smile even on the day of my Dad's funeral.

"If there's a heaven, I'm pretty sure female boxing will be outlawed."

"How would we know? Christians are always saying 'Let God be The Judge'."

"Very funny. Just imagine it though, Dad arriving on a big, white fluffy cloud and Irene and my Mum both there, hands on hips, waiting to see which one he chooses."

"Your Dad is a master of diplomacy. He'd find a way around it."

"I'm not sure he would."

As I was pondering death's questions, I could see out the corner of my eye that Cathie and Maggie were standing up along with the elderly couple they were with. I can never take my eyes off Cathie for too long, my eyes are always drawn to her and I could see she had gone from looking very friendly and cheerful to repeatedly glancing over at me with a concerned expression. I knew her well enough to know something was wrong. The elderly couple looked very frail and seemed much older than Maggie. At a guess, I thought they were a similar age to my Dad, late eighties.

"I'll help you over to him," Maggie was saying, in a loud voice, to the lady of the couple.

"Who's this heading over?" Andy asked.

"Your mother."

"I meant the old dears with her, as well you know."

"No idea, but I've a feeling we are about to find out."

I felt apprehensive. I didn't enjoy meeting new people in circumstances such as this. Meeting new people with work when it was official and you could hide behind the mask of professionalism was fine, but friends and family type introductions involved awkward small talk which I didn't find very comfortable. I had very little experience of it. Maggie was helping to steady the lady whilst Cathie was leading the man.

"Harry," Maggie called out, "I need to introduce you to two very important people."

I immediately stood up. I was face to face with them. As soon as I looked in the ladies eyes I knew who they were. I was even more scared now.

"Harry, this is Joan and Kenny Craddock. They're your grandparents."

I was thirty three years old. In my entire life I had never met these people. I didn't have an outpouring of emotion as they didn't feel like my grandparents. They just felt like strangers. I was numb.

I gave Joan a polite kiss and said hello and then I shook Kenny by the hand. He looked at me quizzically.

"Who are you son?" Kenny asked in his strong London accent.

"I'm 'H'."

"'H'?"

"Or Harry."

"Do I know you?" Harry said, look confused, "You'll have to excuse me, I've got pneumonia."

"He's got dementia," Joan Craddock explained.

"Oh, I'm sorry," I said and felt a whole combination of guilt, guilty for apologising in front of him and guilty for feeling sympathy for a man who had threatened my father.

"You know the questions you were asking me about the letter your father left?" Maggie asked me. I was feeling really uncomfortable by this point, like I was hurtling towards some sort of disaster and could do nothing to stop it.

"Yes."

"Well, I think Joan may be able to explain a lot of things for you. How about if Andy, Cathie and I looked after Kenny for a bit and you had a good chat with Joan? How does that sound?"

I felt I was being railroaded into this but I was too polite to argue.

"Good," I said probably unconvincingly, "can I get you a drink, Joan?"

"No, I'm fine thanks love," Joan answered, once again with that unmistakable accent.

Andy helped her into the seat he had just vacated.

"We'll just be in the other room if you need us," Cathie said as they began to guide Kenny through.

"Is Joan coming with us?" Kenny asked, unsure what was happening.

"She will be, honey, in a minute," Maggie said softly.

I half-smiled half-grimaced, at my grandmother. It felt like someone had removed half the pieces of my life's jigsaw and we were now about to start the process of putting it back together. The thing was, I knew from all the concerned looks that everything had been turned upside down and once it was back together, it was going to reveal a completely different picture.

Chapter Sixty Eight

My mother was back on the rainbow. It figured. I shook my head disdainfully as I looked out at her. Several hours had passed since my conversation with Joan but the anger I felt towards my parents had not subsided.

"I notice you've not got the guts to come and sit beside me this time."

"Harry, I'm sorry, I'm so sorry, I didn't want you to find out like this."

I laughed with a sneer.

"Mum, I had almost thirty four years to find out in a different way."

"Not from me," Mum said defensively, which appeared to me like she was looking to shift the blame, "it was your father who kept procrastinating. I think he was just scared how you would react. Scared he might tarnish everything."

My mother and father had always previously displayed a united front. Even in death I had never heard my mother saying anything but good things about my Dad. I briefly played with the idea that he may have found Irene in heaven and that my theatrics may be unnecessary. I then remembered what they had done to me and my fury returned.

"So you're saying my father should have told me? My father? That's a joke! I don't even know who my father is any more."

Chapter Sixty Nine

My mother had her mother's eyes. It was a little bit freaky how similar they were, like my Mum's eyes had miraculously been transported into the face of this fragile old lady. They were injected with the same sorrow I saw when I pictured my Mum on the rainbow. Five minutes into our chat at 'The Cemetery' we were still skirting around the truth like we were still on the edges of the tornado.

"We lost your mother twice, Harry or at least I did. Kenny doesn't really understand any more, In fact, I don't think I've ever told him since I found out. It would break his heart and then five minutes later he'd forget so then what would I do? Keep breaking it over and over again? What would be the point in that?

"How long have you known?"

"About your Mum?"

I nodded.

"Only about twelve months, love. When she first left with George, as you can imagine, we were heartbroken. It was the 1970's and things then weren't like they are nowadays. There was no internet for starters. We had no idea where they had gone or how to go about finding them. They had just vanished off the face of the earth. I looked frantically for a while, believe me I did. I asked hundreds of people who knew either of them. I even went to the police but Kitty wasn't a child, she was in her mid-twenties and she had not gone under duress, as far as we were aware, so the police did very little to help. Your grandfather, Kenny over there, he was very angry about it all and one day, maybe a couple of months after they left, he told me for the good of our four other children we had to stop torturing ourselves and just let them go. He said we didn't know where Kitty was but she would always know where we were and she would come back when she was ready. As you know, she never did come home."

I was starting to soften to Joan and even to Kenny too, who had seemed like the bad guy on the rare occasion Mum spoke of them. I picked up on the fact that Joan hadn't told me how she had managed to find out twelve months ago. I didn't try to prise it out from her. I just figured that story would eventually find its way out.

"Did Mum ever contact you?"

"No."

"No birthday cards? No Christmas cards? Nothing to let you know about me?"

"No. I only found about you when I found out your mother had died. Things made more sense when I found out about you."

"Why do you think Mum completely cut you out of her life?"

Joan would not have known I had been told this story by my parents. I wanted to hear her version of events. Mum's version was that Kenny would have arranged for Dad to be killed if he had caught up with him. I figured Kenny wouldn't have ever told Joan about threatening my Dad and, in effect, chasing them out of town. I was keen to know why she thought they had left.

"I can only imagine George had persuaded her that it wasn't in their interest to contact us."

"Why though? From what I remember of my Mum and Dad's relationship my Dad couldn't have stopped my Mum doing anything she wanted to do. My Mum was quiet but she was strong minded."

"Well, that was what we had thought at the time anyway. We obviously didn't know back then about your Mum being pregnant with you. We'd have come to different conclusions if we'd known that. It was still very much frowned upon to have a baby outside wedlock in those days. These days I think more babies are born outside wedlock than inside."

I felt it my duty to set the record straight a little.

"Mum was married by the time she had me though. Obviously she wasn't married at the time she fell pregnant but she was by the time I was born."

"Not to your father though."

"Yes, to my Dad. They got married in July '76."

"Oh, sorry love, I mean your biological father."

Joan stressed the word 'biological' like I didn't know what it meant. I'm not sure how daft Joan thought I was. She didn't think I knew there wasn't any internet in the 1970's and nor did she think I knew what biological meant. I clarified for her.

"Yes, to George, the man she slept with to produce me. They married in July '76, like I've just said."

Joan seemed very muddled. I put it down to her age. Coming all the way up to Rochdale had probably taken a lot out of her. Caring for Kenny probably did too. Joan moved her chair closer to mine.

"Love, I really couldn't say anything for certain and I don't know what you've been told so forgive me for saying this but I really wouldn't have thought George could be your father."

I distinctly remember looking at my arms when Joan said this. I recall looking at the colour of the skin around my wrists where my cufflinks shone. My father was mixed race, my mother was white and I had the colouring and features of a child produced by them. I had been told a thousand times I looked like my Dad. For this woman to even suggest that I wasn't their child seemed preposterous. It also seemed like an insult to their memory. She seemed like a pleasant old woman but what she was insinuating wasn't very pleasant at all. To do it on the day of my father's funeral seemed particularly wrong.

"Joan, when Dad died, I thought that was the end of family life for me. For you to show up here, on the day of his funeral, is a bit overwhelming and I really want to like you and build up a relationship with you. I think it's going to be difficult though because I loved my Dad as much as it is possible to love another human being and you seem to hate him. I understand that because he took your daughter away but look at me. Surely you can see I look like my father?"

"I am still angry with your father, love, but no, I don't hate him. I realise he sacrificed everything for you and your mother but it could all have been dealt with in a much better way."

"True, but why would he sacrifice everything for my Mum and me if he didn't love her and I wasn't his son?"

"I'm sure he loved you both very much but he did what he did because of Micky."

I was a little distracted at this point because Andy was at the bar and stuck his head into the room, motioning over asking me if I wanted a pint. I nodded and gave him the thumbs up. I felt like I needed about twelve.

"I'm sorry Joan, you've lost me. I don't know who Micky is."

Whether it was her age or the circumstances, Joan excelled in pulling faces that highlighted her shock and confusion.

"Are you telling me in all these years your Mum and George have never mentioned Micky?"

"No, I'm sorry, who is he?"

"Micky is the man I'm saying could well be your biological father."

Andy brought my pint over and put it on the table, I said 'thanks' and made a quick grab for it, drinking a third of it in one large gulp. After I'd swallowed it, I blinked hard and long. I remember shaking my head.

"You've lost me. If my Dad was, as you suspect, not my real father and wanted to keep this from me, then why on earth would he ever talk about the person who was?"

"Because Micky McCoy is George's son."

"What?"

"Micky is George's son. I can't believe they never mentioned him although given the type of man he was, I guess it makes sense. That's what I'm trying to tell you. I really don't think George is your father, my darling, I think he's your grandfather."

Chapter Seventy

Everything about Joan Craddock's story felt uncomfortable and upsetting but I had to admit when I reflected on it, a lot of it made sense. I sat with Joan for a further twenty minutes to hear her account of what had happened in the days, weeks, months and years before I arrived on the scene in Rochdale.

Much of what my Mum and Dad had told me was undoubtedly true. Dad had been married to Irene and she had died tragically of cancer. She had also miscarried several times. The twist in the tale was that my Dad and Irene did manage to have one son together, Michael 'Micky' Winston McCoy born back in 1950.

My Dad had always been a hard worker but when Irene died, when Micky was only ten, he threw himself into work. He used to ask various neighbours to keep an eye on Micky, who soon developed the ability to fend for himself but not always in the most legitimate of ways. Joan said in his early teens Micky wasn't a bad child he was just easily influenced and was manipulated by some unsavoury characters at school. As time passed, he lost interest in schoolwork altogether and spent the majority of his time with five or six lads who Joan described as the 'local no goods'.

One traditional routine Micky did maintain with my father was having his Sunday dinner around at 'The Craddocks'. By the time Micky was sixteen, it became apparent that his willingness to go there each Sunday was not to build bridges with his father but to try to foster a relationship with Kitty Craddock.

Joan described how beautiful my mother had been when she was sixteen. Mum had long straight black hair at the time and Joan said if she walked down the road with her, she would watch with a mixture of pride and fear as every male head would turn. It was an innocent beauty though and unfortunately Micky McCoy exploited that innocence. He had the bad boy charm that teenage girls have always seemed to find exciting and attractive. Before my Mum was seventeen, Joan discovered they were secretly dating. It was the start of a relationship that would continue into their mid-twenties. A few months after Joan became aware of the romance, Kenny and my Dad also realised that Micky and Kitty were 'courting' and were both horrified. Joan said she always remembered how George confided to her that most parents, when their son is seventeen or eighteen, are excited about what the future holds for them but he just looked to the future with dread. He felt it was already too late to get him back on an honest pathway and bore some of the responsibility himself due to his neglect. My Dad's fears proved well founded and over the next few years Micky was in and out of jail for a string of misdemeanours including assault, burglary and drug dealing. By his early twenties, not only was he in and out of prison, he was also in and out of hospital due to drink and drug issues. There were several times that Kitty broke up with him but each time he managed to convince her to forgive him. My Mum was, Joan explained, too trusting and loyal for her own good.

My father tried various means to get Micky back on the straight and narrow but nothing worked. He had tried compassion and understanding and when that failed he tried to be a disciplinarian but neither method led to any significant changes in Micky's approach to life. Whilst Dad's relationship with Micky was becoming increasingly strained, his bond with my mother was strengthening. She would often confide in my father about Micky's erratic behaviour and how difficult it was making her life. Once, when Micky was serving one of several short-term prison sentences, Kitty had broken down in tears at the dinner table one Sunday as she wanted to go to see a newly released film but as Micky was in prison she had no-one to go with. Joan said she couldn't recall what film it was but she did remember my father suggesting he took her.

"It was Catch-22," I told Joan, "Mum and Dad have both told me about that trip to the cinema together."

Joan explained that although she knew there was a special friendship developing between Kitty and George, she had never even considered the possibility of them getting together romantically. Joan and Kenny just saw my father as a tortured widower who had lost his wife and had now lost control of his son. When Kitty was in her mid-twenties, Kenny was fuming when my mother had reconciled once again with Micky after a temporary break up, so arranged to meet with Dad at 'The Old White Lion' pub to discuss ways they could work together to bring an end to the toxic relationship. They met up but for reasons unknown to Joan, an argument ensued and after that they never saw my parents again.

"What about Micky, where is he now?" I asked once Joan finished telling her tale.

"We don't know love. After George and your mother left he was furious. I remember him smashing George's house up and when he called around to ours, trying to discover their whereabouts, he said he would break his father's neck once he tracked him down. We used to see him occasionally around Whetstone, often the worse for wear due to his drinking and drug taking. One day, perhaps eighteen months after your Mum and George left, Micky just disappeared too."

"Where do you think he went?" I asked, intrigued.

"There was a lot of talk around the town that he had strayed into another dealer's drug territory and had fled to Ireland in fear of his life but Kenny and I think it's just as likely that he's buried under someone's patio or has a rock tied to his ankle at the bottom of the Thames."

I felt a strange sense of relief when Joan said this. Whether or not Micky was my biological father I would not have wanted to meet him. George was the only father I ever wanted to have. I guess it would have already happened if it was ever going to happen but I did not want him to ever come looking for me.

I had another question.

"Joan, what happened twelve months ago that allowed you to come here today?"

"Your father wrote to us. He had just had a heart attack and I think it must have made him realise his time was running out. He wouldn't have known whether we were still alive or not but he wrote a letter and sent it to our old house. Our eldest daughter, Harriet, lives there now so she brought it over to us. He apologised for taking Kitty away and broke my heart by telling me she had died. Up until then I had always kept hoping that one day she would walk through the door. The blessing though was that I got to hear about you. A grandchild I never knew I had."

I gripped her hand tight when she said this. I had only ever had two family members but perhaps now I would get an opportunity to meet Aunties, Uncles and cousins and they would get the chance to meet Cathie and our children.

"Why did it take you a year to come up?"

"George just said he had moved with Kitty to Rochdale and they had remained there but he didn't give an address."

"Why do you think that was?"

"Probably to make sure you never found out about Micky. Anyway, I've been reading the Rochdale newspapers on the internet for the last twelve months hoping for something that would lead me to you and eventually it arrived."

"What?"

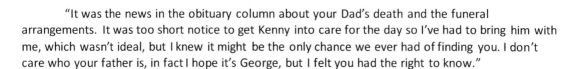

"It was the news in the obituary column about your Dad's death and the funeral arrangements. It was too short notice to get Kenny into care for the day so I've had to bring him with me, which wasn't ideal, but I knew it might be the only chance we ever had of finding you. I don't care who your father is, in fact I hope it's George, but I felt you had the right to know."

"Thank you."

I wasn't completely sure how I felt about knowing but I was glad my grandmother had found me.

"I don't want to lose you again, Harry."

"You won't, Joan. I'll make sure you won't."

Chapter Seventy One

With the exception of Cathie and me, by eight o'clock everyone who had attended the funeral had left 'The Cemetery'. We were just clearing the remainder of the buffet into black bin bags. Cathie had surprised me by lasting this long.

"I think you gave your Dad the send off he would have wanted," Cathie commented as we cleared up.

I begged to differ.

"I doubt he'd have been too keen on Kenny and Joan Craddock turning up and telling his son that he probably isn't his son," I replied.

"You said she said 'might not be'," Cathie pointed out, "that means you might be."

"Cathie, that's not the point."

"What do you mean?"

"I honestly don't give a toss who my biological father is. I've been here nearly thirty four years now. Whoever was there at my conception to create me is immaterial. George has been around for every moment of my life and will always be my father. The point is, Dad should have disclosed the whole story about Micky to me at some point. Whatever the truth was, he could have just been honest about it. I might not have liked it but I would have handled it. I stood up in the crematorium today and spoke about how honest my Dad was and it turns out he wasn't honest at all."

"Yes, he was."

"He lied to me for the whole of my life, Cathie."

"He did what he thought best to protect you for the whole of your life, 'H'. There's a big difference. I'm sure the sole reason he kept it from you was because he loved you and didn't want to see you get hurt."

"Maybe."

"Definitely. Your father adored you, 'H'."

"I know. I just feel a bit annoyed with him and my Mum right now."

"OK, I understand that but don't let the wound fester. There's nothing either of them can do about it now."

Chapter Seventy Two

The rainbow wasn't fading away. I would have liked to move away from the window, climbed back into bed and dreamed a new dream but something powerful was stopping me. My mother had already offered her apologies and now she wanted to offer her explanation.

"Harry, I have never witnessed a bond like the one between you and your father. It was something incredible. He is unquestionably your father."

"Mum, you don't need to tell me things I already know. I'm never going to stop loving him. All I want now is to be told the real story rather than the one that you and Dad have concocted."

"Most of what we actually told you was true, Harry."

"Not really. Neither of you ever mentioned Micky."

"There were justifiable reasons for that."

"Then tell me what they were."

For five minutes or so (it's difficult to put a definitive figure on dream time), I just let my mother speak. Most of what she spoke about just corroborated the story that Joan had told. Irene's death when Micky was ten, created distance between father and son rather than bringing them together. Through the years of them coming to Sunday dinner, Mum watched Micky develop into a handsome, confident teenager and by the time Mum was fourteen (Micky was twelve months older) she had become infatuated with him and would fill her diary with tales of how much she loved him. Every day of the week was just another step towards Sunday when she would see him again.

On Sunday in June 1966, when Mum was fifteen, Kenny had asked Mum to wash the dishes and Michael had politely offered to dry them. Mum said she could feel a different vibe to other Sundays that particular weekend. For the first time ever, she was convinced her feelings were being reciprocated. Micky was flirting with her. She was shy but was increasingly becoming aware of how attractive young men found her. Mum sensed this was her opportunity with Micky and flirted back, blushing, smiling and laughing as her heart pounded. Before the dishes were finished, Micky asked if he could meet her one night, after she finished school, at 'The Pits', a slang name given to 'Swan Lane Open Space', a park in Whetstone. Micky had left school by this time and despite his father finding him several jobs, he had not stuck with any of them for more than a fortnight. He always seemed to have money though. Mum said she had almost fainted when Micky asked her out but remained calm enough to say she had plans for the whole of the week other than the Monday night. The real reason she had said this, Mum confessed, was because she couldn't bear to wait any longer than twenty four hours.

Micky and my Mum made arrangements to meet by the 'Wendy House' in the park. The following day was a scorcher but Mum said she couldn't help herself running all the way to 'The Pits' as soon as school was finished. She then had to sit in the shade for five minutes once she arrived so Micky couldn't spot her red face or detect any signs of perspiration. When they did meet up, they walked around for a while, nervously at first, not used to being solely in each other's company. Once they grew in confidence though, they both found it easy to talk to the other and after half an hour of walking, Micky led her to a secluded spot in the upper park above the keeper's lodge. Whilst sitting down, Micky unexpectedly lunged forward to kiss her. Mum said it came so out of the blue that she instinctively leant backwards leading Micky to clumsily kiss thin air. Embarrassed, Micky stood up and without speaking began to walk away. Mum started to panic. She blamed herself and immediately worried that Micky would now assume she didn't love him. She quickly got to her feet and ran after him, shouting his name. Once Micky stopped, Mum said she kissed him passionately and from then on, their romance took off.

For almost ten years after that, there was some sort of relationship between them. Mum explained that it seemed wonderful for the first two years and then increasingly awful subsequently. She learnt that Micky had two sides to his character, a charming, sensitive side and a self-pitying, aggressive side. By the time he was in his late teens, he stopped even turning up for the jobs his father had arranged for him and increasingly relied upon unlawful ways to make money. This started with him dealing in stolen goods and buying and selling marijuana and then, through developing a network of unsavoury contacts, he became involved in a group that would burgle houses in the Barnet area. One night, just before Christmas in 1969, he had been the last of the group to leave a house and was spotted by a local 'bobby on the beat' who made chase and rugby tackled him to the floor. Micky had various items in his possession that could be traced back to a string of burglaries that evening and he was subsequently charged and imprisoned. Micky had a number of previous arrests for minor crimes so by this stage a custodial sentence was the only option the courts had.

Mum explained that she didn't even consider splitting up with him at this point. She swallowed all his stories about the fault lying with everyone else; a bad group of friends, an unsympathetic and unhelpful father, poor job opportunities and an inept government. He vowed to change and she vowed to help him. In reality, however, the only changes Micky made were for the worse and spells out of prison were soon followed by spells back in.

Throughout this period, when my father wasn't working, he would continue to go around to the Corcoran's for a Sunday roast. Kenny and Joan had politely told him that Micky wasn't welcome as they didn't approve of Mum's relationship with him. The afternoon that my parents arranged to go to see 'Cathch-22' together, Mum said her parents could not have been more encouraging. They knew George was a gentleman and although they would never have expected a relationship to develop between their nineteen year old daughter and a forty eight year old man, they wanted Mum to realise that not all men were trouble like Micky McCoy.

Mum said that gradually, bit by bit over a five year period, she found herself falling out of love with Micky and in love with my Dad. She was scared of Micky though. He had started dealing in all sorts of drugs and had resorted to taking them too. His visits to hospital were almost as regular as his visits to jail. He just wasn't detained for as long at the hospital. Mum had tried to break their relationship off on a number of times but stopped even threatening to end things once Micky began to say he could not and would not live without her. He said he would kill them both rather than see her with another man. In 1973, in a row over his drug taking, he had struck her in the face for the first time. He had cried after he hit her and promised it would never happen again. Two months later it did and eventually it happened so regularly that Micky stopped apologising and started blaming my mother,

"Why do you do these things that make me hit you, Kitty? You need to learn to stop winding me up."

My Mum explained that eventually my father offered her a way out. One day she blurted everything out to him and revealed how desperate things had become. My Dad proposed a solution and although it meant abandoning everyone Mum loved, it seemed like the only way out. Kenny got wind of the fact that my parents were plotting something and met up with my Dad to suggest a solution of his own. Kenny didn't threaten to kill my father, as I had previously been told, but did say to my father that he knew some men who could ensure Micky disappeared for good. My Dad hated what Micky had become but he didn't want him dead nor did he want Kenny jailed for his murder. After the meeting, my Dad implored my mother to stick to the original plan of fleeing to Manchester. Mum said she was completely in love with my father by then so would have done whatever he suggested.

I listened to the whole disturbing tale and as the rainbow began to fade, I asked,

"There's one thing I don't understand. If you were so in love with my Dad, what made you choose to continue sleeping with Micky?"

"Harry, believe me," she said sadly, "there was never any choice."

Chapter Seventy Three

I was around at Maggie's (Dad's) house the weekend after the funeral. Andy was there too as he was still off work. I'd been clearing out some of Dad's stuff, clothes, shoes, photographs and keepsakes mainly. The photos had made the whole process take far longer than it should have done as I kept looking through them and there were thousands of them, especially from when I was a child. My Mum loved taking photos. There were a few black and white ones from my Dad's childhood, the occasional photo they had somehow managed to take in the prisoner of war camp too but none of my mother's childhood. I am guessing Mum left London too quickly to pack photographs. I even managed to discover one photograph of Dad, Irene and Micky. It wasn't with the other main box of photos but there was an old wallet under Dad's side of the bed with half a dozen photos in. It was a summer photo, with Micky sitting in between Dad and Irene on a settee. Irene was wearing a summer dress and Dad and Micky were in t-shirts and shorts. Micky looked about eight. Micky was looking towards the camera with a cheeky smile and both Dad and Irene were looking down at Micky with a sense of pride. Irene was smiling broadly, Dad looked like he was talking or cracking a joke. I don't think I had ever seen a photo of Irene before. She was prettier than I had imagined her to be, in an old fashioned way. She had cropped dark hair, full lips and a big straight smile. It seemed really strange to me that Dad had this other experience of family life before the one he had with my Mum and me. It still saddened me that neither experience ended well for him. After a couple of hours of dividing everything into three groups, 'Keep', 'Charity' and 'Bin', I had stopped for a coffee. Andy was in the kitchen so we sat at the table and I updated him with developments from the week, including my latest visit from my mother.

"I take it you know this doesn't really make sense, 'H'? You can't reach a conclusion on how you were conceived based on something you've dreamt up."

"Dreamt," I stated, "'dreamt up' makes it sound worse."

"Even worse than it already does? You've just told me you've concluded that George isn't your father because your mother told you he wasn't in a dream whilst sitting on a rainbow."

"Andy, I'm starting to think they're more than just dreams."

"Mate, they're not."

"Mum told me about Ludovico Einaudi in a dream."

"We've been over this before. Somewhere deep in your sub-conscience you had stored that music from a time you had heard it being played. This time around all you are doing is making up a plausible story in your head when you're asleep but the bizarre thing for me is that you still believe it when you wake up."

"Because it could be true!"

"It could be true, 'H', but not because of your dream. Just imagine if I did that at work! Imagine how crazy I would sound. Your honour, I am totally convinced Mr Bloggs is guilty of the murder. I know there isn't a scrap of evidence that places him at the murder scene but last night, after I'd had a couple of bottles of champagne, I fell asleep in front of the TV and whilst I was asleep, I dreamt Bloggs here came riding through the desert on a unicorn and confessed he'd done it. On that basis, I suggest you jail him for life!"

Andy started laughing but I wasn't finding it funny.

"Don't take the piss out of me, Andy."

"Then get a grip of yourself! If you want to find out who your father really was, have a proper look into it. Go down and meet your family, ask the older ones questions about your Dad's past and do whatever you can to come to a sensible conclusion. I don't know much about DNA but perhaps you can find out whether there is a way of discovering whether George was your father or grandfather. Do all these things or just some of these but don't just go to sleep and wait for your Mum to arrive on a rainbow and give you all the answers."

I reluctantly realised Andy was right.

"Fair enough, I take your point."

"Good. Found anything in my Mum and George's room of any interest?"

"Not really, the odd photo."

"No hidden treasure?"

"Unfortunately not."

From the Building Society passbooks in Dad's drawer, there was certainly no indication that I would be packing in the job at 'Avon & Severn' and retiring to Barbados. Dad had just under £4,000 in his accounts but his main asset was his house. Selling the property wasn't a short-term option as that would mean I would have to kick Maggie out and I wasn't prepared to do that. I would let her leave when she was ready to.

"Have you asked my Mum?" Andy queried as he drank a coffee machine Latte from a long glass with a small handle.

"Asked her what?"

Given I had been thinking of her residential status, I was hoping I hadn't somehow spoken my thoughts out loud.

"Whether George mentioned anything to her about who your father is?"

"No, I really don't want to know either way."

"I think you do. It's obviously been on your mind day and night since the funeral which is why you're having weird dreams about it. Come on, let's go into the lounge and ask her."

Andy marched into the lounge with me languishing behind. The television was blasting out far too loudly. It was on QVC but Maggie didn't appear to be watching it. She was smoking a cigarette and looking vacantly at one of the walls. It was lunchtime and she was still in her nightie and dressing gown. She hadn't smoked in the house whilst Dad was alive either.

"Mum, 'H' has got something he wants to ask you," Andy blurted out without even a hint of a hello.

Maggie looked up at me from her seat. She had no make-up on and seemed to have aged ten years in a week. She stubbed her cigarette out guiltily.

"Oh, hello love. How've you been doing?"

"Up and down, Maggie. You?"

"Less of the ups, more of the downs. People seem to think you should brush it off when someone over eighty dies, just because they've had a good innings but it's not as simple as that. I felt like punching people right in the gob at George's funeral when they kept saying,

'Never mind love, he had a good innings.'

I know he had a good innings but it doesn't bring him back, does it 'H'? He was the love of my life and now he's gone. I know it doesn't say a lot about the rest of my sorry existence if an eighty eight year old man is the love of your life but that's what he was. 'The Love Of My Life'."

Maggie gulped and her eyes filled up with tears. I was expecting her to start sobbing but she didn't. She just wiped the corner of her eye, sniffed and said,

"Anyway, it is what is. What was it you wanted to ask me, love?"

"I just wanted to ask if you'd give me a hug, that's all, Maggie. You're the only person who really understands how I'm feeling right now."

"Of course I will. Come here you big soft thing."

I went over, sat next to her, opened my arms up and allowed Maggie in between them for a hug. She gave me a kiss on the lips which I could have done without as her mouth tasted like it had caressed a million cigarettes since its last brush. I genuinely felt sorry for her though. I think my father thought a lot of her but it was a fondness not an obsession.

"Ask her," Andy was mouthing to me from behind her back.

"Leave it," I mouthed back.

Andy wasn't prepared to leave it though. He would only wait until our hug was concluded.

"Mum, what did you think of Joan?" he asked.

"Joan?"

"'H's grandmother who turned up at the funeral," Andy explained.

"The old lady from London? I only chatted to her briefly but she seemed very nice."

"She upset 'H'," Andy stated.

"I wouldn't quite say upset," I protested.

"Did she love? I thought you looked like you were enjoying speaking to her. I thought she might have been able to help you with some of those questions you were asking me. The ones I couldn't answer at all," Maggie said, indicating that she had been deliberately obtuse when Joan's name was mentioned. We didn't need a polygraph test to know Maggie was lying about not knowing anything as she looked awkward and uncomfortable. My father had obviously told her something.

"Joan suggested I may not be George's son," I explained further.

"Really?" Maggie said feigning shock, "well, I never."

"Mum, drop the act. I've seen better actors at infant school nativity," Andy said tersely.

"What?" Maggie said with the palms of her hands showing.

"Just tell 'H' what you know, Mum. It's only right that he should know."

"Now look, I'm not saying I do know anything, but if I did, I may have found out by promising I would not say a word. If I did saying anything I would then be betraying the trust of someone I loved."

I had heard enough. If I was George's son there would have been no need to promise a thing. I may have conjured up the whole story in my head but it seemed like I was pretty close to the mark.

"Maggie, please don't say another word. If my Dad made you promise, I would expect you to keep your promise to him. It's the right thing to do. OK, I'm off upstairs to sort the rest of his things out."

I left as swiftly as I could. My father had only ever had one son and now I knew for sure that it wasn't me. It mattered little, in fact, it didn't matter at all. For thirty four years he had been my father, for eighteen years he had been my single parent and if, in death, he became my grandfather too, then that meant he was everything to me. Everything had changed but as far as feelings go, everything remained the same.

Chapter Seventy Four – Twelve Months Later

When we only had Max, I had an office at home. Once our daughter Melissa arrived, I was on Cloud Nine about her arrival but the one drawback was that I had to forfeit my office. It was converted into her nursery, paid for on credit, adding more pressure to our crumbling financial position. As a replacement, I now had a table in our bedroom with various files, a printer and a Laptop on. I would either work in there or as a fall back option on the dining room table. We could have done with moving somewhere bigger but with Cathie not working and largely due to my poor financial management we could barely afford to stay where we were.

It was seven thirty on Monday morning and I had just put Melissa down in her cot in time for my weekly Monday morning Conference Call. We had been up since four. Cathie was asleep in the bed next to me and I knew I would probably wake her up once the call began but Max was watching Children's TV downstairs and there was no way I could keep him quiet for an hour before school whilst I took this call.

Every Monday morning at seven thirty, Benny arranged a Conference Call for his team to review the week before and to discuss plans for the week ahead. It always lasted about an hour. Once we'd all dialled in, Benny would give an introductory speech for five minutes and would then spend forty five minutes going through his team members one by one to discuss our successes, pinpoint our struggles, offer solutions or look for suggestions from colleagues and ask us to describe how we planned to go forwards. Each week, the last ten minutes seemed to be reserved for a character assassination of Wilbur Kennedy.

I tended to do the night feeds with the baby over the weekend and was always shattered by Monday morning so, for many reasons, it was always an uncomfortable hour. I'd be sitting there in my pyjamas, with hair on end, hoping the sound of my demanding daughter, Melissa, would not be heard across the region. It may have been uncomfortable for me but it must have been downright painful for Wilbur.

Benny Victory despised Wilbur. He had been put into Benny's team by a Human Resources department complying with a government condition that a nationalised bank could not recruit staff externally if there was an internal candidate available. Wilbur was sixty six years old and in the eighteen months he had been in Benny's team he had done his level best to understand mortgages but despite asking lots of questions, often the same ones repeatedly, he still hadn't got to grips with the finer details. As a result, mortgage brokers in Northern Ireland had appeared to lose faith in him and would seemingly use alternative lenders whenever the opportunity allowed. Wilbur's sales figures were poor and this impacted on the results of the team. This was the first example I had come across of Benny 'not suffering fools gladly' and it didn't make for pleasant viewing. It had seemed to have become a mission of Benny's to force Wilbur out of his job. Each Monday morning on the Conference Call, he would ritually humiliate Wilbur by asking him questions he could not answer, highlighting his poor sales figures and using him as an example of what not to do in this job. From other conversations both me and the rest of the guys had with Wilbur, it appeared Benny did not go any easier on him during the rest of the week.

I have to confess I had very little sympathy for Wilbur. He was doing a well paid job that required excellent mortgage knowledge and he just wasn't up for it. I could empathise with Benny's frustrations. Wilbur's inability to do the job properly didn't just impact on Benny and the mortgage brokers of Northern Ireland, it impacted on his team mates too. Every month 'Avon & Severn' would pay their top sales team a £1,000 bonus each on top of their normal bonuses. My credit card debts were becoming more and more difficult to manage as the bank's attitude to bonuses toughened due to its nationalised status. I had been a fool in allowing them to build up but the extra £1,000 would have been a huge boost. In my opinion, Wilbur was costing me money. I wanted him out almost as much as Benny did.

Michael Moriarty, who was no fan of Benny and had been through his own difficult times in the cross hairs of Benny's fury, was about the most neutral team member. He pointed out to me that although it was clear that Wilbur wasn't the most knowledgeable Business Development Manager, you always had to remember that Benny always liked to have a team scapegoat. Michael was unsure whether Wilbur's failures were down to his lack of ability or if Benny had just set him unachievable targets to undermine him. Michael knew better than most about Benny's underhand methods. He had fought a six month battle to keep his job when Benny had tried to force him out via Avon & Severn's infamous 'Formal Action Plan' process. In modern banking terms, the 'Formal Action Plan' was like the black spot had been for pirates in 'Treasure Island', if you were given one, you were doomed. Michael wasn't willing to accept his fate though. He had ensured he complied with every demand Benny and Human Resources made and also involved the 'Staff Union' representative. Other than me, no-one in our team knew of the battle Michael was fighting but I was impressed how he eventually fought them off. The battle between Benny and Michael was like a fight between a lion and a rhino. Michael was a thick skinned heavyweight. The battle between Benny and Wilbur was like a battle between a lion and a fawn.

On this particular Conference Call, Wilbur took his usual weekly ear bashing, but to the casual observers such as me it seemed to take on a new degree of ferocity. To try to compensate for his lack of ability, Wilbur tried to act as enthusiastic as possible. It didn't lessen Benny's rage. In fact, it probably stoked it up. This week he had asked what 'M.I.G' stood for. It hadn't gone down well.

"For fuck's sake, Wilbur! How long have you been selling mortgages now?" Benny yelled this so loud I remember taking the phone a safe distance away from my ear drum.

"Eighteen months," Wilbur replied timidly.

"And how long have you had a mortgage?"

"I've had various different ones over the last forty years."

"And you've never thought to ask before now what 'M.I.G' stands for? Jesus Christ, give me strength. I've had worms in my shit more intelligent than you. It stands for 'Mortgage Indemnity Guarantee'. I seriously cannot believe I am having to inform one of my Sales staff what 'M.I.G' stands for. It's going to stand for 'Man In Grave' if you don't sort yourself out. OK, everyone, with the exception of Wilbur and Harry, please get off the line and get out there selling. Wilbur and Harry, stay on, I need to speak to you both urgently."

Everyone quickly said their goodbyes and got off the call. Melissa had just started to cry for her bottle downstairs and I could hear Cathie trying to soothe her (Cathie had dragged herself out of bed just after half seven). I could really have done without having to spend any further time on this call, especially with the mood Benny was in, but he was my boss so I was in no position to object.

"Are you both still here?" Benny asked.

"Yes," I replied.

"I am too," Wilbur added.

"Right, listen up the pair of you. Harry, you have management potential. Wilbur, as far as I can make out you have no potential at all, none. Now my time is too precious and my blood pressure too high to be dealing with fuckwits like you any longer. I'm wiping my hands of you. Harry, unofficially, I want you to become Wilbur's mentor. Wilbur, if you have any questions from now on, like do we still operate in pounds, shillings and pence or is the world flat then go and annoy Harry with them not me. I don't want to see you or hear from you for the next three months. I don't want you on my Conference Calls and I don't want you at my meetings. I just want you to piss off out of my life. Come back in three months' time and if you still know nothing I will personally drive over there, stick a 'Tiocfaidh ar la' T-shirt on you and dump you on the Shankill Road. Is that clear?"

Benny didn't wait for an answer. A robotic voice announced,

'The Call Leader has now left the session. This call will terminate in thirty seconds.'

I could hear Wilbur breathing out a long sigh.

"Wilbur, let me give you a quick call on your mobile."

I rang Wilbur straight back. I have to admit mentoring Wilbur was the last thing I wanted to be doing. I was working flat out as it was from half seven on Monday morning to ten o'clock on Friday night. I barely saw Cathie or my children during the week for more than twenty minutes each evening which was just enough time for me to stuff my tea down and have a cup of coffee. At weekends, as well as doing the night shifts with the baby, I was trying to maintain some sort of bond with Max by taking him to the park to play football or running him around to friends' birthday parties which seemed to happen at least once a weekend. Someone must have invented a rule that stated if your child was aged between five and eight the whole school year needed to attend the party.

On top of all this, my ridiculous financial decisions of the past were taking bite size chunks out my backside on a daily basis. I was overdrawn in the bank from the day I was paid and was over my formal overdraft limit from a week before the next pay day. My credit cards, of which there were several, were all up to their maximum and I had resorted to using a payday loan company called 'Loanzamoney'.

All of this was putting unnecessary pressure on my marriage. Cathie was often asleep before I finished work and if she had been up in the night, I was often out in the morning before she had properly surfaced. Life was stressful enough without Wilbur Kennedy adding to my woes.

"I'm sorry, Harry," Wilbur said as soon as he answered the phone.

"What are you apologising for, Wilbur?" I said in an irritable tone.

I wasn't sympathetic to his needs at all. All I was thinking about was his impact on mine.

"I'm sure you're busy enough as it is without having to mollycoddle an old bloke like me."

I realised I wasn't being fair. This poor bloke had come into our team and everyone, including me, had just let him suffer, thanking their lucky stars that it wasn't them that Benny was venting his spleen on.

"OK, Wilbur, let's just start from scratch, shall we? How do you feel right now and how do you want to feel?"

"At the moment, I feel hopeless and hated and I just want to feel appreciated. I can't concentrate on trying to learn new stuff when every time I make a mistake I feel the whole team are laughing at me."

Wilbur had a point. He had become a figure of ridicule. For the first time I started to see things from his perspective. I hadn't given Wilbur a hard time personally but at no point had I made any attempt to stop others mocking him. I remembered the old saying,

'The Only Thing Necessary For The Triumph Of Evil Is For Good Men To Do Nothing.'

Benny Victory probably wasn't evil but he was unnecessarily harsh, if I wasn't prepared to stick my head above the parapet on Wilbur's behalf, the least I could do was give him a bit of guidance. He was almost sixty seven and was struggling through for the good of his family in a job he knew nothing about. He should have been enjoying retirement or at the very least enjoying the pleasures of a care free job.

"OK, I'm going to do what I can to help. I promise if anyone in our team takes the mickey out of you from now on, I'll get them to back off and that includes Benny."

It was a brave statement for me to make. I was not sure how true it would be in reality but I could tell Wilbur appreciated me making it.

"Thanks Harry."

"No problem. All this is ultimately about Wilbur, is you building some trust up amongst your brokers. Once you do that, sales will pick up and once your figures are good, Benny will leave you alone."

"How do I get their trust though?"

"By adding value. Get the basics right first of all. Know our lending criteria inside out. Sometimes things can be a bit ambiguous so if you aren't sure about something chat it through with an underwriter before giving the broker a call back. Don't over promise. Over the next three months, I promise you my first job of the day will be to give you a ring. If you are stuck with anything I'll help you. Ring me too, if I'm in appointments, I can always bell you back. Enjoy this period but make sure you use it to your advantage because if you don't, Benny will make your life a living hell once it's over."

"I will."

"I know it's a cliché but none of this is rocket science. No-one dies if you get anything wrong but it's one hundred mile an hour stuff every minute of every day and it's a shitty job if you aren't keeping on top of it and you think everyone around you hates you."

"Benny does hate me."

"Wilbur, I think Benny hates everyone. It's just on various levels."

"Well, I'm on the highest possible level of hate."

"Let's see if we can change that."

This was the first time since I had started at Avon & Severn that I felt I had done anything to help a fellow staff member to any great extent. Over the next three months, Wilbur and I spoke every day. I learnt a lot about Wilbur. I grew to understand his personality, listened to his problems, rejoiced in his successes and although I thought we were very different, I learnt that we had a lot of similarities. We were both sensitive souls. After four weeks, Wilbur told me one Monday morning that he had got through a Sunday evening without tears for the first time in six months. I was pleased for him but admittedly I did think he must have been over dramatizing things previously if he had let it get that bad. I wasn't a stranger to tears myself though so I would have been a hypocrite to tell him to get a grip.

Over the three months, to my surprise as much as everyone else's, Wilbur's figures showed significant improvements. The fact that I had assisted Wilbur sort out the Northern Ireland territory was not only picked up on by my fellow BDMs but also by some of Avon & Severn's management team. I received a few phone calls from the Senior Management, including the North West Regional Manager, Graham Cunliffe, congratulating me on my part in Wilbur's sales resurrection. I appreciated receiving the praise and although I enjoyed helping Wilbur turn his working life back around and reluctantly be welcomed back into the Benny Victory team fold, it was a small positive when a forest of negatives seemed to be growing around me.

Away from work, depression began to introduce itself into my life. My father's death and the revelations about my parentage were not issues that sent me from being perfectly happy to incredibly sad in one fell swoop but I think they were significant enough to push me off the springboard of level moods, sending me somersaulting towards the cesspit of sadness.

Initially, I blamed my overwhelming feelings of sadness and the inability to sleep for more than an hour at a time on Melissa's sleep patterns and then I blamed it on the amount of extra hours I was putting in on the LAPTOP, especially at night. Some nights I could manage two or three hours sleep but there was the occasional night when I didn't sleep at all. My mind just seemed to be full and I couldn't unwind enough to switch off. I thought about work, I thought about our money troubles and I thought about life and death.

The knock on effect of my lack of sleep was increased levels of irritability especially with Cathie and the children. As far as I could tell, Cathie didn't seem to understand that the hours I spent on the LAPTOP weren't a shrewd tactic to avoid parenting duties or a way to deliberately avoid spending time with her. I was putting in the hours for the good of our family unit. I needed to keep in a well paid job because I knew we had significant enough debts that if I was earning any less, we would drown in them. Since Avon & Severn had been nationalised our revised targets and movement away from a commission pay structure had already led to my net wage dropping by over a third but if another bout of redundancies came about and I wasn't keeping on top of everything in the territory then Benny wouldn't hesitate to get rid of me.

There was absolutely no way Max or Melissa could have had any comprehension of what was going on in my work life but for some reason I expected them to, at least to the point that they could pick up on when I was especially stressed out and make an effort to behave. If Max had a petty crying fit over something trivial or Melissa wouldn't settle because she was teething, it just seemed like one big conspiracy to make my life harder than it already was. There were times I resorted to smacking Max's lower legs out of sheer frustration and although it wasn't hard, I knew it reflected the fact that I had lost control, not just of Max but of my own life. Sometimes I would sit in his room with him and we would both cry.

For twelve months, I think I had the capability of masking my depression from everyone at work and just about well enough at home so Cathie just suspected I was overworked and bad tempered. There was a lot more to it than that. I knew I wasn't being a good father or a good husband at that point and I had a lot of feelings of guilt about that. Other than my parents, I had everything in my life that I had ever wanted but I felt I was gradually screwing it all up. I felt work was providing the camouflage to stop everyone seeing the real me. I knew I was good at my job and for a while that area of positivity was what kept me going.

Chapter Seventy Five

I was finding my mother was becoming more demanding. I didn't sleep a lot but when I did I seemed to find my mother and the rainbow on a regular basis. Mum wasn't as calm as she had been whilst Dad was alive. She seemed to focus on certain things and repeatedly talk about them. One of her issues was Maggie.

"You need to get Maggie out that house, Harry. You told me she'd only be there for a couple of months after your father died but twelve months have gone by now and she's still there. She's laughing at you behind your back, Harry, I've seen her. She thinks you're a fool. I can't tell you how frustrating it is for me as your mother, watching you struggling financially, when you could sell our old house and free yourself of all that debt. If that woman had even a shred of decency she wouldn't have needed prompting to leave. I can't believe you aren't even taking rent off her. Have you spoken to her?"

"About rent or about evicting her?"

"Both."

"I've spoken to her about rent and I've said I don't want any. She's a family member and I just think it would be wrong to take money off her."

Mum scoffed at this comment.

"Harry, she isn't family either by blood or marriage."

"If Dad had lived another twenty fours she would have been."

"Anyway, taking a few hundred quid off her every month wouldn't solve all your problems. Selling the place would though. You just need to give her ample warning that now is the right time to find somewhere else. She could go and live with Andy."

I knew that would not be happening.

"Andy's an independent soul, Mum. He wouldn't want Maggie living with him."

"For goodness sake, of course he would! She's his mother."

"I know, but I know Andy, he wouldn't entertain it."

"Well, he could at least contribute to her finding somewhere new."

"I'm not asking her, Mum."

"Be brave, Harry. You need to put your real family first now."

Chapter Seventy Six

I am not sure whether I sensed there was going to be an issue with Benny Victory when he came up to the North West for his visit in May 2011 or whether other factors were taking control of my life but prior to his Wednesday visit I did not sleep at all. The only positive I could take from the sleepless night was at least I didn't have my mother in my ear urging me to evict Maggie or to stop working "these stupid hours" (another area of focus). My plan was still to let Maggie leave when she was good and ready. When my Dad was alive, I had two close friends, now I only had one so wasn't prepared to end up with none.

Benny Victory was what my parents would have described as a rotund or 'broad in the beam'. He was small and almost the shape of an enormous die with arms, legs and a head poking out from various sides. Personality wise he was outgoing, talkative, quick witted and under normal circumstances you would even go as far as to say he had a sunny disposition but his ability to turn in an instant and become fiery tempered was legendary. He was about to show me an altogether different side to his character, the cool and calculated assassin. Benny had been in London the night before for a banking event so I had arranged to meet him at Preston train station and after I picked him up we drove North to a succession of different mortgage brokers before dropping him off at Carlisle train station just after five so he could jump on a train to Edinburgh.

The conversations I had with Benny between appointments were less work focused than I had had with him before and revealed unpleasant new layers to his character.

"Are you happily married, Harry?"

Benny knew I was married, I think the emphasis was on the 'happily'. Interestingly not one of the Regional Sales Managers at Avon & Severn was still with their first spouse.

"Very much so although I'm not sure how happy Cathie is with the amount of hours I work these days."

"Do you begrudge the amount of hours you need to work for this job too?"

Conversations with Benny often required tactical rather than candid responses.

"No, I understand it's a necessity for this role. We're a popular lender and popularity brings volume. Volume of business, volume of phone calls, volume of emails and everything else that goes with it."

"But your wife likes to moan about it?"

"Sometimes. We have two children, one at Primary School and a baby so I'm sure she feels she could do with a little more help with them."

"Does she work herself?"

"Not at the moment. She's still on maternity."

"So she enjoys the perks of your role, like the money, but doesn't like the fact that you have to earn it."

"I just think she'd prefer it if I worked a little less."

"If you don't do this job properly it's not worth doing at all. Ignore her, Harry, women can only do three things better than men, give birth, bleed and moan. I would have said jiggle their tits too, but I reckon I can outdo them on that score these days," Benny laughed raucously at his own misogynistic wit.

There was not one thing that Benny said throughout the course of the day that endeared me to his character. I hadn't slept and my ability to function in my appointments was based on adrenalin alone, so perhaps I was feeling particularly irritable but several times throughout that day I reflected on the fact that I was selling my soul for money. I would have absolutely nothing to do with this prick or even this job if I wasn't financially trapped. I enjoyed the interaction with the mortgage brokers but I felt more than a little dirty inside about the collection of loathsome individuals I was representing. I didn't think I let it show but perhaps, looking back now, it was all too clear.

At the end of Benny's visit he suggested we go for a coffee at Carlisle station as he had forty five minutes to kill before his train and wanted to discuss our day on the road. I felt it had gone well. Several of the mortgage brokers, not men or ladies I knew particularly well, had taken it upon themselves to tell Benny I was the best Business Development Manager they had ever had and a credit to Avon & Severn. Once our cappuccinos arrived, the discussion began.

"So," Benny asked pouring several sachets of sugar on to the layer of chocolate powder, "how do you feel today went?"

This was the opening gambit every month and I gave a pretty standard response.

"I thought it went well. The brokers all seemed committed to use our product offering and are happy with the service provided by myself and our processors. I'm confident I can build on our market share with all of them."

"Not how I saw it," Benny replied bluntly as he stirred his sugar into his drink.

I knew his game instantly. I was already shattered but a sinking feeling spread through my body, starting in my stomach and spreading to my limbs, chest and brain. I was about to be placed on his scapegoat list. I was officially fucked.

"How do you mean?" I asked.

"Every appointment was disjointed and lacked structure. Once the brokers deviated from the path you were leading them down, it took you an age to rein them back in. It was unpleasant to witness and I've never seen you struggle so desperately. What's going on?"

Things were going on. I was in a financial mess. I was physically drained. I had no sex life. My relationship with my wife was strained. My children rarely saw me. I was unhappy, bad tempered, aching and missing my father, despite all this though, I was pretty damn sure I had just performed in exactly the same manner as I had in the previous visits over the last two years when Benny had signed me off as 'excellent'. What was going on was that I had inadvertently done something to piss Benny off and he was now about to ram a red hot poker up my arse, turning it whenever he deemed necessary to make me dance.

"Nothing is going on."

"Well, you could have fooled me. Today has been a disaster, 'H'. I can't put my finger on why but perhaps you've reached the end of your shelf life."

I wanted to punch the arrogant arsehole in the face. I bit into my cheek.

"I've what?"

"Reached the end of your shelf life. A sales job requires a huge amount of ambition and drive. Perhaps you've used up your supply. Perhaps the pressure your wife is putting on you is getting to you. Perhaps you've peaked and you are on the slide. Perhaps it's time to look for another job."

I was no Michael Moriarty when it came to fighting back but I wasn't just prepared to roll over on my tummy and let Benny tickle it either.

"My sales figures are better than anyone else's in our team, Benny," I said through gritted teeth.

"Well, that's something else I need to talk to you about. I've made some adjustments to targets going forward. Have a look at these figures for next month."

Benny passed me a sheet with a set of figures on. Everyone's target figures had come down, especially Wilbur's which had reduced by 40%. To balance this out, my targets had increased by over 80%.

"What do you think?" Benny asked.

He knew only too well what I thought. I thought I was being stitched up. I managed to keep my composure.

"I think there's been a sharp increase in my target."

"That isn't a thought, 'H', that's a fact. Do you think you can achieve it?"

"I'll try."

"That's not good enough. I need you to say 'I will'."

There was no way I was going to achieve an 80% increase in my target. There weren't enough hours in the day or brokers in the territory.

"Why am I the only person with an increase?"

"I hope you aren't questioning the validity of the targets I have set, Harry."

"No, I was just wondering why there has been such a significant increase?"

"I think you're coasting, H. I think it was obvious today in your appointments and it's very obvious in this conversation."

"How?"

"Well you aren't rolling up your sleeves ready for the fight, are you? You're just feeling hard done to. I need you to be smarter and more dynamic. You're my best paid BDM and you need to start justifying your wage."

Was my wage the reason that everything was changing? Was this just a simple cost cutting exercise? Was our status as a nationalised bank putting pressure on the bigwigs to cut costs so much that it had filtered down to my level?

I expected it was something more personal. There were two possibilities that I quickly considered; either Benny did genuinely feel I had lost my selling mojo or his wife, Liz, had said something to him about me that had got his back up and he was after revenge. Either way things had just become a whole lot tougher. I decided rather than put up a fight, I would just go along with whatever targets I was given. It would buy me some time to decide a proper course of action. Benny had all the power and I figured that if I put up a fight it would serve no purpose other than antagonising him further.

"OK, if that's what you think, I'll review how I do everything. I'll look into who I'm seeing and when I'm seeing them, brush up on my sales skills and work out if I could make more of my time."

It was all very clichéd but it was what I expected Benny wanted to hear.

"Do that, H. I'll write up a report about today, send a copy to Human Resources and copy you in. I am rating your appointment skills from today as 'Poor' and your overall rating as 'Underperforming'. To address this huge dip in your skill sets, I am going to come out with you one day a week for the next six weeks. I'm going to put you on an 'Informal Action Plan' with immediate effect and if there's no improvement over the next six weeks, I'll have no choice but to make it a formal action plan."

There it was – the 'Black Spot'. Benny Victory had just slapped the palm of my hand with a 'Black Spot'.

"OK," I said sullenly.

"Right 'H', it's gone five, you get yourself home. I'm going to wander over to buy a magazine before I catch my train. Enjoy your evening and I'll fire across a few emails whilst I'm on the train. Have a read of them later on this evening. See you next week!"

Without speaking I shook his hand and left. I was completely bewildered about everything that had just taken place. I thought there had been a clear distinction between my work life and my emotional state but it seemed like the two had just been formally introduced. Had I really been as bad as Benny was suggesting? I kept going over the day minute by minute in case I had missed something but the more I thought about it, the more I was left to conclude it was something personal. I felt very uneasy about Benny disliking me. It wasn't as though I liked him either but I was not in a position to make his life difficult. If he'd have said I hadn't been at the top of my game, I would have accepted that but there definitely hadn't been a fundamental shift in my performance from excellent to poor. All I could think of doing was working even harder to see whether I could change his mind but something was telling me Benny's mind was already made up – everyone had their shelf life and I had gone stale.

Chapter Seventy Seven

I was working in the dining room. It was a Sunday and I knew how much Cathie particularly resented me working at the weekends but it was a necessity. From time to time I could hear Max running around in his unique delirium or Melissa gabbling away in her newly found nonsense language but I just tried to shut it out as much as I could. I needed to crack on with my work.

It must have been around lunchtime when the doorbell rang. I ignored it at first as it wasn't going to be for me. The only ever person that ever called for me was Andy and I had turned down a few offers of a drink over the previous few weeks, including the night before, but I did remember saying he was off to Tatton Park for the day with some of his barrister buddies.

The doorbell rang a second time. I didn't understand why Cathie hadn't answered it the first time.

"Cathie!" I shouted, "Someone's at the door!"

There was no response. Where was she? I didn't really want to be answering the door. I was in a tatty old dressing grown and a less than modern pair of pyjamas which I had intended on remaining in for the rest of the day. I had only anticipated leaving the dining room for meals so there seemed little point in getting dressed.

The doorbell rang a third time, a more prolonged ring.

"For fuck's sake! CATHIE!"

Still nothing. Had Cathie gone out and left me with the two children? If she had, I didn't remember her saying. I wasn't sure though.

The doorbell rang a fourth time. Whoever it was, wasn't intending on going away. I was tempted to leave it until they finally called it quits but a sense of duty forced me up off my chair. I grumbled all the way to the door and pulled it open.

"Keith!"

We stood and stared at each other for what seemed like an hour but perhaps may only have been less than a minute. Max's father looked a million times better than me. He still looked youthful, his face was tanned and carried a smell of expensive after shave that mixed well with his moisturised and cleanly shaven face. I hadn't bothered to shave that weekend. I couldn't remember if I had bothered to shave that week. He wore a Ralph Lauren shirt that it appeared someone had spent twenty four hours ironing to remove every sign of a crease. His jeans looked expensive too and certainly weren't frayed at the bottom or threadbare at the knees like all mine had become. I needed to go shopping but I didn't like the idea of going out on an unnecessary journey. I was finding it difficult enough to get out the door from Monday to Friday. I looked admiringly at Keith's black shoes that were either brand new or freshly polished. I knew my appearance would not generate a similar feeling of awe from Keith.

Whilst I was still staring at Keith, I heard Cathie running down the stairs.

"Keith, I'm so sorry, I was in the bathroom getting Max dry. He wanted a bath. Are you OK? 'H', invite him in."

I didn't say anything I just stepped aside so Keith could enter. I was going to return to the dining room but I was intrigued as to why Keith had suddenly shown up at our door. As far as I was aware, he should just be going to bed in Australia. I looked at Cathie. She was wearing more make up than I had seen her wear for a long time and clothes she would only normally have worn on a night out. It was a long time since we had had a night out together. Her naturally curly blonde hair looked like it had been blown dry, hair sprayed and given some extra volume. Cathie looked beautiful but there was a knot in my stomach as I knew it was all for Keith's benefit. I was losing her but felt so deeply entrenched in all my problems that I didn't think I could do anything about it. Anything I tried to do would have as much impact as shouting at the television.

Cathie smiled at Keith.

"Max has been so excited about you coming, hasn't he 'H'?"

I knew I was just expected to agree but I couldn't. Was I supposed to have been aware that Keith was back? That he was coming to take our son away? I had no recollection of any of it.

"I don't know," I answered honestly.

I inadvertently made Cathie feel awkward by my unexpected response.

"'H'! He's hardly stopped talking about it for weeks. Ignore 'H', Keith, if it's not something to do with mortgages, 'H' just lets it go in one ear and out the other. Don't you?"

"I suppose I do."

"Max!" Cathie shouted up the stairs, "Are you coming? Your Dad's waiting."

Max came running down the stairs far more quickly than his mother had managed. He jumped down from about the fourth stair up and sprinted into the outstretched arms of his father. He was wearing a Manchester United top that I didn't even know he had.

"Max and Keith are off to Old Trafford to watch United against Blackpool," Cathie explained. I must have looked bewildered so Cathie must have correctly concluded an explanation was necessary.

"Very good," I replied.

"Yes," Keith added, "it's a bit of a dummy run. I've managed to get hold of two corporate tickets for Club Wembley for next Saturday. If Max enjoys himself today Cathie says I can take him down to London for the weekend next week."

"What is it that's on?"

"It's the Champions League Final. United against Barcelona," Keith answered.

I knew very little about football but even I knew that was a big game. The cost of the tickets could probably wipe out half our debt.

"I'm sure Max would love that," I replied honestly.

"I would love it," Max said, "I'd get to see Giggs and Rooney and Messi. I'd get to see Messi! I'd also get to see my Dad," Max said almost squealing with delight.

I looked at Max bouncing around excitedly. He was a wonderful child, a little male version of his mother. He was tactile, caring and fascinating just like Cathie but somehow over time, I had managed to distance myself from them. I wanted them back in my life. I wanted to put them before everything else but I was starting to wonder whether I was sinking and in the process dragging them down with me. If I was out of their lives maybe Cathie could get back with Keith and they would all be happy. Melissa would have a richer, brighter father than me.

After Keith and Max left I started to head back towards the dining room.

"How long is Keith over here for?" I asked.

Cathie sighed the sigh of a frustrated woman.

"Permanently. You know this 'H', I've told you a thousand times. He managed to get a transfer back at work last month but he's been in their London office for the first few weeks. He's back up North now."

"Where?"

"Cheadle Hulme."

"Alright for some. He looks well."

"He looks very well.

"In my imagination, at this point, Cathie started licking her lips and thrusting her hips but in real life I think she did nothing other than pass comment. The comment alone still did enough to wind me up.

"Good to see you tarted yourself up for him."

It was a spiteful, unnecessary comment but I couldn't help myself making it. I was jealous.

"I know I should be annoyed with you for saying that, 'H', but to be brutally honest I'm just glad you noticed. You're so wrapped up in your work these days that I feel I could walk around the house naked and you wouldn't even blink."

Cathie looked stunning naked. It used to take my breath away how beautiful she was. I briefly remembered how I used to lust after her but nowadays when I got into bed at night, I just hoped she was already asleep. I felt so guilty for everything.

"I'm really sorry, Cathie."

"Don't be sorry 'H', just do something about it."

I carried on walking towards the dining room.

"I wish I could, Cathie. I really wish I could."

Chapter Seventy Eight

"Talk to me, 'H'. What's going on?"

Andy had finally managed to persuade me to go out with him for a drink. We had been out for half an hour and I hadn't been a great deal of company. I didn't feel like I wanted to be there. I felt gloomy. We were in 'The Bamford Arms' and from the groans of the football watching drinkers it was safe to presume Manchester United were losing. Some of them looked as despondent as me but luckily for them theirs would be temporary. Max had gone to the game. I knew he would be disappointed too but he was just loving the fact that he was getting to spend a weekend with his Dad. I was really pleased for him. It provided a spark of warmth in my cold heart.

"Oh, I don't know. I just seem to be overwhelmed by this constant feeling that everything is falling apart."

"What's falling apart?"

My life was the correct answer but I watered down my response so not to faze Andy too much.

"Work mainly. My boss has shafted me with targets and all of a sudden he seems to have decided he wants to make my life difficult. It's all very strange. I thought he loved me until a couple of weeks ago."

"What's triggered that then?"

"I wish I knew but I honestly have no idea. He says I might have gone beyond my shelf life."

"What a wanker! You're not even thirty five yet. You're a salesman not a bloody footballer."

"I know. I thought if I worked even harder than I did before I might win him around but it's not happening. You know in Treasure Island when the pirates get given a black spot and they know they're screwed, that's how I feel."

"Can you not leave?"

"It's not easy finding jobs in the mortgage industry at the moment. Half the mortgage brokers have packed in and half the banks can't take anyone new on because they've been nationalised."

"Can't you find a job in Sales in a different industry?" Andy asked. I think he was genuinely interested but I think he was also pleased that he was managing to engage me in conversation. It was actually feeling OK to talk which made a change.

"I'm not sure I want to. I'm good at what I do. On a day to day basis, when my boss isn't around, I actually enjoy it. I used to anyway."

"Cathie says you never stop working."

"I know. I don't."

"That can't be healthy. I don't ease off much myself, I must admit, but I haven't got a wife and two kids at home."

"I think I'm probably doing them a favour."

"How come?"

"I'm not good to be around at the moment."

"In what way?"

"I don't know, every way. I'm stressed out. I'm irritable, I'm miserable, Keith is back on the scene and I keep thinking Cathie and the kids would be better off with him."

Andy had always believed in me, often more than I believed in myself. He wasn't prepared to accept that statement.

"Keith is a tosser, 'H'. Why would you even think for a second that you wife and kids would be better off with him than with you?"

"You don't have to live with me."

"Cheer up then."

"I can't. Believe me I've tried."

I don't think Andy was expecting me to be quite this low. It seemed to have confused him. He was trying to think very carefully about what to say. He was still spouting some garbage though, 'Cheer up' being a particularly annoying choice of words.

"Maybe you need to see your GP. You might need some anti-depressants."

"I'm not taking anti-depressants," I responded stubbornly.

"Why not?"

"I don't want to rely on tablets to get me through the day."

"What do you want to rely on then? Your natural charm and wit because take it from me, mate, if that's the case they're letting you down big style at the moment."

I almost smiled when he said this. That was more like the old 'Andy'.

"If I went on tablets I think I'd never come off."

"Do you not think working flat out from the moment you wake up until the moment you go back to sleep might be a significant factor? Maybe if you went to your GP, got yourself signed off work for a few weeks with stress, recharged your batteries and enjoyed some family time then you might go back to work as a new man."

I shook my head. I noticed when I did so I brushed the bones in my chest with my chin.

"There's no way I'm doing that," I said dismissively.

"Why not?"

"Avon & Severn don't do stress. They think it's a made-up term invented by lazy employees who fancy a few weeks off. Any time anyone goes off with stress they try to bully them out of work with an ever greater passion once they come back."

"Sound like a nice bunch."

"They're a bunch of arseholes...the bosses are anyway, the people who do my job are alright. Anyway, if I tried to get a job somewhere else it'd look crap if I had a gap in my employment history due to stress."

"It's not like you're going to put it on your c.v, 'H'!"

"They'll go for a reference."

"So, what you seem to be saying is that you need to plod along allowing things to get worse and worse until you get sacked and your wife leaves you?"

"No, I'm just saying I haven't worked out a solution yet."

"Maybe you need to start appreciating what you've got, 'H'. I reckon there're ten million people in this country who would gladly swop their life for yours. Good job, all be it with a knobby boss, beautiful wife, amazing kids and a lovely house. Think about it, what have you got to be depressed about?"

Over the last twenty five years, I had rarely lost my temper with Andy. He was one of life's good guys. He was my best friend. I loved him dearly but spouting stupid sentences like that really didn't help.

"Look Andy, I know you mean well but basically telling me to get a grip and pull myself together is total bollocks. Do you think I have somehow missed the fact that I have a beautiful wife and fantastic kids? The fact that I have and I'm still miserable makes me even more miserable. I don't understand what's happening to me at the moment. It's scary shit. I feel worthless. No, I feel worse than worthless. I feel like I'm sucking the enjoyment out of anyone who comes near me. I feel like I'm doing it to you now. You wanted to come out for an enjoyable glass of wine with an old mate and you'll go home feeling like shit. That's what I keep doing to everyone. I'm like some weird fucked up vampire who feeds off good people and tries to make them feel as miserable as I do."

"'H', I love you. Cathie loves you too. You aren't making us miserable. You're just making us worry about you. You need some help to get through this, professional help from someone who is used to dealing with it day in day out."

"I'm not going to the Doctor's."

"Believe me, 'H', you need to. Do it for Cathie and the kids."
"Thanks for caring, Andy, but I'm sure I'll be fine."

I didn't believe that any more than Andy did.

"Mate, I really don't think you will."

Five minutes later we were stood outside. I was about to phone for a taxi to take me back up to Norden and Andy was all set to walk to his Mum's. Without warning, Andy just grabbed me, hugged me and kissed me on the cheek. His face felt wet against mine like he'd been crying. It was raining outside so it may just have been that.

"I hate seeing you like this, 'H'."

"I hate being like this. I feel like I've been taken over by a robot, a bloody miserable one."

"Have you ever heard Catherine Feeny's Mr Blue?"

I shook my head.

"No."

"That's who you remind me of now, Mr Blue. Please for everyone's sake go and get it sorted out before you feel any worse. We all need the old 'H' back."

He looked me in the eyes and tried to smile. He had definitely been crying. There was no way I was going to the Doctor's. I rang a taxi.

Cathie put her head around the door into the dining room. It was quarter to eleven.

"I'm going to bed, 'H'. Goodnight!"

"Night."

I was having a relatively good day. We were talking a little, not like we used to but I felt well enough to ask about the children and had a good chat about football with Max. I didn't really know what I was talking about when it came to football but I was trying to learn. I was trying to give him a hug every day too but there were certain days I really didn't want to.

Cathie went away and I carrying on looking at the figures on my LAPTOP. No matter how hard I looked they weren't getting any better. There had been a fractional increase in my figures over the last six weeks but it was minimal. I was heading on to a 'Formal Action Plan'. I was trying to work out how I could improve things further but there didn't seem to be a magical solution. The products we were offering weren't as good as they'd been six weeks earlier and as an organisation we had struggled. I was bucking a trend by having an increase in figures but, thanks to the target changes, I was the only one in our team not to have hit 100% in June. Unexpectedly, Cathie opened the door again.

"Things have been better today, haven't they?"

"Yes," I agreed, "I haven't felt as flat, maybe things are picking up."

"I hope so. You're supposed to work to live you know, H, not live to work. Just give yourself a break for once and come to bed."

"I can't, Cathie. I'm under pressure at work right now, I've told you. I need to work out a way of improving things. I also need to be prepared for tomorrow, for all I know Benny could turn up again."

I kept a lot of information from Cathie. She knew I had a power crazed boss who was putting a lot of pressure on me and coming out with me on a regular basis but that's about all I'd disclosed. She still didn't know about our debts either. I'm sure she knew we had some but certainly didn't know the extent of them.

"OK hun, you do whatever you think you need to do. Goodnight."

Cathie left and headed up to the bedroom. At first, I was grateful that she was being supportive but I started to over analyse the conversation and then I started worrying whether she was having a dig at me. Perhaps she was suggesting the right thing to do was to spend more time with her. I wasn't sure. Whatever she was suggesting, it made me feel guilty. I was forever feeling guilty.

As promised, Benny had been out with me at least once a week during my 'Informal Action Plan'. In four of the six weeks, he had also made unannounced visits turning up outside the office of various mortgage brokers a couple of minutes before my appointments. The first couple of times, he had arrived before my first appointment of the day and accompanied me to every visit and the other times he turned up at lunchtime just for the afternoon. In total, he had therefore visited ten times over the six week period. Not once had he said I had performed well. 'Progressively worse' were the words he used most frequently.

At five past eleven, the light on my mobile flashed. The phone was on silent so as not to wake Cathie or the children. It was Benny. I was tempted to let it go to Voicemail but decided, ridiculously in hindsight, that it might impress him if I picked my phone up. Every time he forced that poker further up my backside, his manner with me became softer and more sympathetic. Each time I tried to pull it out though, his anger was back.

"I hope I'm not disturbing you, Harry."

"No, no, it's fine."

It was after eleven, how could he possibly be disturbing me?

"I thought it would be. I noticed you had just read one of my emails so thought I'd give you a quick call to let you know I'll be heading over to your territory again tomorrow."

"Oh ok, that's good."

Just what I needed. I was doing everything in my power to ensure he didn't know he was destroying me.

"We're one big team in my region and with everyone else hitting target I just thought you could do with me there."

"Thanks."

I hated sucking up to him but couldn't see an alternative. I was already going to miss out on my bonus this month. I didn't want to find myself without a basic either.

"I'm not coming out with you tomorrow though, mate. I want you to ring your brokers at nine to cancel all your appointments. I want to talk through how this 'Formal Action Plan' is going to work and I then want to have a look through your 'Broker Appointment Summary' sheets to see where we could be getting more business. Only a few of your records appear to be on the 'Shared' drive, mate, so I presume they'll be on your 'local' drive. Get some sleep, mate, and I'll see you in the morning."

As soon as Benny put down the phone I bashed my head on the desk a few times. I felt like he was pushing my face down into a bath full of water, waiting until I'd nearly drowned then pulling me up before repeating the process. The bastard, who I think was repeatedly calling me 'mate' just to antagonise me, knew only too well my appointment summaries would not be fully up to date. After every appointment we were expected to write a comprehensive review document which generally took about an hour to complete. We averaged six calls a day so if we wrote up every one it'd take us six hours every night. This would be six hours on top of all the other work I needed to do every evening, it was impossible. For audit purposes, we had to send through four a month so most BDMs I knew only completed four. I actually saw the benefit in completing them for any new mortgage brokers, so I'd complete about twenty a month. If it was someone I'd seen several times before, I would just jot down a few notes or not bother at all. I knew Benny would expect every single one to be completed which equated to one hundred and twenty a month. I had two choices, I could either go to bed and just let him come down on me like a ton of bricks or I could stay up and try to fill in as many of the blanks as possible for the last month. I chose to do the latter.

Benny rang me at seven o'clock in the morning to say he would be getting the train into Manchester and to meet him at the Midland Hotel for half past nine. He woke me up when he rang. I had fallen asleep on the dining room table at about quarter past six. When I met him, I think he was pretty taken aback that every broker he selected to look at from the last month had a comprehensive appointment summary completed. There had obviously not been enough time to complete records for every single broker but I started with those that had provided the most business and thankfully Benny had picked out the new ones (which I had done already) and the volume business providers. Temporarily, I felt elated and relieved. The night's work had paid dividends.

"OK, that's all great," Benny commented, "just how it should be. Now let's have a look at last month's."

"Last month's aren't as comprehensive, Benny," I explained, knowing the all too familiar feelings of anxiety and gloom were heading back my way.

"Why not? These should be done every day without fail. No wonder you're struggling if you don't have accurate records."

The main reason I was struggling was because he had put my target up by 80%. Everyone else had hit their target and they only filled four a month in.

"I've never fully completed them before this month," I confessed. I had to, he was about to see for himself anyway.

"Why the hell not?"

"No-one does. There isn't a single member of your team or any team that fully completes them. Go into your shared drive and have a look."

There was a very teacher and pupil feel to the meeting. Benny made me feel like a naughty schoolboy for pointing out a fact. He used compassionate tones when he was torturing your mind but angry tones if you attempted to fight back.

"'H', I don't give a flying fuck what everyone else is doing. Everyone else in my team is hitting their targets. You're the only one I have serious concerns about."

"I was hitting my target before you put it up!"

If looks could kill, I would be dead but I'd like to think Benny Victory would have been dead first. We stared at each other with testosterone fuelled hatred.

"Who the fuck do you think you are? How dare you challenge your target when you know I set those targets? How dare you? Do you want to go and settle this outside?"

Benny Victory took his jacket off. Was he suggesting we go outside in the middle of Manchester and scrap this out? I remembered all the fights I had lost after Mum's death. The last thing I wanted now was for Benny to give me a battering. I would have liked to have swung a punch at him though, I really would.

"No, I don't. I'm not twelve."

"Stop fucking acting like you're twelve then. You jumped up little prick."

I was pretty sure any chance of me salvaging any sort of relationship with my boss had just gone. I might as well give him some back.

"Stop acting like a fucking bully then."

"Are you finished?"

I was finished. Well and truly finished.

"No. What's your problem, Benny? What have I ever done to you?"

"I haven't got a problem. I just want to see this job done properly. You, my friend, are not doing this job properly. Go and grab yourself a drink of water, come back, apologise and we'll move on."

I stood up and walked to the bathroom. I washed my face in the water. I couldn't believe that had just happened. I was trying so hard to keep my cool and not let Benny know he was getting to me. It was all out in the open now. I was screwed. As I rubbed my face, I looked in the mirror. My dead father was standing next to me.

"Son, he's getting the better of you."

"I know he is. What am I supposed to do now?"

"You're expecting me to say 'apologise', aren't you?"

"Yes."

"I wouldn't. The man's a bully. You stand up to bullies."

"Are you suggesting I hit him?"

"What do you stand to lose?"

"My job plus any chance of getting another job."

"Don't do that then," Dad said with a wry smile, "just go back there, sit down and carry on as if nothing has happened. You're going to have to get away from him though. He's not doing your fragile mental state any favours. You shouldn't be seeing your dead Dad in the Gents toilets in the middle of the day!"

I was about to say 'thanks' but Dad was gone. I knew he wasn't really there, it was just my brain playing tricks but I felt calmer for having seen him. I washed my face again then left the toilets and went to sit next to Benny. He was messing with his Blackberry. He deliberately kept me waiting.

"Calmed down?" Benny asked once he put his Blackberry down.

"I'm fine."

"Anything to say?"

I wasn't going to let my father down by apologising. I wasn't going to give Benny the satisfaction either.

"I'll make sure I keep the right side of my target from now on."

"I suggest you do that. I also need to have a word with you about something else. Whilst you've been in the toilets drying your tears, I have been speaking to Human Resources department about another matter. You're making my life difficult at the moment, Harry, you really fucking are. Have you read Avon & Severn's Staff Behaviour policy document?"

I had no idea what he was going to throw at me now. I figured it was probably something to do with threatening behaviour towards a superior, it was my word against his after all and I knew who Human Resources would believe. I had flicked through the 'Behaviour' document the day I had started and hadn't even glanced at it since. It had probably been recycled.

"Yes," I lied, "why?"

"Well, you may recall there's a section about the 'Formal Action Plan' procedures and within that section there's a few paragraphs about what I am permitted to do as your line manager which includes accessing your business emails. Having done that and having sought support from Human Resources, I'm afraid I am going to have to issue you with a documented 'Formal Warning' about your conduct."

I had no recollection of doing anything inappropriate via emails. Michael Moriarty had sent me quite a few emails slagging Benny off but I was careful not to respond. There were various other staff members who I knew had forwarded on joke emails often with light hearted adult themes. I was always careful not to open them. As far as I could recall, I had never taken a step out of line. I had always thought with business emails that 'Big Brother' could be watching. I was now aware he most definitely was.

"I haven't done anything inappropriate on my emails."

"Are you certain about that?"

"100% certain."

"Well, MATE," Benny said the word 'mate' more sarcastically than I had ever heard it said before, "I'm afraid you are 100% wrong once again. On 7th April, you breached staff policy on promoting an external website."

I had no idea what he was talking about.

"Which external website?"

Benny passed me a sheet of paper.

"Justgiving? This was for Helen in underwriting's sister. She was running the London Marathon. Their mother had died of breast cancer and she was running for a Breast Cancer Awareness charity."

"I don't care. You breached policy. You forwarded a link to an external website to over fifty different staff members. I've asked HR to email a copy of the 'Formal Warning'. A hard copy will also be sent in the post."

"Is this some sort of wind up?"

"The only winding up anyone is doing, H, is you winding me up with your deplorable attitude. Look at the state of you! Unshaven, your shirt needs ironing, your personal aroma isn't the most pleasant and you look like you've been sleeping in a cardboard box. In every single way your conduct is not becoming of an Avon & Severn BDM. I'm really not sure you are doing yourself any favours by continuing in this role. I really think you could do with recharging your batteries then starting somewhere new. Have you given that any thought?"

I had given it lots of thought. Three months ago, I was flying, but now thanks to this power crazed fat bastard I seemed to be clinging on to my job by my fingernails. I couldn't walk away though. I now had about £25,000 worth of credit card debt and I'd just taken a second payday loan with 'Baa Baa Loans' (the ones with the sheep adverts about people flocking to borrow from them). Everything seemed to have unravelled since Dad had died. My finances were out of control, my marriage was not in a good place and even in my job I had, all of a sudden, become 'Public Enemy Number One'. I wanted to be how my Dad had been, springing out of bed every morning and being thankful for another day but my self-worth had never been lower. The future scared me. My fingernails wouldn't be able to cling on much longer if Benny kept stamping on them.

Chapter Eighty – Nine Months Later – March 2012

I might be wrong but as far as I am aware autism has been given a spectrum but mental health has not. There's probably a very good scientific reason for this, a logical reason or perhaps, for all I know, there is a spectrum for the mentally ill. If there is a mentally ill spectrum, between 2010 and 2012 I was a lot of different colours within it and a lot of different points along it. My moods were up and down like a cardiograph.

My unhealthy mind had a tendency to focus on specific things, some for justifiable reasons, others just because I wasn't well and had an inability to rationalise properly. I focused a lot on the fact that Benny Victory hated me, which as a line of thought had at least some credibility. In early 2012, however, I found a new thing to obsess about. My depression had stolen almost every sexual impulse from my body and, as a consequence, I began worrying that Cathie would have an affair.

Prior to this, the back end of 2011, leading up to Christmas, I had actually been relatively mentally well. Once Human Resources staff became involved in my 'Formal Action Plan', Benny had to show a certain level of consistency with how he managed me and couldn't manipulate targets to the same degree as he had in the past. Human Resources even questioned his 80% hike in my target and a compromise measure was introduced which meant my target was only increased by 20%. To Benny's dismay, thanks to an incredible amount of hard work, some brilliantly supportive mortgage brokers and a bit of good fortune with mortgage products, Human Resources suggested in August that I should be taken off the plan. Once you come off an 'Action Plan' with Avon & Severn, you cannot be put on another one for six months so I was handed a brief stay of execution. It was like being 'barley' in a childhood game of 'Tick'. For a while, Benny could not touch me.

Without Benny chipping away at my soul, most days I felt brighter. My mental issues weren't (and still aren't) black and white, so it would have been expecting too much to have been happy, contented and worry free every day, especially with some other underlying issues such as our debts, but I did feel a whole lot better.

Buoyed by this improvement and a 'New Year, New Start' sense of optimism, just before Christmas I ordered a bumper pack of twenty four condoms off the internet. My belief was that if Cathie and I could manage to have sex twice a month in 2012, then things must be going well. To a fairly young male brain, sex and happiness are inextricably linked.

Once during Christmas and once in January, we actually managed to get amorous enough to get the condom out of the foil but we never reached a stage when we had penetrative sex. I'm not quite sure why my body failed me but perhaps it was because my mind and body had been so overloaded with so many negative emotions for so long that it was asking too much. Cathie was very understanding, held me close and re-assured me that it didn't matter, but I gradually convinced myself that my impotence was a massive problem for our relationship. I began to believe that Cathie would seek to satiate her sexual needs elsewhere.

From February onwards, every day I came back from work, I would count the condoms in and out of the box. Twenty two. Each time I reached the magic number of twenty two my levels of fear, panic and anxiety would diminish a little.

Work wise, the New Year had not started well. For reasons I could not explain, the figures in my area were not good. Perhaps I had managed to hit targets in the summer of 2011 by working up to twenty hours a day and that level of devotion was not sustainable. My body would no longer permit me to survive on a couple of hours sleep like I had before. I started getting migraines if I did too much work or slept too little and I had no choice but to sleep them off. By mid-February 2012, Benny announced that he had approached Human Resources about putting me back on a 'Formal

Action Plan'. By the end of February, I was back on it and the black dog of depression that had spent several months sleeping or whimpering was now back growling, barking and showing its teeth.

Chapter Eighty One

Cathie was very unsure whether I should be heading to the Quarter end Sales Meeting. She had had a month of watching my moods slide and my self-worth shrinking. My sickness record had been exemplary throughout my time at Avon & Severn but in March I had two separate three day spells when I was off work due to a 'stomach bug' and 'flu'. I was genuinely unwell but not with the illnesses I disclosed. My moods had become so low that I would refuse to get out of bed. Cathie really should have got a Doctor out to me at that point but I begged her not to, saying if she left me alone I would bounce back and eventually, to a certain degree, I did.

If mental illness was logical, the week leading up to our Quarterly Sales Meeting would have brought about a worsening of my depression. I was performing badly and to have to face my principle adversary was a thought you would have expected to darken my moods but surprisingly that week my moods were bright. When Human Resources sanctioned my second 'Formal Action Plan', they had involved the 'Staff Union' who had insisted that Benny must not be permitted to put undue pressure on me. I think his reputation went before him. As a result, second time around, he only spent one day a month on the road with me. Thankfully, he chose the 1st March, so it was over and done with early and I didn't have to fret about it. It passed without major incident or drama. It was most definitely the calm before the storm.

Whilst my moods were a little brighter, I wanted to go to the meeting. Even I was aware at this point that my time at Avon & Severn was coming to an end. At the end of my second 'Action Plan' period, if the company felt I was not performing adequately they could bring about measures to terminate my employment. I could fight this with internal hearings and subsequently legal proceedings but I knew my mental state was not strong enough to fight those battles. The war was lost but I just wanted to drag it out as long as possible before I finally surrendered. I realised my non-appearance at the Sales Meeting would hasten my departure.

Cathie only eventually allowed me to go, without further protests, when I agreed not to drive. I booked a train to Bristol Temple Meads for Thursday 29th March with a return booked for the following day with an overnight stay booked at the Marriott Royal.

As soon as I woke up that Thursday morning I knew things weren't right. Everything felt very flat and dark. I had a shower and a shave hoping the negative feelings would subside a little, but it came as no surprise when my father stood over my left shoulder as I had my morning shave. The mother my mind re-created didn't deviate too much from the reality and the same applied to my father. My Dad remained pragmatic and had a wisdom I couldn't normally find within myself. He explained that he knew I was fighting hard against the demons within me and he understood I just wanted to get back under the bed sheets and remain there for the rest of the day. He was proud of the fact I was battling against that urge though.

"You can only do what you can do, son," he said," I understand how you feel but just know your mother and I are rooting for you and we're here whenever you need us."

As far as pep talks go, it was very simple and straightforward. I wasn't beating my chest when I came out the bathroom. I wasn't pumped full of adrenalin. Dad just seemed to know that whatever anyone said to try to drag me from despair, it didn't work. It tended to just push me deeper in. He didn't try to steer or drag, he was just letting me know he was there no matter what. It was all I needed. I came out the bathroom, got dressed, packed a bag, counted the condoms one last time and then headed, trance like, towards Rochdale train station.

Chapter Eighty Two

I was manically happy when I walked back through the door at home. I bounded like a fawn through the hallway and fully digested the family scene that played out before me in the lounge. Melissa was sat in her high chair being fed pieces of eggy bread by Cathie and Max was sprawled across the lounge carpet watching television.

"How was the meeting?" Cathie asked with cautious tones.

"Brilliant," I replied joyously, "absolutely fucking brilliant!"

Those words, said with a full dose of sarcasm can mean the exact opposite but I delivered them with such enthusiasm it was obvious to Cathie I wasn't being sarcastic. The fact that I had just used the 'f' word in front of Max, however, alerted her not to get too carried away by my euphoric statement. Having witnessed a significant proportion of my down moods, Cathie was aware the pendulum could temporarily swing the other way. It always swung back.

"What made it so good then?" Cathie asked, before adding, "and remember this time that Max may be listening."

"Oh sorry," I said, putting my hand over my mouth.

"It's OK, he's probably too busy concentrating on his programme to have noticed anyway. Go on, tell me why it was so good."

"Because I quit my job," I said standing straight and proud as I said it.

"You have?" Cathie queried.

There was a sceptical tone to her words like she very much doubted that what I was saying was true.

"No, seriously I have. I went to the meeting which was boring as usual but I got through it. Afterwards though, for the evening meal, the managers in their infinite wisdom, thought that given it's Good Friday next week that we would have some sort of satirical 'Last Supper' theme. So, we were divided into four groups dependent on where we were in the Sales League Tables. Have a guess what the four groups were called?"

"No idea, 'H'."

"Just guess," I pleaded.

"I've no idea," Cathie said shrugging.

"Please just have a guess," I begged.

"I don't know....Gods, disciples, angels and devils."

I was impressed.

"Not a bad guess actually but sicker than that. Disciples, Jews, Gentiles and Lepers."

"You're kidding."

"No, straight up. They managed to pretty much offend everyone. We've got people of all religious persuasions and they were all pissed off. Of course everyone on the leper table was far from impressed too."

"Didn't anyone complain?"

"Loads of people did. They just said anyone complaining had had a sense of humour bypass and when had anyone at Avon & Severn been politically correct?"

"I'm guessing you were on the 'Leper' table."

"Of course. The disciples were all given a slap up meal and all the managers sat with them too."

"What did you get?"

"Benny just threw us a baguette over and told us we could fight over it."

"That's horrible. What have lepers got to do with the 'Last Supper' anyway?"

"Nothing, it was just another opportunity to humiliate the people who are struggling against target. I've told you before the managers there are a bunch of wankers."

"So you just quit there and then out of protest, did you?"

I could tell Cathie didn't believe I'd quit. Her tone was a 'playing along' one. She did that a lot with me if I was over talkative.

"No, to be honest I didn't. I was as offended as everyone else but I didn't quit there and then."

"When did you quit then?"

"At breakfast this morning. All the managers were sat on one table, laughing and joking amongst themselves as they do, so I just went over."

"What did you say?" Cathie asked, but I could tell she'd stopped properly listening. She'd gone back to feeding Melissa some eggy bread and Max had turned the volume up so he could hear the television over my chatter.

"I just told them I was quitting. I said I only had one life and for two years I had wasted it by pledging my undying devotion to the biggest bunch of obnoxious wankers the world had ever produced."

"Did they take it OK?"

"Not particularly but I'm not bothered, it's over now."

"That's good, hun. You go and get your pyjamas on and I'll sort out some tea for you."

I wasn't sure whether Cathie believed me. I suspected that she probably didn't. She knew I'd been weak and wouldn't have had the nerve to go through with it on my own. I needed to be honest with her. Tell her something I'd kept from her before."

"You don't believe me, Cathie, do you?"

"Of course I do."

"I don't think you do. You think I'm too weak to stand up for myself but I was helped to make the decision you see. We had a vote on it. The three of us, Mum, Dad and me. We voted 2-1 in favour of me leaving. I was actually the one who voted for me to stay but it didn't matter. It was a majority decision. It didn't need to be unanimous."

Cathie came over to me, hugged me and I hugged back which had been unusual in recent times. I think the capability had returned because I felt a massive weight had been lifted.

"Are you pleased?" I asked.

"I'm delighted, 'H', I really am. We need to have a nice relaxing weekend and then on Monday, given you aren't working any more, I think it would be a good idea if the two of us went to the Doctor's. Do you not think it's a perfect time to make a fresh start?"

I normally fought against any visit to the Doctor's, but I was in such a good mood I wasn't going to argue, not completely anyway.

"OK, but I'm not taking any tablets."

"That's fine, H, let's just take it one step at a time."

Chapter Eighty Three – Saturday 31st March 2012

I slept really well that Friday night. Better than I had for a long time. Mum did still visit me on the rainbow during the night though saying she had her doubts whether Cathie really believed I'd quit. I told her I was unsure too.

Max did football on Saturday mornings at Matthew Moss High School. As I was feeling spritely, I suggested to Cathie that I take him. Cathie didn't like that idea though. She thought it best if I stay at a home because I'd had a couple of busy days and she didn't want me to start feeling down again because I'd worn myself out.

I suggested that if I was staying at home, I could keep an eye on Melissa but Cathie thought the baby needed some fresh air so she ended up taking her too. She told me just to stay in our room, put some music on and chill out. I hadn't listened to any music for ages, I hadn't been able to take it in with everything going on around me, but I was feeling happy and content so decided to do just that. I watched from the bedroom window as Cathie put the kids in the car. I noticed as she was leaving how anxious and edgy she appeared. She had that furrowed brow look. My concern for Cathie started to eat into my happy mood a little.

I watched the car go up the road and then put my music on. I decided on Angus and Julia Stone's 'Down The Way' CD. I'd got into them after Andy recommended 'The Wedding Song' for Cathie and me. It was my favourite album of theirs. I found it difficult to listen to that morning though because something was bothering me. I kept skipping through the tracks until I got to a track called 'I'm Not Yours' at which stage I was distracted by other matters.

The edgy look on Cathie's face came back to me. It wasn't right that she should have that look on her face. She should have been smiling. My job had made us both so unhappy but now that was out the way things were brighter. I had been thinking of asking Andy if he would want to buy Maggie's house off us for a cheap rate. It would help us clear our debts and give me some breathing space to find a new job.

Something was definitely wrong. I started to panic. I pulled out all my bedside drawers. I grabbed the box of condoms. I was starting to struggle to breathe. I started to count. I must have started afresh perhaps half a dozen times but eventually I counted them all out. I counted them a second time in case I had miscounted. There were definitely only twenty one. I counted a third time to make sure. Twenty one. There were only twenty one.

"Shit! Shit! Shit! SHIT!"

I ran down the stairs to the front door. It was locked. I started searching frantically for my keys. They weren't there, none of them. No car keys, no front door key and no back door key. What was happening? My brain was trying to figure it out. The penny dropped. Cathie had locked me in. She was running away with Keith, taking the kids with her and leaving me.

Chapter Eighty Four

I remembered there was a spare car key in the small bottom drawer next to the oven. I needed to get to 'Matthew Moss' school. I thought there was still a chance she had taken him to football. Max was like me, he liked routine. If Cathie was going to go off somewhere with Keith, she might have decided to do it straight after football. I got the key out.

I needed to get dressed so just threw on a pair of jeans and the first t-shirt I could find. I went to my overnight bag to get a pair of shoes out. There were a load of muddy clothes in there which I just piled up on the floor but when I went to pull my black shoes out the bag, I pulled out an old pair of paint splattered brown ones. I stared at them in my hands. They had lots of scuffs on, had weird holes deliberately cut into them and a buckle on each shoe. For a split second I had a vision of where I'd got them from. I'd traded them. I remembered they did fit me. They would have to do. I didn't have time to go hunting around the house for another pair.

I climbed out the window in the lounge, got in my car and went in search of my family.

Chapter Eighty Five

My Mum and Dad were in the car with me, neither of them had bothered to get in the front seat, they were both sitting together, holding hands, in the back. They were both urging me to slow down and to calm down. If I had driven at the speed Dad used to drive, Cathie and Keith might have been back in Australia by the time I got to the football pitches at 'Matthew Moss'. Mum did, however, come up with a suggestion that I did think at the time was a good one though.

"Why don't you stop at Tesco on the way up to Matthew Moss and buy Cathie some flowers, Harry?" Mum suggested, "If you want to want to win her back you need to impress her."

"I don't think I've got any money."

"We'll lend you some," Dad said with a cheery smile.

"OK."

I wasn't sure whether they were going to get back in once I stopped. They looked petrified.

I needed to be quick so rather than hunt for a car parking spot near the entrance I just parked up at the edge of the car park. I didn't bother about getting in a bay or at the right angle. I just stopped, jumped out and started running towards the entrance. Halfway there, I remembered I'd forgotten to get the money off Dad. I ran back. I was panting. I was designed for comfort now not for sprinting.

"Do you have that money, Dad?"

Dad passed me two notes.

"Thanks!"

I looked at it. It didn't look like notes I'd seen before.

"Are these real?" I asked.

"They're legal tender. Go on, hurry up!"

I sprinted again back to the store entrance. I was sure people must have looked at me strangely given I was expending a lot of energy to move reasonably slowly but I was on a mission so didn't look back. Fresh flowers at Tesco are in a collection right at the entrance so I ran over and started to find the nicest bunch.

Whilst sifting through the flowers, I saw him, Keith Corden. He was pushing a small trolley through the fruit & veg section. All he had on was a pair of navy blue Speedos and a matching blue swimming cap. He had shoulders like those on an American football player and muscles that looked like they could explode out of his body and grab you by the throat but as soon as I saw the lettering on the back of his trunks I was ready for the fight. In white capital letters it read,

'I SLEPT WITH YOUR WIFE, HARRY MC COY.'

Keith had not just used one of my condoms, he was gloating about it. He was walking around Tesco advertising it to all of Rochdale. I was going to kill him. I dumped the flowers and ran once more. I chased after him. He wasn't going to get far with his trolley and I didn't suppose those budgie smugglers would allow him to pick up much pace. I ran down various aisles looking for him. He was nowhere to be seen at first and then I'd catch a glimpse of for a second or two before he would disappear once more.

Keith and I eventually came head to head in the alcohol section. I thought I would have charged at him but I didn't. I just stared at him with his gym fit body. I wasn't sure what 'pecs' were, but whatever they were, he looked like he had borrowed his from Lou Ferrigno. I then stared at myself. I was wearing some odd brown, scuffed, paint splattered shoes, jeans that had lost their colouring so they were white at the knees, a white Prince t-shirt that just said Prince on it, underlined and in black lettering and then underneath it, it said four words, one below the other 'DANCE, MUSIC, SEX, ROMANCE'. I wasn't particularly fussed on Prince. It must have been Cathie's. I must have grabbed it in my haste to get out the house. For the first time I realised it was several sizes too small and my hairy beer gut was taunting me from underneath it.

Keith laughed as he saw me looking at myself.

"Can you blame her, H? Can you really blame her?"

It was at that point I started smashing bottles. After that, I remember very little.

Chapter Eighty Six – ANDY CORCORAN

I was having lunch with a colleague at 'Pier Eight' at the Lowry Theatre in Salford Quays. We were all set for an afternoon and evening of wine and song. We'd bought tickets for the opening performance of 'Wonderful Town'. I was beyond excited. We had third row tickets. Connie Fisher was starring in a Leonard Bernstein fifties musical which had the whole Halle orchestra performing. It wasn't just a pit orchestra like you normally had at a show, oh no, I'm talking the whole caboodle, sixty eight accomplished musicians.

I must confess I may have uttered the word 'Bugger' when my phone vibrated and I saw the letter 'H' spring up. I had just ordered a 'Corned Beef & Sweet Potato Hash' starter with poached egg, dried onion and sauce viande. I had already begun to salivate.

There were a multitude of reasons to curse. First and foremost, I feared this visit to the theatre, without 'H', may be deemed a betrayal. He had been very down in the dumps recently and I wasn't sure if it was the right thing to do to invite him. I told myself that he would have preferred me not to ask but I think it would be more honest to say I preferred him not to go. I knew the background noise would reveal I was eating out so I was tempted to divert him and call him back late in the evening after the show or the following day. I'm so glad I didn't.

"Hello 'H'! How are you on this fine day?"

It was almost impossible to hear him. As well as the clattering of cutlery and general chatter at my end, there was an abundance of noise from his end too. It sounded like traffic. He was chuntering too which was irritating and alarming in equal measure.

"I can't hear you, 'H', speak up."

It was still too noisy. I articulated apologies to Edward, my work colleague and sought out a quieter location. The first two sentences I heard cranked up the alarm levels and extinguished the irritation.

"I'm scared, Andy. I'm on a bridge and I can only see one way off."

You may or may not know I'm a little bit crazy about music. As soon as he said it, I thought 'Running to Stand Still, U2.' I know that's not the lyric, it's something to do with ways out and towers but nevertheless that was what immediately sprang to mind. The second thing that sprang to mind was fear. 'H' was continuing to ramble. I wasn't picking up any of it other than the word 'fucking'. He seemed to be using the word 'fucking' a lot.

"'H' calm down. Just very calmly and very slowly tell me which bridge you are on."

It took a while to get it out of him. I eventually established he was on the Thelwall Viaduct on the M6. I have no idea how he had managed to get there in the mental state he was in. I still don't. He could have had the decency to choose Barton Bridge that was right on my doorstep.

"'H', just stay in your car and keep talking to me. I'm going to walk to my car now and then drive over to you. I've got hands free though so it's fine. We can keep talking."

I walked back over to Edward whilst I kept 'H' on the line. I motioned to Ed to get a pen and paper out. He had a pen in his jacket pocket. He didn't have any paper though so I had to write on the back of a 'Wine' menu.

I wrote:-

'Call the police. My friend is on the Thelwall Viaduct. He's not in good mental shape. Tell them I'm worried he might jump. His name is Harry McCoy. I'm going to have to go. I'm so sorry.'

Chapter Eighty Seven – ANDY CORCORAN

I lost mobile signal on the way to Thelwall which was a tad annoying but perhaps speeding along at over a hundred miles an hour didn't help. 'H' had stopped speaking coherently by the time I lost him. I tried several times to ring him back but it just went to Voicemail. He sounded a lot better on his Voicemal than he now did in real life. I rang Edward instead.

"Hi Ed. Can you do me a favour please and find out whether there's been anything on the radio about a traffic problem on the M6 at Thelwall Viaduct. If I turn up going Northwards and he's going Southwards or vice versa, I'll be on the wrong bridge. There're two bridges at Thelwall. I need to be coming at it from the right direction.

Ed probably knew that there were two bridges at Thelwall. He was a clever man but he was gentlemanly enough not to stamp his feet about me insulting his intelligence. He just said he would check it out and come back to me. Five minutes later, Ed rang back to say the stoppage was Southbound. Thankfully, I was coming at it from the right direction.

I have to confess when it comes to telling stories about this dramatic turn of events, I have a tendency to take a seed of truth, plant it, water it, let the sun shine on it and let it grow into an Oak tree so I'll make sure I tell you what really happened rather than the embellished version I have formulated since.

There was only one lane open Southbound when I arrived at Thelwall. The police had blocked the three inside lanes off but it was easy enough for me to weave between a set of cones and speed forward to the police road block. I parked up ten metres short of a dozen police vehicles and walked over to see who was in charge.

The police, quite reasonably, questioned who I was. I explained I was Andrew Corcoran, a barrister and Harry McCoy's closest friend.

"Lover?" one of the Constables asked.

"Friend," I repeated.

I could see 'H' at the highest point of the bridge. He was about seventy five metres further along than us. He was wandering around outside his car which was parked on the hard shoulder. A number of heartless rubberneckers were hurling abuse at him which I have no doubt was doing nothing to help.

I asked the policeman in charge if I could approach him. I wasn't given an immediate 'Yes' or 'No' answer but after a lot of debate and radioing on walkie-talkies I was given a cautious go ahead. I was told to keep a safe distance from the edge. I totally ignored that one. I could see 'H' approaching the edge himself and peering over then pulling himself back. I was good with heights. 'H' never had been.

I think I have forgotten to mention the fact that it was pissing down at this point. You tend to take that as a given when you live near Manchester. Despite the rain, 'H' had clambered over the framework and on to the ledge. He was holding on to the railing with his two arms. I clambered over to join him. It wasn't as significant a drop as it looked when you drove over but still significant enough to kill us if we let go. Thankfully, it wasn't windy. The rain was coming down vertically.

"Hi Andy. You OK?" 'H' asked matter of factly.

"Bit wet," I answered.

"Horrible day."

"I was thinking that. What's with the shit shoes, 'H'?"

I motioned with my head towards his shoes. There was no way I was pointing. I couldn't really make out exactly what he said as he was rambling but it was something along the lines of,

"I bought some new black ones. They were giving me blisters on the heel so I swopped them for these. These are shit too."

'H' then flicked the shoes off so they dropped down into the murky waters below. I tried to create a bit of empathy by doing the same but mine were on too tight, so making sure I gripped for dear life with one arm, I stretched down with one hand and removed my shoes and socks then dropped my black Magnanni double monk shoes into the water. This really pissed 'H' off.

"What are you doing, you mad man?"

Takes one to know one.

"You did it!"

"My shoes were shit. How much did yours cost?"

"£350."

"For fuck's sake! I could have had them."

I was six inches taller than 'H' but bizarrely our feet were the same size.

"They won't be much use to you if you jump off here."

Once again 'H' looked at me like I was mad. He had a bloody cheek.

"I've no intention of jumping off here. I'm scared of heights."

"What are we doing here then?"

"Getting some fresh air."

I eventually managed to bring the conversation around to what had prompted him to drive on to the bridge, park up and get out. His confused mind had developed a hobby of 'condom counting' on the basis that he thought Cathie was having an affair. The very idea is ridiculous because that woman adores him but nevertheless he had managed to persuade himself a condom was missing.

Whilst he was telling this story, which seemed to take an age because he was repeating himself, mumbling, chuntering and getting very worked up, the rain stopped and the sun started to emerge from behind the clouds. It was an absolute stroke of fortune. A rainbow began to form. I remembered the stories 'H' had told me about his poor, gorgeous Mum, Kitty and how she used to appear to him in his dreams on a rainbow.

"Look 'H'," I said, "your Mum's come to talk some sense into you."

He looked emotional at first but then a big smile spread across his face. 'H' stopped talking to me and started talking to the rainbow. I just let him get on with it, figured it might help. I just kept my mouth completely shut (which if you knew me, you would know is very difficult). At one stage, I wasn't sure if my tactics had backfired as he started to get all choked up.

"Can you hear that, Andy? It's Ludovico Einaudi."

I smiled. I recalled him telling me a tale before about this guy. I couldn't hear a thing but I knew 'H' was hearing 'I Giorni'. A sublime piece of music. 'H' does have quality musical taste.

"It's beautiful," I said.

"I didn't even know my Dad could play the piano," 'H' said, his face full of snot and tears. God knows what tricks his mind was playing. He started weeping so uncontrollably his shoulders started to move and I worried he may lose his grip. He composed himself though, apologised for everything and asked me to take him home. I said I would but with a few dozen police officers watching our every move, I knew he wouldn't be heading back to Norden.

Harry was detained under Section 136 of the Mental Health Act and subsequently spent the next eight weeks on the John Elliott Unit of Birch Hill Hospital.

After spending half an hour waiting for Cathie at Birch Hill and then a further ninety minutes telling her everything that had happened, I returned to the Lowry in time to see the evening performance of 'Wonderful Town'. I cried from the first minute to the last. It was nothing to do with the show.

I know very little about ECT. I have chosen not to look into it too much. If you had asked me about it before I was given it, I would have told you it was the 'Electric Shock' thing they gave to Jack Nicholson's character that sent him over the edge in 'One Flew Over The Cuckoo's Nest' before the big Red Indian guy smothered him. I now see it very differently. It may have taken Randle McMurphy's life away but at least to some degree, I felt it gave me my life back.

I have no recollection of having ECT. I don't remember being strapped down and I don't remember coming around after it. I just remember how I felt before and how I felt afterwards. I remember feeling like I was lying face down at the bottom of a dark ocean for days or even weeks with no desire to move or come up for air and then all of a sudden spotting the sun's rays gleaming on to the surface of the water and wanting to investigate. Slowly having the desire to swim back up to the surface and wanting to follow the light. Once I put my head above the water all I could see were blue skies and sunshine.

Cathie came to see me every day at Birch Hill Hospital. Once I was well enough she helped me piece everything together. Andy helped too. He used to visit every couple of days. I think he used to enjoy coming to the Unit. You certainly see things you wouldn't see every day in Chambers.

There were certain things I remembered about being ill that I definitely knew were part of the fantasy world I had created. I knew, for example, that my parents hadn't actually come back from the dead. I also knew that Keith Corden hadn't been through Tesco in his Speedos. Apparently I did smash all the bottles in the alcohol section though. I had to pay for them.

There were other things that I was surprised to find out. An example of which was that I hadn't actually been down to Bristol for the Quarterly Sales Meeting. That was a figment of my imagination. I must have gone into Rochdale with the intention of going but then become very agitated by the thought of going to Bristol so had instead invested in a bottle of vodka and gone to share it with few of the regular drinkers and pot smokers on the sloping piece of grass up by Spotland. I had been arrested that night on 'Public Intoxication' (drunk and disorderly) charges. Police records show I ended up spending the night at the Custody Suite of Bury police station. Andy said I must have swopped my new black shoes with a fellow drinker as when he saw me on Thelwall Viaduct I was wearing paint splattered old brown ones. I do vaguely remember them.

I was also relieved to hear the explanation about the missing condom. I had been very hyperactive having returned from what turned out to be an overnight stay in a prison cell in Bury. Cathie was trying to be as nice as she could to me but was also a little bit concerned by manic behaviour. There was no doubting in her mind by this point that I needed professional help. I had apparently woken her up at three in the morning that night struggling to get an unresponsive penis into a condom and suggesting we make love. Cathie said she politely declined which I didn't take overly well and I had thrown the unused condom at her. She had wrapped it in tissue paper and popped it in the bin. Not my finest moment but a better explanation than the one I made up.

The following morning, for their safety (not because I was dangerous just because I was irrational) Cathie had taken Max and Melissa to her sister's. She was planning to get me assessed by a Mental Health Professional at some point that Saturday so had locked me in the house for my own safety. Little did she know I would take matters into my own hands.

The reason I ended up on Thelwall Viaduct is unclear. There's a possibility I went to 'Matthew Moss' and when I discovered Max wasn't playing football there, I may have gone randomly looking for them and got myself a bit lost. Another theory we have come up with is that I was feeling guilty about lying about packing my job in to Cathie so was driving down to Bristol to actually resign. As I'm scared of heights at the best of times I probably just freaked out when I reached Thelwall. No idea why I then went to stand on the ledge though.

Avon & Severn were eventually sympathetic to my illness. A couple of the Human Resources ladies visited me at home whilst I was still recovering and suggested a pathway for me to get back to work. They said if I returned I could have a different line manager as their feeling was that Benny Victory could have done more to help me. They didn't apportion any blame to Benny though and I know he is still making lives difficult to this day. I talked it over with Cathie and we decided a fresh start elsewhere would be a more sensible decision.

Over the last five years, I would say my mental illness has been controlled. I have had some dark days, especially when they were trying to get my medication right in the early days. I will probably have to take pills for the foreseeable future, perhaps for ever, but that does not bother me one iota. For at least four years though, I have been doing great. It has definitely helped that we are not under any financial stress. When Andy found out about my debts he offered to pay them all off as a gift but I didn't want him to do that. Instead, he bought Maggie's house. I think he paid us a bit more than we would have received through an estate agent, if we had sold it on the open market and we saved in estate agency fees, but it still didn't feel like charity.

These days Andy and I meet up at Maggie's every Sunday night for an evening of music. Two Sunday's a month we listen to our old stuff and one Sunday a month we each get to choose some new music to introduce to the other. My absolute favourite album that Andy has introduced me to in the last twelve months is 'Dream Darling' by The Slow Show. Andy was so excited about me hearing it. He said it was as if the band had been approached by him and asked to write an album designed for my musical taste. I remember him saying,

"Imagine Leonard Cohen was born fifty years later in England rather than Canada, was given singing lessons but still retained that distinctive tone and all his songwriting magic...well that's what it sounds like."

The first time I listened to it, Andy made me switch all the lights out and listen to in total darkness with a glass of wine in my hand. Within thirty seconds of hearing the piano introduction and Rob Goodwin's opening words on the first track 'Strangers Now', I knew I was going to love it. It's an absolutely stunning piece of work and somehow, each time I hear it, I fall in love with it a little bit more. Andy and I went to see them at the Gorilla bar in Manchester last November and I was completely blown away.

Work these days is great. Once I was mentally well I started to do some voluntary work for mental health charities. I was no expert but I had my own unique experience and wanted to hear other peoples. We are all fragile creatures, I have just come to appreciate some of us are just a little bit more fragile than others.

The voluntary work actually ended up introducing me to some people who were recruiting staff and in 2013, I started working for a private medical insurance company in Salford Quays. I have bought tickets to go to shows with Andy and Cathie at 'The Lowry' pretty much every month since I have been working nearby. One day I'll go to one without him mentioning the fact that I ruined his experience of 'Wonderful Town'. Andy is still acting too, a couple of times a year Cathie and I go to watch him. I'm pretty confident we'll end up seeing him at the Lowry one day. I'm hoping it will be in 'Wonderful Town'!

Out of the blue, in January this year, Avon & Severn's Human Resources Director, Susan Hislop, contacted me. She seems a very pleasant lady and explained that in 2016, mental health related issues had become the number one reason for absenteeism amongst their staff. They wanted to ensure their management staff handled any mental health issues in a professional and sympathetic manner so were inviting various mental health professionals to talk to 2,250 of their management staff at a 'Mental Health Awareness Day' at 'The Centaur' building at Cheltenham racecourse in late March. The reason she was contacting me was because they were also asking some colleagues and ex-colleagues who had had experience of mental illness to speak for ten minutes each on the matter. Susan asked whether I would like to take part. I said I would be delighted to.

The event took place a week after the racecourse had hosted its annual horse racing festival. I made sure I was early as I had never been to Cheltenham before but was taken aback by how amazing the racecourse is. It's a stunning location, the racecourse forming a natural amphitheatre below the Cotswold hills.

I wasn't nervous at all about speaking, just excited, but didn't want to need the toilet during my late morning slot, so rather than having a coffee, I went for a wander around the main spectator part of the course during the refreshment break. The Centaur building is a big indoor venue by the main entrance but I quickly walked down towards the racecourse. The place was very quiet other than a few workmen taking down some of the remaining temporary marquees and bars that had been erected for the Festival.

I walked in front of the huge Main Stand and down a significant slope that I imagined the horses had to race up towards the finishing line. There were plenty of wooden benches scattered around in front of the stand so with a few minutes to spare before I needed to return I took a seat.

I swear these days rainbows come looking for me. It had been a bright sunny morning but some dark grey clouds began to cluster together over Cleeve Hill, the largest of the Cotswold Hills. As I sat there, I reflected on the last five years. Everything had progressively improved. My marriage was strong and our children were developing into thoughtful, compassionate human beings. My job was enjoyable and we were financially on an even keel. My friendship with Andy was as good as it had ever been. I was now forty and although I had no personal work related ambitions any more, all I wanted was for Cathie and I to be healthy and our children to enjoy whatever they chose to do with their lives.

I felt content. I think sometimes we lose track of how important it is to feel content. As a rainbow broke out over Cleeve Hill, one of the songs by The Slow Show called 'Ordinary Lives' came into my head and for a few moments I swear I could picture my father's smiling face above that rainbow. It was time to say goodbye. It felt like the words of the song that were coming into my head were Dad's message to me:-

"I'm proud of you boy,

Look how far you came,

Proud of who you are,

Happy how you changed,

I won't see you much more,

But that's OK,

I can rest assured,

That you're happy,

But I am not afraid,

I can see so clear,

Proud of who I am,

It's time to disappear,

This is my farewell,

I can't stay here,

I'm looking at the crowd,

I hope they understand,

That everything is changing,

Everything is changing,

Everything is changing,

Everything is changing...."

THE END